P9-BJK-126

The
Quade
Inheritance

By the same author

Antipodes Jane

The Quade Inheritance

Barbara Ker Wilson

St. Martin's Press
New York

Library of Congress Cataloging-in-Publication Data

Wilson, Barbara Ker.
    The Quade inheritance.

    I. Title.
PR9619.3.W582Q34   1989   823   88-30521
ISBN 0-312-02700-1

First published in Great Britain by Martin Secker & Warburg Limited.

10 9 8 7 6 5 4 3 2

Prologue

SELBURY QUADE, THAT perfect country house set amid green wooded combes in the pleasant county of Somerset, seemed to every stranger's eye a serene and comfortable dwelling place, one that had surely sheltered generations of tranquil family life. Built of honey-coloured stone that had mellowed and deepened through the centuries, the house appeared as much a part of that gentle countryside as the great oaks, the sycamores and elms clotted with rooks' nests in its surrounding parkland. Yet just as each slab of stone, each joist and beam had been positioned by the hand of man, so too each sapling had been planted with foresight. Vanished long since was the primeval forest that once flourished here; everything that now stood in its place had been designed and fashioned and disposed with consummate skill.

The paradox was this: Selbury Quade was conceived and built three hundred years ago by an ambitious, scheming and ruthless woman who saw it as the culminating triumph of her life.

The legend of Dame Margery Quade hovered about the house through each generation of her descendants. She had married three times; Nicholas Quade, her third husband, was a well-to-do silk mercer from the City of London, knighted by Queen Elizabeth I. By him, Dame Margery had a son – the only child she ever bore. Her two previous husbands had suffered untimely deaths, leaving large fortunes entirely in her hands. And when Sir Nicholas died after five short years of wedlock, she amassed still greater wealth. Although she was comparatively young, retaining the enigmatic, unsmiling beauty that had ensnared three wealthy men, she now eschewed all thought of further marriage. The curious, compelling force that seemed to emanate from her dark eyes (it was the feature that women as well as men were most aware of) was now diverted from sexual conquest and material gain towards that project which would fulfil her deepest desire: the building of a country house and its estate.

Sir Nicholas Quade had inherited a freehold farm in Somerset, some distance from Yeovil. His widow, having inherited the freehold in her turn, chose this pleasant site for her dwelling place, ruthlessly demolishing the ancient farmhouse which had sheltered generations of plain yeomen Quades. The task she set herself occupied the rest of her days; utterly obsessed by it, she spun out the building of the house and the acquisition of land for its estate as though such elongation might in some way achieve her personal immortality. The thought of her own death was repulsive in the extreme to this self-absorbed, cold-hearted woman who had buried three husbands with equanimity. And linked to her fear of death was a horror of the dark: she was extravagant with candles. Nor did she show affection for her son, named Nicholas after his father. She scarcely saw him as an infant, giving him to the care of a wet-nurse in Selbury village, and after his father's death young Nicholas spent his boyhood in study with a grave-faced tutor who nurtured a vain and secret passion for Dame Margery, and wrote love sonnets which he never dared to show her.

With the master mason she employed, Dame Margery achieved a closer union than she had known with any of her husbands ... a congress concerned with stone and timber, design and effect, rather than flesh and gold, fornication and material gain. It took ten years to complete the house to her satisfaction, and she proved a hard taskmistress in her quest for perfection. Incapable of love for any other human being, she was in thrall to this pile of honey-coloured stone and superintended every detail, from the raftered ceiling, minstrels' gallery and oriel window of the high great chamber to the oak-leaf carving of a newel post, the linenfold panelling of the long gallery, and the tapestries hung in her parlour.

And while the house was a-building, Dame Margery turned her attention to the grounds, laying out a formal knot garden, stone-flagged terraces, a walk to be flanked by clipped yews, a walled orchard with espaliered pear and quince trees and two sweet cherries, which were first grown in England in old King Harry's time. She made a pleasure garden filled with musk and damask roses, and in the kitchen garden she grew newfangled vegetables, carrets and the exotic potato, which many held to be an aphrodisiac. And it was her peculiar enjoyment to oversee the planting of close-set hedges for a maze, an intricate Elizabethan puzzle which in time would grow high and dense.

With the help of her factor, Master Shadbrook, a petty tyrant whom she despised but found indispensable for her purposes, she acquired rich farmlands, settling a score of tenant farmers and humble cottagers who received harsh treatment from her.

By the time Dame Margery and old age came within nodding distance of one another, her son had left this perfect dwelling place and his unnatural mother. (It was said that even when he was a grown man, Dame Margery would not suffer him to sit in her presence.) The second Sir Nicholas achieved a minor administrative post in the service of his aging queen and spent most of his life at Hampton Court, philosophically awaiting his inheritance. He was well aware that his occasional visits to Somerset irked his mother, reminding her of her inevitable demise. Sometimes she made half-hearted efforts to acquaint him with the affairs of the estate, but

3

Nicholas paid little attention. He knew he would reverse many of his mother's schemes, and especially the manner of her dealings with tenants and cottagers. One of his first actions would be to dismiss the bullying factor.

On those rare visits, Nicholas would pause before the memorial to his father in the church at Selbury, a bas-relief set beneath a stained-glass window. He wondered if there were truth in the rumour he had picked up at court, that his mother had slowly poisoned each of her three husbands. He retained a childhood memory of his father, a man of gentle nature, fond of family life. Doubtless he had hoped for an affectionate marriage in his middle age, watching his children grow and enjoying the companionship of his wife. His only child, that second Nicholas, thought it more likely his father had died from simple disillusionment and everyday despair.

The most shameful episode in the history of Dame Margery's obsession belonged to her declining years, when the sometime allure of her compelling gaze had hardened to a flinty shrewdness. For years now, that gaze had been fixed upon a certain parcel of land alongside Foxhollow wood, dark, mysterious last remnant of the primeval forest. The wood was part of her estate; to gain the few acres of arable land beyond would neatly extend her boundary. An old mill stream ran through this land, and she had plans to divert its course and create an artificial lake to provide a pleasing prospect from the house. She called Master Shadbrook to her presence one day and instructed him to purchase Miller's Green, as those few acres were called.

The factor shook his head dubiously. 'The land belongs to old Agnes Selbury. I doubt she will agree to sell.'

Agnes Selbury – her forbears, according to old custom, had taken the name of the village they inhabited – was much of an age with Dame Margery, though she seemed older, wrinkled and weather-beaten, with a hooped back. She had been born at Miller's Green – her father and his before him had ground corn there. An only child, Agnes had grown into an ill-favoured woman. She had never married. After her parents died she

4

went on living in the tumbledown mill cottage with three cats for company and a row of bee skips set beneath a beech tree. She seldom visited the village, and the only times folk sought her out was when they came to procure honey, or a remedy for some ailment. Agnes was skilled in herb lore; her cottage garden was stocked with country remedies: bugleweed for bleeding of the lungs, marigolds to cure ulcers, golden rod for stomach pains, feverfew to expel worms, celandine mixed with poppyheads as a cure for nightmare . . .

Perhaps it was inevitable that in her old age, Agnes should be dubbed a witch. The villagers spoke of the three cats as her familiars, and told how she went into Foxhollow on nights of full moon to seek toadstools for spells, and murmured incantations to her bees. Yet still they came to the cottage to seek a cure for rheumy eyes, a palsied tongue or the wasting disease . . . or perhaps a potion for a barren wife or an impotent husband. There were those who said that Agnes could conjure up such ills as well as cure them.

When Master Shadbrook called at Agnes's cottage, she would not open her door to him, and he was forced to shout Dame Margery's request in a voice that echoed through the trees. She shrieked her refusal, and suddenly a grey cat came up behind him, arching its back and spitting at him.

Dame Margery was displeased at his lack of success.

'She is so old, mistress, that we need only bide our time,' the factor pleaded, attempting to exonerate his failure. 'She has a nephew will inherit Miller's Green. If I know Peter Selbury, he will dispose of the land to us right eagerly.'

Dame Margery sat very still in her high-backed chair. They were in her parlour, which overlooked the orchard. It was springtime; standing cap in hand beside the window, Master Shadbrook glimpsed the trees below, a froth of pear, quince and cherry blossom. It was impossible to read his mistress's thoughts; her face was expressionless, her eyes hooded.

'I am not prepared to bide my time,' she told him in an even voice. Although she would scarcely admit it to herself, she realized it was possible Agnes Selbury might outlive her. She

5

was determined to see that piece of land enclosed within her boundary, and to create the fair lake she desired. 'You say this nephew would sell the land as soon as he inherited?' she continued calmly.

The cunning old vixen was hinting at something, Master Shadbrook could tell. It was not her way to brew mischief plainly; he had acted on veiled suggestions and half-formulated plans before this.

'The land is entailed to him in law,' he said. 'Nothing will please Peter Selbury more than to get his hands on Miller's Green and pocket the gold it would bring him.'

'I have heard the villagers believe Agnes Selbury to be a witch,' Dame Margery remarked in the same cool tone. You had to take care when you spoke of witchcraft; it was well known that the Queen was opposed to all such superstitious belief . . . for good reason: her own mother, Anne Boleyn, had been accounted a witch, and sentenced as such at her trial to be beheaded or burned, according to the King's pleasure.

Master Shadbrook chose his words with equal care. 'It is the fate of many an old crone with healing powers,' he said. 'I hear the last time she ventured to the village, the children threw stones and dirt at her, and two days later Ned Fletcher's little son died in a fever. The villagers believe she put a curse on him.'

Dame Margery said slowly, 'I would not be surprised to learn of a witch-hunt one of these spring nights . . . and perhaps that the mill cottage had been burned down.' She paused to let her words take effect. 'And now, Master Shadbrook, we must speak of increasing the rent for Combe Lacey farm . . .'

During the next few days, Master Shadbrook made it his business to speak to Peter Selbury, old Agnes's nephew, and a month later a band of villagers, recklessly drunk on strong cider provided by that same Peter Selbury, surged forth to have their sport with the witch. They were led by Ned Fletcher, who was convinced his little lad had died because the witch had cursed him, and they carried flaring torches through the moonless night.

They were cheated of their sport; Agnes Selbury did not emerge to be hounded to death through the leafy coppices. She stayed within her stoutly barred door as they came trampling through her garden, crushing the sweet healing plants underfoot and shouting obscenities to keep up their courage. Drunk and reckless they might be, but they were still fearful of this place. The cats stayed with old Agnes inside the cottage, pied Betsy, Greymalkin and Tabitha, a brindled Cyprus cat, their fur hackled in terror.

The cats perished with old Agnes after the torches were used to fire the dilapidated roof thatch. Their piercing yowls mingled with her thin human screams above the crackle of flames. Meanwhile, the bees, driven from their skips by the smoke, came flying forth in a great swarm, and those who were stung cried out that Satan was defending his own kin.

Sobered at last, their frenzy spent, the men dispersed, and in the grey dawn two or three returned to drag Agnes's charred body from the smouldering ruin. At the place where the Queen's highway met the rough track that led off to Selbury, they dug an unhallowed grave and buried the witch with a stake driven through her heart, lest her master the Devil should raise her to life again.

In due course Master Shadbrook and Peter Selbury conferred with a lawyer from Yeovil; Dame Margery signed her name to the document that was drawn up, and Peter Selbury made his mark and took his payment of a few gold coins. Next year the ornamental lake at Selbury Quade was contrived, water being ingeniously diverted from the mill stream and controlled by a weir.

The old queen died about this time, and Dame Margery did not live much longer. Unlike the Queen's passing (it was said that in her extremity she had a vision of hell and stood for hours defying death, to fall at last upon cushions her maids of honour heaped around her), Dame Margery's end was singularly peaceful. In truth she did not deserve such a gentle passing. Musing no doubt upon some improvement to house or garden as she sat upon a window seat in her high great

7

chamber one summer day, she simply nodded off, closing her eyes with a sigh, and did not wake again.

So Nicholas Quade, now approaching his middle years, came to Somerset to take up his inheritance, and before the year was out he married a gentle lady who was to bear him a quiverful of children. He quickly dismissed Master Shadbrook; none were sorry to see him shamble from the stage. During the years of Sir Nicholas's habitation the estate prospered and a sense of loyalty towards the family sprang up among the tenants and cottagers. And so the long history of Selbury Quade began.

Chapter One

I T WAS THE winter of 1861 when Annette Duval came to Somerset as governess to the daughter of Sir Oswald and Lady Louisa Quade. Snow furred the bare trees and mantled the hedgerows as the station cab bore the new governess to Selbury Quade. She had travelled by train to Yeovil; now she peered out at the wintry countryside as the driver urged his horse along the highway, past a crossroads where a sign pointed to Selbury village. A little farther, and they turned off the road into a driveway. Massive wrought-iron gates stood open beside a gingerbread lodge. Halfway along that winding drive, she caught her first view of the house, and held her breath in admiration and delight. A pleasant place indeed to earn her living!

This was to be her first post; she had obtained it through a scholastic agency in London. Her aunt Harriet, in her reserved manner, had congratulated her on her good fortune. But Annette herself held strange misgivings about the appointment. She had yet to meet her nine-year-old pupil, but during her interview with the formidable proprietor of the agency, she had sensed that Imogen Quade was an unusual child.

At nineteen, Annette Duval was embarking upon an occupation for which she had very little enthusiasm; but, since circumstances decreed she must now earn her livelihood, there seemed no alternative – save, perhaps, to become paid companion to some old lady, an even more undesirable fate. If only, Annette thought for the umpteenth time, there had been some rich and handsome young man to fall in love with her, carry her off to Gretna Green, cherish and provide for her!

Her parents had been killed in a carriage accident while she was still an infant, and she had been brought up by her father's sister, a spinster lady who lived in London, in the highly respectable suburb of Kensington. The relationship between Annette and Aunt Harriet Duval was strict and kindly on the one hand, respectful and dutiful on the other, lacking spontaneous affection and real warmth. Then, six months ago, Jeffcott's private bank, in which most of Aunt Harriet's capital and the whole of Annette's patrimony was invested, had suddenly failed. Sufficient remained of Aunt Harriet's funds to provide her with a significantly reduced income, but Annette was left penniless. Fortuitously, Aunt Harriet had seen to it that her niece received an unusually good education. She had enrolled her as one of the first pupils at a collegiate school for girls, begun ten years ago by a gentlewoman called Miss Frances Mary Buss, who aimed to provide a liberal education as well as the accomplishments necessary for ladies. Annette had consulted her former headmistress, and was given the opportunity to assist for a while with the younger pupils at the school. Armed with this small experience and a helpful note from Miss Buss, she had then visited Mrs Maxwell's scholastic agency.

Mrs Maxwell, a somewhat intimidating female who wore gold-rimmed pince-nez, told Annette quite frankly that the previous governess at Selbury Quade had relinquished the position because of 'the unpredictable character' of her charge, who was an only child.

'This is the reason I am able to offer you, inexperienced as you are, Miss Duval, this excellent opportunity,' Mrs Maxwell said.

Annette at once suspected something amiss. What exactly did that phrase 'unpredictable character' denote? Was it a euphemism for appalling disobedience, frightful temper tantrums . . . even, perhaps, bouts of insanity? She could not help but recall *Jane Eyre*. Was Imogen Quade, to put it plainly, a little monster?

Mrs Maxwell had interpreted her dubious expression. 'Regard it as a challenge, Miss Duval.' Her voice held brisk encouragement; privately, she doubted this young woman's ability to stay the course. But she desperately needed some candidate to fill the post at Selbury Quade. Miss Nuthall, the previous governess, who held the highest references, had now found a new position with a ducal family in Northumberland. It seemed unlikely that Miss Duval could succeed where the experienced Miss Nuthall had failed. Mrs Maxwell surveyed the slim figure before her. Annette sat upright, her narrow hands in immaculate kid gloves lightly clasped, neat ankles demurely crossed beneath her skirt. She was rather too elegantly attired for a governess, Mrs Maxwell considered, but of course her unhappy change of fortune was quite recent. Yet the impression of elegance did not solely emanate from Miss Duval's dove-grey costume and feathered toque. The young woman had a certain air of quiet containment; it was quite difficult to assess the character that might lie behind her pretty face and wide violet eyes. Who could tell, her very youth and ignorance might help her to cope in what was clearly a difficult situation. She would enter into it without expectations founded upon previous experience.

'Very well,' Annette had said finally with a decisiveness she did not really feel, 'I accept the post.'

The child Imogen had watched from an upper window overlooking the main entrance of Selbury Quade as Miss Nuthall was swept away for ever from Selbury in the shabby station cab that had been summoned to collect her. Imogen's face held an expression of grave satisfaction that seemed to belie her lack of years. Another child would surely have demonstrated simple glee.

Miss Nuthall had resigned her post in a spirit of dignified regret. Imogen's parents never properly understood her objections to their daughter's conduct. But then neither Sir Oswald Quade nor Lady Louisa really knew their daughter, whose character bore so little relation to her courteous, rather scholarly father or her fragile, charming mother.

'Apparently it was something to do with the lodgekeeper's child,' Lady Louisa had told her husband in a plaintive voice.

'I have never known such a child in all my years of governessing, Lady Louisa.' Miss Nuthall's manner of speech matched her appearance: imposing, ample, middle-aged. 'Ordinary, high-spirited mischief we are quite able to understand.' (She habitually used the regal pronoun.) 'But Imogen's mischief, I am sorry to say, can be quite extraordinarily heartless.'

'Oh, come, Miss Nuthall,' Lady Louisa had protested gently, 'that is a strong word, surely. *Heartless?* I always find Imogen so affectionate during our time together each evening, before bedtime.'

Miss Nuthall had compressed her lips, keeping to herself the recollection of her pupil intently dismembering a butterfly, tearing away the wings to observe the still palpitating body with dispassion. 'Imogen,' she had remonstrated, 'that is one of God's creatures. Think of the lovely hymn we sang last Sunday, "All things bright and beautiful, the Lord God made them all." '

But Imogen did not sing in church. 'God may have made it, but *I* am unmaking it,' had been the child's unnatural response: surely a blasphemy, Miss Nuthall thought. Other children had been known to tear wings off insects, of course, but Imogen's little cruelties seemed particularly calculated.

It was the incident of poor little Edie Kitto, the lodgekeeper's daughter, that finally drove Miss Nuthall to resign. One morning at breakfast, the only meal that Imogen's parents shared with their daughter and her governess, Lady Louisa had spoken of Edie with sorrowful compassion.

'Poor child, wasting away in her poky little room day after

day. I fear she is not long for this world. I shall send over a basket of fruit —'

Imogen had looked up from her boiled egg. 'Let me take the fruit to Edie, Mama!' she said. 'I should like to visit her. I didn't know she was *dying*.'

Miss Nuthall, helping herself to kidneys and bacon at the sideboard, wondered at the emphasis in Imogen's remark.

'Dear child,' Lady Louisa said approvingly, 'that is a good, kind thought. And perhaps you could read a story to poor Edie.'

So Imogen and her governess had taken a basket of hothouse grapes and nectarines to the gingerbread lodge, and Mrs Kitto had curtsied and shown Miss Imogen to Edie's little room, while Miss Nuthall sat in the stuffy parlour. Chatting to Edie's mother, the governess suddenly realized she still carried in her holdall the book Imogen had brought to read to the sick child: *Pious and Pretty Verses*. Rising majestically, she went along to Edie's room at the end of the passage, then paused outside the door. She could hear Imogen speaking; her words were all too plain.

'. . . and you are going to die soon, Edie, my mama said so, she said you weren't long for this world. And then you'll be put into a dark hole in the ground, under a tombstone with your name on it, and the worms will begin to eat you up, ever so slowly, until —'

'Imogen! Stop that this instant, you wicked child!' Miss Nuthall had burst into the room to find Imogen seated comfortably in a rocking chair, the basket of luscious fruit upon her lap. Poor Edie was bolt upright in her narrow bed, ashen-faced save for two consumptive spots of hectic colour in her cheeks, shrinking against the wall in horror, as if to escape her tormentor.

There was no trace of confusion in Imogen as she turned towards her governess. 'I am only telling Edie the truth,' she had said, her voice sweetly reasonable.

'That is enough, Imogen. Go to Mrs Kitto,' Miss Nuthall told her. 'I will stay with Edie for a while.'

It had taken several pious and pretty verses, spoken in Miss Nuthall's most soothing voice, while she held Edie's paper-thin hand, before the child's terror at last subsided. Then the governess had returned to the little parlour, leaving the dying child with images of angels and a heaven shining with celestial light and studded with semiprecious stones, to replace a stark headstone and slimy worms.

'Miss Imogen be that kind to come a-visiting our Edie,' the unsuspecting mother had declared. And Miss Nuthall was dismayed to observe that Imogen's bland gaze did not waver as she acknowledged the compliment.

Later, at that final interview between governess and fond mama, Miss Nuthall had declared, 'It is Imogen's moral character that poses problems,' which remark seemed to her employer to verge on the impertinent. Lady Louisa did not listen with any real attention to the governess's account of her daughter's behaviour at the lodge.

'Perhaps a genteel boarding school for young ladies might be considered,' Miss Nuthall persisted. 'The company of other children –'

Now she succeeded in reclaiming Lady Louisa's full attention. Although the governess did not realize it, she had laid open an old wound. *Other children*: that was what Lady Louisa so earnestly desired, had desired for so long. Especially a son, an heir to the baronetcy and to Selbury Quade. But after Imogen's birth, no other child had been conceived. It was a situation that she knew saddened her husband; and self-reproach, a submerged sense of failure, lay continually beneath her serene countenance and charm of manner.

'We would not dream of sending Imogen away to such an establishment,' she told Miss Nuthall in an unusually icy tone. 'Other considerations aside, it would break Imogen's heart to leave Selbury. She is devoted to her home.'

That was certainly true. During her year with this family, Miss Nuthall had come to realize the quite extraordinary feeling, amounting, she would have said, to a passion, that Imogen held for Selbury Quade. It was during Miss Nuthall's time that Imogen had first become aware that she would inherit this lovely house and its estate . . . unless, of course, a brother should chance to arrive upon the scene. Her father had acquainted her with this fact on her last birthday.

'Well, Imogen, I daresay all this will be yours one day – your inheritance and your responsibility,' Sir Oswald had said as they took a favourite stroll around the one-acre lake. His tone was fairly light-hearted, and he was surprised and a little taken aback by his young daughter's response.

'I will dedicate my life to Selbury, Papa,' she told him solemnly.

'Come now, dear child, it is not the throne of England, you know . . .' But at heart Sir Oswald had been gratified by such evidence of family feeling. If only his daughter were a son! It was a wish he sought constantly to suppress. After that day Sir Oswald took to calling his daughter 'Dame Imogen' from time to time, in a gently teasing manner. He never realized how Imogen closely identified herself with her Elizabethan ancestress. She had, of course, grown up with the legend of Dame Margery Quade, whose portrait hung above the great staircase, whose memorial she saw each Sunday in church . . . young Imogen Quade received the distinct impression that Dame Margery remained the guardian of the house she had built so long ago.

When Miss Nuthall heard the cold disfavour in Lady Louisa's voice she was aware she had offended; she had departed forthwith, bearing a lukewarm reference in her employer's delicate handwriting, which she kept apart from those other glowing tributes she had received over the years. There had been no difficulty in obtaining her new position, at the ducal seat of Stamford Itton, a world away from Somerset.

Chapter Two

THE FIRST PERSON Annette Duval encountered at Selbury Quade, apart from the young footman who opened the massive door to her, was not of flesh and blood. As she stood in the great entrance hall facing the double staircase, her glance travelled upwards to rest upon a portrait hung where the first wide flight divided to left and right: a full-length portrait of a woman in a stiff, wide-skirted Elizabethan gown, the bodice worked in silver-gilt embroidery. She stood beside a table on which a parchment lay half unrolled. One hand rested upon the parchment, the other was held outwards, palm and fingers spread in a gesture of display. The painting was conventional enough in most respects: the painstaking depiction of the embroidery, the frosty lace of the ruffled collar above it, the tapering fingers thin and lifeless as ivory fan sticks. It was the smooth, composed face of this unknown woman that was so arresting – no, not the face: the eyes. Annette could not repress a slight inward shiver. It seemed as though that penetrating gaze could spike your very soul. Those dark eyes held pride, arrogance and worldly knowledge – and, surely, triumph. Later, Annette was often to avert her gaze from the portrait as she mounted the stairs, knowing that those painted eyes would follow her whichever way she turned to attain the long panelled gallery that ran across the top of the branched staircase.

'I see Dame Margery has you enthralled.' A pleasant tenor voice broke into Annette's preoccupation.

She turned to see a tall, scholarly-looking man who appeared to be in his forties, wearing a velvet smoking jacket.

'I think,' Sir Oswald Quade continued, 'you must be my daughter Imogen's new governess. Welcome to Selbury Quade, Miss Duval.'

Annette extended one gloved hand. 'Yes, I am Annette Duval. And I look forward to meeting Imogen.' With some apprehension, she might have added.

Sir Oswald nodded. 'I believe we are to take family tea in the library so that we may become acquainted.' He was recalling the well-upholstered, middle-aged Miss Nuthall. Impossible not to draw a comparison in favour of Miss Annette Duval. 'Duval,' he continued musingly. 'Is that not a French name?'

'My father's family is descended from Huguenot lacemakers who fled to England during the times of persecution in France.'

'In that case our families have something in common,' Sir Oswald replied. He nodded towards the portrait on the staircase. 'Dame Margery's third husband, Nicholas Quade, was a silk mercer.'

'And did he build this lovely house?'

'Oh no!'

Annette was a little startled at the positive manner in which Sir Oswald refuted this suggestion. 'Selbury Quade was entirely the creation of the formidable Dame Margery. She built it after his death.' He smiled. 'I believe the fortune he bequeathed her was of some assistance. Those are the plans for Selbury, on the parchment beneath her hand. I have always assumed she is making that expansive gesture with her other hand as if to say, "Look around you: this is *my* achievement."'

At this moment the young footman came forward bearing Annette's light luggage, which he had retrieved from the cab. 'Your trunk will be sent up to your room later, miss,' he told

her in a respectful tone, impressed by the quality of her luggage
– a travelling portmanteau from Nicoll's of Regent Street, no
less, and a mohair tartan rug with the Scott Adie label. He
guessed that Miss Duval was a young lady come down in the
world. A good-looker all right, though a little too cool and
stand-offish for his taste. He wondered how long she would
stay. Miss Imogen certainly seemed a handful. The footman's
seemingly impassive regard absorbed every detail of the new
governess's appearance to relate below stairs.

'We shall meet later in the library, then, Miss Duval,' Sir
Oswald said as Annette prepared to follow the footman to her
room. 'I am sure Imogen is every bit as eager to meet her new
governess as you must be to make her acquaintance. And Lady
Louisa, of course, is waiting to welcome you.'

By five o'clock it was quite dark. Heavy damask curtains had
been drawn against the winter evening beyond the library
windows. Soft lamplight revealed the bookshelves lining the
walls, the marble busts of Greek philosophers brought home
by some earlier Quade after a grand tour in the last century,
and a wide leather-topped desk piled with papers. Fragrant
apple logs were burning in the hearth and a couple of indolent
spaniels sprawled in front of the glowing fire.

Annette paused in the doorway to regard the Quade family at
home, grouped as though for a portrait. A painting of Sir Oswald
and Lady Louisa with Imogen had in fact just been completed
and hung alongside other family portraits in the long gallery.
Perhaps the commissioning of this portrait was a tacit admission
that Imogen was destined to remain the only child.

Sir Oswald stood with his back to the fireplace. Lady Louisa
sat on a sofa, engaged in a tea ceremony involving spirit kettle,
silver teapot and Rockingham china. Her delicate hands
moved gracefully in practised gestures. And their daughter, a
thin, rather lanky child wearing a brown velvet dress, with a
big black bow set in her dark hair like a huge moth, was
perched on the edge of a deep armchair, beside a tea table piled
with muffins, conserve and cake.

Lady Louisa was wearing black, of course, decreed by the recent death of the Prince Consort. Imogen's sombre dress and big black bow were also a mourning gesture. 'So inconsiderate of Prince Albert to die just before Christmas!' one of Lady Louisa's more frivolous women friends had exclaimed. 'We shall all resemble gatherings of crows around our festive tables.' Annette herself had changed from her grey travelling costume into a restrained grey-and-lavender plaid dress, with an agate brooch pinned at her throat. Sir Oswald's plum-coloured jacket looked positively flamboyant in contrast to the womenfolk.

'Ah, Miss Duval,' he said now, seeing Annette in the doorway.

'Welcome to Selbury, Miss Duval,' Lady Louisa added in her soft, rather languid voice.

'And this is Imogen,' Sir Oswald said. The child slid off her chair, keeping her eyes lowered as she shook hands with her new governess.

'How do you do, Miss Duval,' She said in a totally expressionless voice. How composed she seemed for her nine years, Annette thought as she took Imogen's fine-boned hand in her own. No sign here of appalling disobedience or temper tantrums, or worse. And yet . . . Imogen Quade did not appear as though she were a particularly acquiescent child, either. She seemed – simply her own person, self-sufficient and, somehow, on her guard. Then she raised her eyes to regard her new governess fully, and Annette gave an involuntary start. That penetrating look! It reminded her . . . of course! She had experienced it just a little while ago, in a much more mature face within a gilded frame. Surely those were Dame Margery Quade's dark eyes. Annette recalled Sir Oswald's description of Dame Margery: 'formidable'. Well, by all accounts Imogen Quade might be a formidable child.

The new governess sat on the sofa next to Lady Louisa and accepted the cup of tea that was proffered her, annoyed with herself because, in spite of her outwardly calm demeanour, her hand trembled slightly. She looked at Imogen.

'We are going to enjoy our lessons together,' she told the child with a certain bravado. 'We shan't spend all our time in the schoolroom. There will be nature study out of doors, and musical gymnastics.' She turned to Lady Louisa, who was looking fairly surprised. 'At the school I attended, Lady Louisa, callisthenics designed to promote graceful movement were considered most important.'

Sir Oswald suppressed a smile. Gymnastics, indeed! He began to suspect that Miss Annette Duval, pretty face and violet eyes notwithstanding, might prove to be one of a new breed of female. Impossible to imagine the imposing Miss Nuthall indulging in gymnastics!

'Was it not Castiglione who urged tutors to "joyne learnying with cumlie exercise"?' he asked. A rhetorical question: neither Annette nor Lady Louisa were acquainted with Castiglione's writings.

Annette noticed that her words did not appear to have any effect on her pupil. No flicker of interest showed in Imogen's face. Her main hope, she suspected, would be to try to keep this child thoroughly occupied.

The tea ceremony completed, muffins, cherry conserve and lemon sponge cake consumed, Lady Louisa turned to her daughter.

'You may leave us now, Imogen dear. Your papa and I wish to have a grown-up talk with Miss Duval.'

After Imogen had left the room, Lady Louisa took up Annette's remark about nature study.

'I assume the study you intend, Miss Duval, will be confined to botany – plants and trees and so forth? It will not include a study of – of the *human being*?' Her tone was anxious. 'In due course I shall give Imogen a little book that has been recommended to me for that purpose – *The Seed of Life – Birds, Butterflies and Bees*, by the Reverend Henry Marcus. Possibly you are acquainted with this work. But I do not wish Imogen to receive such knowledge at her present tender age.'

Annette lowered her eyes modestly, as she was sure Lady Louisa expected her to do. Sir Oswald had half-turned to gaze thoughtfully at the bookshelves. Annette was young enough to recall very well her own consuming childish curiosity about the mechanics of human reproduction. She still expended considerable thought upon the act of love, yearning for, yet half dreading that experience. And she was indeed familiar with the Reverend Mr Marcus's euphemistic little book, universal standby of mamas embarrassed by intimate questions. Aunt Harriet had discreetly left a copy on her niece's dressing table about the time of her fourteenth birthday. Annette was grateful that more explicit information had been forthcoming at Miss Buss's school. Now she recalled a conversation on the subject with Miss Buss last year, when the latter had quoted Miss Florence Nightingale's criticism of the education of the average girl, 'left in ignorance of her own body'.

'By nature study,' she replied to Lady Louisa's question, 'I mean the observation of our surroundings – plants, trees, the changing seasons, wildlife. The grounds of Selbury Quade should provide ample scope for such study, I imagine.'

Sir Oswald nodded approvingly in the background. Lady Louisa was visibly relieved.

'My method of education,' Annette went on, surprising herself with such a pompous phrase, 'is based upon the system of Pestalozzi, the Swiss educator, a great believer in relating words and ideas to observation and practice. I hope to devise for Imogen a course of study which will include drawing, original composition, the musical gymnastics to which I alluded before, and such activities as mapmaking and compiling collections of natural objects.' She paused for breath, then added hastily, 'As well, of course, as the usual lessons of divinity, arithmetic, grammar, French, history and geography.'

Miss Buss admired and emulated Pestalozzi's theories and method; Annette had practised them during her few months of teaching instruction.

'Capital!' Sir Oswald exclaimed. 'That sounds a great deal better than merely reciting history dates and multiplication tables and parroting verses learned by heart.' Then he went on in a more serious tone, 'You should bear in mind, Miss Duval, that one day Imogen will very likely inherit Selbury Quade. She should in due course be able to take an intelligent interest in the affairs of the estate.' He waved one hand towards his burdened desk. 'I shall instruct her to some extent in such matters later on, and when the time comes there will of course be an estate manager to advise her, but meanwhile a thorough grounding in arithmetic, the ability to concentrate on a problem and seek logical solutions – these are most important.'

Annette nodded, suddenly aware of how tired she was. Her journey had occupied the whole day. Vaguely she realized the implication behind Sir Oswald's last remarks. But he had said that Imogen would *very likely* inherit . . . perhaps, then, all hope of a son and heir had not quite vanished?

'Have you everything you need in your room, Miss Duval?' Lady Louisa seemed anxious to deflect the drift of the conversation. 'You will find Mrs Arkney, the housekeeper, most helpful.'

As Annette stood up, Lady Louisa looked at the new governess reflectively. Miss Duval, with her slim figure and graceful movements, was really quite like a gentlewoman. Lady Louisa recalled that Mrs Maxwell, who ran that scholastic agency, had mentioned a change of fortune. The governess might even be able to make up the numbers at a dinner party on occasion. She was certainly most presentable. Suddenly an image of her favourite brother, happy-go-lucky, handsome Edwin, sprang into Lady Louisa's mind, and she seemed to hear his voice saying, 'Most presentable? She's damned attractive, Louie, and you know it!'

Lady Louisa was smiling gently as Annette replied, 'It is a charming room.' And so it was, a square apartment furnished with antique pieces and India chintzes, on the same floor as the schoolroom and Imogen's bedroom. From the window, Annette had caught a twilight glimpse of a lake, its surface steely under the snowy sky.

'The schoolroom was formerly the old day nursery,' Lady Louisa told her. 'We decided to make the change when

Imogen's old nanny retired. Nan was my nursemaid when I was young, the dear old soul.'

In fact, there had been some heartache for Lady Louisa when the day nursery was relinquished – another tacit admission that there would be no more children. The night nursery remained untouched, however, the high cot stripped of its muslin frills, the rest of the furniture draped in dust covers.

Returning to her room, Annette found that her trunk had been sent up. She began to unpack, disposing little treasures about her room: the daguerreotype of her parents, strangers she had never known, stiffly posed; a heart-shaped pin-cushion; her Bible and prayer book; the round tortoiseshell box that held her few pieces of jewellery . . .

Now it was time to hear Imogen say her prayers: her first official duty. She went along the passage to the child's room and listened wearily as Imogen recited her petitions to the Almighty by rote, clearly regarding this as a duty to be disposed of as quickly as possible. Then Annette tucked the bedclothes around the child and removed the stone pig that had made the bed warm and cosy. And hesitated for an uneasy moment, looking down on Imogen's face with those curiously knowing eyes. Somehow, she felt, one did not kiss Imogen Quade goodnight. Checking the nightlight, she left the room.

Imogen turned her head to watch the little candle burning steadily, floating in its dish of water. She was afraid of the dark. She lay in bed thinking about Miss Duval. It was a change to have a governess who was quite young . . . and it would be nice not to stay cooped up in the schoolroom all the time. Listening outside the library door, Imogen had over-heard her father's remark . . . and how flustered Mama had sounded when she spoke of that little book about the birds and bees! Last year, one of the housemaids had told her all about babies and how they were made. It seemed a curious arrange-ment – but intriguing, too. Molly, the housemaid, had had to leave because she was going to have a baby herself. The bulge beneath her apron had grown larger and larger, and at last Mrs Arkney had dismissed her. Imogen wondered vaguely what had happened to Molly. Not that it mattered; she did not really care. Molly was only a servant, after all. Imogen wriggled her toes in her warm, soft bed. Nor did she care about Miss Duval. She was just another dreary governess, to be opposed and made to look ridiculous, and to be got rid of if possible.

Before Annette herself retired to bed, she wrote to Aunt Harriet. Easy to sound enthusiastic about this lovely house and her comfortable room, less easy to relay her first impression of her pupil. 'Imogen seems a rather remote little girl,' she said finally, 'but I daresay we shall soon get to know each other.'

She climbed between the sheets, grateful to find her own bed warmed by a stone pig, and drifted into sleep reflecting on the fact that Imogen was the only child in this ancient family. Perhaps one day she would indeed find herself mistress of Selbury Quade . . . like that Elizabethan ancestress whose painted eyelids never closed. But then the direct line of descent would be broken, after all those hundreds of years . . . Annette resolved sleepily to discover more about the formidable Dame Margery. How strange, she mused dreamily: already, in such a short space of time, she was beginning to feel a part of this place, this family. And on the verge of sleep she pushed away the unwelcome thought that perhaps she was destined to remain at Selbury Quade for ever, like the old nanny Lady Louisa had spoken of, to become known years hence as Imogen Quade's former governess, 'Miss Duval, the dear old soul' . . .

Chapter Three

CHRISTMAS AT SELBURY Quade that year was more subdued than usual, echoing the grief-stricken royal Christmas at Osborne. The tree at the foot of the great staircase was a young fir uprooted from Foxhollow wood, decorated with candles, baubles and sweetmeats to be borne off by the children of the estate. In a sense, all the Chistmas trees in England that year were memorials to the Prince Consort, for it was he who had made the *Christbaum* of his native Germany so popular.

However, the customary ball for the tenants and servants was held in the raftered entrance hall that had once been Dame Margery's high great chamber. A noble yule log burned in the enormous hearth, and the musicians in the minstrels' gallery played quadrilles, waltzes and gallops. Annette joined in the fun and the footmen and tenant farmers were eager to partner the pretty young governess. She was quite sorry to retire from the scene at an early hour.

'The festivities are apt to become a trifle boisterous as the evening wears on,' Lady Louisa confided.

Trailing out after the family, Annette listened regretfully to the strains of a lively polka.

It was such a different world to the one she had known with Aunt Harriet in the quiet Kensington house, where social life had consisted of church functions, small card parties and musical evenings. The novelty of her new experiences succeeded for a while in distracting Annette's thoughts from her new, humble status.

In the New Year, Lady Louisa arranged a dinner party for some of the neighbouring gentry. At the last moment one of her intended guests was smitten by a feverish cold, and cried off.

'Oh, Miss Duval,' Lady Louisa said casually at breakfast one morning, 'I should like you to make up the numbers at dinner this evening, otherwise we shall be thirteen at table.'

Bidden to dine as a duty rather than for the pleasure of her company, Annette nevertheless looked forward to the occasion. After she had seen Imogen safely tucked up in bed, she went to her own room to dress with a pleasant feeling of anticipation. Jessie, the little between-maid, had brought up a can of hot water, and there was a bright fire burning in the grate. Eager to help (it had caused some comment below stairs that the new governess was to dine with the gentry that evening), Jessie poured water into the china washbasin and folded the serviceable serge skirt and shirtwaist blouse Annette had discarded.

'Would you like me to brush your hair, miss?' she asked Annette. 'The way her ladyship's maid does?'

Annette smiled at Jessie, loosened her hair and sat on the stool before the looking-glass. It was not difficult to dream a little . . . that she was a cousin of the family, perhaps, staying at Selbury for Christmas and New Year . . . the dinner party arranged so that she might meet a neighbouring squire . . . And if Annette could dream, so could young Jessie: that she was a real superior lady's maid with smooth white hands instead of her own grubby little paws that were for ever raking out ashes, sweeping and dusting, fetching and carrying . . . all the menial chores that fell to a tweeny's hapless lot . . .

'*Ouch!*' Annette's cry broke both their reveries.

Jessie's inexpert wielding of the hairbrush had tangled a long strand and brought involuntary tears to Annette's eyes.

'Oh, miss, I'm ever so sorry!' The vigorous brushing changed to a timid, ineffective stroking.

Annette completed her coiffure herself, sweeping her dark, gleaming hair into the usual demure style she wore – except that tonight she allowed a few soft tendrils to curl over her temples and forehead. Then she went over to the oak press beside the window.

'What are you going to wear, miss?'

'This, I think.' Annette brought out a gown of grey moiré silk shot with blue and green, with a creamy froth of antique lace, a Huguenot heirloom, at the neckline. It had been made by Aunt Harriet's dressmaker, a clever seamstress, from a bolt of Spitalfields silk.

Jessie caught her breath as Annette clasped the gown to herself. 'Ooh, miss, it's lovely!'

Annette slipped into the gown and arranged the lace becomingly about her neck and shoulders. Then she took a necklace of seed pearls and a small diamond brooch out of her tortoiseshell jewel box. She fastened the pearls about her neck and held the brooch to the dress to gauge the effect in the looking-glass. It was the only piece of any value she possessed, a floral spray constructed so that the tiny diamond flower heads trembled and glittered with the wearer's movement.

'I think,' she declared with a sigh, 'this brooch would not be quite the thing.' Governesses were not supposed to glitter.

'Oh, what a shame, miss!' Jessie exclaimed as Annette replaced it in the box.

Annette recalled what Aunt Harriet had said when she had given the brooch to her, 'Your mother wore it on her wedding dress. Perhaps you will wear it on yours one day.' Perhaps, Annette thought now with a tinge of bitterness. She looked at her reflection wryly. What hope had she of finding a husband now? Who would propose marriage to a penniless governess? It had been painfully obvious how that young lawyer, who had attended the church socials in Kensington, and Mr Venables, the handsome, silver-haired widower who used to come to Aunt Harriet's musical evenings, had withdrawn their former marked attention towards her, once her fortune changed. The world was a pragmatic place. Then she remembered how Mr Venables' baritone had always sounded a tiny bit flat as he sang soulfully 'Drink to me only with thine eyes', and how the young lawyer's lingering handclasp had always felt quite clammy, and she smiled in spite of herself.

She surveyed herself carefully, standing away from the glass to obtain a full-length view. The gown fitted perfectly; the creamy lace and the pearls complimented her smooth neck and shoulders. Her spirits revived and her mood of fantasy returned. Perhaps one of Lady Louisa's guests was destined to fall in love with her! She pinched each cheek to encourage a rosy flush; there was a natural sparkle in her eyes.

Then she heard the mocking voice behind her: 'You look quite like Cinderella, Miss Duval. But I don't believe Mama has asked Prince Charming to dine tonight.'

Annette spun round. Imogen was standing in the doorway in her flounced white nightgown. More than the sneer in her tone, it was the way she had seemed to pounce upon a secret thought that made Annette feel disconcerted.

'It doesn't really matter how you look, you know, Miss Duval,' Imogen went on. 'Mama only asked you to make up the numbers at table.' Her cool, almost mocking gaze travelled over the shimmering dress.

For an instant Annette felt quite reduced – Cinderella with her shining ball gown turned back to rags.

'Well, *I* think Miss Duval looks beautiful,' Jessie ventured boldly.

'*You* shouldn't be hanging about up here, Jessie Lambert,' Imogen retorted cruelly. 'Pretending to be a lady's maid, with your dirty sooty hands –'

Jessie hid her hands beneath her apron and hung her head. She was only twelve years old; it was easy enough for Miss Imogen to belittle her.

Annette frowned. How long, she wondered, had Imogen been watching her? 'Go back to bed, Imogen,' she said crisply. 'And Jessie, you had best return downstairs. Thank you for your help.'

'My nightlight has gone out,' Imogen complained.

Annette resisted the suspicion that the child had probably blown it out herself as an excuse to leave her bed. 'Then Jessie will light it again for you,' she said. It was high time she went downstairs herself, she realized – she had been dawdling over the pleasant task of putting on her finery.

Gathering up her shining skirt, she began to descend the narrow back stairs that served this wing of the house. But after the second flight she diverted her route by way of the long gallery to the main staircase. It seemed a more fitting beginning to the evening ahead to glide down the last flight, her skirt fully spread in its sheen of peacock blue and green. In the hall she turned to glance at Dame Margery's portrait. It was almost as though Imogen had followed her downstairs. The same eyes, the same mocking regard looked out at her from the painted canvas.

As Imogen had foretold, there was no Prince Charming at the dining table. Annette found herself seated between the rector of St Michael's, the parish church, and the master of the local hunt, Colonel Grace. Opposite her was Dr Giles Fonteney, who looked after the health of the Quade family. It seemed unusual for a medical practitioner to be a member of the gentry; overhearing snatches of his conversation, she guessed he was more interested in scientific research than in his medical practice. At one point he and Sir Oswald, obviously friends of long standing, had a brief discussion about the efficacy or otherwise of country remedies.

'I tell you, Oswald, if one of the villagers really believes an infusion of marigolds and powdered adder scales will cure him of whatever disease he is suffering, then the odds are it will do so,' the doctor asserted.

'Possibly the disease, in such a case, is an hallucination in the first place,' Sir Oswald suggested, 'with false symptoms to attest to the power of the patient's imagination.'

'An imaginary cure for an imagined disease?' Dr Fonteney shrugged and glanced across the table at the rector, noticing as he did so the charming young woman who had come to Selbury as governess to that difficult child Imogen, heaven help her. 'Perhaps we are straying into metaphysical territory,' he suggested, wondering how long it would be before the new governess packed her bags and departed.

Every man at the table was married except for one deaf and elderly widower on Lady Louisa's left, Sir Nigel Blount. Annette had entertained a vague romantic hope when she first read his place card before dinner and realized there was no corresponding card with 'Lady Blount' inscribed upon it. How very foolish of her! The wives seemed extraordinarily similar in their style of dress, opinions and accents; Annette classified them as 'county folk'. Conversation across the candlelit table was for the most part studded with references drawn from a pool of shared experiences and mutual acquaintances, all of which she found quite bewildering.

There were two exceptions among the female guests. Mrs James, the rector's wife, was dressed quite dowdily and her voice, when she spoke, held a pleasant West Country burr. Lady Dowling, by contrast, was much overdressed and bejewelled, and her voice was excessively refined. Her husband, Sir Percy, spoke loudly and unabashedly in a Cockney accent; Annette gathered he was a rich manufacturer of some kind, recently settled in the neighbourhood. A self-made squire. She did not care for the way he laughed at his own sallies. Nor, as she observed from the raised eyebrows and looks askance around the table, did some of the other guests. Colonel Grace was mostly too engrossed with chewing and swallowing his food to talk to her, and clearly at a loss to know what he could say, after she told him she did not ride at all, let alone to hounds. Mr James, however, she found courteous and much interested in local history. Between the fish and rack of lamb she seized the chance to ask him about Dame Margery Quade.

The rector sipped his claret, considering his reply. 'On the whole, a lady I should prefer not to have known, I think – save as the merest acquaintance. There is, for instance, a legend about a witch-hunt she is supposed to have instigated to gain a piece of land. The witch herself is said to lie buried at the crossroads above Selbury.' He paused as a footman deftly removed his empty plate. 'Dame Margery was also suspected of having poisoned her first two husbands, and possibly the third, Sir Nicholas Quade himself. One seventeenth-century writer, Aubrey, I believe, refers to it somewhere. But he was a dreadful gossip and it is most likely a malicious rumour. There was such a deal of remarrying in Elizabethan times, the accusation of poisoning was quite common.'

Annette's eyes widened. 'I had no idea Dame Margery was such – such an intricate character. Although the expression on her face in her portrait is scarcely that of an innocent.' She smiled. 'The trouble with historical portraits is that one is apt to regard them as no more than subjects in fancy dress.'

The rector nodded. 'And the fancy dress – and those lifeless hands you see so often – were often painted in by some hack assistant. But the face – that was always the work of the artist himself.'

'Well, Dame Margery certainly built a beautiful place here at Selbury.' Annette turned slightly to help herself from the dish of vegetables offered to her.

'And made sure that accomplishment was recorded on her memorial,' the rector remarked.

'I've noticed her memorial at St Michael's – I must study it more closely,' Annette responded. She promised herself a visit one free afternoon to take a proper look at the parish church. The walk to Selbury and back would be very pleasant once the weather improved. She glanced at her other neighbour: Colonel Grace was now deeply engaged in talking to the horsy-looking lady on his other side. '. . . so Carberry's boy got blooded,' she overheard, and '. . . damned fox went to earth beyond Combe Lacey.' She felt free to pursue her conversation with Mr James.

'There is one curious circumstance which seems to indicate that Dame Margery was – how shall I put it – somewhat fearful of her ultimate destination,' he told her. 'There used to be an old custom practised hereabouts known as sin-eating. When the corpse was brought out of a house and laid upon the bier, a loaf of bread and bowl of milk were produced as well, and some poor wretch was paid a few pence to eat the bread and drink the milk. The idea being that in this way he took upon himself the sins of the deceased, who would thus be freed from walking . . . that is, remaining upon earth as a ghost.' He glanced towards Sir Oswald at the head of the table. 'Our host once told me that his famous ancestress made provision for a sin-eater at her funeral.'

'I trust the provision achieved its object,' Annette remarked.

'I have not heard that Selbury is haunted by *her* ghost.'

'You seem to imply there is another?'

The rector gestured as if to deprecate superstition. 'In the last century, one of my predecessors summoned the bishop of Salisbury to exorcise strange happenings in the long gallery. Pictures fell from the walls, ghostly footsteps were heard, that sort of thing. Oddly enough, the exorcism succeeded. But that might have been anyone's ghost – the spirit of some vengeful retainer, possibly.'

Bell, book and candle, Annette thought. It must be superstition, of course. And yet . . . She recalled how Imogen's youthful, unwavering gaze seemed to echo those compelling dark eyes in Dame Margery's portrait. Were there such beings as ghosts? If 'beings' they might be called. And – could they perhaps return to *inhabit* the living as well as haunt them? A disturbing speculation. She decided against broaching that hazy notion with the rector. She did not want him to think she might be one of those who dabbled in the craze of spiritualism – he might well consider that quite unsuitable for a governess who instructed her pupil in divinity. There had been a fashionable spiritualist circle in Kensington which engaged mediums and held séances. And papers such as the *Psychic News* were popular. She had bought a copy once to try to find out what it was all about. Mostly rubbish, she had concluded.

'Sir Oswald told me that the first Sir Nicholas Quade was a silk merchant,' she remarked.

Mr James nodded. 'Many of the Elizabethan families who rose to fortune had fairly humble origins, often in trade, and were proud of the fact. Which is not to say they could not assume arrogance and relish their power newly gained. But on the whole they were free, I think, of the petty snobbery we know today, when parvenus attempt to gain acceptance in society and are sneered at for their pains.'

Annette could not resist a swift glance towards red-faced Sir Percy Dowling, once more laughing uproariously at his own wit, seemingly oblivious of those raised eyebrows and pained expressions around him.

The week before, Sir Oswald and Lady Louisa had dined at nearby Wilton, seat of the great Herbert family, and had clearly counted it an honour. ('Mama is wearing her emeralds,' Imogen had commented.) Doubtless, Annette thought, these 'lesser gentry' around the table regarded their invitations to Selbury Quade in something of the same light. For the newly arrived Dowlings it must rank as a singular mark of 'getting on in the world'. The rector, she supposed, was respected for his cloth – after all, the church was one of the three professions a gentleman might consider – while Mrs James, with her pleasing West Country voice, was simply his appendage. Dreadful word! Almost as distasteful as 'relict' to denote a widow. As for herself, Annette thought, she was a complete outsider. Miss Duval, from another world. Yet Kensington, too, had had its ascending scales of social standing. And she had clearly observed the pecking order among the servants here at Selbury – with poor little Jessie at the very end of it. How complicated it all was! What must it be like in new countries such as America or Australia? she wondered. Human nature, she suspected, would not be much changed even in the Antipodes. Snobbery was light luggage, easily exportable. And then the sudden thought came to Annette that if she had been a young man instead of a female, she could have gone to Australia and tried her luck on the gold fields . . . and perhaps restored her patrimony. Much more adventurous and surely more agreeable than governessing. Certainly more exciting. Moleskins instead of serviceable serge . . .

During dessert, someone mentioned the current rumour that the death of the Prince Consort had proved too devastating a blow for the Queen: it was said her reason had given way and that was why she was hidden away on the Isle of Wight. 'It was always on the cards . . .' '. . . the hereditary strain – poor mad King George, her grandfather.' How eager some of the guests seemed to give the rumour credence, Annette thought.

Then Lady Dowling spoke up indignantly, shedding much of her assumed refinement. 'I for one don't believe a word of all that! She – Her Majesty, I mean – and Prince Albert built royal Osborne together. Ain't it her favourite 'ome? Only natural she should choose to go there, if you ask me.'

Annette caught an amused aside from Colonel Grace's other neighbours. 'They say that Osborne is furnished with *tartan carpets*, my dear! Do you imagine the Dowlings will do likewise at the Grange?' She appreciated Sir Oswald's attempt to defuse the issue.

'There's a mad ancestor lurking in the background of most families, isn't there? We are rather proud of ours: Carew Quade, who ran amok at the time of full moon back in Charles II's day. A lunatic, in fact. He was also quite renowned, in his saner moments, as an astonomer, which seems to have a certain deranged logic.'

But Lady Dowling continued zealous in her sovereign's defence. 'Mayn't the poor widow grieve in private for a while? She was devoted to the dear prince. And now she 'as – *has* – nine fatherless children.'

A royal relict, Annette reflected. But of course queen in her own right. If *she* had died, Prince Albert would have been the relict.

Lady Dowling's last remark proved too much for sensible Mrs James, herself the mother of six. 'Come now, Lady Dowling,' she remonstrated in her soft voice. 'The Princess

Royal was married five years ago and has children of her own –'

'Poor little Princess Beatrice is only four,' Lady Dowling insisted, 'and Prince Leopold seven – and besides, he has that dreadful haemo- haemo-something.'

'Haemophilia,' Doctor Fonteney, cracking walnuts, supplied precisely.

'Nine children,' Colonel Grace's horsy lady observed idly, peeling a choice nectarine and resolving never to ask Lady Dowling to anything except afternoon tea. 'And three other sons apart from the unfortunate Leopold. She *has* ensured the succession.'

Relinquishing finger bowl and napkin, Lady Louisa seemed to rise a little abruptly at this point to lead the ladies from the dining room. As Mrs James left the table she cast a wistful glance at the luscious hothouse grapes. Such luxury! She had been about to snip off a cluster.

It was another idle remark that eventually sent Annette to bed that night in a despondent mood. Following two of the ladies into the drawing room, she overheard one say: 'Do tell me, who exactly is the young person in the slightly unsuitable peacock-coloured dress?' And then the heedless reply, 'Oh, she's nobody, only the new governess Louisa has found for the impossible Imogen.'

Could anything have sounded more negative than that? *Nobody, only the new governess.* In the drawing room, well-meaning Mrs James came to sit beside Annette and complimented her on her gown. But Annette could not help wondering whether she, too, had overheard the unfortunate exchange and was merely being kind. Kind and Christian, a dutiful rector's wife. She responded listlessly and Mrs James was disappointed, for she had observed her husband enjoying his conversation with this young woman at the dinner table.

At the end of the evening, when all the guests had departed, Annette trailed up the back stairs to her room, shoulders drooping, her silk skirt dragging unheeded in the dust, her candle making huge shadows on the wall. *Nobody, only the new governess.* It was at this moment that the novelty of her new way of life quite dispersed and she recognized for the first time the reality and loneliness of her position.

Chapter Four

URING THE MONTHS that followed, governess and pupil achieved a tolerable relationship. By devoting herself assiduously to her work, Annette largely succeeded in overcoming despondency, though at heart she retained a profound dissatisfaction with her fate. Sometimes, usually on overcast, gloomy days, or when Imogen had been particularly trying, she would be overtaken by an acute sensation that she had been lured away from life's broad highway into a disagreeable side alley that led nowhere, bypassing all those experiences she longed for: romance, travel, elegant clothes, a comfortable home of her own. At such times she might look into the glass and stem a rising panic by saying aloud to her reflection, 'You are only twenty-one. There is plenty of time.' But was that true? Twenty-one, after all, was quite old for the marriage stakes.

As for Imogen, she was kept so busy by the new governess's teaching method that there was scarcely time to concoct mischief. Collections of pressed leaves and flowers now filled several albums. In spring, pussy willows, violets and cowslips adorned the schoolroom; successive crops of mustard-and-cress sprang from flannel squares on the window sill. A map of North America was pinned to one wall, dotted with tiny Confederate and Union flags made by Imogen to follow the progress of the Civil War. Beside it was a large diagram of the Selbury Quade estate. Governess and pupil planned to visit every part of the estate, to add noteworthy details to the diagram. This was a project of special interest to the heiress of Selbury. Last week they had gone to Combe Lacey farm, where a vast and ancient tree known from time beyond memory as the Druids' Oak stood in the sheep pasture. Imogen had drawn it naively, each green leaf carefully indented like a jigsaw-puzzle piece.

Sir Oswald was enthusiastic about the project; he considered it an excellent way to acquaint Imogen with her future responsibilities. Sometimes he even accompanied them on their explorations. Annette welcomed his presence; he was an attractive man and she found his conversation stimulating. She felt closer to him than she did to Lady Louisa; her communication with the latter was mostly confined to conventional exchanges concerned with Imogen and the schoolroom regime. But Sir Oswald would discuss such subjects as the theory of evolution, with which Mr Darwin had stunned the world a short while ago. (Below stairs, Cook had always called the gardener's boy 'you little monkey'; nowadays the epithet seemed to have acquired a new significance.) One afternoon, Annette went to the library to return the copy of *The Origin of Species* which Sir Oswald had urged her to read. She paused by his desk to study a perfect fossil shell that lay there. Looking up from his books, he picked up the fossil and said, 'I found this in a cliff near Lyme. The Dorset coastline is honeycombed with them, you know. You should take Imogen on a treasure hunt.' He turned the fossil in his hand. 'Perfect, isn't it? A sea creature perhaps a million years old. I wonder which truth it holds, Mr Darwin's or that of the fundamentalists who are so earnest to refute his theory.' He gave a short laugh. 'Do you know, Miss Duval, one such fellow, who also calls himself a scientist, has put forward the preposterous notion that Mr

Darwin has allowed himself to be misled by false evidence; he asserts that when God created the world in six days precisely, he peppered the rocks with fossils to give it the *appearance* of having evolved over a long stretch of time. Presumably with the express purpose of deluding Mr Darwin and enabling him to become the Devil's advocate, some billions of days later.'

Annette smiled incredulously. At the same time, she could not help feeling some sympathy for those who feared the rapid changes overtaking the world today. So much seemed incredible in this modern scientific age ... wonders like the electric light, gas-filled balloons that sailed across the sky, chloroform to relieve pain, and the deadly new magazine rifles to inflict it. During her last year at school, Miss Buss had arranged an expedition to the new Science Museum in Kensington. When they emerged from its handsome portals, it had seemed to Annette there was nothing man might not achieve. Perhaps it was not really so surprising that the fundamentalists should view science as the enemy of religious belief.

With a sudden gesture of recollection, Sir Oswald went over to one of the bookcases and rummaged along a shelf until he finally pulled out a manuscript work bound in peeling calfskin. Opening it, he found the passage that had come to his mind. 'Sir Carew Quade wrote this in 1650 or thereabouts,' he told Annette. ' "That the World is much older, than is commonly supposed, any man may be induced to believe from the finding of Fossils so many Foot depe in the Earth." I dare say Sir Carew went about chipping them from the rocks in his day, too.'

'Sir Carew – the lunatic!' Annette blurted out before she could stop herself. His name had remained in her memory ever since the dinner party in the New Year. She was immediately covered in confusion.

'Only at the time of the full moon,' Sir Oswald responded in an amused tone, thinking that Miss Duval looked even prettier when she blushed. 'He cannot have been such an idiot to have written that. But it has been left to Mr Darwin, famous or infamous according to one's viewpoint, to formulate a precise theory.'

Annette said hesitantly, 'I – I suppose one might deduce something of the theory of evolution from the Book of Genesis itself. I mean, the order of creation, first heaven and earth, and the oceans, then plant life, next the fishes and birds, then all the beasts and creeping creatures, and finally man. And woman,' she added.

Sir Oswald considered this. 'I believe you have omitted the fourth day, Miss Duval. Was not that the day on which the sun, moon and stars came into being? *After* the grass, seed-bearing herbs and fruit, as I recall from the many times I have had to read that particular lesson at divine service. It is, surely, quite unscientific that plants should flourish without warmth or light.' He smiled wryly. 'So far as the creation of man – and woman – is concerned, Genesis seems to provide us with two versions. The first, that God made male and female simul-taneously, the second, that woman arose from Adam's rib.'

'The story of Adam's rib is – more picturesque,' Annette remarked demurely.

'"And God caused Adam to fall into a deep sleep." While the operation was carried out. I believe that sentence is sometimes quoted to justify the use of chloroform.' Sir Oswald smiled at her – much as he might have smiled at Imogen, Annette realized. Sometimes she observed him smiling at his wife in a quite different way, intimate and secret-sharing, excluding the rest of the world. At such times she would look away again quickly, feeling as though she were an intruder.

Annette and Imogen read a good deal together. Sir Walter Scott's novels, *Tom Brown's Schooldays*, *A Tale of Two Cities*. There were tears in Annette's eyes as she read Sidney Carton's final words, 'It is a far, far better thing that I do, than I have ever done; it is a far, far better rest that I go to, than I have ever known.' But Imogen, dry-eyed, was more interested in the mechanism of the guillotine about to descend upon his head. Annette obtained a new anthology, *The Golden Treasury*, and they read verses aloud out of doors, acting 'Lord Ullin's Daughter' beside the reedy margins of the lake. '"Come back, come back!" he cried in grief, "And I'll forgive your Highland chief! – My daughter, O my daughter!"' Imogen declaimed, a tartan travelling run flung across one shoulder. But Annette would not allow her to use for further dramatic effect the punt kept in the little boathouse. The lake Dame Margery had made was deep, and neither Annette nor Imogen could swim.

Lady Louisa thoroughly approved of the musical gymnastics, Imogen bending and stretching gracefully to the accompaniment of the schoolroom piano. She even consented to a pair of dumb-bells being ordered from London.

A little hesitantly, aware that she was invading Imogen's most private territory, Annette spoke of her own interest in Dame Margery. Imogen's response was guarded at first; she seemed to have an almost sacred reverence for her ancestress. But she could not resist helping Annette to find out more about her. One afternoon Sir Oswald showed them two musty volumes, one a record of estate affairs dating back to the building of Selbury, the other a curious collection of miscellaneous lore and recipes which appeared to have been compiled by Dame Margery herself. Carefully they turned the fragile pages, sharing discoveries.

There were ancient complaints: 'The Gentlemen who goe a-hawking across my shepe pastures have dalliance with ye Shepherdess, and the shepe straye from ye flock to their greate harme.' Again: 'A cunninge rascal stole a cow from my dayry grasing. He hath made a hole in a hott loafe newly drawne out of the oven, and put it on the Oxes-horn for a convenient time to soften it, and then was able to turn the horne of ye cow the contrary way: So that Master Shadbrook could not sweare to it being my beast.'

'Master Shadbrook was Dame Margery's factor – his name occurs many times,' Sir Oswald told them. He smiled as he read another entry. 'How would you like to try this cure, Dame Imogen? "For a Scarlet Rashe, Take a living Frog and hold it in a Cloth, that it does not go down into the Child's Mouth; and putt the Head into the Child's Mouth till it is dead; and then take another Frog . . ."'

Imogen made a wry face.

Among the cures, Annette spied this sinister entry: 'A Drench of Yewgh pounded is a potent poison.' Imogen saw it too, and stored it in her mind.

The estate book held records of the amounts paid to 'joyners, carpenters and masons' when Selbury Quade was built, occasionally overwritten with a complaint. This peevish comment appeared beside the amount paid 'to Ned Eason, wood-carver, for Oake Leaves to ye Staircase': 'Too bigge withal and acornes too few.'

On another page, Annette drew Imogen's attention to a rough cross scrawled beneath a note concerning the sale of a parcel of land, Miller's Green. 'Peter Selbury, His Marke' was written beside the cross.

'That was how people not able to write used to sign documents,' she told her pupil.

'We haven't been to Miller's Green yet,' Imogen said, thinking of the diagram pinned to the schoolroom wall. 'It's just beyond Foxhollow. I don't believe I've ever been there.' She turned back to the recipe book. 'Listen to this, Papa: "A Horse-shoe nailed to the Threshold of a Door is to hinder the power of Witches." I've seen horseshoes nailed above cottage doors in the village!'

'I dare say quite a few people still believe in witchcraft,' her father said. 'Superstition dies hard. I'm sure I have seen *you* touch wood for luck, Imogen.'

Annette remembered the rector's allusion to a piece of land and a witch-hunt. 'I have heard a witch lies buried at the crossroads above Selbury village,' she remarked.

'We should dig her up!' Imogen said ghoulishly. Then she saw how her father frowned. 'Oh, Papa, I did not really mean that.' But she did. How satisfactory to find a bundle of witch bones!

'I shall come with you when you visit Miller's Green,' Sir Oswald promised.

There was no more talk of witches.

42

One day in March, Annette and Imogen walked to Selbury to visit St Michael's church. Imogen took a notebook so that she could copy the inscription on Dame Margery's memorial. Leaving the parkland, they went through narrow lanes where ash and holly branches met overhead. Imogen picked wild flowers: pale wood anemones, yellow primroses, modest snowdrops, their petals delicately veined with green. There was a stiff breeze with a hint of salt in it: Tor Bay, with its high cliff and pebble beach, was only a dozen miles away.

They had the church to themselves. It seemed strange to stand amid empty pews which every Sunday overflowed with faithful saints and sinners both. Dame Margery's memorial was set beside her husband's, below a stained-glass window. The two figures, both in bas-relief, knelt to face each other. Sir Nicholas wore doublet and hose and a long cloak hanging in stiff sculptured folds; Dame Margery's gown had ruffs at neck and wrist. A hood concealed her hair, its veil flowing in precise pleats behind her. Her inscription was brief and to the point:

> *I beseche all peple fer and ner*
> *To prey for me Margery Quade*
> *Which did rais a goodely hous*
> *And beside gaf almes to the poore*
> *And the viii day of June was buried her*
> *On hoos soule God have mercy*

Annette recalled the rector's account of the sin-eater provided for in Dame Margery's will. Did this last prayer contain a hint of fear?

'What dreadful spelling!' Imogen commented smugly.

'Even worse than yours,' Annette replied. 'It would be the spelling of the stonemason who made the memorial. Perhaps Dame Margery dictated it to him before she died.'

Imogen put away her notebook and said, 'I want to visit Edie's grave now. That's why I picked these flowers. Edie Kitto – she was the daughter of our lodgekeeper. She died not long ago. She had a dreadful cough and used to spit up blood.'

Somewhat dismayed by Imogen's matter-of-fact tone, which held no hint of regret or sorrow, Annette went with her to a new granite tombstone behind the church. This inscription read:

'Sacred to the memory of EDITH MARY KITTO, who departed this life 20th November 1860, aged 7 years 4 months. "Suffer the little children to come unto Me."'

'How sad,' Annette commented. 'Were you friends, you and Edie?'

There was impatience in Imogen's tone as she answered, 'I told you, she was the lodgekeeper's daughter. She had to die because she was so ill.' She placed the little bunch of spring flowers beside the tombstone. 'There's plenty of space left below the bit about Edie. I expect that's for her parents. People like that are apt to have weak constitutions. I heard Mama say so. They will probably die too.'

Annette stared at Imogen in dismay. Why, the child spoke as though she herself were assured of immortality! An astonishing possibility entered Annette's mind. Did Imogen . . . could she possibly harbour some grand delusion concerning death? Disturbed, she followed as Imogen led the way to another, much older grave, so sunken in the unkempt grass around it that they had to crouch to decipher the weathered words carved on the stone:

Edward Fletcher's Son lyeth here, John Fletcher
    was his Name,
His Father's love was so to him, he caus'd to
    write the same:
He was but 6 Yeares 2 Moneths old, and then was
    buryed here,
And of his Body the Wormes did find a Dish of
    dainty chere.

Recoiling from those final words, Annette exclaimed, 'How

dreadful! Poor little soul.' Rising to her feet, she brushed down the hem of her navy-blue skirt.

'It just says what happened,' Imogen asserted with a shrug. 'I wonder how long it takes for the worms to eat someone up.'

What a morbid child she was! But did she really not relate the fact of death to herself? As they left the churchyard Annette said tentatively, 'A child's grave always makes me think of something Shakespeare wrote, "Golden lads and girls all must, As chimney-sweepers, come to dust." '

Imogen trudged along beside her in silence for some moments. Then she said, 'Chimney sweeps often die, I know that – their masters don't give them enough to eat, they keep them thin on purpose so that they won't get lodged inside the chimneys. Cook told me.'

Clearly, to this extraordinary child, chimney sweeps were counted among those who had 'weak constitutions'. Annette summoned up her courage. 'Everyone must die, Imogen,' she said gently. 'Every single person who ever lives. That is what Shakespeare is saying. And after death, we hope to go to Heaven and find eternal life.' Did she herself believe that? The question remained unanswered in her mind.

Imogen had stopped still; in her eyes was a look of incredulity mingled with dawning horror. She said slowly, 'That means . . . *I* am going to die!'

'One day, yes,' Annette answered in the same gentle tone. 'But I feel sure you will have a long and happy life, Imogen.' To another child, it would surely have been possible to stretch out a hand, offer the reassurance of human contact. Not so with Imogen Quade. 'But – did you not realize,' Annette went on, 'going to church each Sunday, praying for the departed, singing hymns about Heaven – surely you realized, Imogen.'

But Imogen looked back at her with total despair in her stony gaze. 'Nobody told me. I thought . . . I knew other people died, very old people, sick people . . . people who were murdered, or killed in war, or shipwrecked, or –'

'I see.' Annette sighed. 'So you truly imagined yourself to be immortal. It is not so.' And had the child also imagined she

45

would not grow old, or that she would achieve maturity and never decline? But there was no logic in delusion.

Suddenly Imogen began to run on ahead, perhaps in a vain attempt to outstrip a terrible reality. Annette, hurrying after her, attempted breathless words of comfort that were blown away on the wind: 'We do have our immortal souls, Imogen – that is what Heaven is about . . .' She was deeply unhappy to be the instrument that had shattered such a delusion. But someone, some time, would have had to force Imogen to confront the fact of her mortality.

Safe home again, the cosy ritual of teatime, the reassuring presence of parents and familiar surroundings restored Imogen's spirits; but the terror returned to her that night. The same terror that she had once inflicted upon poor Edie Kitto. Curled beneath warm bedclothes, Imogen conjured up the inscription for her own headstone: 'Sacred to the memory of IMOGEN CLAIRE QUADE' . . . And beneath, her dead self in its coffin. Put away inside a tapering box. Never to feel, think, move again. When would she die, where, how! *No!* Her whole living, breathing being revolted against the dreadful vision. She gasped denial aloud, then cast aside the bedclothes and flung herself upon her knees at the bedside. The steady glow of the nightlight threw her shadow, monstrously distorted, on the wall. 'Not me, not me! Let me be different, make me immortal. Please, God, don't let me die!'

It was a strange, pagan prayer. Had Imogen but known it, a similar plea had often lain upon the lips of her ancestress. And like Dame Margery's, Imogen's newfound terror would never wholly subside, but would lurk like a black, evil insect, hiding from the light of day, scuttling out in the dark hours of night.

Father, daughter and governess set out to visit Miller's Green on an April day of sun and sudden showers. Foxhollow wood, as they tramped through it, was filled with the affirmation and renewal of life: glossy young leaves unfurling about the boles of ancient trees, a tide of green shawling the stark boughs of winter. Birdsong gave shrill warning of their coming; a flame-red squirrel scampered around a tree trunk. A hedgehog crept through the undergrowth with a brood of prickly young.

'Mrs Tovey at Combe Lacey keeps a hedgehog in her kitchen to catch black beetles,' Imogen remembered. There had been apple cake and clotted cream in the Tovey kitchen the day she and Annette visited the farm.

'The gypsies cook hedgehogs in a covering of clay,' her father said. 'Baked hedgehog is supposed to taste like chicken. The gypsies visit us each year,' he told Annette. 'They make their camp here in Foxhollow for two months or so. Better to allow them here, all above board, than have them trespass and damage the coverts. Vinnicot doesn't agree with me – he sniffs the air for pheasant stew simmering in their pots.' Jem Vinnicot was the gamekeeper. 'He's not the only one to distrust them. Dan Trefoil keeps a close eye on the stables, and the farmers' wives watch their clotheslines like hawks.'

Annette ducked under the hooped bough he held aside to allow her to pass unhindered along the narrow path. 'Does the same tribe return each year?' she asked.

'I suppose so. They all look the same to me. Swarthy, unkempt, wearing outlandish clothes, speaking their own strange lingo.'

Imogen, skipping a pace ahead, glanced back over her shoulder. 'One of the gypsy women always comes to the house to tell fortunes,,' she said. 'Perhaps she'll tell mine this year. Last time, Mama said I was too young to have a fortune.'

Annette smiled. 'Perhaps she'll tell mine, too.' On this lovely day of sunshine, she felt some golden future might easily await her after all.

Miller's Green, when they reached it, began as a grassy clearing just beyond Foxhollow. It had a strange, deserted feel about it. After the birdsong, the cracklings underfoot, the rustling foliage of the wood, it seemed to impose a sudden hush. A huge tree stump with gnarled grey roots, all that remained of a massive beech tree, stood at one side. Other, lesser trees had sprung up to shade the clearing: slender ash, sturdy rowan, tall elms.

'I don't like this place,' Imogen told her father. She shivered, and there was a fearful expression in her eyes. 'It feels as though . . . as though we are not wanted here.'

'That is purely your imagination, Dame Imogen,' her father asserted almost brusquely. He looked around the clearing. Almost – the thought came to Annette – as though to challenge any hostile spirit that might inhabit there. 'I wonder where the mill cottage stood,' he went on. 'It must have been beside the stream so that the water could turn the wheel to grind the corn.'

But it had all vanished without trace.

Imogen settled herself on the grass beside the great tree stump and spread out their picnic tea. They had brought fruitcake wrapped in a cloth, and a bottle of barley water, with thick white cups to drink from. Sir Oswald wandered off to trace the path of the old mill stream, now a mere shallow ditch overgrown with pink campion, wild garlic and yellow colts-foot. Annette searched the ground for signs that a cottage had once stood here, but it must have fallen down long ago. Not even the chimney stone remained, always the last relic of former habitation. Suddenly she spied a patch of darker green among the grass. Stooping, she peered closer and plucked a crown of tiny leaves, then pinched it between thumb and forefinger and sniffed. Chervil, she thought. And close by she found straggles of flowering burnet. She went over to the tree stump to show Imogen.

'The last remnants of some forgotten garden, perhaps,' she told the child. Did a thread of smoke once curl from a vanished chimney, and the miller's family sit down to bowls of herb-flavoured broth? She could not know that long ago, an ill-favoured girl had grown up in this place, lived out her solitary existence here, and died with a scream on her lips.

'Let me see!' Imogen darted up and ran across to the place where the herbs grew. Stooping, she rooted up great swatches of chervil, of burnet and crushed them together to inhale their fragrance. Watching, Annette saw the child suddenly begin to act strangely, to swerve and dodge about as though she were

48

trying to escape from something ... a horsefly or wasp, perhaps. Imogen ran towards her father, shrieking, 'Papa! Papa! A bee is stinging me!'

Sir Oswald did not care for behaviour verging on the hysterical. 'Stay still, child,' he called. 'It will go away. You are only making it more agitated. A bee sting will not harm you.'

He was wrong. Imogen let out another shriek as the bee, trapped beneath the folds of her scarf, lodged its sting in the soft white hollow at the base of her throat. She put up both hands to tear away the scarf, then swayed and slowly toppled in a heap on the grass.

Her father sprang up and sped over to her, Annette at his heels. He swept the child into his arms. She seemed to have lost consciousness, although her closed eyelids fluttered slightly. She was deathly pale save for the rapid swelling on her exposed throat, red and angry-looking. Her long hair spread in dark strands over her father's tweed-clad arm.

Annette hurried after Sir Oswald's fleeing figure in a desperate rush to the house, gasping for breath as they sped back through Foxhollow wood. In such a short space of time the happiness of the golden day had been overshadowed.

It was an hour before Dr Fonteney came, summoned by one of the stable lads. Both parents hovered by their daughter's bed as she lay fighting for breath, half-conscious now. The swelling on her throat had broken out into a weeping mass, as though she had been scalded.

The doctor, it transpired, had dealt with such a case before. He told them gravely that to some people, a bee sting could prove as fatal as snakebite. There was little he could do except reduce the swelling by laying on cold compresses.

'Luckily her constitution is sound,' he said. The remark inevitably reminded Annette of Imogen's delusion concerning death. Well, she had come within sight of death today. She looked very vulnerable as she lay there.

Gradually the child's breathing became easier and she was pronounced out of danger. But she was ill for another ten days or so.

'Needless to say, she must do all she can to avoid being stung in future,' Dr Fonteney said when at last Imogen was up and about again, with only a faint scar at the base of her throat to show for her ordeal.

And now Imogen had a new dread to mask her deeper fear. All through the spring and summer she went about shutting windows in case a bee should stray indoors. Outside, she would gaze about the landscape in apprehension, listening for the sound that would herald the approach of the enemy. Annette herself became alert to every flying insect. It was almost as though a curse had been laid upon the child, she thought.

In fact, Imogen only became aware of the mortal danger she had passed through after it was over; while it lasted, she was too ill to realize it. But afterwards there was time to brood upon it, and one day she asked her father a certain question that weighed upon her spirit. They were at the stables, waiting for her bay pony to be brought up. Lady Louisa had thought a gentle canter would help restore colour to her cheeks. Imogen was beginning to shoot up these days; she looked quite tall, an impression accentuated by her long-skirted riding habit.

Standing in the cobbled courtyard, she chose the words to frame her question. 'Papa . . . I have been wondering. What would have happened to Selbury if – if I had not got well? Who would have inherited instead of me?'

Sir Oswald put one arm about his daughter's shoulders in a protective gesture. 'A thoughtful question, Dame Imogen.' He sighed. 'You should be aware of the situation, I suppose. God knows, I hope it will never come to pass. I have a cousin, Philip Wanslea, and the house and estate would pass to him in such circumstances. Then to his son, Peter . . . But I doubt Philip would wish to live here. He has his own place, in Gloucester-shire. He might decide to let Selbury, even to sell it –'

He broke off when he saw the stricken look of dismay upon Imogen's face, then continued, 'Or else Peter might decide to come here. He is a little older than you. You might meet the Wansleas one day.' He glanced at his daughter tenderly and added gently, 'You know, it is possible that you yourself may decide not to live at Selbury eventually.'

Not live at Selbury? Imogen began an indignant denial, but her father went on speaking. 'Yes, my child, it is a distinct possibility. When you marry, you may well live at your husband's property. You will become part of his family. In such a case, I dare say you might decide to find a tenant for Selbury.'

'Then I shall never marry!'

'In that case, you would have no children to inherit Selbury Quade, no son – or daughter – to whom it could pass in years to come.'

Imogen frowned darkly. 'Then I would make my husband live here! He should belong to *my* family! I will never leave Selbury, Papa. Never!'

Sir Oswald sighed and shook his head, and wished for the thousandth time for the son he did not have. An heiress created so many problems; for herself, perhaps, most of all. He was afraid that Imogen's intense loyalty to Selbury might cause her real unhappiness in the future.

Later, as they cantered as far as Combe Lacey, where the Druids' Oak stood resplendent in summer greenery, the fresh air helped to dispel Imogen's dark thoughts. But from that day she began to harbour an irrational hostility towards those unknown Wanslea cousins, assigning to them the quite unwarranted role of would-be usurpers of her inheritance.

Chapter Five

LIFE BELOW STAIRS at Selbury Quade was on the whole harmonious, capably organized by Mrs Arkney, the housekeeper. 'Mrs' was purely a courtesy title: middle-aged Grace Arkney had in fact never married, a circumstance which, in her maturity, she considered a matter for self-congratulation rather than lament. She had begun her life of domestic service at a hiring fair at the age of twelve, and took pride in her subsequent rise to a position of responsibility.

A drama like the wretched Molly's unwanted pregnancy was a rare occurrence. All the servants, especially the younger females, were aware that both Molly and her babe had died in the poorhouse at Yeovil; they knew, too, which lusty village lad had put her in the family way. He still strutted about the place, but Molly had simply vanished from the world . . . and the world spared scant sympathy for her fate. Well, that was the way of things.

Once a year, in early summer, the coming of the gypsies to Foxhollow touched the lives of those above and below stairs alike with the suggestion that an alien, exotic world existed apart from their own ordered lives.

This year, it was Jessie who first sighted the gypsy encampment and brought news of their arrival to the servants' hall. She had spent her free afternoon at her mother's cottage down at Selbury Combe, and returned to the big house by way of Foxhollow. One glimpse of wood smoke spiralling above the trees, the Romany caravans and tethered horses cropping the sweet grass, and Jessie fled, heedless of thorns and brambles, her mind a jumble of childish terrors instilled by country lore. The gypsies! Blackies! Queer, dark-skinned heathens. And as she fled, sobbing for breath, an old refrain pounded in her head: 'My mother said – I never should – play with the gypsies – in the wood'. She used to skip to that rhyme as her sisters twirled a piece of rope, chanting the words all gay and carefree, in the days before she entered service. She ran breathless through the vegetable garden and came at last into the great kitchen at Selbury, one hand pressed to the stitch in her side.

'They – they blackies be here again!' she gasped incoherently, leaning against the big scrubbed table where Mrs Robbins the cook, that comfortable provider of meals, was rolling out pastry for pies.

Maggie the parlourmaid was sipping a cup of tea, her little finger cocked genteelly. 'What's all the fuss about, then?' she asked Jessie. 'You look real terrified, you do. Scared out of your wits. If them gyppos are here again, it means we'll have our fortunes told, don't it?' And she smiled to herself and thought of Ned, the young footman with whom she was going steady. Maybe this time next year there would be a gold band on her finger . . . this year, next year, some time for sure.

'It means,' Mrs Robbins declared as she wielded her rolling pin, 'that Dan Trefoil will bid his lads keep special watch on the stables. 'Tes well known that many a painted pony be sold off at the horse fair when they gypsies be about.' She laid a blanket of pastry over a dish of steak and kidney with a loving gesture. 'To say nothing of poaching. Jem Vinnicot has never catched a gypsy poacher yet, but he allus swears their pots be filled with pheasant stew. He can never credit, can Jem, why Master allows them to come to Foxhollow year after year.

'Tweren't so in the olden days – there were mantraps set in the woods then to catch the likes of them. Ah, we live in soft times.'

Maggie shivered. 'A mantrap be a right cruel thing. A man could lose a leg, maybe, all for the sake of a bird bred up to be shot at for the gentry's pleasure.'

Mrs Robbins glanced at her sideways. ''Tes not for us to reckon the whys and wherefores of such things. But Master had all them mantraps done away with, soon as he came into his inheritance, that I do know.'

'I hear the Egyptians have favoured Selbury with their presence once again,' Sir Oswald remarked at breakfast.

Imogen looked across at him, puzzled. 'Egyptians, Papa? From Egypt?'

Her father smiled. 'The lords and dukes of Little Egypt.' He made the words sound rich and rolling.

'The gypsies, Imogen,' Annette interpreted – to be rewarded by a scowl. Imogen did not like to appear ignorant.

Lady Louisa sipped her tea reflectively. For the past few weeks she had not appeared at breakfast. Annette had wondered if she were ill. But she soon dismissed that conjecture: these days, Lady Louisa seemed more cheerful and looked happier than she had ever known her. She said now, 'They call themselves . . . let me see . . . Romany *chals*, in their own language. And they call us . . . *gorgios*.' She smiled at Annette. 'Like everyone else, I read *The Romany Rye* when it was a seven days' wonder and became quite enamoured of the gypsy life for a while.' She glanced mischievously at her husband. 'I assure you, I was quite prepared to be "off with the raggle-taggle gypsies Oh!" Until I recalled how – unsavoury our Foxhollow visitors are at close quarters.' And she exchanged one of those intimate, exclusive smiles with Sir Oswald.

'The gypsy diaspora,' he said. 'Some believe they are the lost tribe of the Hebrews, but many of their ceremonies appear similar to those of the Hindu.' He had fallen into his scholarly mien for the moment, but his next words were brisk. 'They are not very well treated in our green and pleasant land, I fear. In fact, we seized the chance to get rid of a fair few by sending them off to Botany Bay.'

Imogen said pleadingly, 'Please, Mama, may I have my fortune told this year? *Please* let me go down to the servants' hall when the gypsy woman comes!'

Lady Louisa said indulgently, 'I dare say there is no harm in it. All that nonsense! Perhaps Miss Duval would like to hear her fortune, too . . .'

Annette realized she was required to make sure the gypsy did not fill Imogen's head with foolish notions – at least, to ensure such notions were speedily refuted.

'Yes, of course,' she answered brightly.

As Hagar Smith drew up a chair to the long table in the servants' hall, she seemed the very image of Meg Merrilees, Annette thought. 'Old Meg was brave as Margret Queen and tall as Amazon,' she recollected involuntarily. Upright and imposing, with a dark complexion, the gypsy wore a chip-straw bonnet and a long red cloak. Gold earrings dangled beneath her black ringlets. It seemed as though a countess of Little Egypt had indeed come visiting Selbury Quade. Her eyes were very black, and so were her fingernails, and when you sat beside her, you were inescapably aware of a musty, unwashed odour. But mere neglect of soap and water did not detract from the glamorous aura which surrounded this gypsy fortune-teller.

Besides Imogen and Annette, only Maggie, Sarah the second chambermaid and Jessie were present – and Jessie was merely an onlooker. It cost a precious silver sixpence to cross the gypsy's palm, and sixpences were hard to come by. Both the young footmen, Edward and John, affected to despise fortune-telling as a female preoccupation.

The gypsy's brooding gaze rested on Annette and Imogen for a moment, assessing their significance within this great house. The plainly dressed young woman appeared to be some sort of superior servant, the self-assured child was without doubt the daughter of the house.

Maggie was first. She giggled and rolled her eyes at Sarah as she held out her hand, palm upward, to be grasped in the gypsy's brown fingers. In a singsong voice, Hagar predicted a likely enough fortune for a pert, pretty parlourmaid: a wedding within two years and – peering closely at mysterious lines on the heel of Maggie's palm – five children. Something to be lost, then found again, and, for good measure, a journey to the sea. Maggie nodded artlessly as if to corroborate: hadn't Ned promised to take her to the summer fair at Torbridge? She was warned to take care with sharp objects and – a hint of sadness – to expect bad news connected with her family within a twelvemonth.

'Ah, my old granddad,' Maggie remarked in a matter-of-fact tone. 'Poor soul, he's suffered the wasting sickness for a long time now. 'Twill be a happy release when he passes on to glory.'

Satisfied with her lot, she moved aside to let Sarah take her turn, while Jessie gravely regarded Maggie in a new light – the future mother of five children.

Imogen sat with her pointed chin cupped in her hands, listening intently as Hagar pronounced another future for the more staid and subdued chambermaid. Annette, for her part, found the performance rather tedious, predictable in itself. She did not think Lady Louisa need fear its influence upon Imogen. But she remained fascinated by the gypsy woman's imposing, almost arrogant presence, the contrast she presented to the servants clustered around the end of the table. Hers was a wild, free spirit; they were tamed, for ever at their employer's beck and call. That was the real allure of gypsy life: in a word, freedom! To live apart from the everyday civilized scheme of things . . .

Hagar's chanting voice continued, a voice that might surely cast a spell . . . or else utter a curse. Sarah, it seemed, would marry an older man, perhaps a widower –

'Ebenezer Gulover!' Maggie squealed. 'Why, Sarah, 'tes him for sure!'

Sarah's cheeks grew pink. Ebenezer Gulover was the tenant

of Yatting Combe farmstead; his wife had passed away two years since. Sarah recalled the visit he had made to her mother's cottage on her last free afternoon. They had sat together in the front room and exchanged a few words of stilted conversation while her mother made a pot of tea and produced a freshly-baked lardy cake. Now, as the gypsy relinquished her hand, Sarah pondered the likelihood of becoming mistress of Yatting Combe, wife to a man with greying hair and deep-etched lines up on his face.

To young Jessie this seemed a dull fortune. But then, she thought, heavy-featured Sarah was rather dull herself.

Sarah moved away from the gypsy's side, and Imogen said, 'Now it's your turn, Miss Duval. I want to wait till last.'

How very unchildish of her, Annette reflected. Surely most little girls would want to be first, not last. But Imogen Quade was not like other little girls.

So Annette took her place next to the gypsy woman, anticipating a singsong recital of events, the usual fortune-telling patter. Yet she could not help a frisson of excitement. An extra piece of silver was required as token of her superior status, and then her narrow, fine-boned hand was taken in the gypsy's firm grasp.

Hagar said nothing to begin with, exploring Annette's palm intently, turning her hand this way and that. 'Perhaps I have no future,' Annette thought wryly. Then the gypsy raised her eyes briefly to look at her curiously. Annette recoiled slightly from her glance.

'*Apo miro dadeskro vast*,' Hagar muttered. 'There is a strange destiny here.'

Jessie gasped in pleasurable anticipation and Maggie nudged Sarah in the ribs, while Imogen leaned a little closer.

'Your life is long. The road you take leads far across the seas.' Hagar paused impressively. 'It is by your own deeds that you will find contentment and much gold, and become known to the world. I see a man who is able to steal the spirit of a man or a woman . . . or a child. I cannot tell how . . . A man of many eyes. He has an influence upon your life.'

57

Maggie clapped her hand to her mouth to stifle an explosion of laughter. 'Oh, miss! A man of many eyes!' She succumbed to a sharp dig from Sarah's elbow.

Hagar continued unperturbed. 'But first, I see misfortune. There is a great loss. Someone will bring false testimony against you. You will be helpless. You will know sorrow before joy, tears before laughter.' At this point Hagar paused, frowning. How could the fortune of this *gorgio* woman be mixed with that of a Romany *chal*, a child of her own people? Yet she seemed to see in her mind's eye the fleeting image of a little *Romanchal* threatened by the jaws of some fierce beast . . . '*Kusto bacht* – that is all I can tell you,' she muttered, letting Annette's hand fall away.

It was surely enough, Annette thought. Indeed, her future seemed positively crowded with adventure. Yet it was all predicted in such vague terms . . . except for that 'man of many eyes'! Because she shared some of the simple desires of Maggie and Sarah, she was disappointed the gypsy had not mentioned one all-important word.

'And – marriage?' she asked hesitantly.

Sighing, Hagar took up her hand again. But it was a mere gesture; she scarcely bothered to consult the telltale lines. 'I see a marriage that is not a marriage,' she pronounced.

It was clear the two maids were as bewildered by this as Annette herself. And Jessie felt quite distressed for Miss Duval, though the bit about 'much gold' sounded all right, she thought. Imogen merely regarded her governess with an impassive gaze.

In spite of herself, Annette felt a ridiculous pang of dismay. Of course it was all nonsense; she would marry, and it would be a proper marriage; she would be as other women, beloved, secure, serene. Wishing she had not asked the question, she resumed her former place at the table.

Now Imogen went forward to sit beside the gypsy. She produced three silver coins cajoled from her father, and held out her hand in an imperious gesture. Thinking to satisfy the child of this great house with a few easy phrases – for who could possibly predict the future for one so young? – Hagar took the small hand in hers. She peered at the palm – and the next moment recoiled with a look of horror upon her face. '*O Del!*' she gasped and touched her forehead in a quick gesture, as though to ward off evil. Then, recovering slightly, she shook her head. 'I cannot tell – your hand is too unformed – there is no future here,' she muttered disjointedly. Imogen's three coins had quickly vanished beneath the folds of the red cloak, but now Hagar drew them forth again and laid them on the table. 'Take thy silver,' she said in an almost fearful voice. 'I want none of it.' She pushed back her chair so that its legs scraped discordantly on the stone-flagged floor, and rose to her majestic height. '*Dza devlesa!*' She gave the gypsy farewell as she walked away.

Imogen stared after her, an outraged expression on her face. Annette had never seen such a revelation of her feelings.

'She's nothing but a cheat!' the child burst out furiously. 'She's just a – a smelly old hag pretending to tell the future. I don't believe a word she says!' And then, refuting her own words, she shouted after the departing figure, 'I'm not too young to have a fortune!'

'There, Miss Imogen, don't take on so,' Sarah said smoothingly. 'You shall surely hear a grand fortune for yourself another day.'

Imogen gave her a scornful glance. 'I wish I'd never come down here,' she said. 'Just to hear all the boring things she told you and Maggie – and all that rubbish about Miss Duval. Who cares what happens to any of you?'

'Imogen!' Annette interposed. The others at the table did not react; they were used to Miss Imogen and her ways.

Imogen merely shrugged.

It was all too true, Annette thought with a sort of despair: the child simply had no feelings for anyone else. All she cared about, besides herself, was Selbury Quade . . . and that was a strange, obsessive passion.

Striding towards Foxhollow, Hagar inhaled the sweet fresh air to cleanse her soul. She felt an urgent need for the companionship of her own kind. Deep within her mind lay the impression of pure evil she had received when she took the hand of that strange child. A child she seemed, yet she appeared to contain an age-old spirit of malevolence. For, as Hagar gazed upon that hand, she had seen a vision of rotting flesh, crawling with white maggots. It was as though she looked upon the palm of someone long dead.

The next week Sir Oswald and Lady Louisa left Selbury for their annual visit to London. It was to be a particularly gay season this year, with celebrations to mark the Prince of Wales's marriage to Alexandra, the lovely young princess from Denmark. The Quade town house was in a fashionable square, the rooms kept swathed in dustsheets for the greater part of each year. Half the indoor servants were to accompany Sir Oswald and Lady Louisa; while they were away, the atmosphere at Selbury always became more relaxed. Dust was often left unheeded on polished surfaces, and carpets sometimes remained unswept. Jessie was allowed to sleep until six each morning for a few blissful weeks, instead of rising as dawn broke.

Before leaving, Lady Louisa took pains to impress upon Annette the need for vigilance where Imogen was concerned.

'Always remember, Miss Duval, that Dr Fonteney has told us she might not survive another bee sting,' she said quietly.

Annette thought at first it must be anxiety over Imogen that brought her parents back from London a little earlier than usual. This was partly so, but there was another reason as well. By the time they returned, it had become apparent that Lady Louisa was in a delicate state of health. Within four months, another child would be born at Selbury Quade.

Chapter Six

I T WAS INTOLERABLY stuffy in the schoolroom. With a decisive gesture Annette flung wide the window. Imogen, stewing over an arithmetic lesson, made an automatic noise of protest.

'I really doubt, Imogen, that any bee could possibly fly up here. It's ridiculous to stay shut up like this in the middle of summer.' Annette paused by the open window for a moment to release her irritation and enjoy the spectacle of a high, blue, cloudless sky. A little breeze riffled the papers on the table. She had felt the stuffy atmosphere beginning to addle her brain as well as her pupil's. Imogen's attempts at long division had degenerated into a messy page of rubbings-out. 'Now perhaps you will be able to keep that decimal point in its rightful place,' Miss Duval said sternly, returning to her chair.

Imogen looked sulky but did not make an issue of it. After all, it was true that the myriad murmurations of the bees were far below in the bright summer garden, furry brown bodies bumbling from flower to flower. The episode of the bee sting had in fact receded in her memory, replaced by a far more consuming anxiety.

Mama was to have another child towards the end of this year. She and Papa had broken the momentous news soon after their return from London.

'A new little baby will be coming to live with us before Christmas,' Mama had told her coyly, almost, Imogen thought impatiently, as though it would arrive in the middle of a gooseberry bush in the kitchen garden. (The late unlamented Miss Nuthall used to say, absurdly, that babies were found in gooseberry bushes.) In fact, as Imogen knew perfectly well, Mama was *expecting* – that was the phrase they used below stairs. Under the loosened waistline of her dresses, beneath her raised whalebone hoop and carefully draped shawl she would soon be *great with child*, like the Virgin Mary on the way to Bethlehem, like Molly the vanished housemaid. That little unborn baby lay curled inside Mama, and nothing Imogen could do, no wish, no prayer, no bargain struck with Heaven or Hell, could prevent it making its appearance.

Papa had been straightforward about the difference another child would make to Imogen's position at Selbury. Neither he nor Mama attempted to conceal their hope that the baby would be male: a son to inherit. 'So, Dame Imogen,' he had said cheerfully, 'if the baby is a boy, you need no longer worry about those future responsibilities that have been hanging over your head.' As he spoke he glanced at his daughter quizzically. Possibly he guessed a small part of her feelings, but he could never have believed their strength and depth; he simply took it for granted that she would adjust to the new situation.

A son and heir. A brother to – to supplant her! The dreadful possibility had struck Imogen with almost physical force. Her whole being seemed to suffer a grievous wound. What was a bee sting compared to this?

'And if we should have a second daughter,' Papa went on, 'why, then you would have a sister to help you shoulder those responsibilities and share the burden of the estate.'

How little he understood! That 'burden' was the only thing she desired on this earth. Brother or sister, Imogen thought with a bitterness beyond her youth, it was a disastrous situation. To have to relinquish Selbury altogether . . . almost as unthinkable, to have to share her inheritance: either possibility caused her utter dismay. Already she felt resentful and jealous of her sibling. But it would never do to reveal her feelings to her parents. She had listened to the news grave-faced, and when Mama said finally, 'I am sure you must be as happy about the baby as we are, dear,' she had actually managed to smile and nod her head. But afterwards she went upstairs to the schoolroom to brood, pausing to gaze upon Dame Margery's portrait on the stairs. Then, in a fit of impotent rage, she had torn down from the schoolroom wall the lovingly detailed plan of the estate which she had worked on so eagerly. Only the day before, with Miss Duval, she had walked right around the lake, and afterwards, on the blue oblong on the map, had drawn a swan with an impossibly long neck, surrounded by tall bulrushes.

'Why, Imogen, what have you done?' Annette had exclaimed when she found the crumpled sheet of paper lying on the floor.

Imogen did not trouble to hide her feelings from her governess. 'There's no point to it any more,' she muttered sulkily. 'Selbury was *mine*. Now it will belong to someone else . . . or at least I shall have to share it. It isn't fair!'

Without comment Annette had picked up the map and smoothed it out. It would be hard, she realized, for anyone, after ten years as an only child, to adjust to the idea of another member of the family. She only hoped that during the next few months, Imogen would gradually come to accept the idea of a brother or a sister. It was probably too much to hope that she would welcome the newcomer. If only, Annette thought sadly, Imogen had not been so eager to identify herself with her ancestress, had not conceived the fixed, obsessive notion that one day she would become sole chatelaine of Selbury, like Dame Margery herself . . .

Somehow, Imogen managed to assume quite a lively interest whenever her parents spoke of the baby. Annette noticed that they almost always referred to the child as 'he'. Their son.

What a disappointment if it should be a girl, after all! Lady Louisa was looking rather worn; it did not seem an easy pregnancy. She walked about slowly, and frequently spread both hands behind her to press upon her back, as though she suffered a continual ache. Dr Fonteney had advised regular exercise, gentle walks, yet she spent a great deal of her time upon the chaise longue in her bedroom. But she enjoyed supervising the refurbishing of the night nursery and the new day nursery. The schoolroom was to stay as the domain of Miss Duval and Imogen. The high cot in the night nursery was given fresh muslin hangings; piles of tiny garments awaited the unborn child. The Quade christening robe, all Honiton lace and satin ribbons, was shaken out of its lavender-scented folds. Old Nan, Lady Louisa's former nurse – she had also looked after the infant Imogen – was to return to Selbury to help attend the birth and look after the baby for the first month of its life. This was a loving, loyal gesture on Lady Louisa's part.

Annette, turning now from the open window in the schoolroom, felt a sudden wave of compassion for the sulky-looking girl bent over her spoiled page of figures. 'Enough of sums, on second thoughts,' she said kindly. 'We'll put away the arithmetic book for today. Let me see – there are just two chapters of *Kenilworth* left to read; let's try to finish the story before teatime.'

With a sigh of relief Imogen put aside the hated long division. Her face brightened considerably as Annette produced the novel; she was enjoying the swashbuckling romance, eagerly anticipating the inevitable tragic ending. As the shadows lengthened that summer afternoon, governess and pupil took it in turns to read aloud. Horror piled on horror: Robert Dudley, Earl of Leicester, connived to bring about the death of his secret countess, Amy Robsart. He had long been the favourite of Queen Elizabeth; his wife now blocked his overweening ambition. At last the ill-fated Amy fell through a trapdoor at the top of a steep flight of stairs . . .

' "There was a rushing sound – a heavy fall – a faint

64

groan," ' Annette read solemnly, ' "and all was over." '

Imogen listened avidly.

' "Look down into the vault – what seest thou? – I see only a heap of clothes, like a snowdrift . . . O God, she moves her arm!" ' There was a real sense of horror in Annette's voice.

But Amy's neck, to Imogen's satisfaction, was well and truly broken. Too late the hero Tressilian and Sir Walter Raleigh rushed in upon the murderers. Before Annette closed the book, she read the author's note which told how Robert Dudley himself died, from drinking poison intended for his second countess, whom he married after he fell from the queen's favour.

'Do you remember, Miss Duval, there was a recipe for poison in that old book of Dame Margery's that Papa showed us?' Imogen exclaimed. 'The Elizabethans must have liked to poison people.'

She did not add that she had picked some berries, pink and soft and black-centred, from the yew trees along Dame Margery's walk, and put them in a bowl of dog scraps in the scullery. One of the spaniels had cleared out the bowl, but to Imogen's disappointment had shown no signs of being poisoned.

Annette wondered what Imogen would have thought of the rumour that Dame Margery had poisoned both her husbands. She did not consider it suitable to mention that ancient gossip.

'It was good that Queen Elizabeth did not marry Leicester – or anyone,' Imogen went on.

'Why do you say that?' Annette was curious.

Imogen twisted her long, glossy plait in her fingers. 'Because if she had married, she would not have been so much *herself*. She would have had to – to share her life, the way husbands and wives do. She would have been – less royal.'

A queen diminished by a husband? The image of the dumpy little 'Widow of Windsor', as Queen Victoria was called these days, came to Annette's mind: certainly a striking contrast to glorious Queen Bess! Yet Victoria too, had regal qualities . . . as a stern matriarch rather than a proud virgin queen.

'But Elizabeth had no heir,' she pointed out. 'After she died, the son of her old rival, Mary, Queen of Scots, became king of England. If Elizabeth had married, she might have had a son to inherit the throne.'

Imogen frowned at that. 'She might have had a daughter, another queen like herself.' Her face assumed the closed expression Annette knew so well. It was the end of their discussion.

Beyond the formal lawns of Selbury Quade, behind a grove of rhododendrons was a little wooded, neglected place where the ground, rankly overgrown, sloped steeply away, giving a view across miles of countryside: patchwork fields, the glint of water, the church spire at Selbury and in the distance the Quantock Hills. A sturdy beech grew near the edge of this sudden drop, and the remains of an old swing hung on rotting ropes from a high branch.

In the last century, the swing had been the plaything of Laetitia Quade, youngest and favourite daughter of Sir Oswald's great-grandfather – a charming, high-spirited, impetuous girl. Swinging higher and higher, she used to delight in the sensation of flying through space, heedless of peril as she described a heady arc over the combe below. Fox hunting was newly introduced about that time, and Laetitia became a reckless horsewoman. Riding to hounds, she was flung from her horse; she was dead when they brought her back to Selbury. Her father, broken-hearted, never hunted again; the kennels he had set up were disbanded – he could not even bear to hear the music of hounds in the distance. A miniature of Laetitia, a little oval of ivory mounted on olive-coloured velvet, stood on a table in the drawing room. It showed a young woman with delicate features and a mischievous half-smile. As for Laetitia's swing, that was left to rot in its forgotten corner where no one ever went ... until, this summmer, Imogen pushed her way through the dusty rhododendrons and discovered it. She persuaded one of the stable boys, red-headed Charlie Ashell, to rig strong new ropes over the tree branch, and a new piece of board for the seat.

Charlie was dubious about this commission. 'Do you take care, Miss Imogen,' he warned her when the job was done. 'Hold fast to they ropes, else you'll have a terrible long fall.' Charlie himself held on to an overhanging branch as he peered over the edge of the bank. 'I reckon I should never have fixed up this old swing at all,' he gasped.

Imogen glared at him. 'If you tell anyone about it, Charlie, *I* shall tell Dan Trefoil how you take out Papa's stallion and jump hedges on him every time Dan goes to visit his sister in Salisbury.'

Charlie went pale beneath his freckles. 'Never do that, Miss Imogen. Mr Trefoil 'ud give me my marching orders.'

'Then you had best keep quiet,' Imogen threatened him.

The place remained her secret. She would go off there alone and swing to her heart's content, just as Laetitia had once done, enjoying the thrill of danger as she flew farther and farther above the combe below, then gradually let the momentum die down, scuffing her feet in the long grass as the swing came to rest. It was a release for her restless spirit; the rapid movement, the sensation of rushing through the cool clear air seemed to cleanse her mind of dark thoughts. Perhaps a gay, mischievous ghost hovered beside her as she relived the perilous exhilaration Laetitia had once known.

Sometimes Annette would ask Imogen where she had been, but the girl would simply look inscrutable and shrug her shoulders. Her governess never pressed the point; whatever Imogen had been doing on these occasions, she looked almost happy for a change.

In November, old Nan arrived at Selbury. (Annette never did learn the old nurse's true name: 'Nan' was an honoured household title.) White-haired, wrinkled as a spring apple, Nan still retained some portion of her former energy, when she had ruled the nurseries, first at Aylsham, Lady Louisa's childhood home, and afterwards at Selbury. When it had seemed that Imogen would remain the only child, Nan had retired to a cottage on the Aylsham estate. Lady Louisa's eldest brother was now Lord Moulvey; both he and his brother Edwin, the youngest of that family, had been Nan's former charges.

There was a touching reunion between Lady Louisa and her old nurse, but Annette observed that Nan's greeting of Imogen seemed to hold a certain wariness. Young Jessie, to her great joy, had been promoted from tweeny to under-nursemaid. When Nan departed after her month of caring for the babe, a new head nursemaid would take charge. For the moment, Jessie's chief duty lay in providing Nan with meal trays and endless cups of tea. She used to dust the spotless nurseries every day, and each time she passed the high cot awaiting its new occupant she would smooth an already perfect fold of muslin drapery, longing for the babe to arrive, yet somewhat apprehensive of her forthcoming role.

'It's a real chance for your betterment, my girl,' Nan told her. 'I'll show you all I can while I stay here, and mind you watch me well. I ha'n't lost my old skill in minding little babbies, nor never will.'

Nan felt concern for Lady Louisa. Imogen's entry into the world had not been easy, as the old woman well recalled.

'Oh, Nan dear, I have the greatest faith in Dr Fonteney,' Lady Louisa assured her. 'And this time, I shall have the benefit of chloroform.'

Nan did not risk upsetting Lady Louisa by voicing her opinion of that newfangled device. She chose, instead, to express her views to the governess. The old nurse approved of Miss Duval; young as she was, she seemed to have the knack of handling her difficult pupil. Nan was well aware how contrary and unmanageable Imogen could be. She had been a very strong-willed infant, always determined to have her own way. Her mother had been such a sweet-natured little girl; it was a thousand pities Imogen did not take after her. Nan had never known a child quite like Imogen. Lady Louisa's brother, Edwin, had been a naughty child, the young rascal, but that was different . . . besides, his sunny disposition had made up for his misdemeanours. Nan sighed as she spoke of him briefly to Annette one day; by all accounts Edwin was living an extravagant life in London these days, flinging away his patrimony and causing great worry to his elder brother.

Nan broached the subject of chloroform when Annette joined her in the nursery one afternoon for tea. Nan, who had never married, who had looked after other people's babies all her life, firmly believed the pangs of birth to be divinely ordained. Did not the Bible state 'In sorrow thou shalt bring forth children'? – 'The Book of Genesis, chapter four, verse sixteen.' The old woman's voice held a note of pious triumph as she offered Annette the sugar bowl.

Annette, to whom childbirth was veiled in a certain mystery, spoke hesitantly. 'But surely, with chloroform, modern medicine has given women a great boon . . . the easing of pain . . .' She recalled a conversation with Sir Oswald concerning Adam's rib, but decided it might upset Nan if she were to quote Genesis back at her.

Nan pursed her lips. 'You may be very clever at book-learning, Miss Duval, but it is God's truth I speak. Besides, everybody knows that the sufferings of childbed are what make a mother's love so strong.'

Annette supposed there might be some merit in that argument: people were apt to value what cost them dear. But she knew, too, there were women who, after their first experience of giving birth, denied their duty to their husbands from fear of conceiving another child. The world condemned them as selfish and berated them for turning marriage into a mockery. She thought of something else. 'If I am not mistaken,' she said gently, 'the Queen has called it "that blessed chloroform". It was given to her during her last two confinements, was it not?' Striving for a lighter tone, she smiled. 'I read somewhere that the very first woman to try chloroform was a doctor's wife, and she was so pleased with its effect, she christened her baby daughter Anaesthesia! Poor child – it's to be hoped most people called her Annie!'

Nan shook her head, torn between reverence for the Bible

and loyalty to her sovereign. 'It's unnatural, that's what I say,' she maintained stubbornly. She dabbed at her mouth with her handkerchief; cake crumbs clung to the fine white fringe above her upper lip. 'And what's more,' the old woman went on, 'who is to say that poor Prince Leopold's illness is not connected with such going against the word of the Lord?'

How could one argue against prejudice and bigotry? Annette let the subject drop, and simply hoped that poor Lady Louisa would be spared as much pain as possible.

Chapter Seven

LADY LOUISA WAS was 'taken ill', as the saying went, one morning in mid-December. The winter this year was mild. No snow had fallen yet and the lake was not frozen, though the bare corduroy fields were frosted and cat-ice glazed the rutted roads. As soon as it became known the birth was imminent, a palpable hush of suspense fell upon the house above and below stairs. The doctor's carriage stood in the driveway; the two dalmatians which always ran behind it waited, dogs couchant, on either side of the main entrance. Dr Fonteney had brought with him the wet-nurse who had been engaged to suckle the baby. Mary Gibbon, respectable village wife, had a supply of milk more than sufficient for her own lusty child of three months. She sat in the nursery, patiently awaiting her summons to duty while the winter daylight gradually declined. Dr Fonteney had informed Sir Oswald it might be several hours before the child was born.

In the afternoon, Annette and a stony-faced Imogen went for a walk in the crisp, clear air. 'Stay out as long as possible,' Sir Oswald had told Annette. They went as far as Foxhollow, then took a long route back, skirting the lake. Annette's attempts at conversation elicited practically no response from Imogen. For the most part they trudged along in silence.

When they returned to the house some two hours later, a subtle change of atmosphere seemed to have taken place. Sir Oswald sat alone in the library, making a pretence of reading, getting to his feet every now and then to pace the room impatiently. Dr Fonteney was with Lady Louisa, whose bedroom door opened and shut to let Jessie in or out with cans of water. Nan was at the bedside, watching with disapproval as the doctor exhibited the 'blessed chloroform'. He rolled a spotless handkerchief into a funnel, placed the open end over his patient's mouth and nose, and administered a few drops every ten minutes or so. Lady Louisa's struggles were acute; the chloroform, while it did not render her insensible, soothed and quietened her and removed the look of wild pain and panic from her eyes. The birth was proving considerably more difficult than Dr Fonteney had thought. The umbilical cord appeared to be wrapped around the child's neck. He feared strangulation.

Imogen joined her father and Annette left them alone together. On her way upstairs she passed by the closed door of Lady Louisa's room; she was inexpressibly relieved to hear no dreadful screams or moans of pain. Had she but known it, a healthy scream or moan would have indicated better progress. Even young Jessie, who had been present at several cottage childbeds, was aware this birthing was not proceeding as it should. The doctor was using the pincers now. They had a fancy name, though: forceps, they were called. Surely, thought Jessie, the baby should have been safely delivered by now.

It was the second time this week Giles Fonteney had used this same pair of forceps. Lydia Yeo, wife of a prosperous farmer, had died giving birth to her first child, a victim of puerperal fever.

A few moments later, shirtsleeves rolled beyond his elbows, his brow beaded with sweat in the overheated room, he delivered the infant. A perfectly formed male child. But, as he had feared, the cord was twisted around the tiny neck.

Releasing it quickly, he placed the waxen, silent scrap of humanity into Nan's waiting hands. 'Stillborn, I fear,' he muttered briefly before turning back to the mother. At least he would save her life, if he could.

Jessie, standing beside the bath of warm water prepared for the infant, was puzzled and fearful. Why wasn't the baby crying? All day she had been waiting to hear that first whimper of indrawn breath and the air expelled again in a lusty howl. Nan looked down sadly at the pale little burden as she bore it from the bedside. In answer to Jessie's silent question she shook her head, and saw the girl's face crumple with disappointment. Suddenly, the old woman thought she felt the tiny frame between her hands quiver slightly, like the last despairing flutter of a wounded bird.

'Quick, girl,' she said softly but urgently, 'more hot water – we may yet shock this babe into life.' She immersed the child in the water, then held it, dripping, upside down, grasping its heels in one hand and slapping it on the back. Then she began to massage it vigorously in the folds of a thick towel – treating the poor little thing, Jessie thought, for all the world as though it were a turnip watch that refused to tick. A small amount of watery mucus dribbled from the infant's mouth, and at long last – though in fact no more than a few moments could have elapsed – it drew its first uncertain breath and emitted a feeble cry of protest at being thus forced into life.

Giles Fonteney turned in amazement. He could have sworn the child was stillborn . . . what magic had the old woman worked?

That feeble cry brought Lady Louisa back to consciousness. 'Is – is it – a boy?' she asked weakly.

'A son,' Giles Fonteney told her. He knew how she had longed to hear those words.

'Thank God.' Lady Louisa closed her eyes and a great sense of peace flooded through her. A son, after all these years. At last, an heir for Selbury. But, oh, she was so tired. She must sleep now. No more of that dreadful struggle. Why hadn't she been given the baby to hold? No matter, she was too exhausted to wonder about that now. Later . . . there would be all the time in the world to hold him. Her son. She fell asleep at last.

The doctor came over to examine the infant so miraculously restored to life. 'Hmph,' he uttered finally, having assured himself the child was sound in wind and limb, 'they should christen him Lazarus, I think. He owes his life to you, Nan.'

The old woman was well content. Then she looked towards the bed, a mute question in her eyes.

'She needs a long rest.' Giles Fonteney did not voice the anxiety he felt for his patient, but Nan detected it in his tone.

While Lady Louisa slept, Giles Fonteney went down to acquaint Sir Oswald with the news of his son. He found his old friend sitting alone in the firelight – no one had cared to disturb his vigil by entering the library to light the lamps. At his suggestion, Imogen had gone to tell someone to feed the dalmatians that waited so patiently for their master in the chill twilight outside.

The doctor's first words brought Sir Oswald to his feet with a surge of joy: 'Congratulations. You have a son.'

The father's thoughts flew to his wife. 'And Louisa? May I see her?'

'She is exhausted by her ordeal. She sleeps now.' Giles Fonteney hesitated. He knew he should express something of his fear for his friend's wife. 'She – she will need a great deal of rest and care. It was a difficult birth. I thought at first –'

At that instant Imogen appeared in the doorway, just in time to hear his next words.

'– the child was stillborn.'

Stillborn. Imogen stood there without moving, taking in those four words. *The child was stillborn.* So . . . there was no brother or sister after all. Nothing was changed. Everything was as it had always been: there was just herself, no one else, ever, to take away or share her inheritance. For surely there would be no more babies after this. She looked towards her father, whose expression reflected the implication contained in Giles Fonteney's words concerning his wife. How sad and solemn Papa looked, thought Imogen.

74

'Oh, Papa!' She ran across to him and he embraced her mutely, holding her close to his side.

'However,' the doctor continued after pausing to accommodate Imogen's entrance, 'thanks to the skill of the old nurse, the infant finally drew breath. I left him crying lustily for sustenance.'

Imogen, her face buried against her father's jacket, stiffened as she heard the remainder of Dr Fonteney's remarks. It could not be! Cruelly, unbelievably, in the space of a single moment, her world fell apart again. It – it was like the time one of the footmen, unwrapping a newly mended Chinese vase, had let it drop so that it shattered into fragments once more. She recalled those shards of celadon-green porcelain scattered on the drawing-room carpet. The baby was alive, after all. Dr Fonteney had left *him* crying . . . she had a brother. Selbury Quade was his inheritance now.

Neither Imogen's father nor the doctor had perceived her first misapprehension.

'Yes, Imogen, the baby is a boy,' Sir Oswald said. 'Your brother.'

How Imogen resented the unmistakable note of pride in his voice! A son and heir . . . how much more it meant to him, to all the world, than a daughter, an heiress! Her face still hidden against his coat, she squeezed her eyes tight shut for an instant, as though to utter an unholy prayer. Then she broke from her father's embrace and her mouth stretched in the travesty of a smile.

'I am so glad, Papa – so very, very glad.'

Annette was summoned to the library, together with Mrs Arkney and Mr Teague, the butler, to take a glass of champagne and drink the baby's health. Imogen was allowed a sip too.

Sir Oswald proposed the toast. 'To my son, Nicholas Quade,' he said simply. The oldest family name of all had been decided upon before the child was born.

'Nicholas Quade!' The name resounded through the room.

The high cot in the night nursery was filled at last. Jessie looked at the baby lying there, replete with milk, tiny fists curled tight. His colour was now a delicate pink. Jessie stroked one of those little hands with a touch light as a feather. How helpless a newborn baby was! But she was here to play her part in looking after him. She gave a sigh of supreme satisfaction. She was so glad this little boy had come to life. Without him, there would have been no place for an under-nursemaid. But it wasn't only because of that. Of course not! She was happy for Sir Oswald and Lady Louisa . . . and for Miss Imogen, she supposed. But most of all she was happy for the child himself, for little Nicholas. Just think! He would grow up to inherit this grand house and its estate, and one day his son would take his place in turn. It comforted Jessie to think that things at Selbury would continue as they had always been. Father to son, for all those generations . . .

It was very peaceful in the night nursery. A fire glowed behind the high fender, a shaded lamp stood on a table. Fresh white curtains were drawn across the window. Jessie sat in the low nursing chair before the fire, drowsy after the day's momentous events. Then the door opened and Nan entered with Imogen following behind.

'Miss Imogen would like to take a peep at her little brother,' Nan said. Then, to Imogen, 'Mind you don't disturb him.'

Imogen walked over to the cot and stared at the sleeping infant. Watching her, Jessie thought how strange it was that her face showed no expression, no emotion. It was almost like a visit from the bad fairy in the old tale. But how could that be, Jessie chided herself. The two children were sister and brother. They must surely love each other.

But after Imogen had gone to her own room, Nan voiced something of Jessie's feeling. 'She's a strange child, Miss Imogen. And mighty jealous of her new little brother, I've no doubt. You'll need to watch how she behaves towards him in future, Jessie my girl. She could make his young life miserable if she put her mind to it.'

Jessie shivered in spite of the warm, cosy room, as though

she felt some premonition. 'I'll look after him, never fear,' she asserted stoutly.

The baby was baptized a week later, well bundled in a thick shawl against the cold. He was christened with his full names of Nicholas Carew Arthur Quade and cried lustily, with all the vigour of the old Adam, when the holy water was sprinkled on his head. Lord Moulvey and Sir Philip Wanslea, Sir Oswald's cousin, stood as godfathers, and a youthful cousin of Lady Louisa's, Miss Hester Graham, was godmother. Lord Moulvey and Miss Graham had driven to Selbury together: the Grahams lived quite close to Aylsham. Annette attended the ceremony with Imogen, who was wearing a new, squirrel-trimmed cape with a muff to match. When her father took her over to meet Philip Wanslea, Imogen recalled with a start that this was the man who now stood third in line to inherit Selbury Quade, should anything happen to her brother – or herself. Reluctantly she withdrew one hand from her muff to accept his large, friendly clasp.

'One of these days your papa must bring you to Gloucester-shire, to visit us,' he told her. 'My son Peter is a few years your senior – he is at Harrow.'

Imogen remembered that her father had mentioned Peter Wanslea. He was her half-cousin, she supposed . . . or perhaps her first cousin once removed. It was so difficult to work out cousinly relationships.

Then Miss Graham came up to greet Sir Oswald and his daughter. A slender, dark-haired young woman, about the same age as herself, Annette thought. She bore some re-semblance to Lady Louisa – their mothers had been sisters, of course. Annette, wearing the serviceable navy-blue serge coat and skirt she regarded as her governess uniform beneath her warm tweed mantle, glanced at Hester Graham's elegant costume and furs with admiration and an undeniable tinge of envy. Miss Graham so clearly belonged to a wealthy, privi-leged, pampered background. Yet, like Annette herself, she was unmarried. Doubtless she was pursued by eager suitors.

77

Her life would consist of country-house parties, the London season, balls, theatres, visits to Deauville, to Switzerland. Perhaps there was some sort of understanding between Lord Moulvey and Miss Graham . . .

Hester Graham's soft grey eyes held an expression of sorrow as she spoke to Sir Oswald and greeted Imogen. For a shadow lay upon this family gathering. The third day after Nicholas's birth, Lady Louisa had become feverish and was seized with rigors. Her pulse rate quickened alarmingly; by now she had sunk into extreme weakness, with occasional delirium. The bruised and lacerated tissue of her womb had become one huge ulcer; she had succumbed to puerperal septicaemia.

They were all aware that there was little hope she would recover. A competent nurse from Yeovil had been engaged; the thoughts and prayers of the entire household were concentrated upon the sickroom. Louisa Quade herself knew that she was dying. She had insisted, in a lucid moment, that the baptism should take place without delay; she wanted to know that her son had been christened. There would be no celebration at Selbury afterwards; Philip Wanslea was to return home directly; Lord Moulvey and Miss Graham were preparing themselves for the final farewell.

Birth and death, a beginning and an end: how cruelly intertwined they were, Annette reflected. Lady Louisa had provided Selbury with a male heir — at the price of her own life. Annette could not but wonder whether Sir Oswald reckoned that price too dear . . . but of course such things were not to be coldly calculated, the one balanced against the other. For the first time, Annette realized the barren sense behind her Aunt Harriet's consolatory view of spinsterhood. 'At least we are spared the perils of childbirth,' she had remarked more than once. It *was* perilous, for women of every degree. How many women died giving birth! You had only to consider the number of widowers there were, and all those husbands with new wives younger than themselves.

It was extremely sad that Lady Louisa would not grow old in the lovely home she had come to as a bride. The place would hold a perpetual sense of loss. They would miss her serene personality, her light step as she moved from room to room, her tactful handling of difficult situations above and below stairs . . . Annette had never been close to Lady Louisa, but she had come to admire her for all those qualities which together created a calm and somehow reassuring ambience at Selbury. How would they manage without her?

When the christening party returned to Selbury, they found that Edwin Moulvey had arrived unexpectedly. He had occupied the time until they came back by practising shots on the billiard table; now he came strolling into the drawing room, brushing a lock of fair hair from his forehead. Sir Oswald, with Nan and Nicholas, had gone straight to his wife, but the others were assembled in that pleasant room with its long windows opening onto the terrace. Annette took it upon herself to dispense the sherry and cake she found laid out on a tray. Edwin gave her an appraising smile as she approached him. At any other time she might have found his carefree, insouciant manner attractive. Today, it seemed strikingly inappropriate.

'I say, isn't sherry a bit sober?' Edwin said cheerfully to the company at large. 'Shouldn't we be toasting my nephew in champagne? Sorry I was too late for the church, by the way.' He turned to his elder brother. 'I only found your note a couple of days ago, when I got back from Paris. Came up from London on the train.'

Lord Moulvey stood regarding him with an air of embarrassment mingled with exasperation. They all felt embarrassed as Edwin went on talking.

'Had to turn up to see the right thing done by Louie's son! By the way, why won't they let me see Louie? I wanted to dash up to her as soon as I arrived, and tell her how clever she is to produce the son and heir at last. But Teague murmured something about the nurse being with her —'

He broke off, realizing at last that something was wrong.

There was an appalled moment of silence; each of them,

except Imogen, avoided Edwin's puzzled gaze. There were tears in Hester Graham's eyes. Annette fiddled nervously with the stem of her sherry glass. Lord Moulvey gave a nervous cough.

Then Imogen's clear, high voice broke the silence. 'Mama is dying, Uncle Edwin,' she said in a curiously matter-of-fact tone.

It was dreadful to see the consternation that spread across Edwin Moulvey's face. He sagged visibly.

His brother took a step towards him. 'I'm sorry, Eddie. I know how close you and she have always – It has all happened so suddenly. We never – I did not realize it myself until yesterday.'

'I – I can't believe it.' Edwin's voice broke. 'Louie . . .'

Hester Graham went over to him and took both his hands in hers. 'Dear Edwin.' Her voice was filled with compassion. 'None of us can quite believe it.' She led him gently to one of the windows overlooking the wintry scene outside.

Annette considered it high time she removed Imogen from this emotionally charged scene. She only hoped the girl would be spared a deathbed farewell to her mother. Annette herself had never been present at a death; which, she supposed, was fairly unusual. If her own parents had not been killed in an accident, if she had been one of a large family, she must surely have known that experience. Many of her schoolfriends had delicate brothers or sisters who had died. But then, she reflected wryly, there was so much she had not experienced: the triple mysteries of love, birth and death, in fact.

'Did you see – Uncle Edwin was *crying*,' Imogen remarked after they left the room.

'He must love your mama very much,' Annette answered softly.

'I've never seen a man cry before.' There was no mistaking the scorn in the child's voice. Could she really be so heartless, Annette wondered in dismay.

Upstairs, they passed quickly by the door of Lady Louisa's room. It was ajar; they caught a swift glimpse of Imogen's father sitting in a chair drawn up to the high bed. A cloying perfume wafted from the room, emanating from scented pastilles placed beside the lamp. Beneath that false fragrance lay a barely discernible odour of decay. It would have been familiar enough to any soldier on campaign whose comrades lay dying of suppurating wounds.

Suddenly Imogen looked at her governess with an expression that was indescribably bleak. 'Everything has gone wrong,' she said. 'Nothing will ever be right again.'

That evening, Annette sat for a while in the nursery with Nan. Earlier, Nan said, Edwin Moulvey had been up to see her, seeking comfort and someone to confide in. She spoke of him fondly, at the same time shaking her head over his follies. Edwin was in the army, Annette learned, an officer in a crack regiment. It occurred to her that he must cut a dashing figure in his uniform. But it seemed his heart was not in soldiering. Nan talked of his London extravagances, his absurd generosity when he was in funds, the girls whose hearts he captured.

'I dare say he'll settle down, all in good time,' she said optimistically. 'He was telling me about his latest fancy – the photygraphy. He's spent a mint of money on one of those cameras. The reason he went to Paris was to see what they Frenchies are up to with their photygraphs. But that wouldn't be all he did in Paris, knowing my boy Edwin!'

Naughty deeds, it seemed, might be condoned so long as they took place in Paris, or some other exotic location.

'He told me the portrait painters will be out of work soon, that photygraphers will take their place,' Nan went on. 'I don't know, I'm sure. I'm too old to keep up with this modern world.' She sighed and fell silent for a while. Then she said, 'He told me he wished he could have taken a likeness of his sister. They were such friends when they were little, those two. They always did everything together. Many's the scrape my Louisa got young Eddie out of. She was always a good influence on him.' She shook her head. 'I'm sure I don't know who Edwin will turn to now, or who will be able to set him straight when he needs it. He told me he hopes his brother will lend him a sum of money to pay his debts. Lady Louisa would have persuaded Lord Moulvey to make the loan – but she'd have told Edwin not to be so extravagant in future, too.'

Annette was curious about Lady Louisa's cousin Hester. 'Miss Graham seemed very sympathetic towards Mr Moulvey,' she ventured.

Nan gave her a sharp glance. 'There's nothing more than proper cousinly feeling there. Miss Hester was engaged to be married – oh, three years ago now, it must be. Her fiancé was with one of those private regiments in India – Spencer's Horse, that was its name. He served through the Mutiny, and then was killed during a border raid in the Khyber Pass. It was after that Miss Hester took up her work in London.'

'She *works*!'

Nan smiled shrewdly. 'There's some that work because they have to, Miss Duval, and others from choice. Miss Hester is very interested in the movement started by Lord Shaftesbury, to rescue homeless childer from the streets of London. Terrible, some of the tales she's told me. She has a lot to do with them ragged schools.'

Annette digested this surprising information. 'Does Miss Graham teach at one of those schools?' Her voice held a respectful note. She recalled a talk Miss Buss had given once on the subject of the ragged schools, which offered hope to thousands of homeless children "too raggedly clothed" to attend the free Sunday schools – and usually vermin-ridden and near starving as well, Miss Buss had told them, and often fallen into a life of crime. Most of the teachers in these schools were voluntary workers; Miss Buss had said that the novelist Mr Charles Dickens had taught in one.

Nan shook her head. 'When Miss Hester is in London she goes to meetings to do with how the schools are run. She got herself interested in them waifs and strays after Captain Martin was killed. She wasn't one to sit at home moping.'

Annette felt she would like to know Miss Graham better. But that seemed a fairly remote chance. As Imogen Quade's governess, she stood very much on the periphery of the family so far as these cousins and family friends were concerned.

She left the cosy nursery with its atmosphere of peace and security – though surely all peace, all security were illusions which must eventually be shattered – and went to her own room. The hours dragged by. She could not sleep, but sat by the window in her wrapper, with the curtains drawn back, waiting, like every other member of the household, for the news they dreaded. There was a crescent moon; its light silvered the frosty lawns and the distant, glassy surface of the lake. A wintry silence prevailed outside. Once an owl hooted, hunting mice in the shrubbery below.

Annette thought about Lady Louisa's two brothers, so dissimilar in character. Was Lord Moulvey's responsible and authoritative air part of his nature, or did it arise from the fact that he had grown up with the knowledge that he would become the head of the family? Perhaps, for the reverse reason, Edwin Moulvey lacked such characteristics. To be the younger son in an important family must be hard. From what Nan had said, he sounded quite serious about his photographic interests, taking the trouble to visit Paris to see what the French photographers were doing.

Before the bank crash, Aunt Harriet had bought one of the popular stereographic machines to amuse themselves and their visitors in Kensington. An amazing three-dimensional effect was obtained when you viewed the paired images of pictur-esque scenes – the Taj Mahal, the Cheddar Gorge, the Crystal Palace. After the bank failed, Annette, at her aunt's bidding, had taken the machine to the nearest pawnbroker and obtained a few shillings for it, far below its cost. She recalled, too, an exhibition she had visited at the London Photographic Society. One picture had stirred enormous controversy. Critics had declared it was too painful, too realistic. The scene it showed, carefully posed in every detail, was entitled 'Fading Away'. A young girl, in the last stage of some illness, lay propped on a sofa, with anxious relatives around and a man, his back turned, gazing out of the window in the background, presumably overcome with emotion . . . like Edwin Moulvey today, Annette thought. Many artists had painted more disturbing scenes than this, of course. But the photograph showed real people, even if they were only models, friends of the photographer. The illusion was more complete, and far less comfortable.

Suddenly Annette wondered if Imogen, too, were awake . . . and fearful. She recalled the child's morbid fascination with death, and her horror of dying herself. Pulling her wrapper closely about her, Annette went quietly along the draughty passage to the child's room. The little night light was burning steadily and Imogen was sound asleep. Relieved, and yet astonished that she could sleep peacefully at such a time, Annette crept back to her own room.

Lady Louisa died in the early hours of the next day. Hers was not a deathbed to provide a touching picture. The opium she received relieved her agony but she died at the height of her fever, her face ravaged and empurpled. It was a death more fitted for a battlefield.

The funeral, with the pomp and ceremony of plumed horses, sheaves of hothouse lilies, the mournful tolling of the church bell, the sorrowing members of the family and household and grieving tenants and villagers, came hard upon the baby's christening at St Michael's. Lady Louisa was laid to rest in the family vault, to take her repose among all those Quades who had gone before her. A dry and dusty family gathering. And so a second Christmas at Selbury heralded a period of mourning, this time for one who had been at the very heart of its existence.

Chapter Eight

IT WAS 1867. Deep-red rambler roses climbed the low grey walls of the terrace and white pelargoniums spilled from stone urns. Annette wrote in her diary: 'My twenty-sixth birthday. It is seven years since I came to Selbury Quade . . .' Seven years: the words seemed to hold some fateful, cabbalistic undertone. Perhaps this new year would herald change, significant happenings, a new direction. But that was something she wondered about each April birthday. She used to long for some new direction in her life. Now, she half dreaded the thought of change.

She laid down the little book with its gilt clasp and paused to gaze across the lawn, where Nicholas had persuaded Jessie into a game of tag. Flora and Angus, the two Highland terriers, fairly recent recruits to the houshold, ran indiscriminately between the chaser and the chased, barking joyfully.

'Can't catch me!' Nicholas shouted gleefully as he dodged about to escape his nursemaid's outstretched arm.

Jessie lumbered after him, in imminent danger of tripping over one or other of the little white dogs. At eighteen, she had grown quite plump, with a rosy complexion and clear, candid eyes. Her starched white apron strained across an ample bosom. Left far behind was the poor little tweeny whom Annette had first encountered.

As for Nicholas, he was certainly a credit to Jessie's devoted care and the rather stern regime of Nanny Hodges, the head nursemaid, who had been appointed soon after Lady Louisa's death, five years ago. Nicky was a sturdy child with a sunny, open nature. He had inherited his mother's colouring, her dark hair and eyes midway between hazel and grey. Last year he had discarded his baby dresses; now he wore sailor suits, like a proper little boy. How Lady Louisa would have loved him! Annette, watching from the terrace, felt the stab of that old grief. Nicky was everybody's darling, yet he showed no sign of being spoiled. Sometimes, she thought, he seemed almost too good to be true, this bright young heir to Selbury Quade. His father doted on him; Annette had often seen the habitual expression of sadness Sir Oswald wore nowadays changed to joy as his son made some sudden, unexpected appearance.

Yes, Nicky was everybody's darling . . . except for Imogen. Annette's thoughts clouded as they turned to her pupil, fifteen now and rapidly maturing into tall, slender womanhood. A very different process to Jessie's uncomplicated metamorphosis. There was no clear, candid gaze beneath Imogen's slightly hooded eyelids.

Annette was thankful that ever since Lady Louisa's death, Miss Hester Graham had taken a practical interest in Imogen's upbringing, as well as that of her godson. Miss Graham came often to Selbury and had made an effort to see that Imogen met other young people from suitable families in the neighbourhood. She supervised Imogen's clothes, and had instilled a number of social graces into the adolescent girl. Imogen, rather to Annette's surprise, seemed eager to accept Miss Graham's advice and guidance. Perhaps she realized the need to acquire a certain sophistication, the manners of her caste, if she were to succeed in society.

Miss Graham, in fact, had slipped into the role of surrogate mother to Imogen and Nicholas; everyone at Selbury had

86

become used to her frequent visits. It had occurred to Annette – and to others of the household – that Miss Hester Graham would make an excellent second Lady Quade; but it seemed as though she and Sir Oswald had no thought of changing their comfortable, friendly relationship. Annette recalled the fiancé who had died in Afghanistan; perhaps he had fulfilled the role of romantic hero in Miss Graham's life once and for all. Whenever Hester Graham stayed at Selbury, she brought his silver-framed miniature to stand beside her Bible on her night table: the image of an idealistic-looking young officer wearing the dress turban of Spencer's Horse. Imogen had shown Annette the miniature one day, and remarked in the agreeable, well-modulated tone Miss Graham encouraged her to use, 'You don't have anyone, do you, Miss Duval? Not even the picture of someone who has died.'

Sometimes Annette accompanied Imogen to tea parties or luncheons. She did not particularly relish this role, part chaperone, part servant, relegated to an insignificant corner while the careless young disported themselves on the croquet lawn or played charades. She observed the impact Imogen made on those other overgrown, giggling girls about to make the transition from schoolroom to finishing school and ballroom – and on their schoolboy or undergraduate brothers, apt to display gaucherie and arrogance in equal measure. Imogen seemed much more composed and collected than her contemporaries . . . much less spontaneous. The other girls appeared wary of her but she was always the centre of attention for those young males.

'I confess I sometimes find Imogen a little – remote,' Miss Graham said once to Annette: a rare confidence. 'I think she will have a certain style when she comes out – there is an enigmatic quality about her. She is rather – mysterious.'

'She has certainly mystified me many times,' Annette had replied with a touch of asperity. She had experienced a particularly trying French conversation lesson that morning.

'We must always make allowance for the tragic loss of her mother at such an impressionable age,' Hester Graham had responded rather loftily. The governess felt rebuked.

Nowadays, Imogen spent relatively little time in the schoolroom; French conversation and literature were the only regular lessons she and Annette did together. There had been a scene recently when Annette discovered Imogen engrossed in a scandalous new novel borrowed from one of her young friends: *Under Two Flags*, by a writer who called himself Ouida.

'I don't know why you should make such a fuss,' Imogen had said sulkily. 'It isn't nearly as – as suggestive as *Les Liaisons Dangereuses*, which I found in Papa's bookshelves.'

Annette had no answer to this; she had not read Laclos's novel. She did so now, and was both fascinated and repelled by its ambience of evil. She was not surprised that this amoral tale of manipulation had appealed to Imogen; and its covert salaciousness, as Imogen herself had observed, was infinitely more powerful than Ouida's blatant paragraphs of torrid passion.

There was ample time now for Annette to begin Nicholas's instruction; he sat at the schoolroom table, chubby legs dangling above the floor, spelling out the words in Imogen's old reading primers and labouring over pothooks with inky little fingers. He loved the outdoor nature lessons; next week, Annette had promised, they would go to the lake, bring back a jar of tadpoles and watch them turn into frogs. Tadpole metamorphoses were a spring ritual of the schoolroom at Selbury Quade: there had been six generations of frogs since Annette's arrival.

The map of Selbury that Imogen had first delighted in, then torn down in a fit of jealous rage when Nicholas was born, now lay rolled up in a cupboard. But Imogen's obsession with Selbury still smouldered. Last year, she had wheedled her father into restoring Dame Margery's maze, which had been neglected until it was quite overgrown and impassable. There had even been talk of uprooting it. Lady Louisa had never liked the maze and would not venture inside it. She was averse to confined spaces. 'Besides,' she had once remarked, 'surely such mazes were not supposed to grow into huge green fortresses. I imagine they were designed to stand waist-high at most, so that one could watch a knot of people all trying to reach the centre – a sort of outdoor puzzle.'

But now those green hedges, twelve feet high, stood straight and trimmed, and the interior pathways of the maze were raked smooth. Annette shared something of Lady Louisa's aversion to confined spaces; she did not care to explore this newly restored fortress. It had become another of Imogen's private places, where no one followed her. She used to read or daydream on the bench that stood in its secret centre.

Two years ago, the swing beyond the rhododendrons had been discovered, pronounced far too dangerous, and done away with. Its discovery had provided desperate drama for Jessie. Nicholas, still in petticoats at the time, had grown adventurous, and Nanny Hodges often had to send Jessie outdoors to find him. On this occasion, he had wandered across the lawn and through the little jungle that led to the swing. And there he found Imogen propelling herself through space, swinging out above the combe far, far below. The little boy had watched open-mouthed, and at last called out:

'Me too! Me wants to fly!'

The piping voice caught Imogen's attention: she looked down, saw her brother, and slewed to a sudden stop. She was so used to regarding Nicholas as a nuisance that on most occasions she greeted his appearance with something approaching a scowl – unless her father or Miss Graham were present. But now – curiously – it was as though she looked at him through someone else's eyes. What a sturdy little fellow he was! In the softened mood which her visits to this hidden place seemed to induce, she held out her arms to him.

'Swing with Midgin,' she said. 'Midgin' was the nearest he could come to saying her name.

Nicholas ran to her and she pulled him on to her lap, holding him with one arm while she pulled on the rope with the other. They rocked gently back and forth. Then – 'More, more!' Nicky cried.

The swing hung so near the edge of the abyss that quite a small arc took them over the edge, over that sheer, dizzy drop. Suddenly Imogen's mood changed. She let go of Nicky and seized the ropes with both hands. He twisted around perilously in her lap, his arms clinging to her neck. Perhaps he sensed his sister's darkened mood; perhaps, with animal instinct, he was aware of the yawning space that opened up each time they went forward. As Imogen pulled harder and harder, Nicky began to sob and shriek, clutching at Imogen desperately while she swung higher and higher, farther and farther over the edge . . .

Jessie, seeking her charge, came out on to the lawn and heard a distant cry from beyond the shrubbery. There was no mistaking its note of terror. She ran through the bushes, reached the little clearing, saw the tall tree, the precipice on which it stood, the flying swing and Nicky clinging leechlike to his sister's neck.

'Miss Imogen! Miss Imogen!' Jessie cried desperately, fearing at any second to see them both slide off and plunge into the valley . . . or Nicky lose his grip and hurtle from his sister's lap. Her loud calls finally had succeeded in slowing Imogen's frenzied flight. She glanced down and this time saw Jessie waving and shrieking in a frenzy of agitation. Gradually the swing lost its momentum until at last Jessie was able to rush forward and drag on one rope to bring it to a complete stop, the way a brave soul might tug at the bridle of a runaway horse.

'Oh, Miss Imogen, how could you do it? How could you do such a thing?' she cried, half-sobbing. She wrested Nicky from Imogen and gathered him to her, soothing away his panic. 'There, there, my little love, 'tes all over now.'

Afterwards, Jessie had related the incident to Annette, who in turn told Sir Oswald about it. He strode out to the swing and promptly ordered it to be dismantled and the tree from which it hung chopped down. 'I did not expect you would be so foolish and so thoughtless,' he had told his daughter sternly. Imogen sulked for days over the loss of her retreat, where she had so often felt light-hearted and carefree. And as the tree fell with a crash of leafy branches and an alarmed twittering of birds, it was as though some happy influence finally relinquished its slight hold on her, and a gentle little ghost sighed and crept away.

That had happened last September. Musing on last year's events, Annette continued writing in her diary, confiding to the page: 'I do not regret rejecting Mr T's proposal. I have no wish to become someone's wife for the mere sake of being married.' Pensively, she acknowledged to herself that six years ago, she might very well have embarked on marriage for just that reason. Chiefly, of course, for the material security it would bring. Now, the prospect of marriage without true affection and companionship seemed utterly distasteful. As for security – well, that was provided by her position here at Selbury, and she had become used to managing on a pittance. It did not do to dwell upon the future. Six years from now, it would be time for Nicholas to be sent away to school . . .

She thought again of Frederick Tenterden, who had come to Selbury as the curate at St Michael's. Over the years, a friendship had developed between the rectory family and the young governess. Edith James had pounced upon the notion of marriage between the new curate (a bachelor, gentlemanly, in his mid-thirties) and Miss Annette Duval. The curate and Miss Duval were duly introduced to one another and Frederick Tenterden, in his own quiet way, was quite smitten with the elegant young governess from Selbury Quade. He considered it would be a suitable enough match, even though Miss Duval had unfortunately lost her patrimony. And so, amid the potted ferns in the conservatory at the rectory one night, he had proposed to her. Annette had rejected him as kindly as possible, firmly withdrawing her hand from his tentative clasp and looking down on his receding hairline as he knelt on the tiled floor. A few months later, the curate had married the second daughter of a gentleman farmer; she brought him a small dowry and modest expectations. Already there was a pale, podgy little Tenterden boy as issue of the marriage.

Annette's only abiding regret was that no one else had materialized to invest her life with real romantic interest.

And now her thoughts turned to that unfortunate incident involving her employer. *That* could scarcely be termed romantic! She liked to pretend it had never happened . . . but it had, and that was a great pity. Ever since that day, Sir Oswald had avoided her company. Annette missed those occasional agreeable conversations they used to have. She was aware that she had, in fact, become something of an embarrassment to Sir Oswald Quade.

It had been a late summer day of impending storm. The air was close; by mid-afternoon a livid light hung over the landscape, so that it appeared unnatural, like a stage awaiting some momentous event to be played out. The grass appeared intensely green, each leaf of the abundant foliage minutely delineated. Annette, hurrying indoors as the first heavy drops of rain began to fall, seemed to feel her surroundings as well as see them: it was as though she shared the anticipation of grass blade and leaf of the storm about to break.

Inside, the servants hurried to close windows against the impending deluge; at the first rising of the wind, the first flicker of lightning, the little tweeny hid in a cupboard under the back stairs, and Mrs Robbins covered the milk lest it should turn. Annette glanced upward at Dame Margery's portrait as she crossed the great hall. There was a face to defy lightning flash and thunderbolt! How many, many storms had this old house weathered in its time, she wondered. Words from an ancient prayer came into her mind: 'The Lord shall protect you always, so that the Sun shall not burn thee by day, neither the Moon by night' . . . But had not Sir Carew Quade had been burned by the moon?

She had gone into the library to find a book she needed for the schoolroom, and noticed that one of the casement windows stood wide open. She went to close it, kneeling on the window seat to reach the hasp. She remained by the window, gazing at the flash of lightning and the now teeming rain outside. A strange excitement ran through her body. She did not realize Sir Oswald was in the room until he came to stand beside her. He had been sitting in a deep wing chair by the fireplace, and had watched her stretch across to close the window, her slim figure outlined against the dramatic light cast by the storm.

A sudden gigantic thunderclap sounded overhead; instinctively, Annette cringed a little towards him.

'Are you afraid?' To her heightened senses his voice sounded thickened, unusually intimate. She looked at him. How intently he stared at her! She was aware of the current of feeling between them.

'Why – no,' she stammered. 'Thunder – lightning – they seem to put mere mortals in their place. I enjoy the havoc –'

'Then you must be a passionate creature at heart,' Sir Oswald muttered, 'in spite of all your careful speeches' – and suddenly he folded her body closely to him, then pressed her down on to the window seat, tearing open the high collar of her blouse, shaping the contours of her flesh – breasts, waist, thighs – with possessing hands.

It would have been easy enough to succumb to his sudden passion. Annette still felt an illusion of unreality; for an instant she almost responded to his frenzy. But sheer common sense, besides the discomfort of the wooden window seat, prevailed over the electric atmosphere and her own spark of passion. She knew she must bring him back to himself. Disdaining to wrestle his hands from her body, she cried, 'Sir Oswald!' (How ludicrous to recollect rank in such a predicament.) 'Think of Imogen – Nicholas – Lady Louisa –'

Perhaps it was the utterance of that last name which stemmed his urgent need. He released her abruptly and moved across the room to stand with his back turned to her. With trembling fingers Annette smoothed her skirts and her rumpled hair, and tried to fasten her blouse – but its tiny pearl buttons had been wrenched away and were scattered over the floor. Desperately she sought words to gloss over what had happened, to restore the status quo between her employer and herself. Somehow their formal relationship must be restored.

By now the storm was beginning to subside; the thunder had become a distant reverberation. She moved hesitantly towards Sir Oswald. 'We – we must forget this unimportant incident. Storms are apt to affect people in unpredictable ways.' Then, recalling his remark about her 'careful speeches', she added simply, 'I understand – your loneliness.'

Really, she thought, it was all too reminiscent of the Ouida novel she had confiscated from Imogen and sampled for herself – only to put it aside with impatient scorn for the second-rate. Yet somehow this rent in the conventional pattern of Selbury life must be mended.

Sir Oswald raised his head to reply, but kept his gaze averted from her. 'I shall quite understand if you no longer wish to remain at Selbury.' His voice was remote. 'Needless to say, the highest reference . . .'

Annette was taken aback. How curious that *she* should seem the one repulsed. She was aware of a spurt of resentment in her mind as she replied, 'Merely for the sake of a few unfortunate moments . . . no, Sir Oswald, I believe I should stay at Selbury, chiefly for Nicholas's sake. Imogen does not need me so much now, but I believe I can be a real help to Nicky until he goes to school . . . I believe that Lady Louisa would have wished me to remain.' She raised her chin. 'I intend to dismiss this – this incident from my mind completely.' And if, she thought, Sir Oswald considered that a careful speech, why then, it was just too bad.

She stared down at the Persian carpet that lay between herself and her employer. It seemed suddenly to represent an unbridgeable chasm in their relationship. Those few moments of bodily contact had quite destroyed the friendly, relaxed feeling that used to exist between them.

Sir Oswald had looked at her straightly then. 'Very well, Miss Duval. I apologize for my conduct.' There was a harshness in his voice; it was half apology, half dismissal from his presence. Annette had left the room obediently, one hand concealing her torn collar.

Now, with a sigh, she shook the memory away (you could

not really put things out of your mind for ever and ever, amen). She locked the clasp of her diary with its tiny key. Were birthdays ever occasions for rejoicing, once childhood was left behind? She rose from her chair on the terrace. It was time to call Nicholas for his reading lesson.

Annette's recollection of that unfortunate encounter ended when she left the library. After she departed, Sir Oswald had paced the room in a fit of irritation. Damn, damn, damn! To have given way to base instincts – to betray his own code of civilized conduct – it was against everything he believed in. And it had to happen with Miss Duval, too, whom he respected, even liked. Better to have lunged at a pretty housemaid . . . but in truth, that sort of behaviour was simply not in his nature. Possibly Miss Duval was right to elect to remain at Selbury – but he would have been relieved if she had reacted in a more predictable manner, shown offence, resigned on the spot, instead of being so uncomfortably *understanding*.

He sank into a chair, shielding his eyes with one hand. It was time he did something to assuage his loneliness, he told himself, reorganize his life to include permanent female companionship. A second marriage. It would be best for the children, too, if he remarried. And there was someone close, someone they knew and trusted, who already belonged to the family.

The notion of marrying Hester Graham had in fact been forming in Sir Oswald's mind for some time. It would be very – appropriate. She was not too young – above all, she was not a stranger. She too had loved Louisa. But would she accept him? Louisa thought that Hester had closed her mind to marriage when Henry Lovell was killed in Afghanistan. Well, he would find out about that. The Grahams were to spend a season in London. He would go, too, open up the town house – high time it was used again – and take Imogen with him. He would escort Hester around a bit.

He looked out of the window. The wind had died down, the sky was growing lighter by the moment. He decided to take a walk and cleanse his mind of its shame in the fresh air. He knew Miss Duval would keep her word; she would never mention his behaviour to anyone. And after all, he began to persuade himself, was it so very heinous? Little more than an embrace beneath the mistletoe, when all was said and done . . .

Sir Oswald would have been much more disturbed if he had known that Imogen, pausing on the threshold of the library at the height of the storm, had witnessed the little scene with a mixture of curiosity and scorn – and had carefully stowed it away in her mind.

Chapter Nine

'HOLD STILL, DON'T move – not an eyelash, not a quiver . . . How about a nice bright smile, Violet, Lily, Rose – which are you? Ssh!' – As Lily, the new parlourmaid, clapped one hand over her mouth. 'No giggling, if you please!'

A long pause ensued while the photographer vanished beneath his black shroud, with everyone's attention fixed towards that magic box upon its tripod. Several of the servants suspended their breathing. Then: 'Presto!' and the carefully posed group relaxed and came to life again.

The entire household and outdoor staff, from Mrs Arkney and Mr Teague to the little tweeny and the second gardener's boy, had assembled on the lawn for Mr Edwin Moulvey to take a group portrait. It was a new line of business he had hit upon, photographing country houses and gardens, their families and staff. He had known his brother-in-law would not refuse the suggestion he should make such a record of Selbury Quade. The photographs were always presented in a handsome album, on its cover in gilt letters the name of Mr Moulvey's studio: *The Superior Photographic Studio*

(Portraiture a Speciality), London.

Three years ago, much to the disgust of his elder brother, Edwin Moulvey had resigned his army commission to devote himself to the subject which, apart from womankind, interested him most. And, since he was in need of an income, it had become his gainful occupation.

'I daresay this photography mania is harmless enough as a pastime for a gentleman, but to take it up as a trade . . .' Words had failed Lord Moulvey. True to his caste, he recognized only three professions: the church, the army and the law. He forbade his brother to use the family name in his new venture. Undeterred, Edwin had founded his Superior Studio, at somewhat insignificant premises in Oxford Street.

His visits to Selbury after the death of his beloved sister had been infrequent. He had little in common with his brother-in-law. But those rare appearances were greeted joyfully by Nicky, and Imogen was not averse to having her portrait taken each time Uncle Eddie came to stay . . . posing in Grecian draperies on the terrace; as a pensive reader by lamplight; in the punt at the lake's edge, one hand trailing languidly in the water. Annette, too, found herself diverted by Mr Moulvey's insouciant personality and the aura of a different, exciting world that clung about him: echoes of London and Paris, the bohemian life of artists and models. He had made a portrait of her which she sent to Aunt Harriet: posed in a chair, pen hovering above a half-written letter. It had the fashionable soft-focus effect. Edwin told Annette that he had met the inventor of this effect, a Mrs Cameron, at an exhibition. When he complimented her, she had laughed and said, 'My dear young sir, it all happened by accident. My first out-of-focus pictures were a fluke. When I was focusing and came to something which, to my eye, looked very beautiful, I simply stopped there instead of screwing on the lens to a more definite image.' Edwin had emulated her technique with considerable success, though some of his clients demanded a 'good sharp picture, none of that short-sighted fuzzy look'. The Superior Photographer was quite agreeable to tailoring his art to suit his customers.

Edwin's present visit to Selbury had lasted longer than before. He had taken the house from every propitious angle, views of the stables and horses, and sundry garden prospects, as well as the family and staff. And when, one morning, he learned that the Romany caravans had come again to Fox-hollow wood, he declared this was an opportunity not to be missed: he would make a photographic record of the gypsy encampment.

They were at breakfast. Imogen, presiding over the coffee pot, refilled her father's cup as he held it out absent-mindedly, his attention fixed on the *Morning Post*. Most of the news these days was gloomy: riots in aid of Reform up and down the country, a Fenian uprising in Ireland . . . the world seemed in a perpetual state of crisis. Only last year the Russians had attempted to murder their tsar, and the year before last, an American had succeeded in assassinating the president of the United States. Sir Oswald was feeling distinctly pessimistic this morning. Perhaps it had something to do with the presence of his brother-in-law. Surely Eddie had taken sufficient views of Selbury by now. If only he would return to London and leave them in peace! But what was Imogen saying now?

'. . . and you should make a special study of the gypsy woman who used to come here to tell fortunes, Uncle Eddie. She's so picturesque! She doesn't tell fortunes any more, another woman comes instead with a pack of raggy old tarot cards. But I saw her in the village only yesterday, hawking twiggy brooms.'

'Why, yes,' Annette agreed. 'She is a real Meg Merrilees.'

Imogen glanced at her governess from beneath lowered eyelids. 'She once told you that you would never marry, Miss Duval.'

Annette blushed and Edwin looked across at her appraisingly. He admired the poise the governess maintained – he knew how difficult his niece could be, and wondered how Miss Duval had managed to cope with her all these years. As for Oswald, he seemed virtually to ignore her presence. She must feel lonely sometimes, Edwin thought. Moreover, Miss Duval had made an excellent camera study. Edwin considered her portrait to be one of the best he had done; he had a copy on display in his studio. More than one gentleman had enquired the name of the wistful young lady with her half-finished letter.

'If you really want to take the gypsy's likeness,' Imogen went on, 'you'll most likely have to cross her palm with gold.'

There was an irritable rattle of newspaper as Sir Oswald broke into the conversation. 'I'd be obliged, Eddie, if you would refrain from disturbing the gypsy folk,' he said stiffly. 'They might well take exception to the notion of having their likenesses captured by a camera. They are a secretive race – I have read that they never use the name given to them at birth, but are known by another all their lives. They believe that knowledge of someone's real name bestows power over that person. Then think what greater power would lie in a photogenic likeness!'

His words were both rebuke and lecture, and an uncomfortable silence fell upon the breakfast table. Oh, Louie, dearest Louie, Edwin thought. She had always acted as a gentle intermediary between his brother-in-law and himself. He relied on another week at Selbury; to embark upon some gypsy studies seemed a useful as well as an artistic notion. Taking pictures at country houses often proved a useful ploy, enabling him to escape his London creditors until sufficient funds built up to pay their bills. This visit had also marked the breaking-off of his relationship with a certain lady of the musical-comedy stage. There would be no more bouquets of roses for La Belle Esmée, no more champagne suppers *à deux* when he returned to the metropolis. Well, Oswald could hardly throw him out of Selbury. And he was genuinely intrigued by the thought of those gypsies. Edwin made up his mind. He would stay another week, and he would visit Foxhollow, in spite of his brother-in-law.

It was a sadly depleted gypsy encampment this year: only two wagons stood in the clearing, with a quarter the usual number of horses and dogs. Hagar Smith stood surveying the scene from the topmost step of her own *vardo*. She had been busy since daybreak, hoping activity might dispel her gloomy thoughts. Perhaps they should find another summer camping ground, away from this place. She had never forgotten her premonition of some disaster that seemed to link her own people with the family at the great house here, the thin dark *gorgio* girl with her proud young face, the unspeakable horror of the maggots crawling in her palm. A few days ago, as Hagar sold her brooms at cottage doors, she had caught sight of that same girl passing along the village street. She was older now, of course, and taller, but she had the same proud look upon her face. Hagar had quickly made a sign to avert bad luck.

The past twelve months had not gone well for the tribe. They were a small group now: just Hagar herself and her husband Fowk; Fowk's brother Taiso with his small son, little Ishmael; and Hagar's sister, husband and their children. First old Ishmael, Fowk's father, had died during the winter. His passing left Fowk as head of their group. When they burned old Ishmael's *vardo*, according to their custom, with all his worldly possessions inside it, the flames had made a brave sight against the snowy landscape. But while the remnant of the wagon still glowed, a quarrel had broken out between Fowk and his cousin Ithal. The two had never liked each other; while old Ishmael lived, he held the peace between them. There was a fight; and the end of it was that Ithal, together with his wife, his two nephews and their wives and children, had broken away to form their own group. Ithal was a famous horse-handler; there used to be at least half a dozen ponies about the camp that he would be breaking in.

Worse was to come. The greatest tragedy of this past year had been the death of Taiso's young wife, Lurina. She had coughed her life away in the space of a few months, leaving Taiso with little Ishmael. Who could say what evil eye had caused Lurina's sickness? Hagar recalled how one of Ithal's nieces, Salome, used to cast fond glances upon Taiso. It was said that she had baked a cake with seventeen drops of her menstrual blood, as a love potion, and that, unwittingly, Taiso had eaten some of it. But it had not deflected his love from Lurina. Ah, that had been a true love match. Hagar remembered their wedding, in a field somewhere near Exeter, a gypsy *rommerrin* in the open air. It was Fowk who lightly gashed the wrists of bride and groom, so that their blood ran together when they placed their hands palm to palm; and afterwards they jumped together over the ceremonial fire.

Hagar sighed. It was all over now . . . and only Taiso and little Ishmael were left. The child was five summers old, a healthy, lively boy, full of fun and mischief. But Hagar worried about Taiso, who had grown increasingly morose. Standing at her painted door this morning, she thought how strangely deserted the scene before her looked, where only her sister Raia sat twisting a bundle of twigs into a broom while her little ones played about the fire, and young Ishmael brought her more twigs from the wood. The sway-backed mare that belonged to Taiso cropped the grass beside the other two horses. It was Raia who went to the big house now to act the part of the *darbushi fal*, the fortune-teller, but in truth she did not have the gift; she brought out phrases as well-worn as her tarot cards. Hagar shrugged. What matter? Doubtless those who crossed Raia's palm with silver were content to invest her threadbare predictions with their own hopes.

Suddenly Hagar stiffened. Someone was coming through the wood towards the clearing, walking carelessly in the way of a *gorgio*. The three scrawny dogs lying beside the fire pricked up their ears and began to bark.

Hagar called a warning to Raia, who looked up from her broom-making to see who the stranger might be.

Into the clearing came a man – a *rye*, a gentleman, to judge by his clothes. He was carrying some sort of three-legged instrument, the like of which Hagar had seen before, outside a fair booth. An instrument of the devil, to capture your soul by means of mumbo jumbo beneath a black cloth.

Edwin Moulvey paused on the edge of the clearing, thankfully easing himself of the weight of his tripod and the rest of the cumbersome equipment. The dogs circled him with menacing growls. His gaze rested on Hagar, who stood in a defiant attitude at her painted door. By Jove, here was Meg Merrilees herself! He had no doubt this was the gypsy woman his niece and Miss Duval had spoken of. There was also no doubt of her hostility as she stood looking down at him, hands on her hips, head thrown back. He attempted conciliation.

'Good day to you! I should be much obliged if you would allow me to make a pictorial study of your encampment. And please – call off your dogs.'

'Who might you be?' She was declaring war on him, it seemed. She made no move to check the snarling dogs. As for the other woman, she merely sat gaping at him, with her children gathered around her.

'I am Sir Oswald Quade's brother,' Edwin said.

This put a rather different edge upon the matter. Hagar lowered her head slightly. Something of her hostility seemed to evaporate.

That's given her something to think about, Edwin told himself.

Hagar felt herself to be in a difficult situation. Their camp site belonged to Sir Oswald Quade; she could hardly refuse permission for his brother to make pictures here. She shrugged, reluctantly acknowledging his right, and at last called out a few words of command to the dogs, who slunk away.

'But do not try to take our likenesses,' she warned him. 'We gypsy folk do not permit that. It is against our *kris*, our way of life.' With a final glare in his direction, she disappeared inside her wagon.

Edwin was disappointed. Perhaps the other woman, sitting with her brooms by the fire, would prove easier to persuade. She did not have half the character of the other, but one gypsy was better than none, and she looked quite picturesque with her patterned headscarf and the children clustered about her, staring at him with big, dark eyes. He approached Raia with a half-sovereign in his hand. After an initial display of unwilling-ness, she relented and pocketed the gold coin, much to the fury of Hagar, watching from behind her lace curtain. Edwin rearranged the little group more to his liking, and managed to convey to the gypsy woman that she and the children must not move for several moments. Then he disappeared beneath the black cloth to take the picture.

At this moment, young Ishmael emerged from the far side of the clearing, carrying a bundle of twigs almost as large as himself. He saw Raia and the other children gazing – fearfully, it seemed – at a headless monster with five legs and a black body which seemed to have transfixed them with a strange power. The little gypsy boy, to whom black magic was a fact of everyday life, gave a terrified shriek, dropped the whole bundle of twigs, and ran blindly back into the wood, leaving the trodden pathways to weave through thick undergrowth. In and out among the trees he fled, his single thought to get away from that black demon.

This disturbance spoiled Edwin's picture, for Raia and the other children turned to look at Ishmael, whose shriek of terror also brought Hagar out on to the steps of her wagon once more, in a fury. The dogs, made bold by her example, came forward and began to snarl and bark again.

'You – you *limbo gaujo*! You have terrified the child out of his wits! I told you, we gypsies do not like to give away the image of ourselves. Go away! Be off! Leave us in peace!'

Edwin felt deeply aggrieved. A whole half-sovereign relinquished for nothing! One or two seconds longer and his exposure of that scene would have been completed. Crossly he dismantled the tripod, packed up his camera and retreated the way he had come. A wasted morning – and now, since all hope of making gypsy studies had clearly vanished, he had no more reason to delay his departure from Selbury.

Little Ishmael ran himself to a standstill and flopped to the ground, sides heaving, heart beating wildly. Some moments later he had become calm enough to sense a movement in the undergrowth. He swivelled his gaze in that direction without moving head or body, the way his father Taiso had taught him.

A *sho-sho*! The rabbit sat up on its hindlegs, nose and whiskers quivering, not ten paces away. Cautiously Ishmael's fingers crept to the pocket where his catapult lay, while with his other hand he picked up a small round stone. A rabbit was always a welcome offering for the stew pot. He withdrew the catapult inch by inch, then raised it to take aim. But just before he drew back the leather thong, the *sho-sho* seemed to sense its mortal danger and bounded away.

Ishmael ran after it for the sheer excitement of the chase knowing he had no hope of catching it. And though the rabbit escaped mortal danger, the little boy did not. Lurking long-forgotten in tangled undergrowth, amid glistening ground ivy and delicate wood anemones, lay a rusting relic of the last century: a mantrap, set to spring a poacher and pinion him by the leg. No gypsy lore or cunning could save Ishmael now. He stumbled full upon the trap, which snapped on his ankle with a screech of metal, its rusty fangs biting deep into his tender flesh. The little boy gave a piercing shriek of agony and struggled for a few moments before he fell unconscious. In flight from one headless, three-legged monster, he had fallen victim to another, with dragon's teeth.

It was twilight when the frantic Taiso found him. By then the boy was half-conscious and delirious; already those rusted teeth were working their poison in his blood, devouring his life. Half-demented, the father carried his son back to Hagar's wagon. She looked at the terrible wound, saw the red streaks spreading up Ishmael's legs, and felt his burning forehead. By twilight next day the boy was dead, and Taiso's howl of grief echoed from the depths of Foxhollow.

Dan Trefoil, trudging home from the stables, heard that unearthly sound and stopped in mid-stride to ponder its source. It was unlike the cry of any creature he had heard before. ' 'Twas a sound not of this world,' he told his wife. In truth, it was akin to the lost sound of a wolf's howl, in days beyond memory when Foxhollow was an impenetrable forest.

Chapter Ten

NEXT DAY, A subtler emotion took hold of Taiso's mind. It was born when Hagar, indicating the stiff little body that lay covered in one corner of her wagon, said, 'You must go to the big house and ask Sir Oswald Quade to arrange burial for the *chal.*'

The next moment she almost shrank from the wild look in his eyes. 'Sir Oswald Quade . . . if it were not for him and his instrument of the devil, little Ishmael would be alive today!' His nostrils flared. 'And now I am to beg a favour of him—that my son may be buried in his churchyard beside all manner of *gorgios!*'

Hagar knew he was beyond reason. Useless to point out that the mantrap must have lain rusting in the wood for nigh on a hundred years, that Ishmael's death was none of Sir Oswald Quade's doing, that the picture machine had belonged to his brother . . .

'It must be done, Taiso,' she said. 'If you like, Fowk will go in your place –'

'No!' Taiso cried out. 'It is for me alone to go. And after it is done and they have put my Ishmael in the earth, I will never come nigh this place again.'

'I do not think any of us will come here again,' Hagar muttered. She herself felt bewildered and confused by what had happened. Was Ishmael's death the culmination of all the troubles that had overtaken them in the past year – or was there something else to come, yet more evil awaiting them? She was fearful, for she had a premonition that Fate's ravelled cord was not yet run.

It was unthinkable that this wild-eyed gypsy should come to the main entrance of the house, demand admittance of the liveried footman, then push past him into the great hall.

Hearing the commotion, Sir Oswald emerged from the library. Taiso's glittering gaze fastened upon him.

'You killed my son!' The accusation broke from him uncontrollably.

Edward the footman, immobilized by amazement and a certain fear – for it was almost as though some wild beast had invaded the house – suddenly came to his senses and sped off to fetch help.

Sir Oswald looked at Taiso and recognized a man half-crazed by grief. 'Tell me what happened to your son,' he said in a calm and reasonable tone. One did not cringe before a mad dog.

'*O Del* – it were the devil's trap! Set in the trees to catch a *chal* as though he were a hare or a rabbit –' Taiso's voice broke. 'My Ishmael were caught in it – his leg –' He turned aside, unable to go on.

There was no need. A mantrap that had been overlooked. Sir Oswald surmised the rest of the tragic story. The gash left by rusty metal teeth – the blood poisoning that must have ensued, culminating in the wretched child's inevitable death.

He chose his words carefully. 'I am sorry your son died so terribly. Believe me, it was none of my doing, nor that of my gamekeeper. These mantraps were set there in my great-grandfather's time. I gave orders for them to be taken up and done away with, years ago.'

Taiso's hands were clenched. 'But – but that were not the

whole reason Ishmael died. 'Twas that other contraption that did for my *chal* as well. If he had not run away from it he would not have fallen upon the trap –'

Sir Oswald frowned. 'What other contraption?'

'Why, the – the picture-machine the other *gentleman*' – Taiso turned the word into a sneer – 'brought to our camp. Your own brother. He frightened the very life out of Ishmael –' Realizing the literal truth of his own words, Taiso uttered a groan of anguish.

So Edwin had taken his infernal camera to Foxhollow after all. Silently Sir Oswald cursed his brother-in-law, who had finally departed from Selbury that very morning. Grimly he told the gypsy: 'I knew nothing of that. I am indeed distressed that Mr Moulvey disturbed your camp.'

Taiso stared at him fiercely. 'My son! My son!' he shouted in desperation. Tears streamed down his swarthy cheeks.

His grief was almost biblical in its intensity; Sir Oswald seemed to catch the echo of a king's lament for one who was strangled by his own flowing locks within another wood.

At this juncture, Edward reappeared with Tom, the other footman, and Dan Trefoil. Seeing the gypsy's threatening stance, they made to move against him, but Sir Oswald restrained them with a gesture.

Then Dan Trefoil spoke up. He already knew of the tragedy that had struck the gypsy camp; in truth, he hoped it meant they would not come again to Selbury. 'The child will require a Christian burial, Sir Oswald.' As he spoke, he recalled that unearthly cry he had heard from Foxhollow: he knew now who had uttered it.

'Of course.' Sir Oswald nodded. This practicality came as a relief, must indeed be the reason underlying the gypsy's visit, to ask that his son be buried in the churchyard at Selbury. 'It will be arranged.' There was really nothing more he could say.

He was suddenly aware that Imogen had joined the little group before him. He had not noticed her until that second. She seemed to have materialized out of thin air.

'Why, Imogen –' Her presence disconcerted him.

'I heard a noise, Papa.' She turned then to look full at the gypsy, not with compassion, but with a cool, detached regard. And Taiso, returning her gaze, saw in her eyes a cold, remorseless curiosity. Immediately his one desire was to quit these alien people, leave this great house of gloom and shadows. With a sudden loss of all bravado he bowed his head and stumbled away, seeking escape to the dark world outside, the solace of his own folk and the campfire at Foxhollow.

Afterwards, when the servants had left, Sir Oswald said, 'I wish you had not been present at that distressing scene, my dear.'

Imogen shrugged in reply. 'It was only a gypsy boy that died, Papa.' Then, seeing the hint of disapproval that came to his eyes, she added quickly, 'I mean – it isn't as if – as if Nicky had stumbled upon that mantrap!'

Whereupon he covered her hands with both of his, protectively, as though to smother such a notion.

Annette knew nothing of the gypsy tragedy until the next day, when she was startled to hear Nicky relate the grisly details.

'He was the same age as me,' he told her, his face solemn. 'And he was caught in a – a rusty trap in our woods and bleeded to death. And – and he's to be buried today in the corner of the churchyard where they put tramps and – and paupers. That's what Midgin says. What is a pauper, Miss Duval?'

'So Imogen has told you all this,' Annette remarked. Her lips tightened. It sounded appropriately ghoulish. 'A pauper is someone who has no money – nothing that belongs to him in all the world,' she explained.

They were in the schoolroom, preparing for the promised nature expedition to collect tadpoles from the lake. Annette brought a jam jar and two shrimping nets on slender poles out of the cupboard.

'One of the nets has got a hole in it,' Nicky reported. 'All the tadpoles could escape.'

'Then we shall have to make do with the other one,' Annette replied.

At that moment Imogen, almost a stranger to the school-room these days, appeared in the doorway. She seemed to be in an unusually good mood and smiled disarmingly at her governess. 'May I come too?' she asked. 'It's such a perfect day, far too nice to stay indoors. I'm supposed to be writing letters in the morning room, but the curtains keep out all the sun.'

'Why, of course, Imogen,' Annette said lightly. Not wanting to spoil this rare overture of friendship, she said in the same light tone, 'By the way, it seems you have been regaling Nicky with some tale about a gypsy boy –'

'Oh, that.' Imogen shrugged dismissively. 'He fell into one of the old mantraps. Papa says he must have died from blood poisoning. His father came here last night and made a dreadful scene. He said his boy ran off into the woods because he was frightened by Uncle Edwin's camera.' She sighed derisively. 'They are so ignorant, these people.' She looked sideways at Annette. 'Lucky for Uncle Edwin that he went back to London yesterday, if you ask me. Papa is fearfully displeased he went to Foxhollow to take pictures – I've never known him so angry. He even said he would never invite Uncle Eddie to Selbury again, if that was the way he abused our hospitality.'

Edwin Moulvey never to visit Selbury again! Annette was conscious of a distinct sensation of dismay. Aloud she said, 'You seem remarkably detached about the whole business, Imogen. And – I don't think it was quite suitable to tell Nicky about it.'

Usually such a rebuke would have caused at least a minor flare-up. But Imogen appeared determined to remain affable this morning. 'Perhaps you are right, Miss Duval,' she said demurely.

Imogen demure? Annette glanced at her sharply, but there was nothing to be gleaned from the girl's downcast gaze.

A few moments later they trooped down the backstairs and out of doors. The two Highland terriers came running to them and cavorted about Nicky's legs, barking excitedly as he strode ahead bearing the shrimping net and jam jar as weapons of the hunt. Both dogs were utterly devoted to him.

'It seems that Flora and Angus have decided to come tadpoling too.' Annette laughed. Quite suddenly she felt extraordinarily light-hearted. Imogen was right: it was a perfect spring day. Almost too perfect. The foliage in young green leaf, the blue sky patterned with fluffy little white clouds, drifts of daffodils and freesias beneath the trees . . .

Imogen gave a lingering backward glance towards the house, and seeing the look in her eyes, the sudden realization came to Annette: 'Why, she *worships* Selbury! It is her graven image.'

The thought dissolved in the spring sunshine as they drew near the clipped, precise, high walls of Dame Margery's maze, which lay directly in their path. A trim, green citadel, Annette thought. She had not ventured into the maze even though it was now restored; certainly it seemed more approachable now than the rough, forbidding fortress it had been before.

Imogen glanced at her. 'I've never shown you the secret of finding the way in and out again, have I, Miss Duval? The key to the maze. Let me show you now! Come, it will take only a few moments. Nicky can wait for us outside – you know how much he hates little, narrow places.'

Annette hesitated. She saw Nicky stop in his tracks, the two terriers still running joyful circles around him. It was true that he seemed to have a real fear of dark or confined areas. He would always avoid the narrow back-stairs passage, and like his sister when she was younger, he always slept with a night light beside his bed.

'Just wait there, Nicky,' she called, deciding to humour Imogen. 'We shall be with you again as soon as you can say "Jack Robinson"!'

'Well, hurry up,' Nicky said. 'Or else we'll miss all the tadpoles.'

Imogen stood at the entrance to the maze, framed by the dark green branches. How pretty she was when she smiled, Annette thought. She looked quite charming standing there; what a photographic study it would make. And then, as

Annette recalled that Edwin Moulvey might never visit Selbury again, she felt that same curious pang of disappointment.

'Don't worry, Nicky, the tadpoles won't turn into frogs as quickly as all that,' she said over her shoulder as she followed Imogen into the tunnel of foliage. 'Just wait there for us, dear.'

She had no inkling in the world these were the last words she would ever speak to Nicholas Quade.

'You follow the hedge on the right to begin with,' Imogen called back, 'and then – just here – you change to the left as you turn the corner . . .' Her voice faded away.

'Not so fast, Imogen! I must keep up!' Annette called back light-heartedly.

Had Imogen heard her? Annette turned the corner to find the girl had vanished. She was faced by nothing but green leafy walls, and now there was a choice of narrow pathways. Which strip of beaten earth should she follow? She strained to hear Imogen, but the thick hedges muffled every sound.

'Imogen!' she called – and again, more urgently, 'Where are you? Imogen!'

There was no answering call. Annette felt a prickle of panic. Was this intended as a joke – or had Imogen deliberately schemed to trap her in this green prison? A silly practical joke – yes, that must be what it was. She recalled the girl's laughing face as she had glimpsed it a moment ago . . . several moments ago by now. Had Imogen in truth been mocking her, devising a torment for her governess? Bewildered, Annette looked up at the blue sky and those downy white clouds far above the high hedges that walled her in. This was ridiculous! She must simply find her own way out, that was all there was to it. She set off down one green alley with determined steps, her skirt brushing against the branches on either side. It came to a dead end. She retraced her steps – or so she thought – to try another path . . . And she thought of Nicholas waiting there outside. What if he grew tired of waiting and decided to go on to the lake by himself? Trusting to her to follow. She recalled the steep, sheer banks above the deep water. The lake was very full from the spring rains. It would be so easy for a little child to tumble in

. . . and drown. She strove to hear some sound from the world outside. Nothing, not even a shrill bark from one of the little dogs. But Imogen . . . surely she would have enough sense not to let Nicky go to the lake alone, or else to go after him if he had set off. But who could tell what Imogen might do?

By now Annette felt confused both physically and mentally. Could Imogen perhaps be waiting for her in the centre of the maze? Perhaps the girl had merely set her a test of ingenuity. They would meet up again in the centre, and then Imogen would lead the way out in just a few moments . . . yes, that must be it!

She consulted the fob watch she wore on her bodice. Heavens! Already a quarter of an hour had slipped by since she entered the maze. Fifteen minutes: an eternity to a five-year-old. She sent up a silent prayer that Nicky might have returned to the house, have told someone that she and Imogen had disappeared inside the maze. Meanwhile, she must find the path that led to the centre. Feverishly now she set off again, trying in vain to peer through the thick, impenetrable hedges. A branch caught at her head and a long strand of hair fell across her face. The green walls seemed to close upon her as if to forbid her presence. The silence was thick, eerie, unnatural. Dame Margery's maze! An absurd notion slipped into her mind. If – when she reached the centre, would she find that Elizabethan ghost sitting on the stone bench that stood there, embroidered skirts spread stiffly? A sob of frustration and apprehension welled up in Annette's throat, and now she began to utter little useless cries of anguish as she stumbled on . . .

Meanwhile Imogen stepped coolly out of the maze, to be confronted by a very cross little boy.

'There you are at last! I could have said hundreds and hundreds of "Jack Robinsons"! But where's Miss Duval? Why isn't she with you?'

Afterwards, Imogen Quade almost succeeded in convincing herself that everything she did this day was unpremeditated, that she simply and naturally took advantage of the circumstances confronting her. Now she shrugged in response to Nicky's question. 'Oh, I expect she'll come out in a minute.'

'But what about the tadpoles?' Nicky's indignation was shrill. 'If she doesn't hurry up there won't be time to get them before lunch.'

Imogen sighed. 'I don't care about your wretched tadpoles, you silly little boy.' She hesitated for a fraction of a second. 'Why don't you go on to the lake by yourself? Miss Duval will catch you up, I dare say.'

'But Midgin –' Nicky began to protest. He knew the lake was out of bounds unless he was with someone else.

Imogen shrugged again. 'Oh, do what you please. *I'm* going back to the house to do my letters.' She began to retrace her steps towards the lawn without waiting to see what effect her words would have. Nicky would either go on to the lake by himself or he would not. If he did . . . why, anything might happen. No need to formulate exactly what that 'anything' might be. But perhaps Miss Duval would find her way out of the maze and catch Nicky up. Who could say? Chance, sheer chance, would decide the outcome.

Nicholas came to the brink of the lake, its surface a rippling reflection of blue sky. He knew that frogspawn and tadpoles were to be found at the reedy edges where tall bulrushes grew and moorhens and fussy little coots built their nests. But he found that even lying at full length upon the bank, he still could not reach down to the water with his net. Flora and Angus watched his efforts, heads cocked, uttering whimpers of encouragement.

Nicholas was a determined little boy; he decided to take off his boots and stockings and get right down into the water. He did not realize he would be out of his depth almost at once; there was no gentle, shallow margin here. Barefooted, he was about to clamber down when he caught the sound of hoofbeats. Someone was riding along the lakeside towards him: soon he was able to make out a rough-looking man mounted bareback upon a brown horse.

It was the gypsy, Taiso, who that morning had seen his son put away into the earth in an obscure corner of the churchyard, a little pine-wood coffin in an unmarked grave. He had mounted his horse and ridden off as soon as the *gorgio* priest concluded the brief service, not caring where he went. As he cantered by the lakeside, it was the two white terriers that drew his attention. Then he saw the child, who stood up straight to watch him. A sturdy little boy, about the same age as Ishmael, from the look of him, but with a milk-white skin, and wearing a blue-and-white sailor suit like a little gentleman. A gentleman's son! Suddenly Taiso realized who this child must be. The son of Sir Oswald Quade – his only man-child, heir to his great house and all the land surrounding it. Reining the mare to a halt a few yards away, the gypsy looked down at Nicholas with such an intense, brooding gaze that the child grew frightened. The dogs, too, seemed to sense some threat. They began to bark defiantly, circling horse and rider warily.

'Don't be afraid, *chal*, I won't harm ye.' Taiso gave a strange smile, more like a snarl.

Nicky backed away, coming dangerously close to the edge of the bank.

And then Taiso realized that fate had given him this chance to take revenge upon the gentleman whose wicked trap had destroyed Ishmael, his firstborn, his only-born. 'Many children, much luck' – that was the old saying of his people. Well, he had had the luck of the devil! Lurina, then little Ishmael – both gone. Why should that other father not know the selfsame sorrow? He gave a quick, furtive glance around the landscape; there was no one in sight. Swiftly he dismounted, then came towards Nicholas, who cringed before this menacing, swarthy stranger. Angus rushed forward to attack the gypsy's legs, while Flora barked hysterically. Taiso cursed and flung out one foot, hooking the little terrier upwards and out into the water in one movement.

'Angus! Angus!' Nicky cried out fearfully.

The little dog bobbed up and down in circles, frantically

paddling to keep his head above water. Flora rushed to the edge, watching him and making anxious sounds.

Then Taiso made a sudden lunge at Nicholas, grasped him by the waist and leaped back on the mare, holding his captive tightly as he dug his heels into the horses's flanks.

'Let go! Let go of me! Let me go!' But a huge brown hand was clamped across Nicky's mouth, cutting off his cries as they rode away towards Foxhollow.

Nearly two hours had passed. Annette, dishevelled and frantic, her face streaked by tears, her throat sore from shouting uselessly for help, sank helplessly down on the dusty path, leaning against one of the living walls of her prison. She knew for certain now that Imogen had deserted her. Several times she had stumbled into the centre of the maze; the first time, she had rested on the ancient stone bench, trying to devise some rational plan. But her predicament defied logic. It was a nightmare in broad daylight. (At least no image of Dame Margery, risen from the grave, had awaited her.) Then she began to shout, until her voice cracked. And all the time she was filled with dread at the thought of what might have befallen Nicky.

Now, huddled on the path, she seemed suddenly to hear a voice. Yes, surely it was someone calling . . . calling her name.

'. . . Duval! Miss Duval! Be you in there?'

One of the stable lads, perhaps. Annette sprang up and somehow summoned voice to shout back, 'Yes! Yes! Oh, get me out of here!'

'. . . back with a ladder!' the distant voice replied from the world outside.

Then silence, until she heard a scraping noise: looking up, she spied a lad's head and shoulders above one of the outer hedges. It was the red head and freckled face of Charlie Ashell.

'Here! I'm here,' she croaked, and Charlie's head swivelled in her direction.

'Thank the Lord we've found ye, miss. Searching high an' low, we've been. But ain't Master Nicholas with ye?'

'No! He – he's –' But she abandoned speech. The main thing was to get out as quickly as possible.

'Now just ye follow what I say and ye'll be out of there in no time –'

Annette obeyed the lad's directions: take that pathway, then this, now to the right, now left . . . Just a few more turns, and then at last she emerged into the open air. She found herself confronted by a little group of servants: Nanny Hodges, her face marked with grim disapproval; Jessie, flushed and worried, twisting her hands in her apron; one of the gardeners, clutching a rake. They stood staring at her, a silent tableau, amazed at the appearance of the usually neat, impeccably dressed young governess, who now faced them with hair awry, clothes dusty and dishevelled, face streaked with dirt.

Then, 'Where is Nicholas, Miss Duval?' Nanny Hodges demanded icily.

Annette swayed slightly. But there was no pity for her exhaustion in the eyes of those before her; rather, she sensed hostility and closed ranks. These were her judges, ready to condemn.

'Oh, miss, where is he?' Jessie was wrung by anxiety. 'Master Nicky! We can't find him nowhere! And Miss Imogen's been taken ill –'

'Master Nicholas was in your charge, Miss Duval.' That was Nanny Hodges again. She was disclaiming responsibility for herself, Annette realized dimly.

Useless to attempt explanation – if indeed any existed – and a waste of precious time. Nicholas! The lake – there was no time to lose. For the moment the news of Imogen scarcely registered in Annette's mind.

'Quickly – the lake,' she said, attempting to recover some remnant of her usual poise. 'We were going there to collect tadpoles –' Abandoning speech, she gathered up her skirts and set off, half walking, half running, closely followed by the others. Charlie Ashell sprinted ahead of them.

As they neared the lake they heard a mournful howling that froze the blood. It came from Flora, still pattering frantically beside the lake's edge. Upon the grassy bank they found Nicky's discarded boots and stockings alongside the tadpole net and jar, pathetic evidence of his presence there.

Then, looking across the lake, Jessie screamed, ''Tis him! 'Tis our Nicky, drowned!'

Annette's heart lurched sickeningly as she too saw the little body floating on the surface of the water. But the next moment she heard Nanny Hodges assert stoutly, ''Tis not a child – that be the other little dog floating there.' And then Charlie Ashell dived into the water and clambered out again bearing Angus's sodden corpse in his arms. But that did not mean that Nicky had not drowned as well. Perhaps the brave little terrier had tried to save him . . .

Annette turned to Charlie. 'Run back and tell Dan Trefoil to bring help – the lake will have to be dragged –'

The lad sped off as Nanny Hodges and Jessie began to circle the lake in opposite directions, calling Nicky as they went. Annette tried to think coherently. Sir Oswald: she recollected he had said something about visiting one of the distant farms. He might not return for hours yet. Someone should be sent to fetch him home. Imogen: what had Jessie said? That she'd been taken ill . . . what did that mean? She had better go to find out; there was nothing more she could do here. If Nicky was anywhere about, he would surely answer the others' calls. Gathering up her skirts again, she set off for the house, too consumed by anxiety to realize just how exhausted she was.

Imogen, it transpired, had suffered another bee sting. On this day of all days! Annette's heart sank even lower as she heard this news and recalled how desperately ill the girl had been after the episode at Miller's Green.

Mrs Arkney had risen to the occasion with her usual competence and taken charge. Dr Fonteney was now attending to Imogen; word had already been sent for Sir Oswald to return home. Annette came face to face with the housekeeper outside the door of Imogen's room. Briefly, Mrs Arkney related how Edward had found Miss Imogen lying on the terrace steps. Just before she became unconscious, she had managed to tell him that a bee had stung her . . . and she had murmured something about her governess being lost in the maze. That was almost an hour ago, Mrs Arkney said. She had then sent word for someone to take a ladder to the maze. They had all assumed Master Nicholas would be there with her. When Charlie reported that Nicholas wasn't with her, they had begun a general search for him. In the housekeeper's expression and tone of voice, Annette sensed the same disapproval she had encountered in Nanny Hodges, the same reproach Jessie had implied.

'He – he went on to the lake by himself, it seems,' Annette told Mrs Arkney wearily. 'We were to go there together – it was a nature lesson. Nanny Hodges and Jessie are looking for him there. I came back to see how Imogen –'

Mrs Arkney was staring at her in horror. She cut through her disjointed speech. 'The lake!'

Annette bowed her head. Worn out as she was, something puzzled her. 'Are – are you sure Miss Imogen was found only an hour ago?' she asked.

'Quite sure, Miss Duval.' Mrs Arkney compressed her lips.

But she had been trapped in the maze for twice that length of time, Annette thought. What was Imogen doing meanwhile? And why, oh why had she not prevented Nicky from going to the lake?

Mrs Arkney gave the governess's dishevelled appearance a disparaging glance. Miss Duval seemed quite distraught – as well she might! It seemed clear she had shown the most appalling lack of responsibility, neglected her duty, betrayed the trust reposed in her . . . It was devoutly to be hoped that Master Nicholas would be found soon – alive.

'You might care to change your dress before you go in to Miss Imogen,' the housekeeper said coldly.

Chastened, Annette went off to make hasty repairs to her appearance; when she returned to Imogen's room she looked more like her usual self, though beneath the crisp cotton of her clean shirtwaist blouse, her heart was heavier than ever with anxiety.

Imogen had just regained consciousness, it seemed. Deathly white, she lay on top of her bed, propped against ruffled pillows, undressed to her bodice and petticoat. Her eyelids were drooping. Her left forearm, swollen and blistered, was stretched out stiffly upon the counterpane.

Dr Fonteney glanced up as Annette entered the room. 'Ah, Miss Duval.' Knowing nothing yet of Nicky's disappearance, he bestowed on her the first sympathetic look she had received since she emerged from the maze. 'Our young patient does not seem to be suffering as severe a reaction as she experienced on that first occasion, thank God,' he said, glancing down at Imogen.

At this juncture, a murmur came from Imogen's blanched lips.

Annette leaned across the bed. 'What is it, Imogen?'

'I – I left you because a bee came flying at me in the maze, Miss Duval. I was so afraid I – I panicked and ran outside . . . just reached the terrace . . .' Her voice died away.

Annette drew back, biting her lip. Imogen seemed to imply that she had run straight back to the house shortly after they had entered the maze together. Yet Mrs Arkney had said Imogen had been found just one hour ago. Was it conceivable that she could have lain there a whole hour without someone seeing her? That seemed unlikely. Besides, she was still conscious when Edward found her – she had managed to tell him about the maze. And there was absolutely no doubt that she herself had spent the best part of two hours in that hateful place. Well, Imogen had survived her sting, that was one blessing. Dr Fonteney did not appear unduly worried. As Annette's thoughts now reverted wholly to Nicholas, suddenly her legs seemed to give way and she collapsed into a chair.

'You look quite done in, Miss Duval,' the doctor said. 'I would advise you to take some rest. There really is no need to worry about Imogen.'

Would his gentle tone, his kindly smile vanish when he learned of Nicky's disappearance? Assuredly. Annette knew she must tell him herself, before he heard it from someone else.

'It – it isn't on account of Imogen,' she faltered. 'There is – something else.' Haltingly she related everything that had happened – and watched Giles Fonteney's expression change from kindliness to deep concern. When he spoke to her again his voice and eyes held a cold reserve.

'Well, Miss Duval, I would reiterate my advice. Take some rest. You realize that when Sir Oswald returns, it will be necessary to go over every detail of these unfortunate occurrences. We can only pray that Nicky . . . I will go at once to find out what has happened since you left the lake – if anything.'

As Annette trailed off to her room, she knew she had become an outcast, an unwanted presence amid these familiar surroundings. The people who still belonged here were all turned against her. She lay on her bed for a while, resting her body while her thoughts ran in dizzy circles. Had they found Nicky? Had he run out from a clump of bushes, perhaps, in answer to those frantic calls? Maybe in a little while she would hear his piping voice upon the stair.

She pressed her head into the pillow, dreading her forthcoming interview with her employer. She had no doubt of the outcome: she would of course be dismissed without a reference. It went without saying. Her seven years of service at Selbury would count for nothing. All the times she had shared with this family – happy times and times of sorrow alike – would be wiped from the slate for ever. In recollection, she would always be the governess who neglected her duty, who caused Nicholas Quade to . . . oh no, surely Nicky had not drowned!

Even if – *when* he was found, she would still be dismissed for the trouble she had brought upon the household. Was it in fact her fault? Did she deserve to be ostracized? All she had done was to humour Imogen, to follow her into the maze. The girl had been so persuasive, in such a rare good humour. And then the bee . . . Suddenly Annette sat bolt upright. The bee! Why had she not been aware of it inside the maze? Yet Imogen had undoubtedly been stung. Oh, these half-formulated suspicions . . . was she in fact simply trying to deny her own culpability,

Annette asked herself. Or was Imogen in truth responsible for everything that had happened? Imogen – who would once again become heiress to this house she loved if Nicky . . . But that was an evil thought to harbour. There could be no truth in it.

Annette got up and went to the looking-glass to tidy her hair. Whatever the truth, whatever the evil, the result would be the same so far as she was concerned. Dismissal. She would be obliged to leave Selbury immediately. She looked into her own eyes, lit by a sudden panic. What would she do then?

The summons she was dreading came when Edward tapped on her door. As she followed him down the great staircase, she recalled that it was Edward who had opened the great door of Selbury Quade and welcomed her when she first arrived. Now his stiff, liveried back seemed to register hostility.

Sir Oswald chose to see her in the morning room. Haggard with anxiety, he spoke to the point. There was still no sign of Nicky. He cross-questioned her about each detail of the day's events, in a voice which held overtones of extreme dislike. Annette answered as best she could, striving not to break down.

At last Sir Oswald told her, 'They will drag the lake tomorrow. I do not wish you to remain here one more day, Miss Duval. You will be paid the salary due to you and leave in the morning. A cab will take you to Yeovil station.'

Evidently he assumed she would return to London, whence she had come all those years ago. What did he imagine she would do then? Without a reference she had no hope of finding another post. Word would soon spread of what had happened here at Selbury. Aunt Harriet . . . how could she possibly return to her aunt's house in such disgrace, to impose herself upon that elderly, impoverished lady? But of course Sir Oswald neither speculated nor cared about her future. She could not blame him. It seemed a harsh, cruel fate indeed that he should lose first his wife and then the son Lady Louisa had borne him. If Nicky were not found alive, he would be left alone in this great house with Imogen – Imogen, his heiress.

Defeated, Annette left the room, then went upstairs to pack her belongings. There would be a small sum to tide her over for a while. If she sold her diamond brooch, that would provide a little more. Somehow she would survive. She must! Wryly she recalled her explanation of a pauper in response to Nicky's question . . . was it only this morning? A lifetime seemed to have intervened.

She stood before the window with clenched fists and looked out over the spring foliage of the trees towards the lake for a long moment, uttering a silent and heartfelt prayer for Nicky.

As the station fly bore Miss Duval away next morning, someone stood looking down upon her ignominious retreat. Imogen, still pale, but with a gleam of triumph in her eyes, held back a pleat of gauzy curtain as she lowered her gaze to the courtyard. So that was the last of Miss Duval . . . after seven years. And today they were dragging the lake. They would surely find Nicky's body, as sodden and lifeless as the little white terrier that had drowned.

Turning from the window, Imogen examined the place where she had pressed the bee upon her arm. Red and inflamed still, but beginning to clear up already. That sting had happened on a sudden impulse. After she had left Nicky, instead of going back to write letters, she had made her way to the once secret corner where Laetitia's swing used to be. She had stayed there for a long time, sprawled on the grass while haphazard thoughts drifted through her mind. Perhaps she had even drifted into sleep for a while. Then she had gone back to the house; as she approached the steps leading to the terrace, she saw the bee hovering over a mass of spring flowers. And the thought had leapt into her mind: if she were stung, that would provide a reason for abandoning Miss Duval in the maze. She could say a bee had come flying towards her and she had run away . . . It took a sort of courage to approach the flowers and close her hand over the bee, then press it upon her arm until she felt its needle-sting. The poison had worked quickly, just as before; and she recalled no more until she regained consciousness lying on her bed.

And now Miss Duval was going away, out of her life for ever, and she herself, Imogen Quade, would be heiress to Selbury again.

When Taiso rode into the clearing at Foxhollow, he saw that everything had been made ready for an immediate departure. The fire was dug over, the horses stood in the wagon shafts; the rest of the tribe only awaited his return before they took to the road.

Mindful of the churchyard rite the bereaved father had attended, Hagar came forward to give him a soft greeting, but when she saw the fair-skinned child in his fierce grasp, she stepped back, one hand at her mouth.

'*Ap i mulende!* What have you done, Taiso?'

'*Ap i mulende* – by the dead – it is well said, sister. I have taken revenge for Ishmael's death. The lord of the great house has paid his debt to me in kind.' He took a firmer hold on Nicholas, who had begun to struggle wildly once more.

The boy was terrified. Even in those games when Jessie chased him across the lawn, there had always been a little lurking spark of terror: the primitive terror of being caught in the hunt. But this was no game. Exhausted, he gave up struggling and began to whimper.

Hagar berated Taiso, her eyes flashing. 'You fool! You *sleever*! *Dordi, dordi*, you will end up in the transported fellows' country for sure. Let the child go! Otherwise we shall all eat the prison loaf for this deed.'

Her outcry brought Fowk and Raia, her husband and children out of the wagons. They stood staring fearfully at Taiso and at the *gorgio* child he clasped so firmly to him.

'Hagar is right,' Fowk told him, frowning. 'Do you not realize, Taiso, that they will be sure to chase after us as soon as they discover the child is missing? It's *sleevers* like you that give our people a bad name. None of our brothers has ever stolen a child before. A horse or two, maybe, to be painted and sold at the next fair. But a child! Never.'

Taiso faced them defiantly. 'You are wrong, Fowk. They will believe he has drowned. The truth is, I saved the life of this *chal* – he was about to step into the lake. They will find his boots on the grass, and the corpse of the little dog I kicked into the water. I do not wish to see this *chal* dead. I am taking my revenge upon the *rye*, his father, that is all. He shall know what it means to lose his only child, his son!'

'But – what will you do with him, brother?' Raia called out fearfully.

Taiso gave his wolfish smile. 'I shall take him on a long journey and sell him for gain.'

Fowk shook his head. 'This is a bad deed, Taiso,' he growled. 'It is against the *leis prala* of our people.' He drew himself to his full height, and in spite of himself, Taiso cringed. Fowk was a real *calo rom*, a great bear of a man.

While the others looked on sorrowfully and Raia hid her head upon her husband's shoulders, Fowk pronounced the words that must be said. 'You are no longer one of our tribe, Taiso. We are for the *drom*, we take the road. You must go where you will. You are no longer our blood brother.'

'*Kooshti*,' Hagar breathed. 'It is well said.'

Defiance blazed up in Taiso. 'So be it! *Yn iach!* Farewell.'

And he wheeled his horse around to ride away from his tribe for ever, with Nicholas still firmly in his grasp.

Chapter Eleven

ANNETTE DUVAL HAD discovered what seemed to her a foreign country. She was in London, but a London she had never known before, even though she had grown up in the metropolis. This other nation, the East End, was as far removed as Timbuktu from the respectable, genteel neighbourhoods of Kensington or Camden Town. She had found a clean, cheap room within a court of mean houses. The sparse furnishings – iron bedstead, plain wash-set, rag rug on the floor, a few pegs on which to hang her clothes – could not have offered a greater contrast to her comfortable quarters at Selbury Quade. The rest of the house was let off to artisans and seamstresses, and the widowed landlady kept a street kitchen, selling baked potatoes through the window to passers-by. Annette reckoned she had sufficient money to pay for her room and feed herself for about three months. In that time she must find employment – or starve.

Her situation caused her considerable distress. She cringed from the vibrant world of dirt, drunkenness and violence that seethed around Belton Court. She was only too aware that of the five thousand victims of the cholera epidemic which had struck London last summer, all but a thousand belonged to the East End. And yet that awful tally of death seemed to have made little difference to the overcrowding and unemployment of those who lived around her.

Somehow, each day, Annette contrived to emerge from that dingy dwelling looking neat and trim. She then took a fourpenny horse omnibus to the West End, where she spent her time searching for work. She knew it was hopeless to approach any of the scholastic agencies. News of events at Selbury had doubtless spread swiftly through that tight little world. As soon as she gave her name or mentioned her post with the Quade family, she would be shown the door.

A mixture of consideration and pride kept her from seeking shelter beneath Aunt Harriet's roof. After all, it was not as though they had been really close. During the past few years, correspondence between aunt and niece had dwindled to Christmas and birthday letters. After considerable thought she had decided there was really no need to distress her aunt by revealing her altered situation. One day, Annette walked quickly past the Kensington house where she had spent her girlhood, its gleaming window panes looking out on the street with such a sure regard. As she passed by the front door, she knew that part of her life was over for good. So was the second part – her career as a governess, as a hanger-on to life in a pleasant country house. Was all her life to be divided into such well-defined segments, she wondered. For the present, she felt herself to have fallen into a disagreeable limbo; she longed to embark upon the next phase, whatever that might be. Another day, taking an omnibus to Camden Town, she alighted near her old school, and saw a group of laughing, carefree girls streaming out of the door and down the steps. Just for a moment she longed for time to go backwards, so that she might make a new beginning.

There were so few opportunities available: she had no talent as a seamstress, and posts as female companion to some old lady in comfortable circumstances, or perhaps an invalid, were usually obtained by personal recommendation. The only feasible possibility open to her appeared to be that of finding work as a shop assistant. Walking through the shopping streets of the West End, gazing at the tantalizing window displays at Peter Robinson's in Oxford Street, Shoolbred's in the Tottenham Court Road or Farmer and Rogers' famous Shawl and Cloak Emporium in Regent Street, Annette thought she might enjoy serving behind a counter, offering customers a choice of attractive merchandise. She recalled how, before her fortunes changed, she used to visit these very shops, taking her time over choosing new gloves, veiling for a hat, perhaps some lace-trimmed handkerchiefs. How skilfully the assistants had displayed these articles; how desirable they had made them seem! And how deftly they had been wrapped, precious objects to carry home.

So far, she had had no luck in approaching the shopwalkers to make her hesitant enquiries. At first, mistaking her for a customer, they would smile ingratiatingly; then, learning her request, curtly direct her to the back premises. She could offer no previous experience, and there were queues of out-of-work assistants, male and female, at the back door of every establishment.

Walking disconsolately along Oxford Street one rainy afternoon after an unsatisfactory interview at Marshall and Snelgrove, uncomfortably aware that the sole of her left boot had worn through, a sign suspended above a tobacconist's caught her eye: *Superior Photographic Studio.* Edwin Moulvey's studio! Her heart, unaccountably, began to beat faster. She passed by the doorway quickly, her eyes downcast. How embarrassing if she should chance to meet Mr Moulvey coming down that steep flight of stairs beside the tobacconist's window with its display of pipes and snuff! What would they say to one another? Surely, like all the rest of the Quade family and household, he must think ill of her. Doubtless he would not deign to acknowledge her. She recalled how he had doted upon Nicky, the son of his beloved sister. Dodging the traffic, she crossed to the other side of the busy street to seek anonymity in the passing throng.

Often it was dark by the time she returned to that other country where she lived now. The narrow streets around Belton Court were ill-lit and badly paved; sometimes, as she hurried through them, she was vividly reminded of the horror of being trapped in the maze at Selbury. Would she ever escape from her present predicament? There were thousands of women, homeless and destitute, desperately seeking work. One of the shop people whom Annette had approached had told her that the city simply could not offer enough employment to go round. In recent years the population had increased enormously, alarmingly. There were more jobs available during the season, when the great town houses were reopened for a few months and staff for restaurants and shops, and the services of seamstresses and hairdressers, were heavily in demand. But as soon as the season ended, that demand dwindled away.

Annette knew that scores of women took the only way out they could, joining the army of prostitutes that crowded the pavements of the West End and the East End alike. Sometimes, as she walked down some fashionable street, a gentleman would catch her eye as he passed by; just once or twice, in spite of her instinctive rejection of such an advance, she half thought how easy it would be to acquiesce . . . and perhaps by such means achieve a protector, some gentleman to lift anxiety from her shoulders. But she barely acknowledged such speculation to herself.

There was another army, newly founded, that marched through the streets of the East End to the strains of martial hymns, brassy cornets and clashing tambourines. As often as not the 'Salvos' took up position opposite some gin palace lit by flaring gaslight. Here they would mount their challenge to the power of the demon drink. Their rousing appeals for repentance and the hoarse-voiced testimonies of sinners who came forward provided a diversion for believers and scoffers alike.

The Salvos were not the only evangelists abroad: Annette's landlady had told her about an energetic young Irishman called Tom Barnardo, who, it seemed, had hoped to go to China as a missionary. Instead, he had studied medicine at the London Hospital, and toiled heroically during the cholera epidemic. He had also set up a ragged Sunday school in an old donkey stable, in the neighbourhood known as World's End. Annette knew there was a number of such ragged schools in the more disreputable parts of the city; she was aware that she might quite easily have found employment in one of them, teaching writing and grammar, besides religious instruction and moral precepts. But she was frankly appalled by the notion of facing a roomful of rough, smelly guttersnipes as her pupils. Doubtless, she thought ruefully, it showed a great fault in her character. She recalled Miss Hester Graham's association with the Ragged Schools Union. Perhaps pious Miss Graham would consider such work suitable atonement for a governess who had betrayed her trust.

It was usually at night, when she was alone in her room, that Annette's thoughts turned to Nicky. During the day she tried to close her mind to unhappy memories. Part of her yearned to know what had happened since she left Selbury, whether they had found Nicky's body when they dragged the lake . . . She would lie awake, recalling Nicky's sunny face, his affectionate nature. Then a vision of Imogen would come into her mind's eye; and on the verge of sleep she would puzzle once more, to no avail, over the events of that last dreadful day.

Finally, in her sixth week in London, Annette found a position. The suggestion came from a rather supercilious shopwalker at Harvey Nichols, the high-class store at Brompton. 'We've nothing here – you might try Whiteley's, at Westbourne Grove,' he said, his tone clearly implying his disdain both for the shop and its neighbourhood.

Annette vaguely recalled hearing of Whiteley's, a new department store which catered for a more lowly clientele, not for the carriage trade. She found that if she took the new underground railway to Bishop's Road station, it was then only a short walk to the shop. How convenient! As soon as she entered its doors, she was aware of a different atmosphere to that of the more superior stores. It seemed busier, more bustling. The shopwalker who approached her spoke pleasantly and asked her to follow him as he led the way to Mr Whiteley's office, which had an overview of the entire establishment.

Whiteley's, it seemed, specialized in drapery. Skirting a display of umbrellas by the door (how useful to find them there some rainy day and make an instant purchase, Annette thought), she walked through aisles of cunningly draped silks and linens, past a selection of ready-made mantles, through the millinery and artificial-flower department, and finally the haberdashery. It was clever to position the haberdashery at the back of the store, she realized. If all you wanted was half a yard of ribbon, you might easily be tempted on your way there by a fur-trimmed mantle or a delicious hat. The aisles between the counters seemed wider than in other shops – and then she saw there were not nearly so many chairs for the customers. Perhaps that speeded up the buying process.

There was no nonsense about Mr Whiteley, a man of early middle age with a penetrating gaze and a Yorkshire accent. He dismissed his shopwalker with a brief 'Thank you, Mr Barker', and waved Annette to an upright chair set before his desk.

'Your name, young woman?'

'Er – Duval.' Annette was more used to the sobriquet 'young lady'.

'Very well, Miss Duval. We have vacancies in Ladies' Outfitting and Artificial Flowers and Feathers. Supposing I was to engage you, I would expect you to work hard and obey the rules I have drawn up for my staff. The first sign of idleness, the first infringement of a rule means instant dismissal. Hard work never hurt anyone – no one knows that better than I do.' Mr Whiteley was obviously launched upon a familiar recital. 'I was apprenticed to a draper when I was a mere lad – I've served my time behind the counter. Yes, indeed. And so has Mrs Whiteley. She was one of my first female assistants, when I opened my shop – just four years ago, that were. I started with only two helpers. And look at us now!'

Quailing slightly in the face of such supreme self-confidence, Annette managed to nod brightly.

'Whiteley's is in the business of making profits, Miss Duval. We are open from eight in the morning to eight at night, Saturdays included. You won't find Whiteley's closing at six or seven, like Swan and Edgar or Marshall and Snelgrove!' He pronounced those names with a scorn to match that of the shopwalker at Harvey Nichols. 'My customers,' he continued proudly, 'are the middle class, who work for their money. Brass, we call it where I come from, Miss Duval. And we persuade them to part with it. How do we do that? By offering top-quality stock, displaying it to best advantage, advertising in the newspapers and on the omnibuses – above all, by giving good service. As one of my assistants, young lady, you will be a vital link between me and my customer.' He sat back in his chair.

Was he definitely offering her a position, then? Annette did her best to look eager and alert.

'We'll put you in Art Flowers and Feathers, Miss Duval. Ladies' Outfitting demands experience. I can tell you don't have that.'

Annette sat up a little straighter. He was certainly blunt, this self-made Yorkshire man.

'I've a feeling you could do well,' Mr Whiteley went on. 'Call it instinct, if you like. Well, you may start tomorrow, eight o'clock sharp. Mr Barker will let you know about wages and lodging arrangements for our female staff. Our boarding houses are close by.'

Annette nodded. She knew that all the large stores required their unmarried male and female staff to reside in hostels. Escape from Belton Court at last!

Finally, Mr Whiteley leaned across the desk and proffered the hollow palm of a successful draper. 'Welcome to Whiteley's, Miss Duval. I trust you will prove a credit to us.'

Somewhat bewildered, Annette stood up uncertainly. Should she offer profuse thanks to her new employer for this opportunity to join his workforce? But Mr Whiteley had become absorbed in some accounts on his desk; it was clear she was dismissed from his mind. She sidled out of the office, to find Mr Barker awaiting her.

'I am to join Art Flowers and Feathers,' Annette told him.

He looked pleased. 'I'm glad the old man took you on.' Privately, John Barker thought the choice of department singularly apt. There was something coolly flowerlike about Miss Duval herself. He went on briskly, 'About your wage and lodgings, Miss Duval. There is a vacancy in our Hatherley Grove hostel . . .'

Chapter Twelve

THE FATEFUL YEAR of Nicholas's disappearance, Sir Oswald Quade put aside his intention to open his London house for that season . . . and the next. He was in no mood for musical soirées, the opera, exhibitions, art galleries, the sympathy of female acquaintances, the commiseration of fellow members of his club. Nor did he wish, just now, to proceed with his other plan, to propose marriage to Hester Graham . . . though, God knew, during these bleak months he felt more comfortless than ever. But Imogen was there to keep him company, and he reverted to his former practice of discussing the affairs of the estate with her. After all, she was once again heiress to Selbury. There was little heart in these discussions, so far as he was concerned – something of which Imogen was well aware. He had lost the son his dear Louisa had brought into the world with so much pain. Her death now seemed quite meaningless. He viewed the emptiness of his life – save for Imogen's presence, of course – with acute dismay. For the first time he ardently wished he were a religious man . . . like the great and good Lord Shaftesbury, for example, who never doubted the power and wisdom of an all-seeing deity, and a time to come when every soul on earth would receive salvation.

But Sir Oswald was too much an enquirer after the new scientific discoveries to be able to accept the consolation of any established religion. He was in fact a disbeliever. He did not completely eschew all possibility of the existence of some divine force, but he felt that if such existed, it was unknowable to mankind. He found himself in agreement with Thomas Huxley, the biologist, who had written recently that the contemporary confrontation between science and religion had resulted in 'the slaying of a beautiful hypothesis by an ugly fact'. Professor Huxley had coined a new word to ameliorate the ugliness of his theory of biogenesis, that all living matter has its sole origin in earlier living matter. That new word was 'agnostic', which he derived from St Paul's altar 'to the Unknown God'. It was a word to refute atheism, offering a compromise which Sir Oswald found apt to himself.

Nicky's body had not been found when the lake was dragged; it was generally assumed that, being so small and light, it must have drifted riverwards and been carried on the current out to sea. Jem Vinnicott, however, had voiced his suspicion that the gypsies might have taken off with the young master, and there were others below stairs who thought this a likely notion. Were not those heathens notorious for stealing children? And was it not strange the boy should have vanished the selfsame day the Romanies left Foxhollow? Sir Oswald himself did not seriously consider this a possibility – he was well aware of his gamekeeper's prejudice against the gypsies. Nevertheless, willing to grasp at any chance, he had agreed that Vinnicott should saddle a horse and ride after them. He had awaited the outcome with a faint spark of hope.

But Jem Vinnicott did not bring back to Selbury its youthful heir. He reported that he had caught up with the gypsies about forty miles to the north, not far from Bristol. He had spoken to one of the women, a tall, proud creature with glittering eyes. She vehemently denied all knowledge of Sir Oswald Quade's son, and when Jem insisted on searching the camp, she stood aside, mutely resentful, as he looked through the wagons, even beneath the high beds covered with embroidered linen, pride of the gypsy women.

Hagar had recognized Sir Oswald's gamekeeper as soon as he rode up. She had half expected such pursuit and was prepared for his suspicious questions. Though she had whole-heartedly concurred with Fowk's outlawing of Taiso from the tribe, nothing would have induced her to betray one of their own kind to the *gorgios*.

'Ye've wanted riddance of us for many a day, Master Vinnicot,' she told the gamekeeper. 'Well, ye'll never see another Romany in Foxhollow wood so long as ye live. We'll not return to the cursed place that took the life of our *chal* – and ye can tell that to your fine gentleman as he sits grieving over his own lost boy.'

And that was all the news Jem Vinnicott brought back to Selbury. Whereupon Sir Oswald's hope finally expired.

Each member of the household staff grieved over the loss of the young master. Recalling his endearing ways, Mrs Arkney would sniff resolutely and reach for a handkerchief, while Mrs Robbins went about in a state of unrelieved gloom. As for Jessie, she would surely have felt her world had come to an end, where it not for the fact that she was being courted by a village lad. It would not be long before she married and then had a child of her own. But in the years ahead, she was often to fall silent, gazing into space until her husband asked her what she was thinking of. 'I was remembering little Nicky,' she would answer with a sigh. As for Nanny Hodges, she departed to serve another family. Of all the staff, she was the most outspoken against Miss Duval.

'Such a wicked neglect of her duty!' she was heard to fume time and time again.

'Well, she were sent packing with no references, weren't she?' Jessie would remark. She could not help recalling how kind the young governess had been towards her in the past.

'It seemed – out of character,' Mrs Arkney ventured stiffly.

Lily the parlourmaid shrugged. 'I wonder whatever will

become of her. She took the train to London town.'

At this they all fell silent, imagining the worst. For who could hope to survive in this wicked world without a reference, dismissed in such disgrace?

Hester Graham came to Selbury to offer comfort, consolation and what practical assistance she could. As the carriage bore her along the winding drive and reached the place where the lovely house stood revealed, she shivered suddenly, in spite of the warm day. So much tragedy had visited Selbury in recent years. Miss Graham was appalled by the news of her godson's disappearance. His death, as seemed most likely. It seemed blame must be laid upon the governess, that she had shamefully neglected her duty. Imagine allowing Nicky to wander off to the lake by himself! And yet Miss Duval had always seemed so conscientious. Certainly she had managed well with Imogen, not the easiest of pupils. On the other hand, she had sometimes seemed rather youthful for her position. Miss Graham recalled how she had once observed her cast a lingering glance on Edwin Moulvey, during one of his visits to Selbury. Perhaps the foolish young woman had harboured some romantic notion.

It was almost as though a curse had descended upon Selbury ... but instantly Hester Graham chided herself for that superstitious thought. Her face grew graver still as her thoughts turned to the lonely widower. In recent months, she had sensed that he had seemed about to suggest a closer relationship between them. She had carefully contemplated the notion of marriage to Oswald Quade. It seemed to offer advantages to both of them, above all a warm companionship based on mutual respect and liking, and a shared background.

Once, a long time ago it seemed now, Hester Graham had fallen in love . . . with Henry Martin, who had died so far away from England. There was a vast difference between liking and loving. But perhaps love was merely an illusion, sometimes delightful, sometimes exquisitely painful, that belonged to youth. Perhaps liking was the more enduring emotion, after all. In all successful marriages, did not love become transmuted into liking? And in unhappy marriages, where that did not happen, that same love seemed to curdle and turn sour. Although she was in her early thirties, Hester Graham thought of herself as middle-aged. When Henry died, she felt as though youth had slipped from her the way a mantle might fall from one's shoulders.

There was something else. She and Henry had shared a deeply religious belief, verging towards evangelism. That secure belief had helped her to accept Henry's death. She was aware that Oswald Quade possessed no true religious belief. Could she marry a man without faith? Was that a true Christian marriage? Perhaps she should look upon the possibility of her union with Oswald as a challenge, the chance to persuade him towards real Christianity. Such thoughts had often occupied her mind recently. She felt that when the time came, she would probably accept Oswald's proposal, but she knew that for the present, all notion of marriage must recede. This new tragedy overshadowed their lives completely. In Selbury's great hall she found Imogen waiting to greet her. Strangely composed, she stood at the bottom of the staircase, one hand resting on a newel post carved with a garland of acorns and oak leaves. She looked pale. That was scarcely surprising, Hester thought: besides the shock of Nicky's tragedy, she had suffered another bee sting. Then something seemed to compel Hester Graham to glance upward, until her gaze rested on Dame Margery's portrait. She had always been vaguely aware of some resemblance between Dame Margery and her descendant; now Imogen's extraordinary similarity to the woman in the portrait struck her so forcibly that she gave a sharp intake of breath. Imogen had matured a great deal of late; she was a young woman now, Hester realized. It might have been a young Dame Margery herself who came forward to take her hands in a cool, light clasp rather than Imogen . . . who must now be presumed heiress to the house Dame Margery had built.

Many days of journeying had followed when Taiso rode off

with Nicholas, and during this time the boy had learned to depend on his captor for food and shelter, much as a dog depends on its master. Sometimes that shelter was the hedgerow, sometimes the corner of a barn, and their food was scarce enough — potatoes and turnips stolen from the fields along their way, perhaps some scraps begged from an inn kitchen, a rabbit caught with Taiso's gypsy cunning, or a feast of trout tickled from a stream.

Once Nicholas's mother had laughingly confessed a fantastic desire to run off 'with the raggle-taggle gypsies O', never dreaming that in days to come her son would be abducted and fulfil her frivolous wish. The boy was bewildered and sometimes fascinated by everything that happened day by day — he would never forget, for instance, with what gentle movements Taiso coaxed the trout from the water. His vain resistance and fear of his captor were now replaced by a dull obedience. Taiso did not treat him cruelly; he behaved much as he would have done towards young Ishmael, in fact, cuffing him occasionally for some minor misdeed, addressing him rarely with few words. But unlike Ishmael, who had grown up accustomed to the roving, open-air life of his people, Nicholas was tired out by their daily journeying for much of the time. They covered many miles tramping beside the old horse to give it a necessary respite from carrying them. It was a very different pattern to the nursery regime the child was used to.

Taiso kept to unfrequented lanes as much as possible, travelling quickly, usually at sunrise or dusk, through the cobbled streets of the villages and market towns that lay along their way. Always they headed eastward, towards the great metropolis that was the gypsy's destination. As the days passed by, a kaleidoscope of new sights and sounds superimposed themselves upon Nicholas's recollection of his former life. Selbury and its inhabitants began to fade like an ancient tapestry; each hour that passed bleached a little more colour from his memory. All those people he had known during the five years of his brief life began to seem like the characters of some dream world. Nor did the boy resemble the gently nurtured child he had been such a short while ago. Taiso had filched some rough, scratchy garments from a farmhouse washing line and burned the crumpled sailor suit on their campfire one night. Sun and wind and showers of rain soon gave the child's white skin a tanned appearance; his hair was wild and matted as any gypsy boy's.

As they neared their journey's end, they passed through more towns and villages. Inns, churches, houses, cottages and shops crowded upon each other and the stretches of open countryside grew rare. Finally they joined the stream of traffic on a great highway: horsemen, carts, coaches and carriages filled the wide road and streets on every side were thronged with people on foot. They reached a high place that over-looked the great city: the Vale of Hampstead, with its broad heath. Once descended to the city with its crowded streets and busy bridges, tall buildings, pall of smoke and ceaseless clamour, they would lose their perception of it as an entity. But now, ascending the heath, with the tired mare trailing beside them, Taiso stopped with one hand on Nicholas's shoulder and flung out his right arm in a wide gesture.

'The *Boro Foros*!' he proclaimed. 'Behold, the great city of London!'

And now the mare must be disposed of before she dropped in her tracks. There was a gypsy encampment on the heath, where Taiso swiftly concluded a deal. Then on they tramped, making for that part of London known as 'the Potteries', not far from Notting Hill. Dusk fell as they neared this Romany ghetto. Nicky, stumbling with exhaustion, had a confused impression of flaring torchlights, voices speaking in a strange language, raucous laughter, barking dogs, the cackle of poultry – and, rising above the din, the reedy strains of a gypsy violin and the clash of a *cluicoshtourenomengi*, a tambourine. A mishmash of smells assailed him: cooking-pot stews, the stink of open drains, unwashed bodies and the odour of pigs that rooted amongst the waste heaps.

Suddenly: '*Taiso!*' It was a shrill, female cry.

Taiso spun round, alarmed and wary, pulling Nicholas close

to his side. A gypsy girl came running towards them, gold earrings swinging, a necklace of shining coins about her throat. For one wild moment Taiso imagined it was Lurina, in the days before her slender body was racked by coughing. But that was a cruel delusion.

'Salome,' he muttered, recognizing Ithal's brazen niece. He had not seen her since Ithal broke away from the tribe. Taiso had always been half repulsed by Salome, who had never concealed her passion for him. She was young and graceful, with moist black curls and a voice that could draw tears from your eyes when she sang the old songs of their people. But Taiso remembered Hagar's tale of the love cake she had baked, and was repelled anew to think he had unwittingly swallowed her woman's blood. Nevertheless he let her lead him by the hand, with Nicholas close beside, to the place where Ithal's wagon stood beside a campfire.

Ithal rose to his feet in the firelight as they approached. He greeted Taiso cautiously. 'We are here for a few days only,' he told him. 'I have been selling horses near Epping.' He paused, then said, 'We had news of Lurina's death, may her soul rest with God.'

Salome peered at the child cowering beside Taiso. 'This must be Ishmael,' she said. 'Come to me, *chal*.' She pulled the boy towards her, then recoiled as he stood revealed in the firelight, clearly no *Romanchal* in spite of his altered appearance. '*Akai!*' she gasped. 'Who is this?'

Ithal looked closely at Nicholas. 'The girl is right. This one has no Romany blood. He is not even a Diddikai.'

'I was asked to bring him here, to the *Boro Foros*,' Taiso told them, the words coming easily from his tongue. 'His parents are labourers, down on their luck and unable to keep him. They asked me to sell him here.' There would be time enough to tell of Ishmael's death.

His lame explanation did not deceive Ithal, who frowned. 'Many masters come to this place to find children to work for them, it is true. You will be able to carry out your business tomorrow. If you like you may spend the night with us. Then

141

you must leave. We want no trouble on account of a *gorgio chal*.'

Taiso nodded and joined the circle of kinsfolk around the fire, sitting on his heels and stretching out his hands to the warmth. Salome's touch on his arm, the way she folded his hand in hers, felt strangely comforting. More than that: for the first time since Lurina's death, he felt stirred as a man.

Salome whispered shamelessly in his ear, increasing his newly awakened desire, 'You are more attractive to me now, Taiso, than when you were a *shav*, a bold unmarried youth.' Then she turned her head towards Nicholas, who lay curled up like a hedgehog. 'Look,' she said softly, 'the little *raklo* has fallen fast asleep.'

Daylight revealed the whole squalor of the Potteries as Taiso walked with Nicholas over the beaten earth and greasy cobbles to parley with a middle-aged man wearing a stovepipe hat and black suit of clothes. Ithal had pointed him out among the throng of people.

'He will buy the *gorgio chal*,' he told Taiso. 'Do what you have to, then go.'

The man watched with narrowed eyes as Taiso and Nicholas approached him. Samuel Oliphant, master sweep, had come here to seek a new climbing-boy, the smaller the better. He had built up a good business within this great metropolis of smoking chimneys; his customers dwelled in some of London's grandest streets and squares, a world apart from this reeking area of Notting Hill.

It took Taiso no longer to dispose of Nicholas to Sam Oliphant than it had to sell the old brown mare, though the price he received for the boy was considerably higher. If he had haggled longer he suspected he could have got more, but he wanted to get the transaction over as quickly as possible. Six gold sovereigns passed from master sweep to gypsy. The sweep had a bargain: children as small as this one could fetch as much as eight guineas quite easily. Where the gypsy had obtained the child was none of Samuel Oliphant's concern.

As Taiso pocketed the coins, Salome stole up behind him. Her eyes glittered when she spied the money; it would be more than enough to buy the pony on which she and Taiso planned to ride away together. She held a cloth bundle containing her few belongings. A bargain of a different sort had been struck between Taiso and herself last night as he lay between her thighs and she cried out with the triumph of a desire satisfied at last.

Taiso hesitated a moment as Nicholas stood staring up at him. The child did not understand why this black-suited stranger had taken his hand as if – as if he belonged to him. There was a sort of desperation in the child's gaze. But those grey eyes had no power to move Taiso. He recalled Ishmael's dark eyes with their spark of mischief, and his heart hardened.

'This gentleman is the one who will look after you now,' he told the boy. 'I am leaving you.'

Then he was gone, Salome by his side. They were simply swallowed up in the press of people. The familiarity bred during those days of journeying together vanished in an instant. Nicholas, left alone with another stranger, was about to enter into a new bondage.

Mr Oliphant's high-class establishment was situated in a humble terrace bordering those fashionable streets and squares where his wealthy customers resided. Above his door, projecting over the pavement, was an old-style sign put up in his father's day. It showed a master and his boy on their way to a brick house whose chimneys spouted yellow flames. The paint was faded now; but Sam Oliphant kept the sign out of sentiment for the father who had taught him his trade.

Mrs Oliphant, a large lady (to the little sweeps employed by her husband, she was, inevitably, known as 'the Elephant'), was excessively house-proud. It seemed an ironic fate that she should be married to a master sweep. However assiduously she cleaned her house, the metallic smell of soot seeped into every room and little drifts of coal dust, disturbed by her duster, would settle down again on her polished furniture as soon as her back was turned. All the soot shed by the chimneys that were cleaned each day was brought home in sacks and stored in an outhouse in the back yard, eventually to be carted to the waste heaps.

The apprentices themselves were forbidden to enter Mrs Oliphant's rooms. Their quarters were in the cellar, where they slept on grimy straw mattresses; and they ate their food in the back kitchen, around a table ingrained with soot. They were able to wash themselves once a month; in the meantime, all they could do was brush themselves down after work each day. Their hair stood up in sooty spikes and their clothes were beetle-black. Their eyes were red from dust and dirt and their teeth gleamed white as a blackamoor's in their dusky faces.

The new climbing-boy Sam Oliphant brought home this day would replace one of his other apprentices. In spite of the meagre diet provided by the Elephant, thirteen-year-old Jem had grown too large for his work. He was off to join an East Indiaman and become a sailor. The other boy, known as Manny ('Emmanuel' being the name bestowed upon him by the superintendent of the workhouse whence he had come), was ten, and pleasingly small for his age. And then there was Polly, Sam Oliphant's climbing-girl, an eight-year-old scrap of humanity. She could climb the narrowest flues of all; her sticklike arms, amazingly, were strong enough to wield the brush and scraper as well as any boy's. She had been apprenticed to the master sweep by her father, who had then headed off for the nearest den to drown his sorrow and his conscience. Sam Oliphant was proud of his Poll; climbing-girls were rare in the trade. He was often heard to boast that she was the equal of those climbing-girls who swept the narrow chimbleys of Windsor Castle itself.

If Nicholas had been transported on a magic carpet to the dark heart of Africa, he could not have felt more estranged from everything that had gone on before in his brief life. Arrived at his new dwelling place, he gazed in wonder at the faded sign above the door; he was taken round to the back premises, where a large, formidable lady admonished him against ever setting foot beyond the back kitchen; then he was set down at a dirty table and a hunk of bread and dripping was put before him. On account of Mr Oliphant's errand to the Potteries, Jem, Manny and Polly were today distributing their master's trade cards around the neighbourhood. Nicky had yet to make their acquaintance.

Mrs Oliphant surveyed the new climbing-boy unsmilingly. No little Oliphants had appeared to bless her marriage and she felt no vestige of maternal sentiment towards the children who lived on the periphery of her house. She did her duty and fed them daily on mean portions of porridge, small beer, watery stews and slabs of bread and dripping, and that was all.

'Wot's yore name, boy?' she asked the new arrival, unmoved by the pathetic bewilderment in his infant gaze.

''is name's Nicholas, if you please,' her husband told her. 'I bought 'im from a gyppo – no questions asked.' He gave a slow wink. 'We'll call 'im Nick fer short – young Nick. It won't be long afore 'e's black as Old Nick 'isself!' And he guffawed at his own joke.

And so, when the other three returned towards the end of the day, they met 'young Nick', their new companion. At first sight, Nicky thought that they must indeed be three young blackamoors. He found it difficult to make out their speech; it sounded as foreign to him as the gypsies' Romany. He was able to understand Polly better than the two boys.

He was given an armful of clean straw for his mattress that night, and Polly helped him to spread sacking over it, and saw that he was covered by a filthy blanket. A single candle lit the cellar, and when it was blown out, Jem and Manny, as usual, fell asleep as soon as they laid down their spiky heads. But in the gloom Nicky saw Polly kneel down beside her mattress to say a prayer before she crept beneath her own blanket. And then, as she did every night, she lay awake conjuring up memories of happier days before her eyelids drooped in sleep. Tonight, her memories were disturbed by muffled sobs from the mattress alongside her own. There was a world of sympathy and compassion in Polly's nature, and her heart went out to the little boy who lay there.

'Don't cry, little Nick, 'taint so bad as all that,' she whispered. 'We've a roof over our 'eads and food inside of us, and there's plenty young as you wot's down in the gutters an' freezin' to death.' She wondered where their new chum had come from. The few words that had passed his lips had sounded different to their own way of talking. 'Quite the little gentleman!' Jem had observed with good-humoured scorn.

As Nicky's sobs gradually subsided, she leaned over to pat his shoulder with a grimy hand. 'I'll see yo're all right, you c'n trust Polly,' she reassured him.

And that was the beginning of a true friendship, the memory of which Nicholas Quade was to treasure all his life.

Chapter Thirteen

Y THE EARLY summer of 1870, Annette Duval's first
feeling of euphoria at having found employment as one
of Mr Whiteley's assistants had long since evaporated.

'Mr W's bloomin' slaves, more like!' snorted Annie
Meagher, who served in ladies' undergarments and shared
Annette's room at Hatherley Gardens. With her pithy
comments and pert prettiness, she reminded Annette of the
parlourmaids at Selbury – Maggie or Violet, or maybe Lily.

This evening, the two of them had just returned to the hostel
after their long day at the shop. All the way up the four flights
of stairs that led to their room, Annie fumed over a sixpenny
fine she had received for breaking one of Mr Whiteley's long
list of rules. Framed in black, these rules – all 176 of them –
were hung in every room. Last Saturday, Annie had returned
later than the curfew hour of ten o'clock, and the grim-faced
matron of the hostel had to open the front door to her. Today,
her name was among those of other offenders recorded on the
notice board in the hallway.

'Still and all, it was worth it,' Annie declared with a cheeky
grin. 'I didn't half enjoy the music hall! An' Fred promised he'll

take me there again.'

Fred served in gentlemen's outfitting – situated, naturally, as far as possible from ladies' undergarments. He and Annie had met at closing time one day at the staff exit. It had been pouring cats and dogs, and Fred had gallently sheltered her all the way to Hatherley Gardens under his umbrella. He lived in the male hostel, several streets away.

'Bloomin' slaves!' Annie repeated now, easing her boots and wriggling her toes with relief. 'Oh, my pore feet! I'm sure I'll end up with bunions, like your Miss Burr.'

Annette collapsed full-length on her narrow iron bedstead, not caring if she did rest her boots on it. (That was another rule, with a penny fine attached to it.)

'Her bunions are probably what make her so prickly all the time,' Annette sighed. 'She's certainly a thorn in my side.'

'All the same, I think you 'ave a better time of it among all them flowers and feathers than me in unmentionables. I mean, just imagine what it's like selling corsets and camisoles all day long.' With a sudden spurt of liveliness Annie squeezed around to the far side of her bed, and began a droll imitation of serving a very large young lady with a pair of the new bloomer outfits. The craze for Mrs Amelia Bloomer's 'rational dress for ladies' had just reached England from the United States, and Mr Whiteley had reluctantly agreed to stock the garments, torn between his own distaste for them and the desire to cash in. They consisted of a short skirt worn over long, loose knicker-bockers gathered around the ankles. Any day this year you could see progressive young ladies sporting these daring outfits as they rode their bicycles over Clapham Common, along the Ride at Streatham, or even in Hyde Park.

'I'm afraid we just don't have your size, miss,' Annie said in the refined tone of voice she used in the shop. 'The manu-facturer don't make them as large as that, you see. – Oh no, miss, I certainly don't mean to imply that you are too large, not at all! It's simply that all our bloomers are too bloomin' small!'

Annette chuckled and threw her pillow at Annie.

''Ere! If you don't mind, these pillers are 'ard as bricks,' cried Annie, lapsing into her native Cockney.

'If it's any consolation, you're not the only one making a loss this week,' Annette told her ruefully. 'I'm to have a good whack of my princely pay docked. Madam Burr is making me fork out for a bunch of French cherries – those lusciouslooking Napoleons you feel you could pop into your mouth. Only they're intended to trim straw boaters instead.'

'What 'appened?' Annie discarded her aitches along with her boots as soon as she got home.

'Well, along came Mamma and small child. Mamma tries this flower and that flower on her new hat, so enraptured with her own reflection in the glass and so busy asking my opinion of roses *versus* camellias that neither of us notices what said child is getting up to. In fact, the little demon was quietly demolishing a whole bunch of cherries. You should've heard the shrieks and squawks when he found they were filled with cotton wool.'

'I believe I did,' Annie told her. 'There was a noise like a cockatoo from your corner at one point.'

Annette nodded. 'That would be angel-child. Anyway, up storms Madam Burr, and the long and short of it is that I'm to blame and I pay for the damage. Mamma was so mortified that she vanished with her offspring without buying so much as a rosebud.'

'Oh, lor',' Annie laughed. 'What lives we lead!'

Each evening, over cocoa and stale biscuits from unsold stock in Groceries, served in the communal sitting room, the hostel girls – they were all 'girls' or 'young ladies', even though several of them were clearly middle-aged – gossiped and tittletattled and aired petty grievances and jealousies.

'Do you know what I heard today?' demanded one saucereyed young woman from Haberdashery that evening. 'Mr Barker's just had his salary *doubled*! There's a rumour he gets three hundred pounds a year already!'

An older young lady who worked in Accounts remarked judiciously, 'There's good reason for that, seeing as how Mr B's helped to more than double our turnover this year with his new ideas.'

Her remark caught Annette's attention. Mr John Barker, it seemed, was both ambitious and successful. Since the day she first set foot in Whiteley's, she had spoken to him only occasionally. Last Christmas, he had sat next to her at the festive meal provided for the entire staff. Their conversation had extended a little beyond the commonplace pleasantries and banter that dominated the long tables. Annette had listened with real interest as he described some of the new department stores in America. In Philadelphia, he told her, one shop had actually installed an elevator to take their customers from one floor to another.

'Some of the establishments there,' he went on enthusiastically, 'like Marshall Field's in Chicago, or Lord and Taylor's and Macy's in New York, are more like palaces! And all planned around the customer, to induce him – but mainly *her* – to behold, desire and spend.'

'On what she wants rather than what she needs,' Annette said crisply.

'Quite so, Miss Duval,' he responded cheerfully. 'They supply needs too, of course – but their profits mainly accrue from *wants*.'

'And from their customers' desire to outshine their friends and neighbours with worldly possessions,' Annette added.

'Do I detect a note of cynicism, Miss Duval? In my opinion the department store should provide the customer with a sense of wellbeing even if she enters it to purchase no more than a packet of hairpins. To shop should be a thoroughly enjoyable experience.'

Pushing aside a helping of Christmas pudding, Annette had observed, 'I have a feeling, Mr Barker, that some day you may well build a palace of your own.'

He had not denied such an ambition. 'I should always be glad to find a place for you in it, Miss Duval. Please remember that,' he replied gallantly.

In spite of the mean pay and the trivial rules of Whiteley's, Annette had found it easy to submerge herself in the communal life of store and hostel. It provided a breathing space in which she could convalesce from her experience at Selbury and recover self-confidence. She had hoped to embark straight away upon a new phase of her life; instead, the limbo she had fallen into had been prolonged. But now she knew that quite soon she must somehow achieve a more desirable way of life. Her ambition might not be so high as Mr Barker's, but there were certain aspirations rekindling in her breast.

About a month after the incident of the cherries, Miss Duval was arranging ostrich feathers in an artistic display when she heard a voice say, 'How delightful to see you again! Especially framed by pink and green ostriches and all these flowers.'

Looking up, she saw Edwin Moulvey standing before her at the glass-topped counter.

He had the advantage, of course. Desperately she attempted to calm her confusion. Out of the corner of her eye she saw Miss Burr cast a suspicious look in her direction from the other end of the counter.

'Why – Mr Moulvey! What – what a surprise to see you here,' she stammered.

It had been an equal surprise to Edwin Moulvey when, a week ago, he had recognized Imogen's former governess behind the counter as he passed through the shop. That brief glimpse had lingered in his mind. The notion of renewing her acquaintance seemed extraordinarily agreeable.

'May I help you choose something, sir?' Annette asked in a louder voice. 'We are not supposed to hold private conversations,' she added in a whisper.

'Certainly, Miss,' Edwin replied promptly. 'I am in search of props for my studio – a bride's bouquet, carnations for gentlemen's buttonholes, and – a single rose.'

'I shall see what I can pick for you, sir,' Annette murmured demurely. 'But – surely the brides you photograph bring their own bouquets?'

Edwin smiled. 'They often come to have their portrait taken after a three-month honeymoon. By that time the real bouquet has long since withered, or else been preserved beneath a glass dome by a proud mamma . . . and quite often the bride finds her wedding gown a tight squeeze around the waist,' he added indelicately.

'Oh.' Miss Annette Duval actually blushed, Edwin was enchanted to observe. Most of the ladies whose companionship he enjoyed had forgotten how to blush — if they ever knew.

Annette moved about collecting lilies, a spray of stephanotis, some freesias, two or three white roses. In Art Flowers and Feathers spring, summer, autumn and winter flora bloomed all together. Shaggy heads of chrysanthemums clustered beside boughs of stiff cherry blossom; little posies of daisies and forget-me-nots were cheek by jowl with full-blown peonies.

'I am afraid our stock of roses is very low at present,' Annette said apologetically.

'Greenfly? Or black spot?'

She smiled, recalling how she used to enjoy his teasing conversation at Selbury. Then she shook her head. 'The war in France. Our best roses come from Paris.'

She saw a sombre look replace Mr Moulvey's mischievous expression and remembered how he loved France and had so often visited Paris. Now, following France's defeat at Sedan, that city was under siege from the Prussian army. She was vague enough about the reasons for the war . . . something to do with the Spanish throne, which used to be occupied by the Bourbons, being offered to a Prussian prince, to Napoleon III's consternation. It was dreadful to think of Paris threatened by Prussian guns. Why, it was even said the citizens were reduced to eating rats and mice.

'I believe Paris must fall eventually,' Edwin said gloomily. 'And that will be the end of Napoleon's "Parliamentary Empire". Ah well, it was all very gay and enjoyable while it lasted. Things will become earnest and dull after the new revolution, I dare say.'

The flowers lay untended on the counter while Annette listened to the pleasing tone of his well-remembered voice. Then, intercepting a frown from the vigilant Miss Burr, she hastily began to assemble the bouquet.

'I think – some white ribbon from Haberdashery,' she suggested, beckoning to an assistant in the next-door department.

'Magnificent!' Edwin declared when the creation, flowing with satin ribbons, was completed and placed in a box alongside half a dozen carnation boutonnieres. 'Please have it delivered to my studio.'

The memory of a sign in Oxford Street – *Superior Photographic Studio* – entered Annette's mind. How she had dreaded a casual encounter with Mr Moulvey that rainy day!

'I have a new address,' he told her now. 'In Bayswater, not far from here. The Bond Street of the west, they are calling this part of town, with all its new shops – and I swear there's just as much money to be made here.'

Annette recorded the address, then Edwin said, 'We have forgotten the rose.'

'We do have one lovely deep red rose left from our French stock.' She produced it, laying it tenderly on a square of tissue-paper.

'Excellent,' Edwin declared. 'I shall take that with me. And now I have one more request. Will you join me for dinner this evening, Annette? So that we may talk without being frowned upon?' He glanced towards the other end of the counter.

The invitation was as startling as his use of her first name. In the circumstances, with Miss Burr advancing purposefully towards her, there was no space to hesitate over her reply. 'I – I should like that. But I don't get back to the hostel where I live until half-past eight or nine, and there is a ten o'clock curfew –'

His eyebrows rose. 'Quite a Cinderella. Let us meet on Sunday instead. Luncheon. What do you say?'

Annette nodded smilingly and they arranged to meet at the corner of Hatherley Grove.

As Edwin sauntered off, Miss Burr looked after him with vague disapproval. It was really most unusual for a gentleman to patronize Art Flowers and Feathers.

Annette took exceptional care with her toilette on Sunday. She wore a golden-brown silk dress and jacket which had been marked down last season in Ladies' Outfitting and a velvet bonnet trimmed with osprey feathers slightly damaged in consignment. Edwin's appreciation showed in his eyes as he invited her to take his arm, then hailed a cab which bore them to a small French restaurant not far from Hyde Park, where he was clearly a respected and valued patron. How agreeable it was to sit in luxurious surroundings with an attentive companion and be served with delicious food and wine. It all seemed to emphasize the drabness of her everyday life, Annette thought. Over luncheon they talked of everything except Selbury and the Quade family. Edwin's photographic career, it appeared, was more successful now, and he listened with flattering interest as she related anecdotes of life at the shop, laughing outright at the sad story of the cherries.

Afterwards, they strolled in the park and came to rest in a pair of green iron chairs set beneath a sweet-scented lime tree. In some distant corner a military band was playing.

'How splendid martial music sounds muffled by distance,' Edwin remarked. 'It should never be heard close at hand. It should always have that faint, nostalgic air, reminding one of armies in the past and battles long ago.'

Annette guessed that his thoughts had returned to wartime France. 'When were you last in Paris?' she asked.

'Just twelve months ago. No hint of trouble then. I strolled in the sun, visited an exhibition of *les Impressionistes* – Cézanne, Monet, Renoir, Pissarro: I must tell you about their work some day – and heard some of the latest music. Everything worthwhile in the artistic world today is going on in Paris!' He stretched out his legs, elegantly trousered in light grey.

'My family was French originally,' Annette told him. 'But I have never been to France.'

Edwin glanced at her and nodded. 'Perhaps that is partly why I admire you – there is some hint of your French forebears, I think.' Then, quite abruptly, his tone changed and at last he began to speak of those things that lay in both their memories.

'I – I've not been back to Selbury, you know, since . . . Nicky's disappearance. I met Hester Graham by chance one day, here in London, just a few months afterwards. She told me you had been – dismissed.'

Annette looked away as he continued gently, 'She spoke of you in harsh terms, I'm afraid . . . I found it difficult to believe that you of all people could really have been as – as irresponsible as she claimed. I always thought of you, you know, as perhaps the most conscientious and proper young lady I had ever met. Miss Duval, the model governess!'

Annette's head was bowed. The feathers in her velvet bonnet curled about her downcast cheek. Then she looked up at him with an old bewilderment in her eyes. 'I still cannot exactly comprehend what happened. As events fell out . . . so far as appearances went . . . I – I suppose they were quite right to – to make me the scapegoat.' She gave a puzzled frown. 'But surely you must have been back to Selbury?'

Edwin shook his head ruefully. 'I too am *persona non grata* at Selbury Quade. My brother-in-law has made that quite clear. I seriously annoyed him because I visited the gypsy camp at Foxhollow against his wishes. Then, after I had returned to London, I heard about the gypsy boy's death . . . a horrible, beastly way to die.' He shook his head as if to clear it of an ugly image. 'Oswald wrote to me about it. He virtually blamed me for the child's death – said I had frightened the boy with my camera. He ran off, you see, into the woods, and then the man trap . . .' Suddenly he took her hand – it seemed the most natural action imaginable.

Annette looked at him sombrely; their glances met in a shared memory, a mutual anguish. And now she recalled something Imogen had said about how upset her father had been, and that Edwin might never be invited to Selbury again.

'I swear I meant no harm,' Edwin muttered. Annette sensed that these were words he often repeated to himself. It was the same with her: whenever she thought of Nicholas, a familiar refrain came into her mind: *Surely it wasn't my fault.*

'It seems we have each been blamed for the death of a child,' she said sadly.

'The gypsy boy died – no doubt of that, I fear. But Nicky's body has never been found. Hester told me . . .'

And so at last Annette learned what had happened after she left Selbury. Edwin told her of the futile dragging of the lake, the useless chase after the gypsies, Sir Oswald's morose grief . . .

There was a little pause after he had done. Then Annette asked quietly, 'And Imogen? What of her?'

Edwin frowned. 'Imogen is heiress to Selbury once more. A position she is not averse to, I think. It is strange, the intensity of her feeling for that place.'

'She is obsessed by Selbury,' Annette said straightly.

'She was always an unusual child. I admired you more than I can say for coping with her moods. Louie's daughter, my own niece – and yet she always seemed remote from us. I sense she has a dark side to her nature. But I am a stranger to Selbury now,' he ended sadly. 'And to Imogen. It is all in the past so far as I am concerned. I think of Louie so often still. I shall always miss her.'

'We all missed Lady Louisa when – it was so tragic.' Then, still grasping Edwin's hand with its warm comfort, Annette related her account of that last day at Selbury, so clearly and indelibly etched in her memory. At last she unburdened herself of those doubts concerning the sequence of events, the time lapse in Imogen's own tale of what had befallen her.

'I don't suppose anyone will ever know the truth of the matter,' she said finally.

Edwin heard her out and then said gently, 'It is best not to dwell on these things, I think.'

By the time they returned to Hatherley Grove that evening, Annette had told Edwin everything about her subsequent life in London after she left Selbury; she even told him how she had crossed the road in case he should emerge from his studio in Oxford Street.

'I thought you might wish to avoid me,' she said. 'You – you cannot imagine what a relief it is to feel that you do not shun me, as everyone else did at Selbury.'

'I can only assure you that when I saw you again so unexpectedly, I felt a great desire to renew our friendship,' Edwin told her.

'We were not exactly friends before,' Annette reminded him. 'Acquaintances would be more accurate, perhaps.' She glanced at him with a half-smile.

'We shall be friends now ... at the very least,' Edwin declared.

As they parted, he suddenly remembered something and rather sheepishly brought a crumpled tissue-paper package out of his coat pocket. 'A sentimental gesture,' he said. 'Usually I send sheaves of roses as tokens of admiration, but I don't think that would be quite the thing, somehow, for Mr Whiteley's hostel. This substitute looks rather the worse for wear, I fear.'

It was the French rose he had bought from her. She received the poor crumpled offering with as much delight as if it had been dewy fresh.

He clasped her hand. 'I should like to see you smile and laugh, Annette. To enjoy life for a change. To be happy. It – it would be wonderful if you would allow me to try to bring that about.'

She answered him with no more than an enigmatic smile, then turned away to enter the hostel door and climb the four flights of stairs. She felt a curious lightness in her heart, and wondered if this reunion with Edwin Moulvey were indeed a prelude to happiness.

Chapter Fourteen

IN HIS NINTH year, Nicholas Quade was indistinguishable from any other chimney sweep in London. Passers-by were apt to smile indulgently upon these little black-amoors, associating them with good luck, and sometimes proferring a coin. His working day began at first light; after a bowl of thin porridge, Mr Oliphant would lead the way to their first customer, striding through the raw air of early morning, Manny and Nick hurrying behind and carrying the tools of their trade. Jem had gone to sea soon after Nick's arrival, and Polly did not often come out with them these days. She had been suffering from a bad cough for weeks now; at night, after she fell into uneasy sleep, Nick would hear her gasping rapidly and raggedly, as though she ran a continual race to catch her breath. She could not possibly climb chimneys in this state. Instead, she took around Sam Oliphant's trade cards, and the Elephant found a string of tasks and errands for her. The girl had become thinner than ever, and had lost her former wiry strength.

'Don't worry yerelf on my account, Nick,' she told him when one day he found her with a scrap of cloth pressed to her lips, coughing violently. "'Tis only a bad chest from the winter weather. When summer comes agin I shall git better.'

But Nick did worry. He wished he could help Polly, the way she had so often helped him or Manny when they came home scraped raw and bleeding from forcing themselves into the narrowest chimneys. She used to bathe their wounds and rub them with dripping scraped from the stale slabs of bread provided by the Elephant. At first, Nicky came back each day crying from scrapes and sores, but gradually his tender flesh had grown as tough as Manny's, with layers of scabby skin on elbows, knees and heels.

Manny declared that he enjoyed climbing chimneys; he relished the moment when he reached the top and poked his brush clear into the air, then rested his arms on the parapet with a sense of achievement as great as that of any mountaineer in the Swiss Alps. 'I feel like the king o' the bloomin' castle!' he told the other two. 'There's no one higher than wot I am!' For him apprenticeship for the master sweep had been a deliverance from worse treatment in the workhouse. He used to run through the streets with a cheery grin, eyes gleaming in his black face, and always received many more good-luck tokens than either Nick or Polly. Manny had made up his mind to become a master sweep himself one day. Young as he was, he had enough cunning to realize that if he played his cards properly, he might succeed to Sam Oliphant's business, seeing there were no children to inherit. He was obsequious in his behaviour towards his employer and even managed to ingratiate himself with the Elephant to some extent. She showed him such marks of favour as an extra dollop of dripping on his bread.

At the beginning, Nick had faced a far worse ordeal than scrapes and bruises. To have to climb and crawl and insinuate himself into those dreadful, stifling, narrow flues . . . it was like entering hell itself. He never forgot his sheer terror the first time he went up, relentlessly pushed from behind by Sam Oliphant. When the soft, sooty blackness fell upon him, it was as though darkness had taken on a tangible form. He had opened his mouth in a soundless cry, only to have it filled with choking dust. Somehow he stumbled upwards, poking his brush before him. A dingy glow of daylight far above was his one hope – a simple, straight-sided chimney had been chosen for his first climb – and at last he emerged at the top, gulping in the blessed air . . . and dreading the inevitable descent. It was a long time before his terror of that awful darkness subsided: but gradually, since there was no help for it, he grew accustomed to spending most of his waking hours within the brickwork prison of a chimney.

Sam Oliphant had shown him the construction of a chimney: the throat of the fireplace, centred over the coals; the smokeshelf at the bottom of the smoke chamber, built slightly hollow to direct the cold air upwards. Then the sloping walls of the smoke chamber itself, meeting the bottom of the flue. Often there was a damper device at the bottom of the smoke chamber, to regulate the flow of air, and, in some of the older kitchens, a side opening into it for curing hams and bacon. The larger houses often had a bewildering system of interconnecting flues; going up or down, you had to make sure you did not follow the wrong one. Sometimes a grubby little sweep would descend into the wrong fireplace and find himself in a strange room. Sam Oliphant related the tale of a climbing-boy who lost his way in the chimney maze at a castle in Sussex.

''e come down into one of them bloomin' great bed-chambers, an' feelin' tired, blow me if 'e didn't climb into the Duke's own bed, wiv its crimson curtains all wove wiv coronets, an' sheets as white as snow an' pillers all edged wiv lace!'

The greatest fear of every climbing-boy or girl was that they might get stuck in the narrowest flues and suffocate. Both Sam Oliphant and Manny impressed upon young Nick that if ever he got stuck, the most important thing was not to panic.

'Fer that's 'ow yer can suffocate an' die, see,' Manny said. 'If yer struggle an' try to shout yer get that hotted up, yer jest can't breathe no more.'

In those narrowest flues, the two boys were often sent up 'in the buff', stripped of every stitch of clothing. The door of the room was always carefully locked, lest the sight of two naked little black boys should offend some housemaid or other female of delicate sensibility.

'Many a boy's got hisself stuck on account of the waistband of 'is trousers a-turnin' over,' Sam Oliphant said. 'Better to buff it an' make sure.'

In wide flues, Nick climbed with elbows and legs spread out, feet pressing against the sides of the chimney; but in the narrow flues he learned to 'slant it', climbing sideways and making use of all the angles, one arm held close to his side, the other high above his head, with his hand turned outwards to press against the bricks.

Often on Sundays – blessed Sundays, free from toil – Polly and Nick used to go down to the river, to a little pebble beach by Chelsea Reach. One hot summer day they even went into the water, clothes and all, to splash about and cool off. Emerging, they looked at each other in astonishment: much of their familiar blackness was washed away, and for the first time Nick realized that Polly's hair was a pale red-gold that glinted in the sunshine as it dried.

It was on one such Sunday that Polly told Nick the story of her life and how she had been bound to the master sweep.

'It 'appened after me mam died. She took bad wiv a terrible cough an' me dad an' me wuz left on our tod. But afore that we useter 'ave good times, the three of us.' Her voice and face grew wistful. 'Me dad wuz a 'Appy Family Man, an' we wuz a 'appy fambly ourselves, till 'e took to the drink.'

'A – a Happy Family Man?' Nick repeated, puzzled.

'Ain't yer never seen one, young Nick? Yo're terrible ignorant about things, ain't yer? Wiv a cage on wheels, an' inside it all sorts of birds an' animals wot lives togevver as 'appy as if they wuz in Noah's Ark. The public pays ter see them, an' that's 'ow my dad made 'is livin'. My dad allus 'ad a way wiv animals an' birds, an' he wuz taught a secret way to train 'is critters so that even if they wuz s'posed ter be worst enemies, they wouldn't do no 'arm to each other. It weren't such a secret, either – my dad wuz jest kind to 'em all, allus pettin' them an' watchin' ter see what pleased 'em and what didn't. Lots o' folk think 'Appy Family Men dope up their critters, but that ain't true. It's – it's jest that such folk can't believe their peepers when they sees cats an' birds an' mice an' dogs all livin' in the same cage.'

'But how many animals, Polly? An' how big was the cage?'

'Lemme see – it wuz about the size of a huge great cupboard, wiv wirework all round, an' blinds ter pull down when my dad wheeled it from one pitch to anuvver. It 'ad these big wheels, see, an' springs ter stop the critters gettin' jolted over the cobblestones. An' inside the cage' – she began to count off on her fingers – 'we 'ad three cats, two dogs, a monkey, four pigeons, two jackdaws, ten starlings – some o' them could talk, too – two 'ens, a screech owl, five rats, some white mice, two rabbits, an 'edgehog an' a tortoise!'

'But – you mean to say, Poll, the cats didn't catch the mice, an' the dogs 'n cats didn't fight?' Nick's eyes were round with astonishment.

'Nah, they wuz all as 'appy as could be. I forgot ter say as 'ow me dad fed 'em all on the best o' everything – them critters did a sight better than we do, I c'n tell yer. It wuz all part of me dad's secret. There wuz beef for the birds, an' meat fer the dogs too, an' apples an' nuts fer Mr Monkey, an' corn an' seeds an' bread . . . why, jest ter think on it makes me feel 'ungry!'

'The only monkey I've ever seen is the organ grinder's,' Nick said.

He often joined the crowd gathered around a hurdy-gurdy man, whose monkey was dressed in a little jacket and trousers. It would snatch the tasselled cap from its head and dart among the crowd to collect coins as the tunes were ground out.

'Our monkey made a special chum outer one of the dogs,' Poll went on, her eyes misty with recall. ' 'e'd put 'is little arm around the dog an' chitter-chatter away to 'im like anyfink. Mister Monk useter tease the owl an' pull the cats' tails, too, but they never 'ad a proper fight over it.'

'An' – what happened to all the animals, Poll?'

A long sigh. 'Ah well, me mam died like I told you, an' then me dad began ter drink away all our takin's, an' everyfink went from bad ter worse. An' then one day me dad picked up a ferret in the pub – someone give it ter 'im, a nasty long-nosed critter it wuz. Me dad weren't in 'is right mind, else 'e'd never 'ave done wot 'e did. 'E put that ferret straight in the cage alongside all the others, an' a'course it 'unted down an' killed every one of 'em, save fer the tortoise, wot wuz safe in its shell, the 'edgehog, wot wuz too prickly, an' Mr Monk. 'E'd survive anyfink, would Mr Monk. Well, there wuz our way of livin' done fer in one fell swoop, as yer might say. An' me dad, on account of 'avin' ter pay for me mam's funeral an' 'is drinkin', wuz left owin' money fer the first time in 'is life. Then one day he got talkin' wiv our Mr Oliphant, wot he met at that same pub, as if yer 'aven't guessed, an' he offered ter advance me dad enough ter pay 'is debts, if I went ter work for 'im until the money wuz paid off. Well, me dad didn't 'ave no choice really, did 'e? But all I git is ninepence a week, same as you, an' it would take years an' years ter pay orf wot he give me dad. So I reckon Dad good as sold me to Mr O.' Curiously, there was no real resentment in Polly's voice.

'And – have you seen your dad since?'

Polly turned away her head; a red-gold strand fell across her cheek, hiding her expression. 'No, I 'aven't,' she replied shortly.

Nick took hold of her hand, seeking to comfort her. 'I – I think I had a little dog once,' he told her. 'I can't quite remember, but I think it was white-haired an' barked a lot. Or p'raps there were two dogs . . .' He frowned, trying to recall that other life, so dim in memory now.

'Yer know what Manny an' me reckons?' Polly said, tossing back her hair. 'We think yer wuz sold to Mr O by some tramp or gyppo wot stole you from yer fambly! Who yer folks wuz, Gawd only knows.' She looked at him curiously. 'Can't yer remember nuffink, young Nick? Wot about yer mam an' dad, or bruvvers an' sisters?'

Nick hung his head. The word 'sisters' seemed to bring faint recollection. 'I think there was a sister,' he said slowly. 'She was called Pigeon – no, that's not it . . . *Midgin*: yes, that was her name. Midgin!'

Polly shook her head. 'That can't be right. It's like no name I ever 'eard of.' She thought for a moment. 'Most likely it wuz Bridget. That sounds a bit the same. Lots o' gels are called Bridget. Mostly they're Irish . . . I say, young Nick, pr'aps yore family lived in a bloomin' great castle in Ireland!'

Nick looked at her helplessly and they both fell silent, reflecting on how it was to be alone in the world.

Then Polly said briskly, 'Well, never mind, there's you an' me now. We're bruvver an' sister, if you like. An' yo're my chummy, too!'

Soon after that, their clothes dried stiff as boards by the summer sun, they had gone 'home'.

But all this had taken place months ago, and now Polly was ill, and Nick was afraid for her and for himself, because if she went away, then he would be truly on his own. What was it Polly had said about her mam? . . . 'She took bad wiv a terrible cough.' Now Polly herself was racked with coughing every day. Yes, Nick was terribly afraid.

Chapter Fifteen

THE YEAR IMOGEN QUADE turned eighteen, her coming-out ball was the first festive occasion to take place at Selbury since the disappearance of Sir Oswald's son and heir. The great hall was filled with light and music and gaiety as Imogen stood beside her father to receive the guests. She wore a Worth gown in the latest princess style, a creation of pale pink satin moulded to her slender figure. Its deep square neckline was trimmed with pearl-embroidered lace; around her neck she wore her mother's lustrous pearls. There were several guests who, having greeted Imogen and her father, raised their eyes to the Elizabethan portrait set above the splendid staircase and remarked the likeness between Dame Margery and her youthful descendant.

Much of the planning for the ball was due to Hester Graham. 'We could not have managed without you, my dear,' Sir Oswald told her. Imogen observed the look that passed between them, and felt vaguely perturbed. There was no mistaking that tender regard. Later in the evening, she watched them waltzing together and this time she was struck by a cold shaft of apprehension. Before Nicky's death, Imogen had wondered whether her father and her mother's cousin might consider marriage, but she had imagined that possibility to have evaporated. What if it still existed? Hester was not yet forty . . . young enough to bear a child. A son, perhaps. Another heir for Selbury. Yet maybe to speculate on such a marriage was too unlikely. And if there was substance to it – why then, Imogen told herself, there would surely be a way to circumvent such a misfortune. Whereupon, putting aside her apprehension, she gave her hand to the partner who claimed the next dance and whirled across the gleaming floor.

Shrewd matrons, wordly-wise chaperones, wallflower spinsters drooping from more than one unsuccessful season were alike disconcerted by Imogen Quade. It was generally agreed she had striking good looks; she was certainly no pink-and-white, demure English rose. Naturally she possessed all those graceful accomplishments and mannerisms one took for granted. But her quiet self-containment, unusual in one so young, a certain air of aloofness and, above all, her brooding gaze set her apart. Unlike other debutantes, she did not indulge in girlish chatter; nor was her smile easily won. Imogen Quade emerged into society as a curiously enigmatic young woman with an undoubted and unmistakable attraction for the opposite sex.

This evening at Selbury, Imogen was constantly surrounded by a cluster of admiring menfolk who seemed to hang upon her few remarks and that rarely bestowed smile. To those drooping wallflowers watching the emergence of this brilliant butterfly, it seemed grossly unfair that, in addition to her personal attractions, Imogen Quade should be an heiress.

Hester Graham watched Imogen's progress with a wary eye. She was pleased with her success, but at the same time felt an uneasiness which she scarcely allowed herself to acknowledge. Strange, she thought, that men should be so irresistibly attracted to a clear, cold flame: Imogen projected no gentle glow, rather a cool challenge. It was to be hoped she did not have a splinter of ice within her heart.

There were unworldly others at Selbury Quade that evening

who took a simple delight in the gay, glittering scene. Frederick Tenterden had been curate at St Michael's for seven years by now; he and his wife spent most of the evening alongside the Jameses, a sombre clerical group enlivened by Edith James's cherry-coloured gown. Mrs Tenterden, clad in suitably modest attire, was expecting her sixth child. She did not dance but looked about her with a placid pleasure, smiling at everything. The rector walked farther abroad, talking to old acquaintances such as Dr Fonteney, now grown white-haired and slightly stooped.

Watching Imogen dance with a tall young Guards officer, Edith James murmured to her husband, 'I wonder what Annette Duval would make of Imogen now . . . oh, I wonder what has become of her!' Her murmur did not require a response, nor did it evoke one from her husband. Both had been surprised by Annette's seeming negligence of young Nicholas Quade and saddened that she had so suddenly vanished from their lives. It was almost as though she had died. Edith James thought about that tragedy quite often. And then, at the same time, there had been the unfortunate incident of the gypsy child, too. The curate had conducted a brief ritual over his grave – and three months later, her husband had held a service of thanksgiving for the short life of Nicholas Quade. He had suggested to the grieving father that a brass plaque might be erected alongside the other family memorials. But Sir Oswald had turned aside the suggestion. They had found no trace of the boy . . . could anyone still support a hope that Nicholas might be alive?

In the supper room, Lily the parlourmaid waited behind tables burdened with a lavish array of tempting dishes. Edward was in charge of the champagne punch. He and Lily, together with Mrs Arkney, were to go to London at the beginning of next week, ahead of the family. The rest of the staff would be temporary, engaged for the season. If it had not been for the ball at Selbury they would already have left; it would be a real scramble to get everything ready for the arrival of Sir Oswald and Miss Imogen.

Jessie was no longer at Selbury; last year she had quit service to marry her sweetheart and they had moved to the other side of Yeovil, where her husband had inherited a smallholding. They had a son, now six months old, and Jessie lavished upon him all those motherly feelings she had once given Nicky. Whenever she thought of that vanished child, she would clasp her own son to her bosom in a fiercely protective gesture.

As the social columns were to report in gushing style, Imogen Quade's coming-out ball was one of the memorable events of the season. It was duly followed by eager speculation concerning her eventual choice of a husband. That she would capture a husband in her first season was undisputed; it would surely be a brilliant match.

Imogen herself savoured her success and enjoyed the admiration she evoked. But over the months that followed, she was to review her suitors with a calculating eye that looked for unworldly qualities that would have astonished those arbiters of the social scene. Her future husband must be well-bred, intelligent, agreeable, good-looking – all that went without saying. But not too wealthy or distinguished. Above all, he must not have a property of his own, no ancestral home or future inheritance. He must be willing to live with her at Selbury; and he must agree to add her name to his, so that their children would be called Quade. The notion of romantic love simply did not enter Imogen's mind. She was to seem unaccountably wayward in her preferences, often rejecting the most desirable invitations in order to accept others from gentlemen scarcely eligible in worldly terms, however charming and well-connected they might be.

All this, however, lay a little in the future. That night at Selbury, Imogen was content to receive homage and flirt a little in her own cool and enticing manner. She found herself enjoying the new sensation of sexual power, and realized that an exciting and different world lay before her, to be explored and manipulated according to her pleasure.

'*Oeow!* It's a bloomin' bird – 'elp! *Elp!*'

The tweeny hired by Mrs Arkney for the Quade town house in Leighton Square was thrown back on her heels. A shower of soot had suddenly descended as she was polishing the brass fender in the dining room and a London pigeon, turned black as any raven, flew about in a panic, vainly seeking an exit. Its flapping wings threw grains of soot on the mahogany table and high-backed chairs upholstered in antique tapestry. The tweeny ducked and cowered as the bird zigzagged from table to sideboard and finally took refuge on the high curtain rail, where it neatly deposited an offering of guano into a velvet curtain fold. At this the tweeny stopped shouting for help and fled to find it. She had the wit to close the door behind her, preventing the pigeon from discovering a wider aviary.

Ten minutes later the bird was caught by Edward, who bore it off to the basement kitchen, where the temporary cook, a stout individual with an Irish accent, was sorting out pots and pans long unused.

'Fancy a nice plump pigeon to put into a pie?' Edward asked her, grinning, as he went through to the area outside. Released, the bird flew up to pavement level, perched on the street railing an instant, then disappeared into the misty sky.

'All them chimneys could do with cleaning, I shouldn't wonder,' Cook said as Edward reappeared. 'When I was a slip of a girl, a colleen with a waist you could span with your own two hands, we used to send a goose up through the chimney to clean it. A grand job it did, too. White as snow it was when we pushed it up, black as the devil when it flew out again.'

As a result of this incident, Mrs Arkney decided to call in the sweep. 'Of course it would have been done already, if we hadn't been so delayed in getting here. A pity it couldn't have been seen to before the family arrives.' She always referred to 'the family', even though only two members of it remained to be waited upon.

Edward reached out for a taped card that hung on a nail. 'A little girl came down the area steps yesterday with this,' he said. 'Awful thin she were – she looked proper poorly.' He handed the housekeeper a square of pasteboard engraved with the tradesman's message:

*Samuel Oliphant, Chimney Sweeper, 7 Stanton Street, in
returning thanks to the inhabitants of the surrounding
neighbourhood for the patronage he has hitherto received,
begs to inform them that he sweeps all kinds of chimneys
and flues in the best manner.*

Mrs Arkney perused the card swiftly and nodded. 'Oliphant
. . . that's the man. He was last here – oh, three or four year
ago, it must be. Stanton Street's not far away, second turning
past the *Hero of Waterloo* – run and leave a message, Edward.
Ask Mr Oliphant to wait on us as soon as possible.'

Sam Oliphant, anxious to oblige, duly arrived a few days
later with his two climbing boys. Cook was a kindly soul: she
handed the boys mugs of scalding tea and a currant bun apiece
before they began work.

Oliphant grinned ominously. 'Ye'll fatten 'em up so's they'll
get stuck in the chimbley, missus,' he said.

As soon as the last crumb was swallowed and the mugs
drained, he detailed off the two boys. 'You, Manny, start in the
drawing room. And you, young Nick, can go up from the
dining room.'

Edward, sitting at the kitchen table in shirtsleeves and
yawning prodigiously – for it was not yet half past six – got up
to lead the way.

'Sure, I hope you've enough cloths to cover every blessed
thing, Mr Oliphant!' Cook called after the little procession.
'Terrible particular is Mrs Arkney – she'll be down soon to see
what's what.'

'Plenty of clorths, plenty of clorths!' Sam Oliphant
trumpeted, so loudly that Edward put a finger to his lips. 'The
family's still abed,' he admonished.

'D'ye hear that, you young varmints?' the master sweep
shouted to his two blackamoors. 'Mind yer keeps quiet
now!'

The Quade house was a four-storeyed Georgian mansion,
with fireplaces in every room downstairs and each of its six
bedrooms. The flues were not too narrow, and the interior

pattern of the chimney was well laid out. Although young Nick had long since lost count of the number of chimneys he had climbed, he had never quite lost his dread of the pitch-black world wherein he toiled. Today he felt a familiar foreboding at the task ahead.

First he and Manny helped to spread the dustsheets over the furniture in each downstairs room. So many rooms, and such a lot of furniture! Nick had been inside many large houses by now; he was always amazed that anyone could require so much. He saw that the dining room walls were hung with pictures: portraits and landscapes. He liked to look at pictures and he gazed at these solemnly, his eyes round in his black face. Old-fashioned ladies and gentlemen looked back at him out of the gilded frames. There was one picture of a house surrounded by trees. He thought it must be situated in the country. The painted scene evoked in his mind a dim memory of fresh air, green grass and leafy foliage. It was a beautiful house with queerly shaped stone chimneys, but somehow it looked quite homelike, too . . .

'Nah then! Git on wiv it, yer young limb o' Satan – yer ain't come 'ere ter stare at pictures. Manny's already up.' Sam Oliphant entered the room and hustled him towards the cavernous starting-point of his long climb. Resigned to his everyday fate, Nick braced one foot upon the sloping fireplace opening and began his work.

Imogen and her father decided to retreat for the best part of the day while the chimneys were being swept. Sir Oswald took a cab to his club, and after a leisurely breakfast in bed, Imogen dressed and ordered the carriage to be brought round. She would collect Miss Graham for a drive in the park, she decided.

'Take Flora with you – she will enjoy a run on the grass,' her father urged before he departed. He added in a softer tone, 'Please tell Miss Graham how much I look forward to escorting her to the opera next Thursday.'

Imogen concealed her impatience at his first suggestion and

her quiver of trepidation at that request. 'Very well, Papa.' Really, she thought, it was absurd, the way her father had taken to coddling the little Highland terrier ever since Nicky's death. The dog was his constant companion at Selbury, lying at his feet as he worked in the library, following him about the house and to the stables. He had taken it for granted that Flora should accompany them to London. It would have been much more sensible to leave her in the country. Nevertheless, Imogen scooped up the little dog as she swept out of the front door.

Settling herself in the carriage, she brooded on the situation between her father and Miss Graham, and decided not to relay his message – a small gesture to indicate her displeasure in their changing relationship. Last evening she had dined at home with her father. After dessert was served and they were alone together, she had been thoroughly dismayed to hear him say quietly, 'I do not imagine it would come as a very great surprise to you, dear child, if Hester Graham were to become my wife?'

Imogen was slicing a pear with a silver knife. The blade made a little screeching sound on her plate, but her smiling glance denied the disharmony. 'Hardly a surprise, Papa.' There was a brief pause while her father, clearly self-conscious, toyed with the stem of his wine glass. 'Has – has Miss Graham consented to marry you?' she asked calmly.

'No. I wanted first of all to apprise you of the possibility – the *probability*, as I earnestly hope.' Sir Oswald looked almost apologetic as he went on, 'No one could ever take the place of your dear mama. That goes without saying. But Hester is more or less part of the family already, and during the past few years we have grown closer. She is a most sympathetic and very dear companion.'

'I understand, Papa.' Imogen could not avoid a moment's brief compassion for her widower father. Truly, it was a pity that Hester Graham was not yet beyond childbearing age and that, as a consequence, this marriage must be averted at all cost. 'I hope Miss Graham will accept your proposal,' she added demurely.

This morning, she smiled sweetly at Miss Graham as she

joined her in the carriage and they continued on towards Hyde Park, passing close by the splendour of the brand-new Royal Albert Hall to enter through Prince's Gate.

'Such a bore, the sweep coming today,' Imogen remarked. 'I do think Mrs Arkney should have arranged things better.'

'It was difficult for her, with all the arrangements for the ball at Selbury,' Hester Graham said.

Imogen shrugged, aware of a spasm of annoyance as she realized Miss Graham would be responsible in future for giving the housekeeper her instructions if the marriage with her father were to take place. Only she would be Miss Graham no longer. She would be – Lady Quade. No! It was unthinkable. It must be prevented.

They swept round by the Albert Memorial, still surrounded by scaffolding even though work on it had started almost a decade ago.

'Strange that they should have managed to complete that vast hall while the monument, so small by comparison, is still unfinished,' Hester Graham observed. They passed by flower-beds bright with tulips straight as guardsmen. 'Poor Albert,' she went on. 'I believe he was misjudged while he lived. Well, he seems to have acquired a new title now. People are calling him "Albert the Good".'

Imogen turned her head to peer at the monument through the scaffolding. 'It looks rather like an extremely exaggerated mantelshelf ornament,' she said; and then, reminded of the rows of invitation cards upon the mantelshelf in the morning room, she fell to discussing with Miss Graham their plans for the coming weeks.

There were plenty of other carriages abroad in the early summer sunshine, as well as riders in the Row. Nursemaids with baby carriages walked the tidy paths and supervised older children bowling hoops or pushing dolls in toy carts. Small, sailor-suited boys carried model yachts towards the water. Catching sight of one of these, Hester Graham experienced the familiar stab of grief for little Nicholas, her godson. If he had lived, she mused, he would have been – why, he would be nine years old now!

'It is such a warm day,' Imogen said as they completed their circuit of the park. 'Is it done to take ices at Gunter's before luncheon?'

Hester Graham smiled. 'You may take ices there at any time of day. But in the afternoons only if you are escorted by a gentleman.'

So they repaired to the famous pastrycook's with the Pot and Pineapple above its door. Flora lay at their feet beneath one of the marble tables, which were small enough to encourage intimate confidences. Imogen and her chaperone dipped silver spoons into a delectable strawberry concoction, their lavishly trimmed hats forming a flowery ceiling to their low-voiced conversation.

Hester had decided to broach a delicate subject. 'I dare say you have observed, Imogen dear, that a very close friendship has sprung up between your Papa and myself over the last few years.' She lowered her eyes as she spoke and did not observe the almost cynical glint that had entered Imogen's gaze. 'I believe – I think we are reaching the point where we may decide to marry. Oswald – your Papa – has led me to suppose . . . Oh, Imogen,' she continued impulsively, 'your feelings on this matter are so important to me. It does not need saying that no one could ever replace dearest Louisa in both your father's affections and your own. And for my part, I shall always treasure the sacred memory of my dear departed Henry. But your Papa and I are very fond of one another, and I like to think – I feel sure – that you and I have formed a close bond.' She awaited Imogen's response with heightened colour in her cheeks. The girlish blush served to remind Imogen that Miss Graham was still in her thirties.

'Why, Miss Graham, this is not exactly a surprise, you are quite right . . . and of course I cannot imagine anyone I should rather have as my . . . my stepmother. It – it is just that –'

'What is it, Imogen?' It was most unlike the girl to be so diffident. Hester Graham felt a vague foreboding.

Imogen shook her head, seemingly at a loss for words. Then she said, 'It is just that I cannot forget what happened between – between Papa and Miss Duval.'

Quite suddenly, Hester Graham lost all taste for strawberry-cream ice. Carefully she laid down her spoon and pushed aside her plate. She knew instinctively that Imogen was not referring to her father's dismissal of the governess after Nicky's accident.

Imogen felt impelled to abandon her ice as well. A pity – it was delicious. She said, 'Perhaps I should not have mentioned it. Yes, that would be best – please forget that I said anything.'

Hester Graham's blush had faded. She had become quite pale. 'I – I cannot do that, Imogen. You must tell me –'

Imogen sighed. 'Well then – oh dear, I can't . . . it was just such a shock when I – I saw them together in the library at Selbury one afternoon, and realized the situation. I – I don't think I ever quite recovered from it.' Haltingly but quite explicitly she described the passionate embrace she had witnessed upon that day of summer thunderstorm: Miss Duval sprawled upon the window seat, her father leaning over her . . .

There was a long moment of silence. Then Miss Graham said in a confused manner, 'Oh, my dear Imogen, what a dreadful experience for you! And how – how difficult it must have been for you afterwards, to live with that – that knowledge. Oh, that wretched governess! I daresay she inveigled Oswald . . . but, oh, how could he? How could he give way to such base instincts, betray Louisa's memory –'

Imogen felt as though she were acting in a play. How predictable Miss Graham's reaction had been! And how swiftly she had reached the wrong conclusion. Imogen herself was quite aware there had been no real involvement between her papa and Miss Duval. If Miss Graham chose to place a more serious interpretation upon the little scene she had described, that was surely her own fault.

Hester Graham fell silent again for some moments, while their strawberry ices slowly melted away. Then, smoothing her gloves over her hands in a deliberate manner, she said in a controlled voice, 'I am afraid, Imogen, that this – this revelation may alter my feelings towards your father. I do not know quite what to think . . . I shall have to reconsider my position very carefully.' But already she was aware of a certain coolness towards the notion of that marriage she had happily anticipated such a short time ago. It was too unpleasant to think that Oswald had been – intimate – with the governess at the same time as her own acquaintance with him was ripening into what she had sincerely believed to be heartfelt affection. Perhaps she had merely been of use to him, useful in looking after Imogen . . . helping to ensure that the household at Selbury ran smoothly . . . while all the time he had been taking his – his pleasure with that young woman. She was repelled by the thought. And, oh, the betrayal of their beloved Louisa!

'I should be obliged if you would inform your papa that I shall not be able to accompany him to the opera on Thursday after all,' she told Imogen in a stiff, tight voice as they prepared to leave Gunter's. Perhaps, Hester thought, she could avoid close contact with Oswald for the rest of the season. She would do her duty by Imogen, of course, see that the girl was well and truly launched into society. Naturally she would continue to take an interest in her, for Louisa's sake . . .

'Oh, really, Miss Graham? How disappointed he will be! I know he was looking forward to escorting you to the opera.' She had delivered her father's message after all, Imogen realized wryly.

'Perhaps you might accompany him instead.' Hester Graham held her head high as she led the way to the door.

Passing through the crowded café, Imogen was pleasingly aware of the covert glances cast in her direction. It was some sort of achievement, she supposed, to create a stir during her first season, to be pointed out as 'the Quade beauty', 'the Selbury heiress'. She followed her chaperone with an air of supreme self-assurance, satisfied that unless there were some totally unexpected development, she had successfully thwarted any hope of marriage between her father and Miss Graham. She tugged at Flora's lead as the little dog pattered behind her.

'Have you a headache?' she asked the older woman solicitously as they settled themselves in the carriage. 'You are very pale. Would you prefer to go straight home?'

'No, let us return together to Leighton Square, as we arranged. We must decide about those invitations.' Hester Graham was determined not to fail in her duty. And Imogen had said her father was spending the day at his club. As they drove away, she gazed unseeingly at the passing scene. At the Selbury ball she had wondered whether Imogen might have a splinter of ice in her heart . . . now she felt as if her own heart had frozen.

Nick had been diligent in his work, scraping and sweeping all morning, emerging triumphantly above the rooftop to brandish his brush in the blessed daylight and fill his lungs with air. Then the descent into another flue, to repeat the whole sooty process . . . Finally he climbed down for the last time to the morning room and stood shaking off the worst of the soot onto the dust sheet laid upon the carpet, a silhouetted figure against the white-draped outlines of writing desk, chairs, tables. The room led off the circular entrance hall with its gleaming marble floor. The door was ajar; as Nick stood there, he was suddenly aware of the street door opening, a shaft of sunlight invading the house, high female voices and the pattering of a little dog, which came rushing straight towards the morning room.

'Oh, drat the dog!' one of the voices exclaimed, and its owner came hurrying after it . . . in time to witness a strange tableau in black and white. Imogen heard the involuntary exclamation that burst from the lips of the sooty climbing boy – '*Flora!*' – and the next second he was down on his knees, brush and scraper flung aside, while the dog hurled herself into his black embrace with a frenzy of excited barking.

Imogen froze in the doorway as she watched, all her composure thrown into disarray. The awful significance of the scene broke upon her in a single illuminating flash: the little blackamoor must be her brother! Yes, it was Nicholas . . . not dead, but very much alive. She was quite sure it was Nicky who knelt there. There was no doubt at all in her mind. Perhaps there was some instinct which enabled you to recognize a sibling, your own kith and kin . . . But such speculation was incidental. What mattered was whether the wretched Flora, bursting upon him like this, could have acted as catalyst to every dormant recollection that might be in his mind. Would Nicky now recall everything? His name – where he was born – *her* name? Or had that shout of '*Flora!*' emerged as a single, unrealized trick of memory? Four years . . . her thoughts raced as she tried to work out the implications of this discovery. He must be nine now – nine years old. He was so young when he disappeared: how much would he still remember of his previous existence? She supposed he must have wandered away that fatal day, been picked up by some tramp, perhaps, brought to London and sold to the master sweep. It was a fairly common tale, by all accounts. Gradually she felt some measure of self-confidence return. Surely he would never recognize her now: the Imogen Quade of schoolroom days was a different being to her present self. She recalled her image in the glass that morning, her fashionable clothes, the upswept coiffure beneath her flowery hat.

In the moment she stood there, Imogen was aware of the choice that lay before her: to restore Nicholas's identity, or to take the chance that the boy's utterance had been no more than an involuntary dredging up of one isolated word. Her brooding gaze took in the tableau as she lingered at the door. The boy's arms were around the terrier, his black face smudged from her ecstatic lickings.

Suddenly Nick became aware of another presence in the room. Slowly, as though awaking from a daydream to reality, he relinquished his hold upon the dog. He could not tell just why he had called out – he was in fact scarcely aware that he had done so. Now that the moment had passed, if he had been asked what the dog's name was, he could not have answered. What could have possessed him! To clasp and hug the pet that belonged to the lady who lived in this grand house! Horror-struck, he saw that he had left grimy marks on the dog's white body. Looking up, he saw a pair of narrow feet, elegantly kid-booted, below the braided hem of a wide-skirted dress. He knew, somehow, that the lady who stood there was displeased and disapproving, and his heart quailed. Rising awkwardly, he averted his gaze from her face while her furious words broke upon him.

'How dare you touch the dog, boy! You have covered her in soot – just look at her, filthy all over! How *dare* you take such a liberty –'

Nick brushed one hand across his face, shaken to realize how carelessly he had cast aside brush and scraper. The long handle of the brush had fallen against a small table, half-dragging the dust sheet from its polished surface.

Then Sam Oliphant came clumping into the room and took in the scene at a glance. 'Very sorry, ma'am – we shall have this room to rights in just a few minutes,' he said obsequiously; then, changing his tone, he glared ferociously at his climbing-boy. 'What d'ye think ye're about, young Nick, ye varmint! Pick up yer things and go an' 'elp Manny wiv the soot-bags. This instant!'

Cowed, and cringing as though from a cuff to his head, Nick scurried out of the room, out of the front door, leaving black footmarks on the snowy steps, and down to the area, where Manny was tying the first of four huge bags filled with the day's sooty harvest. The terrier tried to follow him, but Imogen swiftly stooped to hold her collar. She had registered the fact that Nicky was still known by his own name – or a variation of it.

'I'm right sorry about the mess 'e made of yer little dog, ma'am,' Oliphant apologized. He shook his head and added, 'The sort o' boys we 'as ter put up wiv these days!'

Imogen merely glanced at him coldly and left the room. Outwardly calm, inside she was trembling from shock.

Hester Graham was standing in the hall, idly examining the contents of the silver card tray. 'What was all that about?' she asked as Imogen reappeared. 'Flora seemed wildly excited.'

'Oh, it was nothing. Just a minor contretemps with a wretched little sweep who forgot his place. – Here, Edward' – she thrust Flora towards the hovering footman – 'for heaven's sake see she gets a good wash.'

What, Imogen wondered, would have been the reaction of the upright, incorruptible Miss Graham if she had known what had just passed? Or supposing – it might so easily have happened – it had been she who had run after Flora and heard the little sweep call out? Would she not have leaped to the same conclusion, that here was her vanished godson? Even now she would have been exclaiming over Nicky's miraculous restoration to his family – Edward would have been dispatched to fetch her father from his club . . . Miss Graham had, after all, readily leaped to that other conclusion concerning Papa and Miss Duval.

Quite unaware of Imogen's dramatic hypothesis, Hester Graham indicated the cards she had been looking at. 'Several callers while we were out. We shall have to return their calls tomorrow. Lady Pierce . . . the Honourable Mrs Fitzmanton – did not Freddie Fitzmanton send you flowers after the ball?'

'Did he?' asked Imogen in an uninterested manner. 'Oh yes – a huge bouquet of pink roses.'

Miss Graham nodded. 'He is heir to his uncle, you know. He will be a very rich man one day. Fitzmanton Hall is a splendid place on the Welsh border.'

Imogen remained unimpressed.

After a light luncheon served in the now immaculate dining room, Imogen retired upstairs to rest and Miss Graham went home. It was Fiona Simonswick's ball that evening. Imogen felt as though she could dance till dawn, but for her part, Hester Graham contemplated the gaiety to come with a great weariness of spirit.

One morning towards the end of the season, Imogen sat writing letters when Edward came to the morning room with a message from her father. Her presence was requested in the drawing room. Putting down her pen, she obeyed the summons and found herself being introduced to Peter Wanslea, the twenty-year-old son of her father's cousin, Philip Wanslea – the family into whose hands Selbury Quade would pass if she herself failed to produce an heir. Taken aback by this unexpected encounter, Imogen bestowed an enigmatic smile upon the young man and allowed her long, narrow hand to be clasped in his; but her heart was filled with a cold, implacable animosity. Young Mr Wanslea's visit was brief; he could not stay for luncheon. He was in London to join some fellow students from Oxford on a walking tour of Europe.

Peter Wanslea was in fact an engaging, open-faced young man with little taste for social life; he felt somewhat at a loss before his elegant, sophisticated young cousin. When he had mentioned to one of his more worldly Oxford acquaintances that he intended calling on the Quades in London, that individual had raised his eyebrows. '*La belle* Imogen!' he pronounced. 'Half your luck, my boy. But beware – they say she's a beautiful witch, a snare and a delusion to an innocent abroad the likes of you.' Peter had merely shrugged; he had no intention of lingering long enough to discover whether those words had substance. At Sir Oswald's introduction, he took Imogen's hand gingerly, afraid he might crush those delicate bones. He was reminded of one of his mother's eggshell teacups. He found it curiously difficult to engage his cousin in a friendly glance, since she seemed to avoid looking at him directly.

'Peter has been telling me he plans to enter for the India Office when he comes down from Oxford,' Sir Oswald told his daughter.

Peter grinned. 'A lifetime of devotion to the cause of Empire,' he said. 'Actually it's something of a tradition in our branch of the family. We used to serve in the East India Company – two of my uncles, in fact, perished in the Mutiny. But you would know all that, sir.' He turned towards Sir Oswald.

'How interesting,' Imogen said, her tone clearly belying her words.

Conversation continued in a stilted manner, then Sir Oswald remarked in a manner he made purposefully light-hearted, 'I suppose you are aware, young man, of the legal provisions concerning the inheritance of Selbury, and how it affects you Wansleas?'

Imogen sat unmoving as Peter answered her father in some embarrassment. Acutely aware of the tragedy of young Nicholas Quade, he strove to keep his response on the same light note, and gave a strained laugh. 'I'm afraid it's as much as we can manage to keep our own place going these days, sir. Father lost a considerable sum when the pepper market collapsed, you know. Peppercorns are cheap as dirt now . . . they used to be worth their weight in gold. Well, almost.' He smiled ruefully. 'He's trying to recoup in whale oil at the moment. But I don't think we'd ever be able to keep up a place like Selbury Quade. I suppose we'd be obliged to sell it to the highest bidder if –' Suddenly he became aware of the stark look of horror, quite undisguised for once, upon Imogen's face. 'Not that such an eventuality could possibly arise,' he added hastily. 'I am sure there will be a row of future little – er –' He had been about to say 'Quades', but realized that Imogen's offspring must bear a different name. 'Children in the direct line,' he finished lamely.

Sir Oswald smiled. He liked this unassuming young relative with his straightforward manner. Briefly it crossed his mind that an alliance between Imogen and Peter Wanslea would unite their families in a most satisfactory way. But he dismissed the thought immediately. The boy was too young; besides, marriages between second cousins were quite undesirable.

When Peter Wanslea departed a little later, taking a hansom cab to Victoria Station, he left an agreeable impression with Sir Oswald; but Imogen's feeling of antipathy towards him and his family had become stronger than ever.

The young chimney sweep, eyes glinting in his black face with the simple joy of being out and about on this fine summer morning, walked jauntily along the street, his tools held musket-fashion across one shoulder. Others abroad at this early hour – hurrying to work, on their way to obtain the best produce at market, or else the occasional toff returning from a night on the town – cast kindly glances upon him. One or two dropped coins into his hand, careful to avoid contact with his sooty paw. And, 'God bless, God bless you, sir,' he piped each time.

The former heir to Selbury Quade had inevitably taken on the characteristics of any little working lad. He had learned to give as good as he got in slanging matches and occasional punch-ups with street larrikins; had learned, in fact, to look out for himself. The gentler side of his nature was revealed mostly in his protective attitude towards Polly, who was now fading rapidly. Her bouts of coughing were more frequent, painful to behold, and she continually pressed a blood-stained rag to her mouth. Lately, she spent much of her time resting on a broken-down couch in the attic room where lumber was stored. Grumbling, the Elephant took up bowls of thin gruel and reluctantly allowed Nick to visit the sick girl, so long as he washed his feet before tiptoeing upstairs. Polly had not been inside a chimney for months now. She was relatively clean, though some of the soot seemed permanently ingrained upon her skin.

There would have been no jauntiness at all in Nick's step today had he known that the Oliphants had finally decided Polly must be removed from their house.

'I'm not 'aving 'er pass away 'ere, that's flat,' the Elephant told her husband as they lay awake through the night, disturbed by Polly's incessant coughing. 'I'll take 'er to the London down at Mile End termorrer.' There was a pause. 'Best git young Nick outer the way so's he don't know about it. Least said, soonest mended.'

Sam Oliphant retrieved a portion of the bedclothes draped about his wife's massive form. 'A Dr Newbold sent a message today, wants one of 'is chimbleys swept termorrer. Young Nick can do that by 'isself, 'stead of comin' wiv Manny an' me to the Lyle house. That'll keep 'im outer harm's way.'

So it came about that as Nick made his way to Dr Newbold's house, feeling a certain pride that he had been entrusted with this job by himself, back in Stanton Street Sam Oliphant carried Polly down to the hansom cab that stood waiting at the kerb.

'She don't weigh no more'n a fevver,' he told his wife as he bundled the invalid into the cab beside her. 'Just like a little bird, she is. A Cockney sparrer!'

Manny stood watching silently as the cab set off down the road. He knew he would never see Polly again.

'I'm taking yer to the 'orspital, Poll,' Mrs Oliphant told her as they set off. 'They'll make yer good as new there.'

Oh, hear what comfortable words are spoken! Polly raised her great eyes in a discomfortingly knowing glance, but did not speak. She had learned to conserve her rasping breath. She had never been in a hansom before; ill as she was, she could still find a shred of enjoyment in the novel experience as the cab rattled on to reach the dingy East End streets.

A bewildering assortment of sick humanity crowded the long benches in the stuffy waiting room at the London Hospital: old, young, silent, talkative, hopeful, despairing. The stench of unwashed bodies was overpowering. Sights and sounds of sickness filled the room: crutches were propped against walls, stained bandages concealed broken flesh, the pallor of disease long endured was visible alongside the flush of fever, and there were spasmodic outbreaks of coughing. The London, together with its doctors and nurses, was held in reverence by the people of the East End. It was only a handful of years since the great cholera epidemic, when nearly every family in that land of teeming tenements had lost one, sometimes several of their number. (Small wonder that as a result, many had turned towards the Salvos and the other evangelist groups, grasping with pitiful eagerness the shining promise of the Second Coming and a new life in the hereafter.)

Mrs Oliphant found a place for Polly at the end of a bench, beside a wall, so that she could lean against it. 'Now Poll, jest you wait 'ere whiles I go ter speak to one o' them nurses,' she said. In a rare, unaccustomed gesture, she took one of Polly's hands and held it briefly. Then she walked away into the throng and out to the cab, which she had told to wait. Her action was similar to that of someone leaving an unwanted kitten or puppy at a stranger's door. And as a result she experienced a similar shallow emotion: her eyes actually filled with tears as she climbed back into the cab. 'Oh, Gawd, oh, Poll,' she muttered, groping in her pocket for a handkerchief.

The Newbold house in Lockett Street was a modest enough three-storey terrace dwelling. The doctor, a young bachelor, shared the house with his widowed mother. He was engaged in research at St Bartholomew's Hospital; a zealot for work, he had already left by the time the young chimney sweep arrived. Nick made his way down the area steps to the kitchen and the maid of all work, a raw-boned female of indeterminate age, showed him up to the doctor's study, ready draped with dustsheets.

'This 'ere's the chimbley wot needs doin',' she told him, and left him to his sooty work.

Nick peered up the chimney, and stepped back in dismay. Besides the fact that it was thick with soot, he judged the flue to be one of the narrowest he had come across. He knew what Manny would say if he were here: 'No 'elp fer it, young 'un, we'll jest 'ave ter buff it!' Nick realized this was exactly what he must do. He went over to the study door and locked it, in case the maid should come back and see him. Then he divested himself of all his garments. Resolutely he began his climb, pressing his feet against one sloping wall of the chimney and levering himself upward. Through the velvety thickness of the sooty lining, rough brickwork scraped his skin. His hands and elbows were calloused enough already, but usually his shoulders and buttocks were protected by shirt and trousers.

Somehow he managed to struggle and twist his way up to the first-floor bedroom, wielding broom and scraper as he went. But between the first and second floors he became stuck fast, unable to move up or down. A line of bricks seemd to have been pushed inwards, making the flue impassable. No wonder the chimney was so dirty; Nick guessed that other boys before him had given it up as a bad job even before they reached this point.

Stuck there in the soot-laden darkness, held fast between

cold, jagged bricks, his old fear of the dark, of enclosed spaces, came down upon him in its full force. He began to breathe rapidly, and felt his throat constrict as panic rose within him. Rolling his eyes upwards – he could scarcely move his neck – he saw no hint of daylight. A flake of soot fell in one eye; he was powerless to move a hand to rub it away. Then he realized the true horror of his predicament: he was alone, without Mr Oliphant or Manny to guess what had happened and help him out. No one knew of his plight; it might be an hour or more before it occurred to the maid who had let him in to wonder what had happened, why he was taking so long inside the chimney. He opened his mouth to shout, even though he knew the sound would be muffled from the outside world . . . only to be choked by another fall of soot. Suddenly he recalled Manny warning him to stay as still as he could if ever he got stuck. 'If yer panic ye're done fer.'

Nick let got his brush and scraper: the brush stayed upright in front of him; the scraper fell a little way, then became wedged across the flue below him. He shut his eyes, trying to force himself to stay calm, taking slow breaths of the stale, soot-laden air. Surely someone must come to his rescue in the end . . . even if he had to wait for hours. The doctor would return home, or the maid send for help . . . Manny or Mr Oliphant would arrive . . . surely he couldn't stay here for ever!

And then – it was so strange – just as he felt tears pricking his eyes in spite of his determined thoughts, he seemed to hear Polly's voice. Not rasping and strained and broken by coughing, but lilting and eager, the way it used to sound before she fell ill. ' 'old on, Nick! Things ain't so bad. Jest don't give up, that's all. . . . I had to go, I couldn't help it. I had to leave you, Nick. But you'll be orlright. Everything will be orlright . . . jest 'old on!' It was the way she had always comforted him, ever since the first day he met her. If she said everything would be all right, then it would be. But – what did she mean when she'd said that she'd 'had to go', she'd 'had to leave' him? Imprisoned in the chimney, Nick felt a nameless dread steal into his mind, far worse than his fear of being enclosed in the dark. Something had happened to Polly, he felt sure of it – and in his heart he knew what it must be.

'I – I think she might have gorn, nurse.' The woman occupying the place beside Polly on the bench, her legs swathed in bandages, watched fearfully as the nurse gently touched one shoulder of the delicate-looking child leaning against the wall. 'Like a little angel,' the woman told her family later, 'wiv gold-red hair and fair skin you could almost see through. Mind you, she could've done wiv a good wash.'

Polly's eyes were closed and her labouring breath had ceased for ever. The nurse bent her head to the child's chest and felt for her pulse. There was no movement. Swiftly she scooped up the frail body and bore it away. It was not the first time someone had abandoned a dying child here, nor would it be the last.

'What a shame!' The little tragedy caused a stir of interest and pity amongst the crowded waiting room. It was not so unusual to come upon a dead infant in the streets of the East End, a little bundle of rags, a child who had died of starvation, or exposure to bitter weather, or perhaps continual abuse and neglect . . . But there had been something infinitely touching about that little girl, sitting there so quietly all by herself. Someone recalled that a large woman had brought her in, then left her.

'A clear case of consumption,' pronounced the young doctor who examined the body. He peered at her skin, ingrained with traces of soot. 'She might have been a climbing-girl,' he guessed. 'Probably abandoned by her master.' He frowned. There were hundreds of master sweeps attending to the smoking chimneys of the metropolis. Impossible to track down the one who might have left her here.

Nelly, the Newbolds' maid, finished brushing the drugget on the stairs. Time now to go down and peel the vegetables for midday dinner. The doctor came home every day to share this meal with his mother. Mrs Newbold was a semi-invalid; she

187

got up at midday, and went to bed early. She'd be up and about any minute now . . . well, at least the stairs were brushed clean of every speck of dirt. Nelly thought she would look into the doctor's study and remove the dust sheets on her way to the kitchen − surely that boy must have finished sweeping the chimney by now. She hoped he hadn't made too much mess. There weren't enough hours in the day to get everything done as it was.

Nelly turned the handle of the study door. In vain. Locked! She rattled the handle, then tried to peer through the keyhole, but of course the key was in it. She knocked urgently. 'What's goin' on? Open up! What are you doin' in there?'

Silence. Well, there was only one thing for it. She pounded upstairs once more and flung open the door of the room above the study. Here she had spread another sheet around the hearth; she was appalled to see how much soot had fallen. She approached the chimney and called up the opening, 'You up there! Can yer 'ear me?'

There was a muffled response which sounded as though it came from the floor above. She sped up the next flight of stairs and threw open the door of the topmost room, where another shower of soot adorned the tiled hearth. This time the answer to her shouts came from below, and she realized it was a cry for help.

It was Marcus Newbold who finally released Nick from his imprisonment. Returning home, he found his mother dis-traught and Nelly doing her best to calm the old lady, while at the same time keeping up a stream of encouragement to the wretched boy stuck in the chimney. Nelly had also had the sense to send a street lad to the Oliphant establishment with a message.

'Great heavens, the boy must have been stuck there for hours!' The young doctor took off his jacket and rolled up his shirtsleeves. 'It's a wonder he hasn't suffocated.'

' 'is voice is gettin' that weak,' Nelly told him. 'Oh, sir, can you get 'im out?'

'I'll try my best,' her employer answered resolutely. Peering

188

up the chimney from the first-floor room, he realized brute force was the only way to release the boy. He managed to dislodge the scraper rammed in the flue, then reached up farther. He was just able to grasp Nick's dangling feet. Taking a firm hold of them, he gave a series of short, strong jerks. There was another shower of soot, a rattle of little stones, and suddenly Nick was free. Scraped, raw and bleeding, he was safely delivered onto the pile of soot on the hearth, where he lay in a crumpled heap.

'Well I never!' Nelly gasped. 'He ain't wearin' a stitch!'

While Nick lay semi-conscious, gasping for breath, the doctor examined the extent of his injuries. 'No bones broken, but his right shoulder needs stitching – it's torn to the bone. I'll take him over to Bart's right away. The poor little wretch is chiefly suffering from shock and lack of air. Fetch some hot tea laced with a drop or two from my brandy decanter, Nelly. This damned flue must be exceptionally narrow. I'd heard that climbing-boys stripped down in such a case, but always thought it a tall story –'

During his examination, he had been appalled to see the state of the boy's heels, elbows and knees, overgrown with layers of leathery scar tissue from repeated scrapes and bruises.

Old Mrs Newbold shook her head sadly. 'It's a disgrace to use children so,' she declared. 'Yet we all enjoy our cosy fires and take these climbing-boys for granted.'

Her son nodded grimly. 'If I can't have this chimney widened, I shall give up the fire in my study. We don't use these two bedrooms above it.'

'That's all very well, but how will you keep warm?' his mother asked practically.

Marcus Newbold shrugged, 'Maybe I shall just wrap myself in a rug. But I cannot bear the thought of another boy going up this chimney.'

'There should be some better way,' his mother said. 'Perhaps someone will invent a great long broom to curve around all the obstacles on its way right up the chimney – then there would be no need for any climbing-boys.'

The doctor had to smash the lock on the study door to get into that room. He looked at Nick's pathetic heap of clothing in disgust. 'Burn these,' he told Nelly. 'We can wrap the child in a blanket. I want to get him to Bart's right away. They'll give him a thorough sponging at the hospital.'

And so, with tea and brandy warming his insides, wrapped in an old blanket, Nick was borne away to St Bartholomew's in the doctor's carriage, a rickety affair that had belonged to his father. After a relentless sponging and scrubbing that included dousing his head with vinegar to get rid of the lice that infested his hair, he was taken into a little room where another doctor put five stitches in his torn shoulder. At the end of this operation Dr Newbold reappeared.

'I suppose you'll be taking him back to his master,' the other doctor said. 'So that he can turn back into a little African again. He's a plucky lad – he never once complained while the repair job was carried out.'

Marcus Newbold had a strong idealistic strain in his nature. He had chosen to work on the problems of infection following surgical procedures because he felt sure the new antiseptic processes would eventually succeed in lowering the mortality rate dramatically. He looked at the bruised, shocked child before him. The ordeal the boy had suffered might have caused his death. How could he, as a doctor with a zeal for reform, send him back to his life of climbing chimneys? Yet, if he were to obtain the boy's release from the master sweep, what would he do with him? It might be possible, he supposed, to find him a situation in the household of one of his wealthier acquaintances – as boot-boy or under-gardener, perhaps . . .

'I'll take him home again for the present,' he said. 'My maidservant sent a message to his master – he may have arrived by now to collect the boy.'

That day, Nick was too shocked and exhausted by his ordeal properly to take in what was happening to him. But he nodded emphatically when Dr Newbold asked him if he would like to end his work as a climbing-boy; there was no mistaking the gleam of hope that came into his eyes. When they got back to the doctor's house, they found Sam Oliphant and Manny awaiting them. A long discussion ensued between the master sweep and Marcus Newbold, which ended with the latter handing the former a handful of sovereigns. For the second time in his short life, Nicholas Quade was sold and bought.

Then the master sweep placed his huge hand on Nick's thin shoulder and bade him a solemn farewell. Manny, too, came forward to squeeze Nick's hand and said goodbye as though he never expected to see him again.

''Alf yer luck, young 'un!' he whispered.

'Well, young Nick, you've got a new 'ome now,' Mr Oliphant told him. Truth to tell, he was delighted with the bargain he had pulled off. The doctor had paid him considerably more than a climbing-boy who would soon become too big for his job was worth. 'I daresay yo're grateful for the good 'ome you've 'ad wiv me an' Mrs Oliphant, an' the way we've allus looked arter you.'

Manny could not restrain a snigger when he heard that remarkable statement. Then suddenly they were both gone, Sam Oliphant and Manny, gone from Nick's life for ever.

It was only later, tucked up in a high bed with clean sheets and a soft pillow, on the verge of drifting into sleep, that Nick suddenly realized something dreadful. He sat bolt upright in that comfortable bed and shrieked out, 'Polly!'

Nelly was drawing the window curtains. She turned round, startled. 'Me name's Nelly, not Polly,' she said.

'No, I mean Polly, Polly at Mr Oliphant's – my best friend in all the world, my chummy! What will she do wivvout me? She's so sick she can't work no more, an' she coughs nearly all the time –'

Nelly laid a roughened hand on his forehead, a surprisingly tender gesture. 'The doctor will take care o' that. Don't trouble yerself wiv worrying about Polly now. Just close yer eyes an' go to sleep.'

And in spite of everything, Nick did just that.

During the next fortnight, while Nick recovered, Dr Newbold

paid a visit to the Oliphants' establishment to find out about Polly. He and Nick had had several long conversations, in the course of which the doctor tried to discover the boy's history, and how he had become a climbing-boy.

'He does not seem to have any other name – just "Nick",' Marcus Newbold told his mother.

'His features are really quite refined,' she remarked. She sighed. 'Perhaps he was the love child of some gentlewoman.' Her mind was inclined to run upon romantic lines.

'I don't suppose we would ever be able to find out the truth.' Marcus frowned. 'All he is able to tell me is that he came to London after a long walk, years ago.'

'Well, at least let us call him "Nicholas" instead of "Nick",' his mother suggested. Then she said gently, 'You will have to decide what is to be done with him before too long, Marcus, for his own sake. He cannot stay here indefinitely. He should really receive some sort of training for the future –'

'A plan is forming in my mind,' her son replied. 'I hope it will prove feasible . . .'

In contrast to that disremembered early life, Nicholas was able to describe quite vividly his experiences as a climbing-boy. The more Marcus Newbold learned of these, the more thankful he was to have rescued the lad from that life. He was appalled to hear that Oliphant had employed Polly as a climbing-girl; from what Nicholas told him about her health, it seemed clear she was in the last stages of tuberculosis.

Only Mrs Oliphant was at home when the young doctor went to visit that house. Knowing all about the dark, dingy basement where Nicholas had lived, he recoiled from the ingratiating smile on the woman's face when she opened the door and learned his quest.

'Oh, sir, it's bad news about our Poll, the worst there could be. She passed away, the poor little angel, just after young Nick came to you. I knowed as 'ow he'd be frettin' arter Poll. They was real close, them two.'

'So she is dead.' Marcus Newbold wondered exactly what the circumstances of her death had been, whether medical help had been sought, where she lay buried . . . in a pauper's grave, no doubt. There really was nothing more he could do. He left that mean house with a sense of overwhelming sadness.

Up and about once more, with the stitches removed from his shoulder, Nicholas received the news of Polly's death with sorrow, but with unexpected calmness. 'I knew she had died,' he said. 'Something in my heart told me.' In bed that night he wept for her; but he remembered how he had heard her voice while he was held fast in the dark chimney, how she had given him the courage to endure, and he felt she was still watching over him in some mysterious way.

Old Mrs Newbold had become genuinely fond of the lad her son had rescued. He had such a sunny nature and thoughtful little ways. He would cheerfully run up or down the stairs a dozen times a day to fetch and carry for her. One day she gave him a Bible inscribed with his name on the flyleaf – just 'Nicholas'. As he looked at it, able to tell that it was his name written there, though he had long forgotten his first reading and writing lessons, he said wistfully: 'I wish I had another name, the same as other people.'

'I dare say one will be provided for you soon,' Mrs Newbold told him. She sighed. If she had been younger, in better health, she might have been able to accept him into their own little household. Instead, she trusted Marcus to think of a suitable scheme for the lad's future.

Chapter Sixteen

THE AFFAIR BETWEEN Annette Duval and Edwin Moulvey had quite swiftly reached its foregone conclusion. There was a Sunday afternoon when, instead of strolling in the park, she went with him to his studio, where he pulled her into his arms upon the wide couch draped with Indian shawls. It occurred to Annette to wonder briefly how many women he might have seduced on that same couch; but she did not really care. She knew she was fortunate that his lovemaking was gentle and unhurried, a true initiation that became shared pleasure. She was vaguely bemused that her deflowering should take place in the daytime, the studio filled with sunlight, and both amazed and delighted that her body should respond so willingly to his, with such a lack of inhibition. Perhaps, after all, in spite of her long years of sexual innocence, she held passion in her nature. Self-consciousness, feelings of guilt, acute awareness of her lack of experience, a peripheral fear of pregnancy: all these simply spun away in a passionate intimacy she had not believed possible. For so long now her virginity had seemed like some valuable jewel always held in safekeeping but never worn; in truth, she was relieved to be unburdened of it.

After that first time, her response to Edwin grew more passionate, demanding as well as yielding. For his part, Edwin was deeply satisfied to discover the sensuous woman he had always suspected lay beneath her elegant, self-contained exterior person. And soon it did not prove difficult to persuade her that they should live together as man and wife. He did not mention marriage, nor did she expect him to. He was not a marrying man. Perhaps she was not a marrying woman? A startling new thought to be considered.

Annette handed in her notice at Whiteley's; she would be helping Edwin in the studio in future. He was to show her the art of retouching portraits, and she knew she would be able to bring order to his rather chaotic book-keeping. Only Annie, her roommate, knew that she was going off with the handsome gent who had appeared in the store one day like the proverbial answer to a maiden's prayer. Half her luck! It was a proper romance and no mistake.

They took furnished rooms in Chelsea, which Edwin insisted on furnishing in his usual extravagant manner. Living there with him, working each day beside him at the studio, Annette believed it would not be possible to grow closer to anyone. She could not tell if this were love or not. She and Edwin were bound together by shared memories, by passion and their mutual interest in the studio. She had at last entered a new phase of her life, filled with rich experiences. But she was also pragmatically aware that all this might change one day. She had always recognized Edwin's weaknesses – the easy charm that overlaid an undeniable desire to take life easily; his extravagance; his obstinate refusal to do without whatever he had set his heart on. His personality – like her own – was flawed. And to her own faults she had wilfully added another, which half the world, that hemisphere of principles and propriety to which she had once belonged, regarded as the ultimate sin. She had broken all the rules. In vulgar parlance, she was a fallen woman.

Edwin took her to Paris. Strangely enough, it was in that city of gaiety and dubious repute – though Edwin assured her that

Parisians took a similar view of London – that Annette glimpsed the more serious side of his nature. They spent a good deal of time visiting art exhibitions; Eddie was eager to show her the work of *les Impressionistes*, as he had once promised her he would. Through his eyes to begin with, but with a deepening appreciation of her own, Annette realized that these modern painters were experimenting excitingly, releasing themselves from conventional attitudes and techniques.

'One day photography will do the same: it will free itself from its present restrictions,' Edwin told her as they stood before a new canvas by Monet, *Lever du Soleil*. 'But first, the camera will have to be freed from the tyranny of tripod and that messy wet-plate process. There's a chap called Maddox who is experimenting with a dry plate, I've heard, using silver bromide instead of collodion. Imagine being able to hold a camera in your hand, take it wherever you may wish to go . . . Imagine being able to record pictures on the spur of the moment!' His eyes sparkled with enthusiasm. 'So many people have a mistaken notion of photography. They think the camera exists to record something accurately, to verify every detail. To tell "the truth". Yet a photograph can no more reveal the truth, whatever that may be, than a painting. Everything is an impression, a point of view . . .' He broke off, smiling suddenly, and tucked Annette's arm in his. 'I must not bore you, dearest Netta. It is time to take champagne . . .'

There was a heady atmosphere in Paris. The last of the Prussian occupying force had now departed following the signing of a truce, and there was talk of the monarchy being restored to France. But the Comte de Chambord refused to accept the tricolour as the national flag, and the restoration trembled in the balance.

When they returned to London, Annette found herself completely absorbed in her work. Edwin's fortunes improved significantly as a result of her business management and her ideas for making his portraiture more widely known. She had suggested he should offer to take studies of two or three well-known actresses and society ladies without charge and display

their portraits in the window. It proved an extremely successful notion.

'What a pity there is no way to reproduce photographs in the
journals,' she observed one day. 'To be able to see some of your
studies in the *Illustrated London News*, for example, would be
the best advertisement of all.'

There was an exquisite skill in retouching portrait studies to
make them more flattering. As Annette deepened a shadow to
emphasize the line of a cheekbone, smoothed away a wrinkle
or deftly concealed a double chin, she felt more like a cosmetic
artist. She noticed that the actresses and ladies of the music hall
who came to the studio used artificial aids even offstage to
enhance their appearance, applying rouge on cheeks and lips,
even a hint of eye shadow. The society beauties were more
discreet: a gloss of colourless lip salve, a dusting of rice powder
was all they dared use.

She did not colour the portraits. The paints available for this
purpose were too crude, more suited to those sixpenny portrait
studios that had sprung up like mushrooms in poorer neighbourhoods. In such places, a 'likeness' was overpainted a
garish pink and blue, and those gullible enough might be
persuaded to expend another sixpence on a 'chemicalized' air
preserver to stop the portrait fading – an elementary
confidence trick. Petty rogues and scoundrels had taken to the
photography trade in droves, knowing their success depended
on human vanity, that trait above all others which cried out to
be exploited.

It was inevitable that Edwin Moulvey's attachment to
Annette Duval should become known to the rest of the
Moulvey family, and through them to Hester Graham. She,
however, refrained from mentioning it to the Quades. She was
aware that Eddie Moulvey had been *persona non grata* at
Selbury since the time of Nicky's disappearance and the affair
of the gypsy boy. Besides, she herself scarcely visited Selbury
now, even to see Imogen. When she did go, she usually
arranged her visit to coincide with one of Oswald's absences.
Recently she had heard that he suffered ill-health, and she was

sorry for it; but she had decided it was more comfortable to avoid him.

It was due to Hester Graham that some three years after Annette's arrival in London, she received a letter forwarded from Selbury. During one of Miss Graham's rare visits, Imogen produced an envelope with a London post-frank, addressed to her former governess, with the words *Please forward* in one corner.

'I simply have no idea where Miss Duval might be,' Imogen said with a dismissive shrug. 'In Timbuktu for all I know – or care.'

'If you give the letter to me I shall make enquiries,' Hester Graham told her, and pocketed the envelope. Later she scupulously readdressed it to Edwin Moulvey's studio, though even this distant contact with the governess was repugnant to her.

Thus Annette learned that her Aunt Harriet had died, bequeathing her Kensington house to her niece. Miss Duval was requested to contact Messrs Preen and Gall, solicitors, at the Inner Temple. She did so, and in due course arranged to let the house, which would bring in a small regular income.

One day she went to Kensington to make arrangements about the sale of her aunt's furniture. She decided to keep a few pieces of china which she knew her aunt had been especially fond of. Standing in the parlour, once the scene of genteel card parties and musical evenings, Annette felt as though she were revisiting another world. She picked up a three-cornered kaleidoscope that lay on a small table beside the wing chair where her aunt used to sit. As a schoolgirl she used to marvel at the mirrored patterns created by the scraps of tinselled paper inside it. She picked up the toy in her gloved fingers, fastidiously blowing away a layer of dust, then shook it and peered into the box. She saw a wondrous pattern of silver and gold, red, green and blue. She shook it again: another design was instantly assembled. With a sad smile she slipped the kaleidoscope into her bag as a keepsake ... perhaps as a reminder that the pattern of life itself might be broken and reassembled from one moment to the next. Nothing, in fact, was permanent except change.

Imogen Quade was married in 1875. Those worldly-wise who had predicted an early and brilliant match were proved mistaken on both counts: the heiress to Selbury Quade was now twenty-four, and her husband the younger son of an impoverished Anglo-Irish family; an army captain who found it difficult to meet his mess bills. (If the truth were known, he was fortunate it was his brother, not himself, who would inherit the family 'castle', a decrepit and draughty country house in Roscommon with leaking roof and untrustworthy floorboards, set amid neglected grounds.) Daniel MacMahon, it was generally agreed, was charming enough in his quiet way and quite good-looking, but ... The remainder of such unfinished sentences did not need to be spoken aloud.

They had met at a house party for Ascot, where Daniel remained wistfully on the edge of Imogen's circle of admirers. To his amazement and delight, she broke away from the others to seek his company, and continued to do so even though he was careful to make his circumstances painfully clear from the outset. They met again in London and at one or two other house parties. In September, Daniel was invited to visit Selbury Quade. It was there they became engaged.

Imogen had had enough of the social scene by now. And she had discovered it was a much harder task than she imagined to find the sort of husband she wished to marry. Much easier, in fact, to have made that early, brilliant match prophesied for her. Daniel MacMahon seemed to fulfil her unique require-ments: without being in the least in love with him, she quite enjoyed his company and accepted his initial devotion with practised skill. When, finally, she led him into a proposal of marriage, Daniel never realized she was manipulating their relationship for her own purpose.

Only one man had succeeded in arousing Imogen's feelings during the few years between her coming-out and her marriage. Feelings not of love, but of sexual passion. She had known immediately that Robert Grange was very different to all those other admirers who circled around her. Robert Grange did not admire her; he desired her. His sole ambition where Imogen Quade was concerned was to seduce her. He dominated the London ballrooms of her third season, causing an alarmed flutter among the chaperones; he was the hero-villain of certain house parties where bedroom doors were often left a fraction ajar. Grange, in his early forties, was an American from Carolina. He had fought a hard war in the Confederate Army during the struggle between the states which had ended seven years ago with General Lee's surrender at Appomattox. There was a certain ruthless air about Robert Grange, an impression of experience and cynicism gained through personal danger and the ability to hold a pistol to another man's head and shoot him. His pride of place and inheritance had once been almost as strong as Imogen Quade's. He had watched his family property, a plantation mansion set among corn and cotton fields, burn to the ground when the Union Army invaded. A Yankee major had ridden his horse up the wide staircase and with drawn sword slashed every portrait on the walls to ribbons before he gave his troopers the order to fire the place.

The war had broken out while Robert lingered as a bachelor among the Southern belles whose lives were to be so cruelly disrupted. Now, displaced, forced to live abroad, he squand-ered life on his own terms. The seduction of Imogen Quade appealed to him as an amusing diversion. She reminded him somewhat of a certain lady in Atlanta, who had been one of the most provocative Southern belles of his youth. (What had happened to Scarlett Butler, he often wondered.) He had picked Imogen out at once from the throng of milquetoast debutantes that season, and had finally persuaded one of the more liberal-minded hostesses to invite them, separately of course, to the same house party.

Imogen's acceptance of Lady Callaton's invitation prompt-ed a worried communication from Hester Graham. 'I have heard you are invited to the Callaton place next month,' she wrote in her small, precise hand. 'It is foolhardy to risk your reputation in this way. I strongly advise you to decline.' Imogen ignored this advice. She did not know her invitation had been prompted by Robert Grange, but she thought he might be a member of the party, and was intrigued by the idea of continuing the flirtation she had carried on with him all season. At Callaton Place their dalliance reached its foregone conclusion. Eagerly she relinquished her virginity within the four-poster bed in the Staircase Room, which Diana Callaton had thoughtfully allocated to Miss Quade. It was separated from the main bedroom corridor by a short flight of stairs, ensuring absolute privacy.

Robert Grange could scarcely believe this was Imogen's first experience of lovemaking. Once aroused, her abandoned prowess reminded him of a certain delicious Jezebel he used to visit at a London establishment. By the time he left that tumbled bed it was dangerously near the hour when the servants were astir.

Imogen lay smiling at him, her dark hair falling about her shoulders and half-covering her naked breasts. It was a curious smile, combining deep satisfaction with a hint of malicious triumph.

'There is a novel I must read again – *Les Liaisons Dangereuses*,' she murmured languidly. 'I first read it when I was fifteen, to my governess's dismay. I shall enjoy it so much more now that I really know what it is all about.'

It was the first time Robert Grant had ever felt at a loss on such an occasion. Remorseful tears, professions of undying love, passionate demands for further encounters – all these he had encountered. But never a literary allusion. Suddenly he had an uneasy sensation that he, the man of the world, the Southern gentleman with the intriguing past and wicked reputation, had been taken advantage of . . . the roles of seducer and seduced reversed. As he prowled back to his own room, he knew that he would return to her bed that night.

The house party, and their affair, lasted a little over a week, and after that they never saw each other again. The following year, Imogen heard that Robert Grant had returned to

America; a general amnesty had pardoned ex-Confederates, and he was no longer obliged to live in exile.

In spite of Hester Graham's foreboding, Imogen's reputation was unharmed. She did not embark on another sexual escapade before her marriage. Perhaps it was inevitable that as a result of her initiation with the worldly, sophisticated Robert Grange, her wedding night brought disappointment. Daniel MacMahon, nurtured on the myth of male pleasure and passive female submission, was hesitant, apologetic and brief. Their wedding was celebrated quietly at St Michael's, that ancient church which had seen so many Quade christenings, marriages and funerals. It was known that the newly married couple were to stay on at Selbury after the wedding breakfast. This was because of Sir Oswald's failing health: he had suffered two heart attacks earlier in the year and Giles Fonteney had given him clear indication that he had only a little time left.

Imogen was given considerable credit for her decision to stay at home rather than embark on a wedding journey to Switzerland or the Italian lakes. Below stairs, Violet exclaimed, 'It's a shame they can't have no proper honeymoon!' She was still head parlourmaid, a rather faded Violet now, whose own expectation of marriage had quietly withered away. She gazed wistfully at the bride in her ivory satin gown, an antique lace veil thrown back over the wreath of orange blossom in her hair. And Hester Graham told Imogen approvingly, 'A very proper decision, dear, considering your father's state of health.'

'Imogen would not hear of going away, Miss Graham,' young Daniel MacMahon assured her earnestly. He was quite a dashing figure in his dress uniform. 'Imogen has such a sense of duty towards her father.' He glanced tenderly towards his bride, her enigmatic beauty enhanced by the lacy folds that framed her face.

In fact, nothing could have been less altruistic than the real reason for Imogen's decision to remain at Selbury. She realized she was on the brink of gaining her inheritance, and she was determined to be there to take possession as soon as her father died.

Hester Graham had felt obliged to attend the wedding. She was quite shocked to see how ill and emaciated Oswald appeared as he took his daughter up the aisle of St Michael's. Perhaps, if he and she had married, she thought sadly, he might not have declined so. Later, at the house, she decided to approach him as he sat huddled in a chair. But their conversation was forced and stilted, a mere mouthing of formal phrases. Imogen, looking across at them, thought how much older Miss Graham herself seemed to have become.

It was after the summer of Imogen's coming-out that Oswald Quade had begun noticeably to decline in health. On his return to Selbury, he spent more time than ever with his books and papers, leaving most of the estate visiting to his agent. His hunter grew fat from lack of exercise; there were no more long tramps through the woods and fields. He had in fact resigned himself to a solitary old age ever since Hester Graham had shown such an inexplicable change in her attitude towards him. One day, hunched over his agent's reports, he experienced a sharp pain in the region of his heart. The pain became frequent, a little worse each time, but he did not consult Giles Fonteney, preferring to endure his disease with a certain detached stoicism. After his first real heart attack, however, he succumbed to medical advice, taking life ever more slowly. Now he was glad to see Imogen married; he hoped her husband would prove a true helpmeet in coping with Selbury and its estate. For himself, he was heart-weary of being only half alive and viewed his approaching demise with equanimity.

So far as the bridegroom was concerned, there was one significant flaw upon his wedding day. Although his brother came over from Ireland to see him married, neither of his parents were present. Proud of their own family tradition, they had been most upset when their younger son announced that he would in future be known as Daniel MacMahon-Quade, so that the children of the marriage might bear the name that had been associated with Selbury since its beginning. Daniel was saddened by this rift with his father and mother; they had been a close-knit family in his boyhood. When Imogen first broached this condition of their marriage, he had been taken aback. It was, after all, no light step to change his name. 'I shall surely feel as though I have become someone else,' he had told her, only half in jest.

She had shrugged in reply, masking impatience with a light-hearted response. 'Women change their name when they marry. Why should a man not do so, for a change?'

The first time he signed himself 'Daniel MacMahon-Quade' was in the marriage register, for of course he had agreed to her request. There was nothing he would not do for love of Imogen.

Daniel's fellow officers had jibed good-naturedly at his engagement to an heiress. 'Half your luck, Danny boy!' declared Brian Kennedy, his closest friend. But now, in order to devote himself to his new life at Selbury, Daniel was to resign his army commission.

During the early days of their marriage, and especially on her wedding night, Imogen was quite prepared to play the part of the innocent young bride. Recalling Robert Grant's skilful lovemaking, the way his touch had aroused her to passionate response and intense pleasure, she patiently endured Daniel's hasty fumbling, successfully creating the impression that she was as inexperienced as he. Turning away from him to sleep with his arm encircling her possessively, she wondered whether in time she might be able to persuade him into greater skill. But what did it matter? The only important aspect of their coupling, the whole reason for their marriage, was the provision of a new heir for Selbury, to ensure the security of her own inheritance. And that could quite easily be achieved without delight.

Sir Oswald Quade died in his sleep six weeks later; so soon Imogen relinquished the pastel colours of her trousseau for sombre mourning garb. The severe black gowns enhanced her beauty in a more striking manner than the pretty dresses she had put away.

Watching as she descended the great staircase at Selbury the day after her father's funeral, Daniel, standing below, said: 'You told me your father used to call you "Dame Imogen". Now I see why.' He looked upward to the painting behind her. 'You and Dame Margery are the image of each other.'

His little speech revived her old pleasure in the resemblance between her ancestress and herself. She slipped her hand through his arm. 'And now Dame Margery's house has passed into the keeping of Dame Imogen,' she said. Her tone, suitable enough, nevertheless held an undertone of fierce pride.

'Into *our* keeping, dearest. I am here to help lighten that burden,' Daniel reminded her.

He did not see the shadow of a frown that came to her face as they entered the library, where Mr August Pinchbeck, the lawyer from London, awaited them. And now at last Imogen Quade, dearly beloved daughter of the late Sir Oswald Quade, was officially apprised of her inheritance. After three hundred years, Selbury Quade was once again the property of a gentlewoman.

The unconventional ménage at Hanbury Mansions, Chelsea, had lasted for five years. But there had been signs of late that the relationship between Annette Duval and Edwin Moulvey was fraying and might soon unravel completely. Annette read these signs with a pragmatic perception: she believed she had always known a day of separation between Edwin and herself to be inevitable. Her aim was to achieve an amicable parting, and a financial settlement for herself which would reflect the significant part she had played in the continuing success of the photographic studio.

There were no quarrels or recriminations; rather, an increasing lack of warmth and spontaneity seemed to descend upon them, as though a fire were gently dying away. Their everyday communication seemed gradually to become more formal. Edwin took to spending many evenings at his club

(Annette surmised 'the club' was often a euphemism for more intriguing entertainment) and went off alone for occasional weekends. She did not question him about these matters; they were not married, after all. Mercifully, neither of them had a jealous or possessive nature. Each had always respected the other's right to a degree of privacy. Edwin's evenings spent away from their apartment – often it was the early hours of the morning when he returned – provided the excuse for separate rooms. For some time now their lovemaking had been infrequent, occasions of habit rather than desire.

Annette wished for a positive conclusion to the whole affair, rather than this miserable dwindling away. She knew that Edwin, so charming and so weak-natured, would never broach the final separation himself; she must take the initiative, before he simply did not return at all one day, perhaps leaving it to some lawyer to arrange a suitable *congé*. When she raised the subject, during supper at the Café Royal one evening (she had decided a public place was the most appropriate venue for such an intimate occasion), Edwin's relief was plain to see. And once they had concluded their mutual sorrow and regret, the evening became quite pleasingly nostalgic. To the refrain of 'Oh, do you recall . . .' or 'That time when . . .' they remembered some of the happiest moments of their association.

At one point, Edwin reached across the little table with its pink-shaded lamp to take Annette's hand, and for an instant she felt the half-forgotten *frisson* of their attraction towards one another. To others in that crowded café perhaps they still appeared as lovers.

'I must say you are making it all very simple, Netta,' Edward said. 'I did not know how to broach –' A sudden thought occurred to him. 'I suppose . . . there's no one else?' Engrossed as he was in a new relationship, the possibility had not entered his head before this.

She shook her head, and the opal and diamond ring she wore glittered in the lamplight as she gently withdrew her hand. 'I just thought it time we . . . made our adieux.' She paused, then asked without reproach, half smiling, 'It *is* Marie Danton, isn't it?'

'So you know!' Edwin looked rueful and a little ashamed, like a boy caught out stealing apples from an orchard. 'Yes, Marie and I – we . . . somehow it just happened. But – when did you realize?'

Annette thought back over the past few months. 'That first day she came to the studio to sit for her portrait as Desdemona, I think.'

'But – that was a long time before . . .'

She sighed lightly. 'It was inevitable, my dear. If not Marie, then someone else would have come along. Our time had passed.'

Marie Danton, the young Shakespearian actress whose lovely face, lissome figure and silvery voice had captivated London's theatregoers, had made several visits to the studio to pose in her other roles, and eventually – inevitably, given the circumstances – to assume a personal role as mistress to Edwin Moulvey. Annette had only once seen her on the stage, as Cordelia to Henry Collard's Lear. A few days later, Miss Danton had come to the studio and changed into Cordelia's costume behind the painted screen. Afterwards, as Annette carefully retouched one of those prints, she realized that no photographic likeness could do justice to the actress's best feature, her wonderful complexion. She said as much when Miss Danton came to collect the print and praised Annette's skilful work.

'I shall tell you a secret,' Marie Danton said with conscious charm. 'My grandmother gave me an age-old recipe for a complexion cream she used. She was a great beauty in her day. I'll let you have a copy of that recipe, if you like.'

In due course, Annette received a carnation-scented note in Marie Danton's careful copperplate, and after the local apothecary in Chelsea had made up the cream for her, she was distinctly impressed by its effect on her own complexion.

That evening at the Café Royal, after they had done with regret and nostalgia and Edwin knew he was set free, Annette decided it was time to broach the business side of their separation. 'You would not wish me to remain at the studio,' she stated calmly. 'The business has prospered exceedingly during the time we have worked together, has it not? And I feel sure it will continue to do so after I am gone.'

Edwin agreed without reservation, acknowledging that, without her business sense as well as her artistic skill, he would never have prospered so. Without demur he acquiesced to the financial arrangement she suggested. It was fair enough; Annette calculated that with her share of the studio profits and the small income she obtained from her aunt's house in Kensington, she would have sufficient to start some enterprise of her own. For she was determined to provide herself with employment and the chance of further gain. She, too, was aware of the excitement of new-found freedom.

'What shall you do?' Edwin asked when she spoke of this.

'I'm not sure. I shall stay on for a few weeks at the studio and help you choose a new assistant. Some young man with an understanding of book-keeping, perhaps, and artistic appreciation.' It was strange – she realized that while she could view with equanimity the notion of Marie Danton replacing her as Edwin's mistress, the idea of another female as his workmate was less congenial. 'I intend to give myself plenty of time to consider . . . I may take a holiday in Deauville.'

'Your life will take a new direction for the third time.' Edwin spoke lightly, but a shadow seemed to touch both of them as the memory of Selbury returned. Selbury . . . that lovely place where so many tragic and ugly events had happened. Recently, Annette had read about the MacMahon-Quade marriage in a society magazine; and there had been an obituary of Sir Oswald Quade in the *Morning Post*.

Edwin's thoughts traced the same path. 'My brother went to the wedding – and then to Oswald's funeral, a few weeks later. He said the MacMahon boy seemed a reliable sort of chap, but somewhat unsophisticated compared to Imogen. I confess I was surprised. One would have thought Imogen would seek a coronet or a fortune – preferably both.' He thought hopelessly how different it would all have been if Louie had not died. His brother Nigel still wrote to him occasionally, but he had no real family connections left.

'Perhaps it is a case of true love.' But there was a dubious tone in Annette's voice. She felt an instinctive sympathy for Imogen Quade's 'unsophisticated, unreliable' husband, joined to that strange, wilful girl. Presumably, now that Imogen was in possession of her inheritance, she had attained her heart's desire. Annette could not repress a little shiver as she recalled the girl's obsession with her ancestress and the house she built. Well, none of it, nothing of Selbury Quade or its people concerned her any longer. And yet, she thought, one was never wholly free of past events that shaped one's life. Events and people . . . and places.

'It seems strange – to hear you speak of taking up a new life in which I shall have no part,' Edwin said then, and in spite of herself, Annette's eyes glistened with unshed tears.

'It is what we both desire,' she answered in a low voice.

'Yes, yes,' he muttered, looking away. Then his gaze rested upon her again, bleakly. 'I'm no good at these emotional crises, Netta. God, how we complicate our lives!'

Annette stayed on at Hanbury Mansions while Edwin went to live at his club, taking with him those familiar, inanimate indications of his presence: his clothes, books, pictures, bibelots, the scent of tobacco and bay rum. Now there was no one but herself to crumple a cushion, leave a magazine lying open, alter the placing of a chair. She was alone.

At the studio, a young man who combined a talent for figures with a fascination for photography was engaged. Annette decided she would go to the Normandy coast for a holiday, but somewhere quieter than fashionable Deauville. A vague idea was beginning to lodge itself in her mind concerning the new enterprise she hoped to start. For the moment she let it lie dormant . . . it would need much careful thought and planning if it were to come to anything.

A few days before she left the studio, an unexpected visitor appeared. Annette was by herself in the reception area, busy with the account books, when the street door opened. She thought she had never seen anyone make such a purposeful entrance. Glancing up from a column of figures, she beheld a short, stocky individual who looked to be in his thirties, perhaps, dressed in a rather dandified style. He moved briskly towards her, then, fixing her with a penetrating gaze from his grey eyes, addressed her without preamble.

'My name is Barnardo. Tom Barnardo. I have come here because I am told this is one of the best photographic studios in London.'

Recollection stirred in Annette's mind, mingled with the memory of those first weeks she had spent in the East End on her return to London. 'Doctor Barnardo, is it not? I know something of your admirable work for destitute children. The ragged school . . . your boys' home at Stepney –'

There was a hint of impatience in the nod he gave her. She had the impression that every second of his time was precious. Energy and determination seemed to emanate from him. Recently, she recalled reading that he had bought a notorious gin palace in the heart of the East End and turned it into a coffee house and evangelical centre. Sometimes the newspapers contained letters written by diehards who deplored the whole system of 'indiscriminate philanthropy'. But how much this man had achieved in a mere decade!

'I should be obliged if you would inform the proprietor of my visit here, young lady. A Mr Moulvey, I believe.'

There was a certain understated dignity in Annette's response. 'I am Mr Moulvey's business partner, Doctor Barnardo. My name is Annette Duval. Miss Duval. Perhaps you would care to tell me the exact purpose of your visit.'

Barnardo looked slightly surprised but gave an acquiescent nod. 'Very well, Miss Duval. My purpose is this. I intend to set up a photographic studio of my own, in the home at Stepney to which you referred. I already make use of photographs for record purposes, and to solicit charitable donations.' Then, rather in the manner of a conjurer, he produced several printed cards and handed them to her. 'They are in pairs,' he told her.

Annette looked at the topmost card. It bore the legend *Once a Little Vagrant* and showed a boy, clad in rags, sitting in an attitude of despair on a pile of crates. The second card was entitled *Now a Little Workman* and showed the same boy after his rescue from the streets. He was standing at a lathe, busily occupied and decently dressed. The reverse side of each card carried an outline of the work done by Barnardo's home, with an emotive plea for funds.

'It has been said these are "faked" photographs,' Barnardo told her bluntly. 'It's true these two photographs were in fact taken on the same day, and in a studio, after the lad had been in our care for a week or so. Nevertheless —' his voice, with its trace of an Irish accent, grew more emphatic — 'the first portrait gives an absolutely true impression of the state he was in when I found him sleeping out at Covent Garden. It is scarcely possible to pose a freezing, starving, vermin-ridden child before a studio camera on the very day of his rescue. We sell the cards for sixpence apiece,' he added pragmatically. 'But pray accept these with my compliments.'

Annette skimmed the wording on the back of the first card:

'. . . the children are educated and taught various branches of Industry, but above all, are carefully instructed in the Word of God, the Director and his co-workers being increasingly assured that the secret of a radical reformation is to be found alone in a TRUE CHANGE OF HEART. We earnestly hope that the view of the bright, or, it may be, the sad faces of our young protégés will lead the friends who purchase the Photographs to sympathize very truly with us in our happy but sometimes deeply trying labours.

'As I remarked before, we do not use photographs solely to advertise our work and aims,' the doctor continued. 'Each time a child is admitted to the home, we compile a history sheet, recording his name, age, physical condition and so forth. As time goes by we add details of the child's subsequent history and where he goes when he eventually leaves our care. These sheets usually carry more than one likeness, and so we have a complete photographic record of every child who comes to us.

We keep the albums available for inspection – sometimes a boy may be claimed by his family, or else by a former master . . . or the police.' Barnardo shook his head. 'There are vast numbers of young runaways, absconders and thieves at large in this great city.' He paused briefly. 'I need advice on the best way to set up my own studio, Miss Duval. It must be fully professional – it will seldom be out of use. I am prepared to spend as much as three hundred pounds on its establishment and equipment.'

Annette's eyebrows rose. A considerable sum. Perhaps, she thought, the money was coming out of the doctor's own pocket – she had heard that he had married a wealthy wife.

'Who has been doing your photography work up to now?' she asked.

'Mr Thomas Barnes, chiefly. His studio is in the Mile End Road. We shall probably appoint him as our first salaried photographer at the home. But I believe in seeking expert advice from all quarters.'

'I believe we shall be happy to help you in any way we can,' Annette responded warmly. 'Come, let me show you our studio and introduce you to Mr Moulvey.'

The outcome of Barnardo's request was that Edwin cheerfully agreed to go to the home at Stepney Causeway a few days later to inspect the proposed studio premises and offer further advice. Like most people who met Tom Barnardo, Edwin found the philanthropist's personality quite charismatic. It would have been difficult to refuse his request.

On the day of Edwin's visit, Barnardo showed him the attic rooms he planned to convert into the new studio, discussing equipment and the best aspect for the windows exhaustively. Edwin was astonished by his thoroughness and photographic knowledge. If this was the way the little doctor approached all his ventures, small wonder that he had achieved so much! Later, as they walked through the different rooms where boys sat learning brushmaking, shoe repairing and tailoring (most of those busy cutting and sewing, Edwin noticed, were cripples), the evident respect and affection which Barnardo inspired in the youths was plain to see.

Finally, Barnardo showed him several of the narrow albums that contained photographs of every child that had entered the home. Turning the pages, Barnardo gave a running commentary, pausing every now and then to enlarge upon the history of one child or another. Edwin found these photographs – most of which, unlike the sixpenny portraits, had been taken on the actual day of admittance – touching and pathetic. Countless pairs of eyes, defiant, hopeless, dulled by pain or sheerly frightened, stared out at him. The boys varied in age from mere infants to well-grown youths. Among them the occasional dark-skinned or Chinese boy caught his eye.

The doctor rested a stubby forefinger beside the likeness of a handsome dark-haired boy. 'When I discovered this lad,' he told Edwin, 'he was a match seller. He's of Italian extraction – his father was a language scholar, a political refugee from his native country. When he died, the boy came to London with his mother. She took to drink. When I found the boy, he had collapsed in the gutter from near starvation, and another waif had seized the chance to make off with his stock in trade.' The doctor shook his head sombrely. 'Heaven knows what happened to the mother.'

Again – 'See this little street Arab? He tramped from Sheffield to London to enlist as a soldier. He was nine years old. He told me his father served in India, was wounded in the Mutiny and later in the Crimea, and died. Terrible proud of his father, he was. His mother had lost her job in a factory and sent him down south with her blessing and one shilling and sixpence – the sum total of her worldly wealth, I dare say. It took the lad three weeks to reach London. Of course, the duty sergeant at the barracks of his father's regiment told him to come back when he'd grown taller . . . I found the boy almost frozen, sleeping out one winter's night.'

Edwin was appalled by some of the doctor's revelations of neglect, cruelty and destitution. They seemed the more horrific because Barnardo spoke of them in such a matter-of-fact tone, without false sentiment. This was a glimpse into another world apart from the secure, luxurious life Edwin had always known.

Every anxiety he had ever harboured seemed suddenly to shrink in importance before this grim evidence of the struggle for very existence.

He returned to Bayswater looking unusually thoughtful. 'That was a visit I shall not easily forget,' he told Annette.

She had seldom seen him so subdued. 'Well,' she said in an attempt to draw him out of his sombre mood, 'I went visiting in Brompton while you were in Stepney, and bought a delicious hat at Harrods, that little shop that used to be just a grocery store. I shall take it with me to France.'

Edwin glanced at her strangely and she said, 'Don't let my frivolity offend you, my dear. I once lived in the East End, don't forget.'

He shook his head as if to clear his thoughts. 'I'm sorry, Netta . . . it is just the complete contrast to everything I have always known that I found so – so disconcerting. I had no idea –'

'And was the good doctor pleased with your donation towards the home – apart from the advice you offered him?'

'How did you know –'

Annette smiled. 'It was not hard to guess. I don't think I have ever met anyone more – persuasive – than Dr Barnardo.'

Edwin's expression lightened. 'He is certainly quite remarkable. I suppose you might call my few guineas "conscience money". Something of the sort at any rate . . . looking at the photos in his albums, I kept thinking: "There but for the grace of God . . ."' In fact, Edwin had donated a fairly large sum towards Barnardo's work.

Annette turned back to the ledger where she had been entering figures, getting everything in order for the new assistant. 'You are well able to afford those few guineas, Edwin, I am happy to say. You have a most prosperous business.'

Chapter Seventeen

'A MOST PROSPEROUS business . . .' Annette's own
words returned to her a month later as she walked
along a lonely beach in Normandy. She was staying
in a small *pension* in the village of Fontaine-sur-mer. The only
other guests were a clergyman and his wife and an English
nanny with two pale, languid children convalescing from the
measles. Annette relished her solitude, enjoying the sea
breezes, the sands washed clean by the tide in the early
morning, tracked only by seagulls and black-capped cormor-
ants. The delicious hat from Harrods lay unworn in her luggage; but she would have the opportunity to wear it in two
weeks' time, as well as the more elaborate gowns in her
portmanteau, for she was going on to Deauville to stay at the
villa of her friend Lilian Morrissier.

A few years ago, Lilian — then plain Lizzy Gump, in the
second row of a music-hall chorus — had come to the
Bayswater studio to have her photograph taken for some
stage-door admirer. It wasn't long before she changed her
name to Lilian Larchmont and became a leading star of the
music hall. Now, having married a Frenchman who had made

his fortune from a popular apéritif, she was Madame Morrissier. From the beginning, a firm friendship had sprung up between Lilian and Annette.

There was a stiff breeze this morning; Annette had tied a chiffon scarf over her simple straw bonnet to keep it from blowing away. As her footprints followed the bird tracks across the sands, her thoughts returned once more to that idea which had lain dormant in her mind for several months. The complexion cream for which Marie Danton had given her the recipe: her plan was to manufacture and market it. Friends whom she had supplied with the cream had all reported on its good effects and begged her for the recipe. Unlike Marie, Annette had given each of them another jar instead. She had discussed the preparation of the cream with the pharmacist she patronized in Chelsea – his corner shop was an old-fashioned establishment with huge china canisters ranged behind the counter, tall glass bottles in the window, and nets of sea sponges and loofahs beside the door. The basic formula, he told her in a bored manner, was quite usual: white wax, oil of almonds, rose water, lanolin, sodium borate . . . doubtless it was the addition of the two extra ingredients specified in the recipe that gave the cream the special quality she claimed for it. Annette received the distinct impression that he had loftier matters to concern him than the preparation of mere cosmetics.

She knew that she would need to find suitable premises and employ at least two people, one with a knowledge of pharmacy. She herself would take care of the marketing and advertising of her product. She had remembered something the ambitious Mr Barker had once said to her when she worked at Whiteley's: 'I should always be glad to find a position for you, Miss Duval.' Well, she would take him at his word. Not to seek a position, but to offer him the exclusive right to retail her complexion cream. She knew he had left Whiteley's a few years ago and established his own emporium in Kensington High Street. Otherwise, she planned to sell her cream directly to the public through the post, advertising it in newspapers and magazines.

She was aware that the way she presented the product would

be crucial to its success. It must appear neither too luxurious nor too medicinal. There was such prejudice against the notion of cosmetic aids. Even her retouching of some of the debutantes' photographs had been criticized by the more strait-laced mammas who came to the studio, though most were delighted to see their daughters' charms so skilfully enhanced. On the other hand, ointments to heal skin complaints were two a penny. She must promote the complexion cream as promoting health *and* beauty . . . a healthy, glowing skin, rosebud fresh.

Surely prejudice against cosmetics could not endure for ever. It had not always existed. She recalled that in Dame Margery Quade's household book at Selbury there had been a recipe for a 'sweet coffer', in which Elizabethan ladies used to keep their beauty preparations. Right up to the last century, it seemed, women – and men, too – had preened and painted and scented themselves to their heart's content. Only this modern age frowned at the use of cosmetic art to beautify face and body. In England, at least – but she had observed that Frenchwomen appeared to see no harm in skilful, discreet *maquillage*. Once, daringly, Annette had procured some French cosmetics and applied them to her own face. A little eye shadow and kohl, a touch of rouge, of lip salve, a dusting of *poudre rose*: the result had emphasized her best features. 'Why, Netta, you look – different, somehow,' Edwin had told her in a tone of warm approval.

In the evenings, seated at the rickety bamboo table in her room at the *pension*, she calculated expenses, takings and profits, and by the time she left Fontaine-sur-mer, bidding adieu to the English nanny, the two convalescing children and the clergy couple, she was beginning to feel excited about her project.

'Duval's Nurturing Complexion Cream . . . oh, Netta, it sounds *absolument superbe!*' Lilian Morrissier exclaimed. She had joined Annette in her room as she breakfasted in bed. Madame Morrissier reclined with studied grace upon the chaise longue, sipping her cup of coffee.

Annette smiled delightedly. Nothing would ever change Lilian. She was such a warm-hearted friend. The often mispronouced French phrases that salted and peppered her speech were positively endearing.

'I shall advise everyone, *tout le monde*, to use it! I know how good it is, for I have used it ever since you sent me that large jar.'

Outside, rain lashed at the window panes. Lilian cast a despairing glance at the weather and pouted prettily. 'We might as well be in *Angleterre*! If only Jean-Paul would buy a villa in the *Sud*, we could now be taking our *petit déjeuner* upon a sunny terrace overhung with bougainvillea!'

The Deauville villa, built in the English style, was perched on a cliff and particularly exposed to weather.

'I dare say you may succeed in persuading Jean-Paul to find another summer residence,' Annette remarked.

Lilian shrugged. 'I shall do my best.' In truth, she was well content with her way of life. Most of the year she spent in the comfortable Morrissier apartment in Paris, and her fond husband lavished upon her more or less whatever she desired. He was a short, energetic Frenchman whose shape somewhat resembled the square, squat bottles of the apéritif which had brought him fame and fortune. Annette had little doubt that if a villa in the south of France was what Lilian really desired, then her wish would be granted.

'I'm sure Jean-Paul can give you good advice,' Lilian rattled on. 'He is such a man of business! And, Netta, I have *une bonne idée*. You must come to Paris with us when we return next week and we shall visit the new beauty *salon* everyone is talking about. The proprietor is an absolutely inspired *coiffeur* called Marcel Grateau. You must have heard of the Marcel wave . . . he is a magician with his curling tongs.'

Annette sighed. 'Frenchwomen are so much more astute when it comes to making the best of themselves.'

Lilian rearranged the folds of her lace negligée. 'You are right. In England, a woman who dares to use the merest *soupçon* of rouge is immediately dubbed a scarlet woman. It has always been different here . . . they say Napoleon loved the court ladies to apply *maquillage*, and of course the empress, so beautiful and sultry, led the way.'

Annette adored being in Paris again, though it was a little strange at first to be there without Edwin. He had made Paris so much his own city, and she had learned to love it through his eyes. It occurred to her that she might even encounter him, with Marie Danton, strolling along some boulevard – the Champs-Elysées, perhaps, or the Faubourg St Honoré. To see Edwin in Paris with another woman on his arm was not an entirely comfortable thought. The most likely place for such an encounter would have been one of the galleries which displayed modern art, but as the Morrissiers did not frequent such places, there was no danger on that score. Jean-Paul, in fact, was voluble in his scorn for *les Impressionistes* and their 'daubs', and Lilian complacently echoed his opinion. Annette was content to keep her own counsel.

Although Annette was determined to save her money for her new venture, she enjoyed shopping with Lilian, visiting some of the great department stores. Lilian loved spending money. At the Magasin du Louvre, she bought an ormulu inkstand for Jean-Paul's desk; at Printemps she found a wondrous maribou wrap; at Samaritaine she examined a Sèvres dessert service, but did not buy it. Each store was a dizzying experience of grand architecture and artful temptation. Recalling the shopping aisles at Whiteley's, the friendly atmosphere of Harrods, Annette thought these French stores far more sophisticated than their London counterparts. There was a hushed, almost sacred atmosphere among the displays of bibelots and furniture; even the mantles and gowns seemed to demand reverence. It was often a little like visiting a museum, or even a cathedral.

One afternoon they duly visited Marcel Grateau's *salon de beauté*. Reposing on a couch in a silk kimono to have her face massaged with fragrant oils and creams, wrapped in hot and cold compresses and finally treated with a skilful *maquillage*, Annette was conscious that the whole process had a more scientific basis than she had imagined.

'But of course, madame,' the masseuse told her. 'There is a scientific basis for every beauty treatment. We are beginning to find out how the skin renews itself, more about the different types of skin, and accordingly which preparations are the most suitable.'

Annette resolved to set herself an intensive course of study. She realized she was about to embark upon a business career which could entail much more than marketing an efficacious complexion cream. If she really wished to succeed, she must do more than she had imagined.

When they returned to the apartment, Jean-Paul Morrissier declared such divine beauty should not be hidden from the world, and they went out to dine at a restaurant.

'I have the good fortune to be accompanying the two most beautiful women in the room,' he declared, ordering champagne.

'In Paris, if you please, *chéri*!' Lilian protested. She sipped her champagne, and decided to broach the subject that had been occupying her mind. 'This new image of yourself, Netta, as a *femme d'affaires*, a businesswoman – it is all very exciting and of course I hope it will prove a *succès fou* . . . but what about a new romance in your life? You should be looking for a husband, *chérie*, as well as filling jars with face cream and pocketing the profits.'

Annette smiled at such directness. 'Perhaps, in time,' she replied. 'But I have learned to rely on myself, you know. It has not been an easy lesson. I – I sometimes feel I am the only person in the world in whom I have complete confidence.'

Lilian shrugged white shoulders above her blue velvet evening gown. 'No woman should rely solely upon herself.' She smiled across the table at Jean-Paul. 'However, it is early days since the end of your *affaire de coeur* with Edwin. But I strongly recommend *la vie conjugale*.'

Annette changed the subject. 'There is one thing that bothers me about my business plans. You know it was Marie Danton who gave me the recipe for the complexion cream. I have been wondering whether I should offer to remunerate her in some way –'

'Certainly not!' Lilian asserted positively. 'She has Edwin to look after her – for the time being, at least. I believe she is quite flighty in her affections. You will need every penny of your capital, Netta. And in any case, where did she obtain the magic formula?'

'From her grandmother, she told me.'

'And where did her *grandemère* obtain it?' Lilian shook her head. 'Don't be foolish, Netta.'

Jean-Paul offered worldly advice. 'In matters of business, my dear Annette, there is no room for such sympathetic thought. It is a self-indulgence you cannot afford if you are to succeed.'

One spring morning in 1879, an unusual procession slowly approached the gates of Selbury Quade. At its head, striding along the highway with a red flag held aloft, was Charlie Ashell; behind him, spluttering along at four miles per hour, came a horseless carriage driven by Daniel MacMahon-Quade, wearing a fearsome pair of goggles. And running gleefully in the wake of the puffing, steam-driven monster was a gaggle of village urchins, shrieking in mingled excitement, derision and admiration.

Peering from a window of the lodge, Mrs Kitto turned to tell her husband, 'He's almost here, Jack – make sharp now.' Whereupon old Jack Kitto trudged out rheumatically to open those massive gates, shaking his fist at the children, who stood for a moment to jeer and defy the authority of the big house before they turned tail and ran away.

Daniel waved nonchalantly to the lodgekeeper as he turned into the entrance, chugging along the tree-tunnelled drive. Then Charlie, tucking the red flag beneath his arm, leaped nimbly into the passenger seat for the daring sweep into Selbury's forecourt, the highway speed limit abandoned in a sudden acceleration of power. The carriage was a light Crompton model, capable of reaching twenty miles per hour. One memorable afternoon Daniel had managed to reach eighteen miles per hour, racing downhill from Great Selbury in total disregard of the Red Flag Act.

They came to a shuddering halt in a spatter of gravel, and after Daniel had dismounted – he and Charlie both were apt to apply the vocabulary of the stable to the steam car – Charlie took the wheel and drove the monster to its lair, a shed beyond the stable block.

Daniel had acquired the Crompton at Imogen's suggestion . . . it was a new toy, something besides hunting and shooting to keep him occupied, as he wryly acknowledged to himself. Doubtless his wife hoped it would help to distract him from 'meddling' in Selbury affairs – for that was how she chose to view his desire to relieve her of some of the burden of running the estate. Gradually, painfully, Daniel had come to realize that the 'burden' of Selbury was all Imogen had ever truly desired. Tactfully at first, then with increasing impatience she had dissuaded him from conferring with her agent; rejected his well-meant suggestions for improvements to the labourers' cottages; frowned on his attempts to understand the latest farming methods. Until, finally, Daniel had really begun to resent his lack of occupation, his powerlessness to make decisions. His days seemed to pass without purpose or the chance of achievement.

It was in direct contrast to the life he had known in the army. There he was trained to plan strategy, take decisions, accept responsibility and command. And, of course, to obey those who outranked him. It seemed now that was all that was left to him: to submit to the wishes of his wife. (Yet was it not Imogen who had promised to 'love, honour and obey'?) More and more these days, Daniel MacMahon's thoughts turned wistfully towards the army life he had relinquished.

The intimacy of marriage as he once imagined it might be had eluded him. 'Just remember, old son, there's more to marriage than four legs in a bed,' some half-drunken comrade had proclaimed solemnly at the mess party on his wedding eve. Well, there was more than enough of the four-legged act with Imogen . . . and precious little else. He had tried in vain to achieve the sort of companionship he craved. In spite of her physical demands on him, his wife remained apart, curiously aloof. He seldom heard her laugh spontaneously or make some simple, impulsive gesture. Everything she said or did seemed, somehow, premeditated.

What sort of a marriage, what manner of life had he fallen into? Sometimes he felt like a child, fobbed off with playtime occupations while Imogen sat at her father's desk in the library, busy with the affairs of the estate. As Captain MacMahon he had known who he was. As Daniel MacMahon-Quade, he seemed in danger of losing his identity.

Of course, Imogen was terribly disappointed they had no child yet. So was he; it would have been jolly to have started a family by now. But there it was – something that just couldn't be helped. Yet they had been married for over two years now. But Daniel had come to realize that Imogen's urgent desire for motherhood was directed solely towards one end: the provision of an heir for Selbury Quade. She did not share his yearning for the sort of family life he had known in his Irish boyhood. She seemed – what was the word – *obsessed* by Selbury, by the legend of that ancestress she so much resembled. Dame Margery. A formidable old biddy, by all accounts. In a sense, he supposed, Imogen was as much a prisoner of Selbury as he had become.

Daniel was troubled by Imogen's seemingly insatiable yet curiously untender physical desire. He had been almost shocked at the beginning to realize her eagerness; then, for a while, he had joyously succumbed to a celebration of un-bridled love and lust. Now that he was aware of her lack of tender emotion, he had begun to dread their couplings, despising himself for the attraction she still held for him. He was unable to resist her, in spite of himself. However, her demands had lessened considerably over the past few months ... perhaps their relationship was about to enter a more harmonious and settled phase. Daniel MacMahon's fund of optimism was not yet exhausted. He had never pretended to understand women, after all.

Each time Daniel entered Selbury by the main door, his gaze went to the portrait of Dame Margery, dominating the house she had built just as she appeared to dominate Imogen, his marriage, and himself. He would have liked to tear down the portrait from the wall, trample the canvas to dust . . . but that he knew, would achieve nothing. You cannot destroy a legend.

Now, as he entered the great hall, his upward glance was arrested halfway when one of the footmen appeared bearing a request from Imogen. She wished to see him as soon as he came in.

Carrying his driving goggles and brushing back his thick mane of hair in a boyish gesture, Daniel obeyed the summons, expecting to find Imogen, as usual, at her desk behind a pile of papers. To his surprise, she was huddled in the great leather wing chair beside the fireplace, nursing a glass of spirits in one hand. She was very pale and looked uncharacteristically vulnerable.

'What is it, my dear? Are you unwell?' There was concern in his voice.

She made a weary gesture with her free hand. 'Sit down, Daniel, don't fuss. It is just that I – I have had some painful symptoms lately, and I decided to ask Dr Fonteney to pay me a visit. He came this morning, while you were out.'

It was true, Daniel thought – she had seemed a bit under the weather for some time, now he considered it. She had got into the habit recently of taking an afternoon rest, and they had cried off one or two neighbourhood engagements because she had pronounced herself too tired to go out. And perhaps it was some indisposition that had curtailed her ardour. How like Imogen not to say anything about old Fonteney's visit until after the event! It was she who had suggested the drive this morning, he recalled . . . to get him out of the way, as it appeared.

Imogen looked at him from hooded eyes. 'It does not seem to be anything serious. It may be a touch of gastric inflammation, apparently.' She paused to sip her brandy and water. 'However, I am not quite satisfied. I have decided to obtain a second opinion – Dr Fonteney has recommended an eminent man in London who specializes in female complaints.' Her voice held no trace of her secret fear that some disorder of her reproductive organs might prevent her from ever conceiving a child.

Daniel was at a loss for words. Talk of female complaints made him feel awkward. His instinct was to go over to his wife and comfort her with a caress, but such an intimation of tender feeling had no part in their relationship. Imogen was passionate but never demonstrative. Now, as always outside their bed, she seemed to set an invisible barrier between them.

'I shall accompany you to London,' Daniel said after a pause.

'No.' Her head came up and he saw the familiar denial of tenderness in her face. 'I would rather go alone.' Her mind turned to practicalities. 'It is scarcely worth opening the London house – I shall only be away a few days. I shall stay at the private hotel in Kensington which Miss Graham sometimes patronizes.'

Daniel shook his head hopelessly. There was nothing for it but to fall in with her wishes. 'Very well, if that is what you want, my dear. But telegraph me at once if you should need me.'

Imogen made no reply. There was no need: they were both aware there was only one area of her life in which his presence was indispensable.

Two weeks later, with shocked dismay Imogen heard the careful opinion of the London specialist.

'But – Doctor Fonteney thought it was most likely a touch of – of gastric inflammation.'

Mr Coblington, eminent physician and shrewd observer of the human condition, regarded his patient dispassionately. They sat facing one another in his consulting room, she – dressed again after that singularly painful and unpleasant examination – on one side of his leather-topped desk, he in his accustomed place behind it.

The physician steepled his fingers. Imogen looked away from those hands which had probed her most secret parts.

'It is true,' he acknowledged, 'that the disease I believe you may have contracted may have something of the appearance of inflammation of the appendix, in its advanced stage. But in my opinion, Mrs MacMahon-Quade, you have a chronic pelvic inflammation which may in fact be the most common venereal disease.' It was possible, he thought privately, that her family doctor had sent her here to absolve himself of the need to pronounce this diagnosis.

'Venereal disease – but how –' Imogen stared at him, her composure shattered.

His voice was impersonal. 'If my opinion is correct, there is only one way in which venereal disease may be contracted. It is transmitted from one partner to another during sexual connection.' He paused, then asked carefully: 'How long have you been married?'

'A little over two years.'

'Then I am bound to say, such is the extent of the inflammation, that I consider it likely you contracted the disease before your marriage.'

This was by no means the first time Mr Coblington had had to acquaint a lady with the fact that she was suffering from a venereal disease. Most often the patient had been infected by her husband. Mrs MacMahon-Quade made no attempt to refute the implication of his words. As much to give his patient time to collect herself as to enlighten her, he launched into a brief description of the disease.

'It is not surprising that you failed to notice any symptoms for some time; many women do not realize they are infected until complications occur.' He paused. 'Sometimes there may be spontaneous recovery – that is, without the need for any palliative treatment. Unhappily, such is not the situation in your case. The disease has extended to the tubes connecting the ovaries to the womb, which accounts for the considerable amount of pain you are now experiencing.'

'Does – does that mean that I have forfeited the chance to bear children?' Imogen was ashen-faced as she asked the question.

The physician was faintly surprised at her reaction. He had not thought her exactly the maternal type of woman. 'I fear that may be so,' he answered in a gentler tone. 'It depends upon the amount of inflammatory obstruction to those organs. I can only advise a short stay in hospital to carry out some treatment to ease the condition.' He looked at her gravely. 'Your husband may well be infected. He should seek medical advice himself. Satisfactory treatment can be administered.'

'So women are affected to a far worse degree.'

He ignored the bitterness in her tone. 'If by that you mean that it can render them infertile, yes. Be thankful it was not syphilis you contracted. A far more uncomfortable disease. I take it you have heard the term "general paralysis of the insane"?'

She inclined her head. 'I acknowledge my good fortune.' She had begun to recover her composure, at least outwardly.

The physician frowned slightly. Whatever lover she had taken before her marriage – he was pretty sure such was the case – might at the time have been unaware he carried the disease. The clap: subject of ribald jokes, one of the most ancient disorders known to mankind. And because of its sexual nature, society regarded venereal disease in a severely moralistic light. Other forms of illness too often provided a mainstay of everyday conversation. Venereal afflictions, needless to say, were never mentioned in polite society. Yet such afflictions were probably as widespread as tuberculosis. Widespread and unmentionable. Mr Coblington looked at his patient with a measure of compassion. He was almost certain her obvious desire to conceive a child was doomed to disappointment.

Arrangements were made for the hospital treatment to be administered. When it was over, Imogen knew for certain that she would never conceive a child. But within a few months, assisted by treatment, she would be healed of the disease.

After she left the hospital she returned to her Kensington hotel. She intended to journey back to Somerset the following day; there was nothing to keep her in London. That same afternoon she walked in Kensington Gardens, along pathways bordered by daffodils and hyacinths, avoiding the main carriage drives. She had no desire to be recognized by any London acquaintance. Eventually she sat down to rest on a secluded bench. She leaned back, closing her eyes, allowing the full bitterness of her thwarted desires to sweep through her. Above, the new green foliage of a great elm arched across the sky. Some children were playing on the grass, calling to each other and laughing. A dog barked joyously as it frisked about their game.

So this was what it had come to, her scheming to provide an heir for Selbury, another Quade to take up that precious inheritance. It was – it must have been – that short-lived affair at Callaton which had proved the marplot to all her careful designs. She recalled how Hester Graham had tried to dissuade her from accepting Diana Callaton's invitation. That advice had been better than she realized. As the result of a few passionate embraces, the mazelike path she seemed to have followed from childhood onwards had arrived at a dead end ... leaving her with a marriage which was now no more than an encumbrance to her.

As her thoughts turned to Daniel, she opened her eyes and her thoughts became more positive. There must be a separation between them. It would be the best thing for them both. To go on with their marriage now would make it more of a mockery than it already was. Perhaps he could rejoin the army, resume his commission. People would gossip, of course – but the opinions of others had never really mattered to her. Divorce was out of the question – that went without saying. She had no wish to forfeit her place in society, to hover on the verge of the *demi-monde*.

What if Daniel should refuse to consider a separation? And now Imogen's thoughts fell into their habitual devious mode. There must be some way to ensure that he would not refuse her request ...

But what would happen afterwards, when she was left alone at Selbury? As she was only to well aware, the property was still entailed to the Wanslea cousins, in the event of her death 'without issue' ... to Peter Wanslea now, since his father had died three years ago. She recalled the naive young student she had met one day at Leighton Square. A fierce resolve welled up inside her. Peter Wanslea should never inherit Selbury! Not if it lay within her power to prevent it. And there was only one means to ensure that would not happen. Quite suddenly she seemed to see her way clear. It was – it was as though she had been shown a path lit by a blinding light. *She must attempt to find her brother.* Nicholas must have his inheritance restored to him. Feverishly she thought how she might begin to search for him. It was a decade since that astonishing encounter at Leighton Square. Who knows, he might have died in the meantime . . . but that was a possibility she resolutely thrust from her mind.

A chilly little breeze had sprung up. Imogen shivered, as much from anticipation of the task that lay before her as from the cold air. How long had she sat here? She had not noticed how the shadows had gradually lengthened as the afternoon drew to its close. Slowly she rose to her feet, then walked briskly back towards her hotel. The confrontation with Daniel could wait; she had decided to remain in London a few more days to start her all-important quest.

The Quade house in Leighton Square had been closed for months, its windows shuttered, furniture and chandeliers dustsheeted. Imogen had brought the key from Selbury, for she intended calling in to collect a gown she had left in her wardrobe last season. But now there was a much more important reason to visit the house.

She rose early this morning with a new sense of urgency, anxious to begin the quest for Nicholas without delay. Arriving at the house, she went into the morning room, dustsheeted as it had been that day when she had recognized the little sweep as Nicholas, her brother. Nicholas, whom she now desired so earnestly to discover. Standing where he had knelt to embrace Flora, Imogen closed her eyes for a brief moment, her mind and spirit forming an unspoken prayer. Then she descended to the basement kitchen and began to look for the first vital piece of information she needed. Where would Mrs Arkney be likely to keep tradesmen's notices? After poking about unsuccessfully in a few musty dresser drawers and disturbing a family of town mice, she opened a cupboard door: there, neatly pinned to the inside, was a row of cards: *Higgins, High-Class Butcher (Families Waited upon Daily); Adey & Son, Fishmongers & Poulterers, by Appointment; Lansells, Wine & Spirit Merchants . . .* and *Samuel Oliphant, Chimney Sweep.* Imogen tore this card from its tape and quickly scanned the address. Stanton Street . . . she would take a hansom there at once. If only the master sweep was still at the same address! A lot could happen in the space of ten years. Perhaps he had retired from his trade. Perhaps . . . As she turned to leave, the dragging pain which had become her incubus momentarily intensified, and she stood by the table gripping its edge, then filled a cup with water and swallowed one of the tablets she had been given. Now that she had a new purpose to spur her on, the pain seemed easier to bear.

Sam Oliphant's trade was indeed still carried on from Stanton Street, but the master sweep himself had 'gorn to 'is reward these two year past', as his widow informed Imogen when the door of that house was opened to her. The woman had taken an unconscionable time to answer her knock; Imogen had been on the point of going away when at last she heard a wheezy voice crying, 'I'm jest coming'!' Then, by way of replying to her request for a few words, Mrs Oliphant bade her enter the house, shuffling ahead into the little parlour.

'An' a good reward I'm sure my Sam'l gained for 'imself. He wuz a good man,' the widow asserted in a maudlin tone. 'But wot can I do for you, my lady?'

Imogen thought she detected spirits on the woman's breath; sure enough, a brandy bottle and half-empty glass stood on a little table by the chair where Mrs Oliphant had evidently been sitting. The woman was a sloven, Imogen thought contemptuously, and her house a pigsty. She compressed her nostrils against the pervading smell of soot, and noticed with some surprise that the brandy bottle was covered in a layer of coal dust. She was not to know that Mrs Oliphant had triumphantly unearthed it from beneath one of the soot-bags in the cellar, where Manny had hidden it. 'How shall us git customers if yo're too poorly to take messages, Mother?' he had often asked despairingly these past two years. She liked him to call her 'Mother', and he obliged her readily; it seemed a small enough return for the chance to inherit his late master's business.

It was a long time since Mrs Oliphant's parlour had gleamed with polish, when each rug was set straight with geometrical precision, every cushion plumped up like a fat hen. It was on account of her loneliness after Samuel's death that she had taken to the bottle. Manny performed the part of dutiful son well enough, but he was out all day. The hours passed on leaden feet. And as a result of her addiction to the brandy bottle she had quite mislaid her house pride. It might be said she had allowed a veil of mourning to descend upon that once spotless room. She no longer fell into a conniption if Manny tracked soot along the carpet, and the furniture she had once dusted and polished with such a prodigal expenditure of elbow grease was now dulled and smeared. Only the mantelshelf was kept immaculate, for it had become a household shrine to the late departed. Draped with a beaded valance and ornamented with a pair of vases, it was overhung by a yellowing, enlarged photograph of the master sweep himself, framed in ebony. A crafty looking individual, Imogen thought, glancing at it . . . though Oliphant himself had considered his camera expression pious and sincere.

Mrs Oliphant had followed her visitor's quick glance towards the brandy bottle. 'I wuz jest takin' a drop for me toothache,' she said glibly. 'Terrible troubled wiv me teeth I be. I sh'll be glad when the last of 'em drops out. Now, wot wuz it you wanted, my lady? Yore chimbley ain't caught fire, 'as it? My son Manny, wot runs this h'establishment now that Oliphant 'as passed on, is out workin' jest now. But if you wuz ter write down where you live –'

Imogen waved aside the ridiculous suggestion. As if she would come in person to request a chimney sweep's attendance! 'No, there is something else . . . something I wish to ask you.' She hoped the old woman's liking for brandy had not befuddled her memory completely. 'About ten years ago,' she went on carefully, 'your husband employed a climbing-boy ... ' In spite of herself, her voice held a tremor of nervousness. 'His name was Nick. Do you recall him?'

'Why, o' course I do!' Then a subtle change came over Mrs Oliphant's expression. 'But wot's that to you? We don't employ no boys now. It's agin the law these days. An' Manny 'as got 'imself one o' those newfangled brushes wot join tergether a' reach right up the chimbley –'

Imogen leaned forward. 'Mrs Oliphant, I have reason to suppose that your 'Nick' may in fact have been my brother Nicholas, who disappeared from our house in Somerset. Nicholas Quade, of Selbury.' She pronounced the last words in a deliberate manner.

Mrs Oliphant bridled, and one hand went involuntarily towards the half-empty glass beside her. 'Well, Oliphant never 'ad nuffink ter do wiv that. Yore bruvver disappearing, that is. He paid good money fer the boy, on account of 'e wuz nice an' small –'

'I am not suggesting your husband was connected with Nicholas's actual disappearance,' Imogen assured her quickly.

'Well, then.' A sip from the brandy glass. Then, reminiscent-ly, 'Oliphant bought 'im from a gyppo, didn't 'e? It wuz all above board in them days to employ climbing-boys, afore the guv'mint began pokin' its long nose into all our bizness.'

'A gypsy!' Imogen's eyes widened. She thought of the Romany encampment in Foxhollow. Perhaps it was the gypsies who had carried him off after all. No wonder they had never returned to Selbury ...

'We looked arter our boys real well,' Mrs Oliphant was saying. 'You can be sure of that. Nuffink but the best for 'em, good vittles an' all 'ome comforts.' She almost believed her own words. 'Yer can tell the truth of wot I'm sayin', else why would Manny 'ave stayed on ter 'elp me?'

Imogen frowned. 'I thought Manny was your son?'

'That's 'ow I think of 'im.' 'E's not really me own. Me an'

232

Sam'l adopted 'im, seein' 'as 'ow we'd no son of our own ter carry on the bizness.'

Inheritance . . . a universal cause for complaint and sorrow, Imogen thought grimly.

'But wot's the use of callin' back young Nick ter memr'y when 'e's dead an' gorn?' Mrs Oliphant drained her glass.

'Dead!'

At Imogen's anguished cry the woman drew a shaking hand across her forehead. 'Why, no, o' course not! There I go, mixin' 'im up wiv our Poll . . . such pals they wuz, them two. An' it wuz Poll wot passed away. I took 'er to the 'orspital, but they couldn't do nuffink for 'er. "You've done all you could've, Mrs O," the doctor sez ter me . . . "all you could've" . . .'

'But Nick – what of him?' Imogen asked urgently, profoundly relieved at this instant resurrection.

Mrs Oliphant cast a wistful glance towards the brandy bottle. 'Well, Oliphant sold 'im to that do-goodin' cove, didn't 'e? Arter young Nick got stuck in 'is chimbley an' well-nigh suffer– sufferated.'

Imogen thought that if this was how Mrs Oliphant began her day, by nightfall she must be completely inebriated, dead to the world most likely. So far as she could tell, Nicholas seemed to have passed out of Samuel Oliphant's keeping into the care of someone else. But who? And how serious was this accident he appeared to have had?

'Mrs Oliphant, do you happen to recall the name of that "do-gooding cove" you mentioned?'

Mrs Oliphant sighed massively. 'The questions you ask. All right, all right, I know it's cos you want ter find yer long-lorst bruvver, an' I c'n tell yo're a lady born, but all these things wot I'm relatin' 'appened a long time ago. Let me see . . . it wuz a doctor, I c'n remember that. 'E lived in a street off the Fulham Road. Linden . . . no, that's not it . . . Lambton . . . *Lockley*, that were the name! Lockley Street. But lor' bless you lady, I can't recall 'is name, nor the number of 'is 'ouse . . .' And quite suddenly her head dropped to her chest and she began to snore.

It seemed clear there was no more information to be gained

233

from this source. Imogen rose, let herself out of the house, went out to the waiting hansom, and told the driver to go to the London Library, in St James's Square. It had been a favourite haunt of her father's; she thought it might supply the reference she now needed to consult. Once there, she asked to see the Fulham street directory that was current ten years ago. She riffled through the pages. Lockley Street . . . but to her dismay, there was no street listed by that name. It was just possible, she supposed, that the name had been changed . . . but much more likely that the wretched Mrs Oliphant had misremembered it. In which case, perhaps the correct name at least began with the letter 'L'. . . . There were several of these. It took a good hour to look up each one; some of the streets were long, and each dwelling was numbered, together with the name and occupation, if any, of the householder. Turning at last from Lobb Place, she encountered Lockett Street and ran her finger down the page. There was only one doctor recorded there, at number 26. A Dr Marcus Newbold. She emerged from the library with a sense of triumph and gave the cab driver the address.

But at 26 Lockett Street she drew a blank. It appeared that for the past five years the house had been occupied by a family called Branston. And before that, for a brief occupancy, by a foreign gentleman. No one at number 26 had ever heard of a Dr Newbold. How transient the life of a great city was in its humbler environs, Imogen thought. The people in these little houses – here one day, gone the next. But there must be some people who sayed in the same house all their lives, for whom Lockett Street was a permanent address.

By now it was afternoon. Imogen was weary, but determined to persevere with her search. While her cabby and his horse dozed at the kerb, she knocked on the neighbouring doors, until at last a timid maid showed her into the presence of an old lady who had inhabited Lockett Street for forty years or more.

Imogen explained her mission and asked Miss Anstruther whether she had ever heard of a Dr Newbold.

There was a pause for recollection. Then, 'Why, to be sure,'

Miss Anstruther told her. 'Such a pleasant young man, and very clever, I believe. He once brought in my little Flossy after she'd wandered out into the road.' She paused to stroke with elderly veined hands Flossy's successor, a pug dog reposing on her lap. 'He lived with his old mother, and when she died he moved away. I don't recall where. He used to go to St Bartholomew's Hospital each day to carry out his work. He didn't put up a plate outside the house, he wasn't that sort of doctor. He was engaged in some sort of medical research, I believe. Perhaps if you were to go to St Bartholomew's they might be able to give you news of him there.' She looked at Imogen with surprisingly alert blue eyes. This young lady seemed extremely anxious to obtain news of Dr Newbold. She also looked quite ill, sitting with one arm held close to her side as if to suppress the welling-up of pain. Miss Anstruther rang a bell and asked the little maid who answered it to bring in some tea, which Imogen accepted gatefully. But in response to Miss Anstruther's gently probing remarks, she divulged nothing concerning the reason for her quest. Perhaps, Miss Anstruther thought, fingering her jet beads, there had been a broken engagement, some misunderstanding long ago . . .

When Imogen left Lockett Street, she felt pleased with the progress of her investigation so far. It was now too late to pursue it further, and she returned to Kensington.

Confident that her good fortune would continue, she visited the hospital at Smithfield next morning. But there her luck ran out. At a long counter where a harassed clerk was recording details of patients being admitted, she was told that Dr Newbold was no longer on the hospital staff. When she persisted in her demand to know more, the clerk sighed heavily and went off to confer with a colleague. He returned with the news that Dr Newbold had gone to Cambridge to pursue his research work and had died only last year as the result of an infection incurred during his anti-septic experiments. Like Kolletschka, like Semmelweis before him, Marcus Newbold had fallen a victim in his own fight.

Imogen was bitterly disappointed. Entering the gates of St Bartholomew's, she had been so sure that before long she would be face to face with the doctor and a step nearer Nicky. 'Is there no colleague of his I may speak to – someone who knew him well?' She broke off to gather her skirts closely about her as two hospital porters brushed past carrying a patient on a stretcher.

The clerk gave a despairing glance at the pile of papers beside his high stool. 'Dr Newbold's former assistant here might be able to help you – with whatever it is you wish to know. His name is Dr Fearnley.'

Imogen's hopes revived.

'But he is presently studying at a medical institute abroad.'

There seemed no end to disappointment. 'I see. Would you be able to give me the address of that institute?'

Barely concealing his exasperation at the persistence of this well-dressed lady who spoke to him as if he were her servant, the clerk went away again, and eventually returned with a piece of paper. 'Here is Dr Fearnley's address,' he told her. 'And now, if you will excuse me – this is a very busy hospital.'

Imogen took the paper and turned away. She would write to Dr Fearnley – surely it was possible that his former colleague might have spoken to him about the climbing-boy whom he had rescued. Such a rescue was not an everyday occurrence, after all. She peered at the paper. Dr Fearnley was in Vienna . . . that meant she would have to wait a considerable time for his reply.

As there was nothing more she could do in London to advance her quest, she decided to return to Selbury without delay. She had neither the desire nor the energy to go shopping or visit acquaintances. Once she had found London an exciting and alluring place, filled with pleasurable possibilities. But she seemed to have grown immeasurably older than the girl who had danced her way through those successful seasons. Then, the culmination of everything she had desired seemed to lie within her grasp. Now, she was returning to her beloved Selbury in defeat, a scarred and barren woman.

Chapter Eighteen

NEXPECTED VISITORS HAD come to Selbury Quade during Imogen's absence. Peter Wanslea, taking a holiday in the West Country with his wife, had found himself passing close by the house. He decided, quite on impulse, to call there. He had not seen his cousin Imogen since her marriage, and he believed in keeping up family connections. Besides, he wanted to introduce Vera to her – he was proud of his young wife, who would soon bear their first child. There was no other motive in his visit; although he looked forward to seeing Selbury, his thoughts never lingered upon the remote possibility that the house and estate might pass into his hands one day, by default. He had not even bothered to mention it to Vera.

The Wansleas found only Daniel in residence. Delighted to have company, he made himself very agreeable. The three of them got on so well together that the visitors were easily prevailed upon to spend a night at Selbury. The next day, Mrs Arkney was happy to take young Mrs Wanslea on a tour of the house. Her pregnancy well advanced, Vera Wanslea was quite content to match the housekeeper's stately progress from great hall to library, drawing room to music room . . . then, on the upper storey, through charming bedchambers and the long gallery . . .

These days, Mrs Arkney was giving serious thought to her retirement. She yearned for a cosy cottage and looked forward to relinquishing the responsibilities she had once been so eager to attain. She did not find her mistress sympathetic; often her thoughts returned nostalgically to Lady Louisa's day.

When they reached the long gallery, Vera Wanslea was quite happy to be left alone to study the paintings there. 'I am sure you have a great many things to attend to,' she told the housekeeper with a charming smile.

If only Mrs MacMahon-Quade had such a pleasant disposition, Mrs Arkney thought as she returned to her duties, Selbury would be a very different place.

At the very moment Vera Wanslea began to descend the great staircase, pausing to gaze wonderingly at the portrait that hung above it, a hired carriage drew up outside the house. It had come from Yeovil station, and out of it stepped Imogen. The huge entrance door stood open; as she came into the hall, she was surprised to see a young woman on the stairs. Clearly, from her dress and bearing, a lady. Why, it was almost as though this stranger were the mistress of Selbury, and she herself a visitor to be welcomed in her own house!

'You are Mrs MacMahon-Quade, I think.' Vera Wanslea reached the hall and came forward eagerly. She had several times seen her husband's cousin at parties and balls in London, but they had never actually met. Vera had hovered shyly on the fringes of Imogen Quade's glittering set. She well recalled her striking good looks – though now, she thought, Imogen appeared somewhat wan and strained. She went on in a rush, 'I am Vera Wanslea. Daniel has been so very kind. He insisted we should stay here overnight. We are touring this part of the country, you see. We were so sorry you were away. Peter will be quite delighted you have returned before we leave.'

Imogen stood still, regarding this unexpected and un-welcome stranger (her husband doubly unwelcome) with a cool gaze. 'Wanslea?' she said. 'Oh, I see. I suppose you have been looking at the house – '

'Oh yes, your housekeeper – Mrs Arkney, is it not – has been most obliging. It is such a lovely place! Our place in Gloucestershire is rather Gothic and gloomy, you know.'

A great sense of resentment welled up in Imogen. This smiling, artless young woman seemed to have no notion of her husband's effrontery in coming here, to – to inspect Selbury!

Then Daniel and Peter Wanslea appeared, and Daniel hurried over to his wife. Peter Wanslea could not help observing Imogen's lack of enthusiasm as she greeted her husband, and was somewhat dismayed.

'My dear Imogen, if I had realized you were coming home today, I would have met you. But your telegraph did not say –'

'I did not need to remain in London as long as I expected. It seemed better simply to return rather than send another message.' Imogen waved aside his words with a dismissive gesture.

How formally they spoke to one another, Peter Wanslea thought. He found himself exchanging a glance with Vera, and knew she felt the same.

'It is good to see you again, Cousin Imogen,' he ventured.

'It is a surprise to see you, Mr Wanslea.' There was no vestige of warmth in her voice.

Imogen's return completely changed the simple, easy acquaintanceship that had sprung up between Daniel and the Wansleas. Her presence seemed to frost the atmosphere.

Glancing again at Vera Wanslea, Imogen perceived the concealing drapery of her costume and realized she was carrying a child. She felt then as though she had been struck by a sharp-edged sword.

After some stilted conversation and a little refreshment in the library, Peter Wanslea announced that he and Vera must continue their journey. 'We are expected at Lyme this evening – that will be far enough for Vera to travel.' He smiled fondly at his wife, who blushed a little at this oblique reference to her delicate condition.

'So you will soon be a proud father,' Daniel remarked.

Peter Wanslea beamed happily. 'I dare say it will not be long before you and Imogen . . .' his voice died away as he saw the stony, stricken expression that had appeared on his cousin's face. There was something much amiss within this pleasant house, he realized.

The Wansleas and Imogen parted with mutual relief. Only Daniel was left a little puzzled as Peter Wanslea's smart barouche disappeared down the curving drive. They had had such a jolly time together yesterday, he and those two Wansleas.

Violet came up to the library to clear away, and quickly returned below stairs with her laden tray.

'Well, it didn't take long for the mistress to get rid of them visitors,' Edward the footman observed. He lounged on one of the kitchen chairs, astride the seat with his elbows resting on the back. 'If you ask me, she weren't too pleased to see them here when she got back. And the master looked like a schoolboy caught out doin' something he oughtn't.'

'It fair cheered me up to see such a nice young couple as them Wansleas,' Violet called back over her shoulder as she left her tray in the scullery. Then she added, 'I should avoid the library for a while if I was you. They're having words.'

Alone with his wife, Daniel immediately asked her what had happened when she visited the specialist. Imogen sat in the same chair where she had huddled in pain a few weeks ago. He thought she seemed a little better now, though clearly the journey from London had fatigued her. She had been away longer than he anticipated. A shopping expedition, no doubt, after her visit to the doctor . . . it was a pity she had not been here when the Wansleas arrived.

But her answer to his question was scarcely reassuring. 'I have beeen told that I can never hope to conceive a child,' she told him flatly.

It was Daniel's turn to look stricken. Her uncompromising statement shocked him. 'Oh, my dear. My dear, dear Imogen. But what – why –'

'Perhaps,' she said deliberately, 'you may be able to supply an answer to that question, once I have told you the rest.'

'I don't understand.' He looked at her warily, realizing she was deeply disturbed. His poor Imogen. No wonder she had behaved a little – oddly – towards the Wansleas. Especially as Vera . . . It must have been a stunning blow when she received the news. And she had been all alone in London.

'I shall explain.' Imogen looked away. 'It is not easy for me to do so. It is something I would rather not speak of.' She laid her head against the high chair back and fixed her gaze at some point beyond Daniel. 'I was examined by the specialist, then had a further examination, under chloroform, at a hospital for women.' She paused, experiencing sudden olfactory recall: the sweet, sickly odour which had heralded brief oblivion.

'You should have let me know.'

'I am letting you know now. I – I have a venereal disease. The clap. That is what it is generally called, I believe. I dare say you have heard of it.'

He was unable at first to believe what she was saying. Unable and unwilling.

'The disease itself will soon be quite cured – I was given some treatment to assist the healing process.' She focussed her gaze directly upon him now. 'But my reproductive organs can never function properly.' She gave a bitter smile. 'Forgive such physiological details. But those organs are rather necessary if one is too conceive and bear a child.'

'The clap!' Daniel was horror-struck. 'But how –'

'How do you imagine?' She paused and said quietly, 'In my case, it would seem, from husband to wife.'

'That's not possible. It cannot be –' Daniel broke off, suddenly unsure of himself.

'Apparently I contracted the disease about the time of our marriage. Its ravages take time to spread.' She watched her husband closely as he got up and began to pace the room. He had turned pale. She wondered what it was he had suddenly remembered.

In fact, Daniel had recalled a half-forgotten escapade a little while before his wedding. A nervous bridegroom about to carry off the most sought-after young woman in London, he had confessed to Brian Kennedy, that brother officer who was so much more a man of the world than himself, that he had never really had a woman. Naive flirtations with properly brought-up young girls, frustrated fumblings with one or two Irish housemaids, an inept experience with an older woman, one of the hunting set at home ... somehow he had never achieved the whole distance.

'What, never?' Brian had regarded him quizzically. 'That will not do for the fair Imogen. – No, don't take offence, I wouldn't dream of suggesting ... it's just that she deserves better than that.' He gave the matter his serious consideration for a full thirty seconds. 'I tell you what: we'll pay a visit to Milly Adair! A good sort, Milly. She'll look after you, set you straight – straight as a ramrod, as the saying goes!'

And she had. Milly, fortyish, easy-going, catered for officers and gentlemen at her establishment conveniently close to Knightsbridge barracks. Daniel had found his visit there a revealing experience, though in the event it had not really helped his wedding-night performance. But now he asked himself uneasily ... had Milly bequeathed him this foul disease? Had he unwittingly passed it on, in his turn, to Imogen, and thereby denied both of them the chance of family life? To say nothing of causing Imogen such pain and anguish. It seemed he must have. What other explanation could there be? Unthinkable to imagine that Imogen could possibly ... In his own anguish he groaned aloud.

'In the beginning, apparently, one may not be aware the disease is present,' Imogen was saying. 'For a male, it may come and go without his knowing he has had it.'

Daniel struck his forehead. 'Believe me, I had no idea of it. I – I should tell you,' he went on, stammering, 'something that does me no credit, I fear. It – it was only because I had never – well, the fact is that I had dealings with a prostitute shortly before our marriage. It was a respectable establishment –'

'Respectable!'

'In its own way. It – it wasn't as though the woman was

some whore off the street. I only went there once . . . ' His voice held a pleading note.

How despicable, Imogen thought. It was the pleading she despised. 'And because of that,' she said coldly, 'that one – indulgence of yours, my life is ruined. Everything I had hoped for –'

'It is dreadful for you. Terrible. For both of us. I cannot of course condone my behaviour. I had hoped as much as you that we might raise a family together.' In a vain effort to rally optimism, he went on, 'Your life is not completely ruined, Imogen. That really is exaggeration, my dear. The – the disease is not fatal, after all. In a sense, it would have been worse if – if I had passed on to you tuberculosis. We still have each other . . .' His voice faltered as he met her uncompromising regard.

'Don't be ridiculous, Daniel. I do not consider my disease a preferable alternative to tuberculosis.' Her voice was icy. 'And I am sorry to say that neither do I consider the fact we still have each other, as you say, sufficient compensation for what I have lost.' She paused, then continued with cool deliberation. 'Since we shall now have no family to bring up together, I think it would be best if we separate and go our different ways.' She gave another bitter smile. 'I always considered it sound sense that marriage was ordained for the procreation of children, as the prayer book has it. Surely that is the only true reason why a man and woman should be – what is the phrase – joined in holy matrimony.'

Daniel stopped his pacing and clutched at a chair back to steady himself. Had Imogen really spoken those words? And yet . . . what was their marriage, after all? His thoughts spun in turmoil as he recalled his own increasing dissatisfaction with life at Selbury . . . life with Imogen. His feeling of uselessness, of being a supernumerary. And now this hideous thing had happened . . .

'It is the only course for us, Daniel,' Imogen said. She stood up to face him directly. 'We shall only make each other miserable if we stay together. I will remain here; at least I shall still have Selbury. And you – you could rejoin the army, resume your commission. I cannot think that would be such hardship for you. I know how much you enjoyed army life.' She paused. 'There is, of course, no question of a divorce.'

Daniel averted his eyes from her gaze. How collected she was! He felt an unmanly constriction in his throat. 'Of course there can be no divorce,' he said. 'I understand that. I dare say I shall . . . the army . . . my old life.' He turned away to look unseeingly out of the window, not trusting himself to speak further.

Imogen settled herself more comfortably in her chair. The whole scene had passed off much better than she had hoped. Daniel's involuntary confession had been much to her advantage. Poor Daniel. What a thoroughly decent man he was, after all. It was a shame he would never be able to remarry – some nice, gentle girl – so long as she herself was alive and they remained man and wife. But she simply could not compromise her reputation. Someone like Vera Wanslea would have suited him admirably, she thought.

Her thoughts reverted to practicalities. There would have to be a legal arrangement. She could provide a settlement of some sort for him . . . at the very least, pay for his commission. Conscience money, perhaps. Well, there was one consolation for him. 'I assume you will revert to your own name,' she said. 'After all, "Captain MacMahon" is much less of a mouthful than "MacMahon-Quade".'

At this he turned to look at his wife sitting there in her elegant travelling costume, still wearing that becoming hat with veil and curving feather. The expression on her face – eyebrows arched, a half-smile on her lips, her eyes coolly amused, head tilted a little to one side: how many times had he seen her just so in the days before their marriage, surrounded by admirers. And he himself very much the onlooker – so he had thought. Yet it was he who had carried off the prize so much desired . . . and, he thought wretchedly, it was he who had despoiled it.

Daniel MacMahon left Selbury Quade that same week, deluded into a false sense of failure and an irrevocable loss of self-respect: feelings which would remain with him the rest of his life.

Imogen was determined to keep her quest for Nicholas to herself, at least until she discovered whether her brother was alive or dead. Perhaps until she found him. There would be time enough for the world to exclaim and wonder. Meanwhile, the MacMahon-Quade separation and Captain Daniel MacMahon's return to the army provided gossip and speculation enough. During the next few months, Imogen channelled all her energy into her plan to restore Nicholas's inheritance. He should find house and estate in impeccable order; she set about a strenuous programme of repairs and renovations. Several farm tenants were amazed when leaking roofs and cracked walls they had complained about for months were mended. Her agent was astonished when she directed him to go ahead with the plan proposed by Daniel which she had formerly rejected out of hand, for improvement to the labourers' cottages.

She shut her mind to the question of what she herself would do if – *when* Nicholas returned. The heiress once more dispossessed. Presumably he would marry – he must marry to ensure this precious inheritance. But Selbury had no dower house to which she might retire.

She had written to Dr Fearnley, in Vienna, soon after her return from London. Although she still awaited a reply, she had not lost faith in the ultimate success of her search. Her optimism accompanied a marked improvement in her health, as the pain at last diminished and the symptoms of her disease finally ebbed away. But it was not only her body that had been damaged; her face was shadowed by her experience, and there were lines of disappointment and bitterness around her mouth. She was still beautiful, but there were times, especially when she was tired, when she looked haggard.

At breakfast one morning she found among her letters an envelope with an Austrian postmark. A reply from Vienna at last. Dr Fearnley's handwriting was small and precise:

... I received your enquiry concerning my late colleague, Marcus Newbold, and apologize for the delay in answering it. I spent some time in Munich earlier this year and found your letter on my return here. . . . As it happens, I well recall the incident to which you refer, when Dr Newbold rescued the climbing-boy from suffocation after he became wedged in one of the chimneys of his house. Dr Newbold was very much perturbed by the boy's narrow escape from death, as well as his general physical condition. Unfortunately, I am unable to give you any further information relating to the boy's subsequent history, as I myself left St Bartholomew's for Edinburgh about this time. I wish you well in your endeavour to trace your brother.

And that was all. After waiting so long for his reply, Imogen was no further forward. She was overcome by a feeling of despair and remained depressed and short-tempered for days. During this period the servants prudently avoided contact with their mistress as much as possible. What could she do now? There was no one she could turn to for advice, since to do so would be to admit that she had failed to restore Nicky to his rightful place ten years ago, when she had recognized and rejected him. What other grounds could she provide for her sudden conviction that her brother must be alive somewhere? Yet still she held to her determination to find him. Surely there must be some way to advance her search.

One day she paused in the long gallery in front of the portrait of her father, her mother and herself, painted before Nicky was conceived. She found she could not meet her father's steadfast gaze, nor her mother's gentle regard. For the first time in her life, Imogen Quade was aware of a feeling of shame and remorse. She had a wild desire to turn back time, to undo everything that had happened as a result of her schemes and plots. But that was impossible.

'I will find you,' she whispered as if it were a pledge to those she had wronged. 'I will find you, Nicholas.'

Annette Duval had established a modest manufactory for her Nurturing Complexion Cream on the edges of Camden Town. She had engaged a clever young pharmacist, two female assistants and a messenger boy. And she carried out her plan to approach John Barker about a retail outlet in his department store. To her singular satisfaction, she received a positive response. Mr Barker not only remembered her, he pronounced himself impressed by her business acumen.

He held up the glass jar with its pale-green lid and butterfly motif which Annette had devised to hold her product. 'I have it on first-hand authority from the womenfolk in my family that your cream really does possess the qualities you claim for it in your advertisements,' he told her. 'I am more intrigued than I can say to discover that you are the manufacturer, Miss Duval.'

'It cannot perform miracles, of course,' Annette replied. 'But regular use certainly improves the complexion. Up till now, Mr Barker, I have sold it only through magazine advertisements, using the postal service – but the response is so encouraging that I should like to try a retail outlet as well. That is why I have come to see you.'

John Barker readily agreed to retail the product, and sales in his store were pleasingly profitable.

Lilian Morrissier was ecstatic about Annette's success; just the other day she had written urging her to market the complexion cream in France; Jean-Paul was prepared to put money into the venture, she said. But Annette wished to become more firmly established on home ground first. She had by now acquired a good deal of knowledge about the skin and different types of beauty treatment. (These days, there was talk about a surgical process of cutting and lifting facial skin to expunge the ravages of time.) She thought that she might branch out into one or two other beautifying products – a glossy hair rinse, lightly tinted lip salve, perhaps a face powder . . .

Annette worked very hard these days. Her social life mainly consisted of occasional trips to France to see the Morrissiers. They had sold the Deauville house and built a villa in the south, not far from Cannes. Lilian called it the Villa Mimosa. Annette could scarcely find time to keep up with her personal correspondence; one day, she decided to devote a morning at home to clearing out her writing desk, which was stuffed with old papers and unanswered letters. At the back of one drawer she discovered an envelope containing the cards Dr Barnardo had given her when she came to the studio in Bayswater a few years ago. She had only really studied the two topmost photographs on that occasion. Re-reading the appeal for funds on the backs of the cards, she resolved to send a donation towards Barnardo's work. How much he had achieved! She riffled through the photographs ... one showed a half-starved child begging in the street, with an infant sister at his side. Then the same lad, sturdy and well-fed, dressed in the uniform of a messenger boy. His sister, Annette read, had become a member of one of the 'families' that belonged to the Village Home for Destitute Girls which Barnardo had established on the outskirts of London. It occurred to her that she could do worse than use this form of advertisement herself to promote sales of her product. A study of a young woman with blemished skin *before* using Duval's Nurturing Cream, and then the same young lady, her complexion perfectly restored, *after* her use of it ...

A forlorn-looking little chimney sweep looked out at her from another card. The other photograph which made up this pair showed him divested of grime annd soot, about to chop a log, with a happy grin on his face as he raised his axe. His face ... for some reason Annette held the card up to peer more closely at the sepia likeness of this fair-haired boy. Suddenly she felt her heart begin to beat more quickly. A surge of excitement ran through her mind. When had this photograph been taken? Presumably about the time Barnardo visited the studio ... the boy looked about ten years old, younger than Nicky would have been then, but she had heard that climbing-boys were often deprived of nourishment to ensure they did not grow too fast. Yes, it was just possible this boy was in fact the same age as Nicky. She made a rapid calculation. Nicky would be eighteen or nineteen now – if he were still alive.

She sat for a long while gazing at the card, then brought out an album from another drawer of her desk. It was years since she had opened it; the few photographs it contained held such painful memories. Now she steeled herself to look at them. There was the likeness of herself which Edwin had taken – the pensive letter writer. Gazing at it, Annette felt as though she were looking at a stranger, whose life was quite separate from her own. She turned to another study: the young Imogen posed in the punt, one hand trailing in the lake . . . Sir Oswald, with Nicky by his side, and the two little Highland terriers . . . and the group study of the household assembled on the lawn at Selbury.

She looked again at Nicky's face and at Sir Oswald's, comparing them with the Barnardo photograph of the boy holding the axe. Was it her imagination . . . or wishful thinking, maybe? Surely there was a resemblance, some family likeness — in expression as well as feature, the way the head was set on the neck . . . Her excitement mounted. Was it possible she had stumbled upon a vital revelation concerning the fate of Nicholas Quade? Had he in fact become a climbing-boy and then an inmate of Barnardo's Home for Destitute Boys?

What should she do? She must take some action — she could not keep this speculation to herself, however far-fetched it might turn out to be. The family at Selbury should be apprised of it. Then, if they wished to follow it up, they could do so: approach Barnardo's, look up the records . . . The family? There was no family left at Selbury Quade in the proper sense. Only Imogen — and Edwin, here in London. Sister and uncle. The former so unpredictable; the latter estranged from Selbury years ago. Annette had learned of the separation between Imogen and her husband in the gossip column of some social journal. And there was Miss Graham, of course, Nicky's godmother. She had been almost a member of the family.

Annette made up her mind. She would tell Edwin about her discovery, and he could contact Imogen if he chose to do so. Surely they must follow up this lead. But even if the little chimney sweep did indeed turn out to be Nicholas Quade, anything might have happened to him in the time that had passed since that photograph was taken. But, oh, if it were Nicky, and if he were still alive!

Annette had installed a telephone at her premises in Camden Town. The next day she put a call through to the Bayswater studio, only to learn that Edwin Moulvey was abroad for a month. As she sat at her desk holding the two Barnardo cards in her hand, the time element suddenly appeared vital. There must be no delay in this business. Even a month, a mere four weeks, was too long to wait. Replacing the telephone receiver, she reached for a sheet of writing paper and an envelope large enough to contain the two cards. Then she composed a letter to Imogen. It was not an easy task; several sheets of paper lay crumpled in the waste basket before she was satisfied with her final draft. 'See that this envelope is sent by registered post, and bring me the receipt,' she told the cheerful lad who ran her messages.

Now there was nothing she could do but await the outcome of her action. Even if Imogen did not communicate with her, she would eventually learn something from Edwin, she felt sure. And if Nicholas Quade were found after all these years – it would surely be an irresistible news item for the public press.

Dispiritedly Imogen Quade glanced at her letters on the breakfast table. It was late autumn, with chill winds beginning to blow. The trees had shed their foliage, revealing shapely winter skeletons, bare branches etched delicately against an overcast sky. The promise of winter increased her feeling of depression. There had been no development in her quest for Nicky. Her thoughts seemed to revolve in circles; she was heart-weary of trying to devise some action that she might take. Her coffee grew cold as she sat wearily contemplating the scene outside the window.

She could scarcely be bothered to examine her post this morning; listlessly she picked up the topmost envelope – addressed, she saw, in Hester Graham's handwriting, which was becoming increasingly illegible as illness weakened her. Miss Graham was dying of cancer; of late she had resumed closer contact with Imogen, who responded to her letters with as much warmth as she could manage. Imogen knew she must go to Gloucester to visit Miss Graham soon, before it was too late. She dreaded the thought of seeing her again – the woman whose chance of happy companionship she had wilfully destroyed. Every dark ghost in her life seemed to haunt her now. None more so than Nicky, the brother she had deprived of his inheritance.

She put aside Hester Graham's letter for the moment. Beneath it lay another, larger envelope with a London postmark. It had been sent registered and was addressed in a firm yet artistic hand which seemed vaguely familiar. Imogen took up her ivory paper knife and opened it. Two photographic cards fell out, enclosed in a sheet of writing paper. She began to read the letter.

In London, two weeks later, Imogen Quade walked purposefully into the offices of Smelton, Pinchbeck and Pinchbeck, close by the Inner Temple. The epitome of old-fashioned legal chambers, they were furnished with Georgian mahogany and overlooked the Temple gardens, now strewn with fallen leaves from surrounding plane trees. Decaying chrysanthemums straggled across the flowerbeds.

The same Mr Augustus Pinchbeck who had come to Selbury after her father's funeral looked after Mrs Quade's affairs. He had no idea why Mrs Quade should have made an appointment to see him today; surely there could be no complications arising from the wretched affair of her separation from Captain MacMahon. He understood the captain, on rejoining his regiment, had gone off to help keep the peace on the border of Afghanistan. The whole business had been a quite simple matter, really, especially as there were no children of the marriage. Simple but unpleasant. Mr Pinchbeck, himself a confirmed bachelor, found anything to do with matrimonial entanglements distinctly distasteful. Luckily such cases were few and far between; most people, thank heaven, had the good sense to suffer their miseries privately and make the best of things – or else suffer the worst, as he acknowledged wryly.

Mrs Quade arrived upon the hour, which pleased Mr Pinchbeck; he considered punctuality next to godliness. She seated herself in the chair by his desk with her usual air of self-possession . . . an air she had retained, as he recollected, even throughout the unfortunate matter of her separation. She seemed, he thought, in excellent spirits today, and was as elegant as ever, doubtless attired in the height of fashion – he knew nothing of such matters. Clearly anxious to proceed with the interview, she responded to his polite remarks about the weather and her journey from Selbury almost abruptly, then came directly to the point with a sentence which quite jolted him.

'Mr Pinchbeck, I have good grounds to suppose that my brother Nicholas, who disappeared almost eighteen years ago, is living in Australia.'

It took a good deal to astonish Augustus Pinchbeck. He was clearly astonished now. He leaned across the desk to look at his client intently. 'You say you have "good grounds", Mrs Quade. May I enquire what they consist of?'

Imogen had always been able to fabricate the truth with complete conviction. On this occasion, however, she merely needed to conceal part of it to respond to his question. Before she had received that letter from her former governess, she would have found it impossible to answer without placing herself in a very bad light indeed. Annette Duval had played the part of a *deus ex machina*. She had provided the impetus she needed to renew her quest.

Now she stated calmly, 'About two weeks ago I received an extraordinary communication from my former governess, Miss Annette Duval.'

The name evoked a neatly labelled recollection in the lawyer's tidy mind. 'Duval . . . was she not dismissed for her negligence towards your brother, who was in her charge at the time of his disappearance?'

Imogen nodded. 'She wrote to let me know that she had come across a pair of photographs which might possibly be likenesses of Nicholas – she could not be sure.'

'And where did she obtain these photographs?'

'They were printed cards issued by the Barnardo Foundation to solicit donations from the public. Apparently she obtained them from Dr Barnardo himself, some years ago.'

Mr Pinchbeck's eyebrows rose. 'Some years ago? Then why, in heaven's name, did she not approach the family sooner?'

'Because, as she explained, she only examined two of the cards at that time. There was a whole batch of them, apparently – she had put them away, and came across them again just three weeks ago. She wrote to me at once.'

'Humph. How old was the boy in these photographs?'

'He looks about ten. If he is Nicholas, then he must in fact have been twelve at the time. But undernourishment –'

'Quite so. I take it you have brought with you both the photographs and the letter?'

Imogen produced an envelope and placed it in his hands. There was a pause while the solicitor absorbed the contents of the letter and scrutinized the photographs. 'Humph. A perfectly straightforward communication, I see. No suggestion of remuneration or further material being withheld.'

'No, indeed.' Imogen sounded almost indignant on Miss Duval's behalf. 'The obvious step to take was to examine the records at Barnardo's,' she went on. 'I dare say I should have left this in your hands, Mr Pinchbeck, but I felt impatient to proceed. I went to the home at Stepney two days ago, and copied out the particulars concerning this boy.' This time she handed Mr Pinchbeck a single sheet of paper.

At Stepney, a clerical assistant had shown her the album which contained the record of the former climbing-boy. *Nicholas Lockett* was inscribed above the particulars of his admittance. Imogen gasped as she recognized the surname. Lockett – that was the street where Dr Newbold had resided! Eagerly she had gazed at the two photographs attached to the record. They were a little blurred, less posed and artistic than those used for the cards. The second had been taken two years before Nicholas left the home; at fifteen, she thought he showed a resemblance to their father. The notes recorded the boy's rescue following near-suffocation in a chimney flue. He was described as diligent, with qualities of leadership. He had been a member of the Woodchopping Brigade, and had attained a good standard in the education provided by the home. At seventeen, he was sent with a work party to a Yorkshire farm, where he had met a visiting Australian sheep farmer, Robson by name. Soon afterwards he had left to work for this Mr Robson in New South Wales. Imogen had made a careful note of the address: Bealiba Station, via Callangarra Creek. What outlandish names! Some sheep farm in the middle of nowhere, she thought dismissively, far removed from all signs of civilization. Well, she would rescue Nicky from that fate.

Mr Pinchbeck read her copy of the notes with careful attention. When he looked up again, Imogen said quietly, 'We all assumed my brother must have drowned, even though no trace of him was ever found. But it seems he may in fact have been abducted and brought to London, then sold to a master sweep.' She lowered her eyes. 'I don't suppose it would be possible to discover the name of the master who bought him.'

'Unlikely,' the lawyer agreed. 'But who would have taken him away from Selbury?'

'There was a band of gypsies who used to set up camp there each year. Shortly before Nicholas's disappearance, I recall there was some trouble – one of the gypsy children stumbled on an old mantrap and died of blood poisoning. Perhaps my brother was abducted in revenge.'

'That is a possible assumption,' Mr Pinchbeck conceded cautiously. 'You must understand, Mrs Quade, that we shall need to verify everything you have told me. Not because we would doubt your word, but for your own protection. One cannot be too circumspect in such a case.' He cleared his throat. 'As it happens, I recall a similar occurrence . . . the son of a former duke of Westminster was abducted and sold to a master sweep in the early years of this century. He was discovered and safely returned to his family. In his case, however, only a few months had passed. The discovery of your brother inevitably raises many more questions and doubts.'

'I intend to travel to Australia to find my brother and bring him back to England,' Imogen said firmly. 'He must take up his inheritance.'

Mr Pinchbeck got up from his desk and took a few steps towards the fireplace. 'I would advise you not to be precipitate, Mrs Quade. Believe me, I well understand your anxiety to find your brother and see him installed at Selbury. But we should proceed with due caution. You must understand, dear lady, that there are unscrupulous persons in this wicked world of ours, only too eager too come forward to claim a name and fortune to which they have no right.' He swung round and returned to his desk. 'Have you heard of the Tichborne case?'

Imogen searched her memory. 'Oh – I believe so. It took place about ten years ago, did it not? I seem to recall some rogue came forward as claimant to the baronetcy –'

'An Australian rogue, Mrs Quade. Or, at least, a rogue, residing in Australia. One Arthur Orton, a butcher at a small township with the unlikely name of – ah – Wagga Wagga.' Mr Pinchbeck grasped the lapels of his morning coat. It seemed as though he were about to deliver a lecture. 'As you may remember, if you read the newspaper reports, Sir Roger Tichborne, quite a young man, was lost at sea, near Rio de Janeiro. Whereupon the baronetcy and estates passed to his younger brother. But the dowager Lady Tichborne refused to believe her son had died. She proceeded to advertise for him in the public press . . . a dangerous undertaking, in my opinion. Eventually she received a reply from Sydney, Australia. She was told that a man answering the description of her son was living in this – ah – Wagga Wagga. In due course, the man in question went to Paris to meet his supposed mother – and she, poor lady, acknowledged him as her son. However' – Mr Pinchbeck took a firmer grasp of his lapels – 'other members of the family contested the claim. There was a lengthy trial, the jury was convinced that Orton was an impostor, and he was sentenced to fourteen years' penal servitude on two counts of perjury.'

'That is very interesting, Mr Pinchbeck,' Imogen remarked. 'But surely, apart from the Australian connection, Sir Roger Tichborne's case has little in common with my brother's disappearance. I do not propose to advertise in the newspapers – I quite agree that might well invite some impostor to try his luck. I intend to travel to Mr Robson's property in New South Wales to meet this Nicholas Lockett for myself. Once I am convinced he is indeed my brother, I shall relinquish all claim to my inheritance of Selbury Quade.' She glanced at the lawyer demurely. 'I realize, of course, that due processes of law will be necessary to establish Nicholas's legal right.'

'Selbury, as you know, is entailed to the Wanslea family.' Tactfully Mr Pinchbeck refrained from mentioning the circumstances in which the entail would come into effect. 'If there were any doubt concerning your brother's identity, I suppose it is possible Mr Peter Wanslea might contest his claim –'

Imogen's chin went up. 'I am sure there will be no doubt.'

Mr Pinchbeck gave a thin smile. 'I can see you have quite made up your mind, Mrs Quade. Very well: but I insist on verifying the sources and facts you have apprised me of before you leave for Australia.' He paused, then said, 'You yourself stand to relinquish considerable wealth and property if this young man, Nicholas Lockett, is indeed proved to be your brother.'

Imogen spoke firmly. 'I may appear stubborn to you, Mr Pinchbeck, to be acting, perhaps, on what is sometimes referred to as "womanly intuition". So be it. All I know is that I must make this journey.' She did not add that she had yesterday visited the office of a steamship company and booked a passage to Sydney.

Finally the solicitor stood up and offered her his handclasp. 'I shall carry out my investigation before you sail. I wish you well in your endeavours, and I can only applaud your unselfish desire to see your brother restored to his inheritance.'

The household at Selbury was stunned to learn that their mistress was to make a journey to New South Wales. They could not understand why she should want to go so far away, all by herself. Australia! Knowing in fact nothing of that great continent, they thought only of convicts and recalled outlandish tales derived from gold-rush days, of bushrangers, shanty towns and wild blacks.

'If it don't beat all!' Violet declared one evening at supper in the servants' hall. 'Why should she want to go all that way when she could travel to her heart's content in Switzerland an' Italy and all them other places where gentlefolk take holidays?'

'Holidays?' a new young footman echoed scornfully. 'Why, their 'ole life's a bloomin' holiday.'

He found Mrs Arkney regarding him with marked disapproval from the head of the table. 'None of that radical talk here, if you please,' she admonished him. Whereupon he looked down at his plate of mutton with caper sauce and grew red about the ears.

'They say there's more sheep nor folk in Australia,' Violet remarked. 'I dare say folk eat mutton every day out there.'

Mrs Arkney had made it known that she intended to retire come Christmas this year. But Imogen prevailed upon her to remain at Selbury until her return in the new year. 'I shall feel reassured to know you are still here,' she told the housekeeper. And added, 'I particularly wish Selbury to be looking its very best when I return.'

Mrs Arkney found there was simply no refusing her. She pondered her mistress's words, sensing some mystery. For the life of her she could not imagine what it might be.

Imogen stayed firm to her original decision not to divulge her quest to anyone – save Mr Pinchbeck, of course. In her letter, Miss Duval had specifically stated that she anticipated no reply, and Imogen did not send one.

The week before Imogen left England, Hester Graham died. Imogen had not visited her after all, and when she heard the news she felt unusually grieved. Miss Graham had loved Nicky; now she would never learn of his discovery and restitution. She learned that Miss Graham had bequeathed her jewellery, which included some fine diamonds, 'to Imogen Quade, beloved daughter of my cousin and dearest friend, Louisa'. Imogen had the grace to doubt that she could ever bring herself to wear those jewels.

It was midwinter when Imogen Quade took ship from Tilbury, bound for Sydney, confident that when she returned she would be accompanied by her brother, Sir Nicholas Quade.

Chapter Nineteen

THE FORMAL GARDEN at Bealiba was modelled as closely as it could be, allowing for differences in soil and climate, upon an English model. But the illusion of an English lawn, complete with rose beds, lavender and wisteria-draped verandah, was dispelled as soon as one reached the low stone wall that bordered it. Beyond lay miles of sheep pasture, still green at this early season. Later it would be bleached and scorched by the fierce Australian sun. Vast paddocks dotted with gum trees stretched away into a distance that seemed infinite. This was no gentle Sussex, Somerset or Hampshire prospect, sheltered by oak, ash and elm; no misty, rugged Yorkshire landscape of moor and crag; it was a remote corner of southeastern New South Wales, three or four days' journey from Sydney.

The founder of the property, Thomas Robson, had come to Australia on leaving Oxford to try his luck on the goldfields of the fifties. He fully intended to return to England. Like so many others, he failed to find a golden fortune, but became so attached to this new country that, using the moderate fortune he already possessed, he took up land, settled on it, and built up his flocks of sheep. Bealiba, the name he chose for his sheep station, meant 'Red Gum-Tree Creek' in the native language. The first homestead at Bealiba was a slab hut, its logs notched together without a chink of light, the inside walls plastered with red soil mixed to a thick paste. But when Thomas's sweetheart sailed from England to become his wife, he built a big, sprawling one-storeyed house surrounded by a wide verandah. It was his English bride who had created the formal garden and furnished the rambling house with massive cedar pieces, a piano and pretty chintzes.

Bealiba, by now a prosperous and important property, had passed to Thomas's son, Arthur Robson. His wife, Alice, was Australian-born, yet faithful to the English tradition as her mother-in-law had been. Alice Robson always spoke of England as 'Home'. She kept the formal garden looking as English as possible, and reverently maintained the English-style interior of the homestead.

Alice Robson was a handsome woman with two daughters, Emily and Laura, aged nineteen and seventeen, for whom she held ambitious matrimonial aspirations. Slender, dark-haired Emily was the more beautiful of the sisters. But Laura, blue-eyed and fair-haired, was usually referred to as 'the pretty one'. Alice Robson was determined her daughters should marry the eldest sons of graziers with properties at least equal to her husband's. In her view, the men of substance who had pioneered their way to positions of affluence and influence on the land (usually with some capital to begin with) were the nearest you could come to an aristocracy within Australia. It was fitting, in her opinion, that such families should inter-marry and strengthen their positions.

Where Emily was concerned her mother held no qualms. Emily was all but betrothed to Athol Sutton, whose family held thousands of acres towards the Queensland border. But Laura ... that, unhappily, was a different matter. Laura seemed strangely uninterested in the eligible young men of the district. Instead, she clearly preferred the company of the young English jackeroo Arthur had brought back to Bealiba after his last trip home, over two years ago now. Laura had been just fifteen then; too late, her mother realized she should have done more to discourage the friendship from the very beginning. It had seemed harmless enough for the child to enjoy some brotherly companionship; alas, it now appeared the brotherly component of that friendship was fast disappearing. In fact, Alice Robson was very much afraid that Laura and Nick had discovered deeper feelings for one another. And that, of course, would never do. Nick was a pleasant enough lad – for an orphan of unknown parentage. A good-looking boy, with clean-cut features and a fair complexion, sunburned now by Australian weather. But he spoke quite roughly and no one had ever shown him how to handle a knife and fork in the proper manner. He was most certainly unsuitable as a romantic prospect for Miss Laura Robson of Bealiba Station.

Standing on the verandah this September day, Alice Robson found the pride and satisfaction she usually experienced as she surveyed her garden and the backdrop of her husband's sheep pastures were clouded by the sight of those two young people talking together beside the low stone wall. She heard Laura laugh at something Nick said, then saw him offer his hand to help her to her feet – for she had perched herself on top of the wall while he lounged against the sun-warmed stones. Surely, thought Alice, that handclasp was unnecessarily prolonged? Frowning, she descended the verandah steps and walked purposefully along the path towards them as they strolled towards her.

'Isn't it a perfect day, Mother!' Laura cried happily. 'Nick and I thought we might ride over to Quilter's Dam – Father has given him the day off.'

'But Laura,' her mother said, scarcely acknowledging Nick's polite 'good morning', 'I particularly wish you to be at luncheon when Mrs Sandison and Geoff drive over from Hurstmere.'

The Sandison cattle property marched with their own land. Geoffrey Sandison, the eldest son, had recently returned from a visit to New Zealand.

Laura's happy anticipation withered visibly. 'Oh, must I, Mother?'

'I hardly think a pleasant luncheon with the Sandisons is some sort of penance, Laura.'

'We can go riding another time, Laura,' Nick put in quickly, acutely sensitive to Mrs Robson's apparent displeasure. It was a heady sensation to be in love and to know that your feeling was reciprocated. What could possibly become of it, however, Nick had no idea. Meanwhile, it seemed imperative not to displease Mrs Robson any more than he evidently had already.

Laura pouted. 'Oh, very well. But Geoff Sandison is so boring! All he can talk about is two-tooth wethers and the like.' She trailed into the house after her mother, looking back once to send Nick a secret smile, while Alice Robson wondered grimly what fascinating topics of conversation Nick entertained her daughter with. Tales of the orphanage, no doubt!

Nick returned Laura's smile ruefully, then walked off towards the quarters he shared with two other jackeroos. He decided he would still ride off to the dam by himself. But half the enjoyment of his rare day of freedom had been snatched away. As he crossed that English lawn in the midst of the Australian landscape, once again he had the strangest feeling he had been here before . . . or somewhere very like it, with green turf, fat cushioned roses, the scent of lavender . . . and a gracious homestead behind him. As always, he shrugged off the elusive half-memory. He fell to wondering once again what could become of his love for Laura, and hers for him. It seemed to have grown so naturally, their affection, to have evolved quite simply from the immediate liking they had felt for each other when Mr Robson had pushed him forward that first day at Bealiba, saying, 'This is Nick Lockett, our new jackeroo, all the way from England. And this, young Nick, is my younger daughter, Laura.'

Laura had given him a shy, warm smile of welcome – unlike her sister Emily, who had merely nodded frostily. And from the very first, Nick had been aware that his employer's wife had not really welcomed his arrival at Bealiba. Mrs Robson's avowed admiration for England and all things English did not, it seemed, extend to members of the lower orders like himself. Now, he knew, she had come positively to resent his presence, the way he hovered uneasily on the edge of the family circle. Perhaps, for Laura's sake, he should quietly take his leave, go off to find work elsewhere. She was only seventeen; after a period of lovelorn despair, she would surely find her tender feelings aroused once more by someone else . . . someone more suitable. As for himself, he knew that he would never meet a sweeter girl. But was not the world filled with broken romances and disappointed loves?

He thought that Mrs Robson must have spoken to her husband about the relationship between Laura and himself; once or twice recently he had caught Arthur Robson looking at him in a puzzled, almost wary manner. It was one thing, Nick supposed, to make a generous gesture and bring a foundling boy to Bealiba; quite another to discover that his younger daughter harboured romantic feelings for that same foundling.

He plunged into a patch of uncleared bush beyond the cow sheds. Here the air held a sweet, peppery smell, the scent of golden wattle, now in glorious bloom. If only he could make a fortune, the way some men had done in those feverish gold-rush days! Although those days were past, with only the abandoned mine workings left like the fortifications of ancient battlefields, there were still nuggets of gold to be picked up. Every now and then you heard a tale of some lucky fellow who had stumbled over a pebble of gold lying above the ground. And yet – even if he were to stumble upon a fortune, would his chances of being accepted as Laura's suitor be any better?

Sometimes, Nicholas had a recurring nightmare. He was trapped in a dark tunnel, unable to move, almost suffocating. That tunnel was of course a chimney, the narrow flue where he had been trapped in the Newbold house. Waking drenched in sweat, gasping for breath, he would tear open the door and go outside. Perhaps it would still be night, with the brilliant stars of the southern sky pricking through the darkness; perhaps dawn, with a raucous chorus of kookaburras in the trees.

Then, to erase his dream memory, he would fill his lungs with deep breaths of the sweet, blessed air, as if he could never have his fill of it.

Often, these past months, he had wondered how Dr Newbold was and how his research was progressing. Letters took so long to come and go between England and Australia. It was over a year now since he had last heard from the doctor. He often wondered what would have happened to him if the Newbolds had not befriended him . . . and if the young doctor had not recalled a fellow student at the London Hospital whose idealism, zeal for social reform, and, especially, religious fervour far outstripped his own.

'Well, young Nicholas,' Marcus Newbold had told him one day, 'we have solved the question of what to do with you. I have had a word with my old friend Tom Barnardo, and he is willing to find a place for you in his Home for Destitute Boys. You'll learn a useful trade there and be able to make your own living by the time you leave.'

And so Nicholas had become one of Barnardo's boys, being registered in the records as 'Nicholas Lockett', his new surname derived from the street where the Newbolds lived. He had joined the Woodchopping Brigade. The Home owned Rhodeswell Wharf down at the docks, and chartered ships to import logs from Scandinavia. Here Nicholas learned to swing his axe joyfully in the open air, making up for all those years of creeping through darkness with cramped limbs.

He had been somewhat taken aback, a few days after his admittance, to be escorted to a photographer's studio by the doctor himself, where he posed for two studies. For the first, he was dressed in ragged clothes once more, liberally smeared with soot (to his great disgust) and handed a brush and scraper. For the second, he stood beside a log, his axe drawn back as if to strike a blow. Dr Barnardo told him the photographs would be used to help bring in funds for the home.

Nicholas had adapted well to community life and reached a high standard in his Sunday-school education. The doctor recommended him for the elite Messenger Boys' Brigade, to which the brightest boys belonged. They wore a smart uniform and ran errands from a central depot in the City. But Nicholas chose to stay with the Woodchoppers.

Marcus Newbold visited him occasionally and took him on outings, usually to one or other of the great London museums. Then, after he left London to pursue his medical research elsewhere, he maintained contact through kindly letters. Old Mrs Newbold had died quite soon after Nicholas entered Barnardo's; he still treasured the Bible she had given him.

The single experience Nicholas Lockett most enjoyed during his years at the home, however, took place towards the end of his time there, when he was sent for a month to a Yorkshire farm owned by one of Barnardo's rich patrons. At Skirlestone he took to farming life with great zest, and in his mind the seed of an ambition was sown: one day he would farm a place of his own. Mr Outhwaite, the gentleman farmer who owned Skirleston – as well as a large woollen mill in Bradford – had a visitor from Australia staying with him. And this was how Nicholas had met Arthur Robson of Bealiba Station. The Australian took a liking to the hard-working Barnardo's boy and talked to him about life in that distant colony. Nicholas confided to Mr Robson his ambition to become a farmer. One afternoon as they stood watching a Skirlestone sheepdog round up some lambs after a busy morning's crutching, Arthur Robson said casually, 'Have you ever thought about leaving England, Nick? Australia might offer you a better chance than this country, you know.'

'As a matter of fact I have begun to think about it, Mr Robson, since talking to you.' Nicholas gazed across the fields to where the high tops of the Pennines were hidden in mist, their lower slopes covered with purple heather and rusty bracken. It was hard to imagine that country half a world away with its eucalyptus trees, dry, dusty paddocks and near-impenetrable bush which must be cleared to provide grazing pasture or arable land. And the relentless sun beating down, with times of drought that dried the rivers in their beds and crazy-cracked the earth. Then, at other times, ceaseless rain that turned those same rivers into raging torrents and flooded the plains. Arthur Robson had vividly described the land of his birth. Such a country would surely present a great challenge. Maybe an orphan boy of unknown parentage would stand a better chance there.

Then the Australian had told him, 'There would be a place for you at Bealiba, Nick. You could come to us as a jackeroo, learn the way we do things out there. If you made good there might be a permanent position for you . . . what d'ye say, lad?'

'I – I would like to talk it over with the doctor,' Nicholas had replied. In fact, his instinct was to seize this chance with both hands.

'I return to New South Wales in two months' time,' Mr Robson told him. 'When I am in London I too will have a word with the good doctor. Think it over carefully, my boy.'

Returning to the home, Nicholas had learned that the notion of finding work for 'his boys' in other parts of the Empire was at the forefront of Barnardo's mind.

'Mr Robson is an honourable and godfearing man,' he told Nicholas. 'I would confidently entrust your immediate future into his hands. I have mentioned the plan to Dr Newbold – he, too, considers that this offer represents a fine opportunity for you.'

And so, in his eighteenth year, Nicholas Lockett had made the long journey to Australia. The sea voyage alone was a tremendous experience – Mr Robson booked a steerage passage for him in that grand old clipper ship, the *Great Britain*. And that was how his new life in Australia had begun.

Nicholas had come to love this land. He never for one moment regretted his decision to leave England. He would gaze into the distance with a sense of wonder that never seemed to lessen, amazed by the countryside that lost itself in such far horizons, the sky that was so high and blue. At the back of his mind lurked that old dream, to work a farm of his own. But that seemed as remote as his dream of marriage to Laura Robson. The days of cheap land here in Australia seemed to have gone for ever. There was in fact a current land boom; prices had never been so high. The great landowners – the squatters, as they were called – were continually increasing their holdings, and it was almost impossible for an ordinary man to come by a smallholding. Nicholas knew he need never want for work, but it seemed as though he was destined to earn wages all his life, never to be his own master.

Yet it was impossible to harbour gloomy thoughts on such a spring morning, and Nicholas shrugged them away as he went to saddle the mare Mr Robson had told him needed exercise. He would pick up some bread and cheese from the kitchen and spend a lazy day at Quilter's Dam – swimming, maybe, if the water was not too chill. He couldn't have gone swimming, stripped to the buff, if Laura had been with him. The idea would never have occurred to him. Nicholas had readily accepted the high moral and religious principles instilled by the masters at Barnardo's. He and Laura had exchanged only the chastest of kisses after they confessed their love for one another. Just to hold Laura's hand seemed sufficient joy.

And then another memory came to Nicholas, that of a summer's day on a muddy beach beside the Thames, when he and Polly, fully clothed, had paddled and splashed about in London's river. Dear Polly! There was something in Laura that reminded him of Polly – a kindness, the warm feeling that she would always think of him lovingly, without reservation. He smiled as he recalled how amazed they had been, he and Polly, to see each other washed clean of all those layers of soot. And how her hair had shone red-gold in the sun . . .

Until she boarded the SS *Kenilworth Castle*, Imogen Quade's notions of Australia were almost as ill-informed as those of her household at Selbury. At first she decided to ignore her fellow passengers, apostrophizing them for the most part as 'a bunch of colonials' – interspersed with a few tea planters and Indian Army officers bound for Colombo and Bombay. To most of the other first-class passengers, Mrs Quade seemed a slightly mysterious figure as she sat on deck in a steamer chair apart from their shipboard coteries.

But it was such a long journey that eventually Imogen grew tired of her own company. Her appearance at dinner at the captain's table became more frequent. There, she was agreeably surprised to find herself in the company of two quite charming and civilized Australian couples and a dignified older woman, the widow of a Victorian pastoralist. 'Pastoralist', Imogen deduced, was the elegant way to refer to a sheep farmer or squatter. Old Mrs Hilyard evidently kept up a country property of some grandeur, and Imogen began to wonder whether Mr Robson's Bealiba Station would in fact turn out to be the 'sheep farm in the middle of nowhere' she had envisaged.

Mr and Mrs Kenton were clearly leading members of Sydney society; they lived in a mansion overlooking the harbour, and spoke of the balls and parties they gave there, and the diversions of Sydney in general, in most sophisticated terms. The Ansteys belonged to Melbourne and appeared to lead an equally prosperous and cultivated style of life. Mere prosperity Imogen had anticipated – after all, Australia had proved itself the new El Dorado. She had equated that prosperity exclusively with vulgarity. Now she began to think she might have been somewhat mistaken.

Also at the table were a taciturn London financier to whom numerals evidently came more readily than words; a stiff and starchy young man called Algernon Chesney, going out to serve on the staff of the governor of New South Wales; and a Lady Fortescue, travelling as far as Ceylon with her faded, thirtyish daughter.

Imogen was amused by the good-natured rivalry between the Sydney-siders and the Melburnians that surfaced in the course of conversation.

'Of course, Mrs Quade,' Lydia Kenton assured her one evening, 'New South Wales is Australia's *first* colony, and Sydney her *oldest* city. If our six separate colonies ever unite, it would be only natural for Sydney to become the Australian capital.'

There was a well-bred exclamation of dissent from Ada

Anstey. 'Melbourne is in fact better located for that purpose, I dare say. And it has a more *varied* population.'

Imogen knew enough of Australia by now to realize that what Mrs Anstey meant by 'varied' was that Sydney, unlike Melbourne, had been founded as a convict settlement.

'Besides,' Ada Anstey continued, 'both Victoria and Melbourne are considerably more populous than New South Wales and Sydney.'

Reginald Anstey intervened at this point, smiling as the ladies' dignified argument got under way. 'You are on rather shaky ground there, my dear,' he told his wife. 'A few years ago, it is true, Victoria boasted some two hundred thousand more souls than New South Wales. And Melbourne topped Sydney by almost a hundred thousand. That was because of the gold rush, of course. But now the two cities are rapidly drawing equal. However, I believe Melbourne may be described as the business centre of Australia.'

Imogen noticed that the London financier silently assented to this opinion with a judicious nod.

'Well, at least we have our glorious harbour,' Mrs Kenton asserted smugly. 'No one could possible compare Sydney's setting unfavourably with that of Melbourne.'

'The river Yarra is most picturesque as it winds through our city,' Ada Anstey remarked demurely.

'I say, isn't there rather a problem about *drains* in Melbourne?' Algernon Chesney drawled. 'Some chap or other told me it is often known as *Smelbourne*.' He sniggered, but no one else smiled, not even the Kentons.

It was left to Frederick Kenton to play the part of diplomat. 'While we have been enjoying ourselves in the Old Country, I hear the railway line between New South Wales and Victoria has been connected. Perhaps that will help to bring home the fact that we belong to one country after all, in spite of border tariffs and separate governments – and our territorial pride!'

The handsome, exquisitely gowned Mrs Quade remained something of an enigma to her fellow passengers. No one could find out exactly why she was making the journey to New

South Wales; she was deft at deflecting questions, whether discreet or direct.

'She has a rather *sad* aura, I think,' Ada Anstey remarked to her husband in the privacy of their luxurious cabin. 'Perhaps she is involved in tragic circumstances . . . one of her family may be a ne'er-do-well, a remittance man. Perhaps she is travelling out to try to redeem him.'

'I take it you are intending to write a novel,' her husband remarked.

Ada Anstey smiled good-naturedly. 'The Quades are a very old family – Mr Chesney told me that Mrs Quade owns the most splendid place in the West Country. She does have quite an air, doesn't she? But she can be awfully aloof at times.'

Her husband grimaced as he fastened gold studs into his dress shirt. 'As a matter of fact, she's a damned attractive woman. A widow, I presume?'

'What can you mean, Reggie? Surely you are not suggesting she may be *divorced*?'

He shrugged. 'I would surmise she has an interesting history.'

'Well, I have noticed one or two of the unattached gentlemen aboard regarding her with marked attention – but she appears quite uninterested.' Ada Anstey looked at her reflection in the glass. She saw a pretty, fair-haired woman with candid eyes. She thought of Mrs Quade's slightly mysterious, hooded expression, and the way she could suddenly glance up with devastating effect. Ada attempted to emulate that gesture in the glass.

'Something in your eye, my dear?' Reggie Anstey enquired.

Ada laughed outright. 'Merely a mote,' she answered happily.

Lydia Kenton was planning to invite Mrs Quade to her house in Sydney; she, too, speculated about the enigmatic Englishwoman. 'What do you suppose?' she asked her husband as they walked arm in arm around the deck one morning. 'About her husband, I mean.'

Frederick Kenton hugged his wife's arm a little closer. 'Oh, she's quite a *femme fatale*, my dear. Intriguing, fascinating, all that; but finally, I think, somewhat pathetic. I would say that one could only feel some sympathy for her husband.'

'Have you discovered something?' Lydia glanced sideways at him.

'I was talking to one of those Indian Army chaps. He happened to mention that until recently, Mrs Quade was married to an army officer — in the British, not the Indian Army. Apparently they parted company.'

Lydia sighed. 'Well, I shall certainly invite her to our coming-home party. She is not divorced, after all. But I do so wonder why she is coming to Sydney.'

'If we possess our immortal souls in patience, my dear, we may in time find out.'

Imogen came nearest to confiding the reason for her journey to Mrs Hilyard. Seated next to her on deck one day, the old lady regaled Imogen with a graphic account of the recent capture of a bushranger at Glenrowan, a small Victorian township.

'When the rogue was sentenced, he said he feared death "as little as to drink a cup of tea". Now, of course, a popular saying has sprung up: "as game as Ned Kelly". The ordinary people, especially those of Irish origin, are on their way to making a folk hero of him.' Mrs Hilyard shook her white head. 'There is nothing in the least romantic or admirable about a bush-ranger, in my opinion. I recall too well the day one such gang came to our property and took our horses from the stables. We had spyholes set beside the main door of the homestead, and my husband took aim with his shotgun, but the ruffians got clear away. There is a good deal of lawlessness in our country, Mrs Quade. I'm told that gangs of larrikins run wild in Sydney. The "Pushes", they call themselves.'

Imogen listened patiently, then asked suddenly, 'Mrs Hilyard, I wonder if you know a family called Robson, in New South Wales?'

'Robson?' Mrs Hilyard frowned. 'Why, yes, the name seems familiar. Let me see ... there was a Judge Robson, and I believe another branch of the family went on the land. Why do you ask, Mrs Quade?' She looked at Imogen with shrewd, bright eyes.

'Oh, it is simply that I have an introduction to some people of that name,' Imogen replied smoothly, avoiding the older woman's gaze. 'They own a property called Bealiba in the southeast of New South Wales.'

'Never heard of it,' Mrs Hilyard said briskly. 'Not my part of the country. A big place, Australia, you know.' She was not deceived by Mrs Quade's seemingly casual enquiry. Such a very unforthcoming lady . . . it was the first hint she had given of any connection whatsoever with Australia. Well, the world was full of mysteries and puzzles. Let those who were younger and more curious unravel them. Of one thing Mrs Hilyard was quite certain: Mrs Quade was not a happy woman.

In Sydney, Imogen stayed at an opulent hotel, all marble and mahogany and heavy velvet curtains. There was even a telephone receiver installed within a little cubicle in the reception area downstairs. Whenever she passed by, there would be someone engaged in a loud, one-sided conversation, as though they must bridge a vast distance by raising their voice.

She had not anticipated the near-tropical atmosphere of the Sydney summer, the warm humidity, the lazy breezes from the harbour that swayed the palm trees. In the city centre, Sydney seemed bent on reproducing the solid, heavy buildings of London's business world, while the General Post Office resembled a temple erected to celebrate the marvels of modern science. There were attractive shopping arcades that provided respite from the overpowering sunshine, filled with goods imported from the four corners of the earth. Most of the city streets were named for rulers, governors and politicians: George and William, Bathurst and Darling, Pitt and Castlereagh . . . and, of course, Victoria.

Away from the central district, the houses of the established families and the *nouveaux riches* varied from pillared mansions

271

in classic style to turreted Gothic fantasies, all set in spacious grounds. And there were streets and streets of humble terraced houses, decked with iron-lace balconies, and primitive little iron-roofed cottages that must be unbearably hot. There were dreadful double-decker steam trams that clanked up and down the hilly roads emitting noisome vapours; most people, it seemed, sensibly preferred to use the horse omnibuses. The steam trams reminded Imogen of that noisy steam car Daniel had driven. Occasionally she spared a thought for him, and wondered how he fared in the wilds of Afghanistan. How comfortably far away he was, she reflected. She recalled the Indian Army officers on the voyage out, their hard drinking, their gambling, their phrases compounded of Indian and English words intermingled, the practical jokes they enjoyed inflicting upon each other. Theirs was the world Daniel had escaped into, a man's world where he would feel at home.

Imogen most definitely did not feel at home in Sydney; she had the disturbing sensation of being an alien here. She knew she could never belong to this city with its dramatic harbour, its oppressive climate and confusing inhabitants whom she felt unable to place in any clear-cut social order.

Soon after her arrival she attended the party the Kentons gave to celebrate their homecoming.

'And what brings you to New South Wales, Mrs Quade?' a genial gentleman with muttonchop whiskers asked her as the guests dispersed onto the terrace of that splendid harbourside mansion after dinner. Chinese lanterns shone above displays of gardenias; below, the sea lapped at a private landing stage.

Since arriving in Sydney, Imogen had devised a routine answer to that question. 'I am here on a business matter, Mr O'Shaunessy,' she said. Every second surname here seemed to be Irish, she reflected. 'I shall be travelling into the country for a while, and returning to England quite soon afterwards.'

Such was the tenor of her reply that even Michael O'Shaunessy, one of Sydney's leading barristers, did not feel he could press her further. Perhaps, he thought, she was here to invest in land.

Imogen had given a good deal of thought to the question of how she was to reach Bealiba. She had discovered the sheep station lay some hundreds of miles from Sydney, and though the train would take her a good part of the way, there would still be eighty-odd miles left to travel. The logistics perplexed her.

Then, 'I should like you to meet one of our dearest friends, Mrs Quade,' Lydia Kenton said; and Imogen found herself in the company of a sensible countrywoman with a deplorably weathered complexion, who might well have been a member of the hunting set at home. As they sipped coffee together, Amelia Sutton nodded in a matter-of-fact manner when Imogen mentioned the Robsons and Bealiba Station.

'You might call Alice and Arthur Robson our nearest neighbours,' she said. 'It's just possible for us to visit and get home the same day — so long as we drive at a spanking pace.'

Imogen hung on her words with flattering interest.

'As it happens,' Mrs Sutton went on, 'Athol, my eldest son, is about to become engaged to the eldest Robson girl, Emily.' She smiled fondly. 'Athol entrusted me with a little commission for a George Street jeweller — and now I am carrying this about with me, just in case. There are some queer characters in Sydney, you know.'

She produced a little leather box embossed in gold from her beaded purse, and opened it to reveal a half-loop of sapphires and diamonds. 'Miss Robson will soon be wearing this ring,' Mrs Sutton said proudly.

Imogen was quite taken aback by the size and splendour of the stones. Lydia Kenton, she recalled, had mentioned that the Suttons owned a large cattle property. Mrs Sutton appeared well pleased by her son's forthcoming engagement. Presumably that meant the Robsons were equally prosperous. Imogen's notion of an isolated sheep farm quite removed from all signs of civilization finally vanished from her mind.

Then she heard Mrs Sutton say, 'Poor Alice Robson has had a difficult time with her younger daughter, Laura. The silly child had a crush on one of their jackeroos, some youth that

Arthur brought back with him after a trip home a few years back. A nice enough lad, but quite without means of any sort, and no family whatsoever. He was brought up in an orphanage, in fact. Imagine!'

Imogen gave a sharp intake of breath. 'How – how old is Laura?' she asked carefully.

'Seventeen. A nice, pretty girl and quite naive. Not one of your sophisticated city girls.'

'And – were her feelings for this – this jackeroo reciprocated?'

'Yes. That was what made the whole thing so difficult for poor Alice. A romance going on beneath her very eyes. It seemed the boy was too useful to get rid of – it's almost impossible to get hold of reliable help these days. I believe Arthur had it in mind to train him up for a manager's job.' She paused. 'In the end they packed Laura off to Melbourne to stay with Alice's sister for a few months. She's an artistic little thing and is taking painting lessons. That was the excuse for her going – but of course we all knew the real reason.'

Imogen asked indelicately, because she needed to know, 'She is not – expecting a child, I suppose?'

'Good heavens, no! Both the girls are very well brought up. No question of that, I assure you. The whole affair was pure romance.'

'A poignant little tale,' Imogen commented lightly.

She decided to cultivate Mrs Sutton, and succeeded so well that within a week, as Amelia Sutton herself ingenuously observed, she felt she had known Mrs Quade 'for ever'. They had even proceeded to first-name terms. Duncan Sutton was in Sydney to visit his banker, his stockbroker and his lawyer, which left his wife free to take Imogen for carriage drives by day. They visited some of the harbour beaches; at Coogee, Imogen cast a wistful gaze at the bathing-machines, with their shark-proof enclosures, but it was clear that dips in the sea did not enter into Amelia Sutton's notions of enjoyment in Sydney. One evening, Imogen accompanied the Suttons to the Theatre Royal, where Sarah Bernhardt was playing in *La Dame aux*

Camélias. Afterwards, she asked them back to her hotel for a champagne supper. It was at this point that Amelia Sutton invited Imogen to return with them the following week to their property, Ningoola.

'We shall certainly be visiting Bealiba one day,' she said. 'Athol is eagerly awaiting our return.'

Duncan Sutton, a tall, sandy-coloured man of few words, endorsed his wife's invitation. He was not sure whether he actually liked this Englishwoman or not – Imogen, as he was supposed to call her. But she and Amelia seemed to have struck up a flourishing acquaintance, and that was good enough for him.

And so it was arranged: Imogen would return with the Suttons to Ningoola, going by train to the nearest railway halt, whence they would complete the journey by carriage.

At Bealiba, some two weeks later, an undercurrent of excitement and anticipation prevailed. This was to be Emily's special day. That was quite understood. The Suttons were arriving in time for luncheon, bringing with them an English house guest, a Mrs Quade, whom they had met in Sydney. The whole party would be staying overnight; guest rooms had been prepared with smooth white coverlets, linen towels, cakes of rose-scented soap. In her note sent the previous week, Amelia Sutton had underlined her statement that Athol would also be accompanying them. Alice Robson had already drafted in her mind the engagement notice for the Sydney and Melbourne newspapers. There were no cut flowers for the house in this hot season, but she had Tilda, the little Aboriginal house-girl, bring pots of greenery from the fern house to decorate the dining room for the celebration luncheon or dinner ... whenever it was that Athol would make his proposal. She rather hoped it would be before luncheon, otherwise the atmosphere would be quite tense, with everyone awaiting the event.

Emily was cool and demure in hailstone muslin, wearing pearls her English grandmother had bequeathed her. Alice looked at her approvingly. She only wished Laura could have been with them. It was, after all, quite a momentous family occasion. But the dear child was not due home until March. Alice's sister had written that her niece still appeared somewhat subdued, but was studying hard at the Collins Street studio she attended. Poor little Laura, her mother thought. It had been quite a wrench, sending her off to Melbourne – but what else was there to do? She was quite a talented little artist; the idea of attending the painting classes held genuine appeal for her. As for young Nick – surely, by now, he must realize the hopelessness of his feelings for Laura. It was a great bore that Arthur apparently considered the lad indispensable to the welfare of Bealiba; much better if he had gone right away, out of their lives for ever. She was satisfied that the two young people were not secretly corresponding with each other. Laura had sent Nick two or three postcards, that was all; views of Collins Street, the cathedral, the banks of the Yarra River, with brief messages scrawled on the back for everyone to see.

But now, from the verandah, Alice discerned a dust cloud along the avenue of she-oaks that marked the approach to the homestead. A moment later that fast but rather dangerous high-wheeled gig which Duncan Sutton had imported from America came into sight, driven by Athol. His father was perched beside him, and on the seat behind were two female figures swathed in dust-coats and veils. Together, Alice, her husband and Emily went out across the lawn to greet their visitors.

Descending with some relief from Duncan Sutton's perilous equipage (she had been sure it would overturn on more than one occasion), Imogen looked about her curiously. So this was Bealiba Station. She was aware of an almost queasy sensation . . . here, at last, she would meet Nicholas; here all her careful plans would reach their conclusion.

Bealiba homestead, she saw, was quite similar to the Sutton place; not quite as impressive as Ningoola, perhaps, but certainly a substantial property. Her room, whither she was beckoned by a barefooted, dark-skinned girl wearing a clean cotton dress and apron, lay along a corridor lined with heavy cedar furniture. It opened onto a wide verandah; Imogen stood by the french window, gazing out at Alice Robson's sundrenched reproduction of an English garden. It must, she thought, take a prodigious amount of watering to keep the lawn so green.

Hearing someone approach along the corridor, then a knock at the door of her room, which still stood open, she turned to see the tall figure of a man on the threshold. He was holding her portmanteau. Imogen's eyes needed to adjust to the dim interior of the room; it was several seconds before she realized that she was looking at her brother.

'*Nicholas.*' She spoke his name involuntarily – she, who so seldom in all her life had allowed herself to act upon impulse. This was not the way she had imagined their meeting . . . she had planned to bide her time, observe, draw conclusions, come to a careful decision before she made the momentous revelation of his true identity. Such cautious intent was thrown aside the moment she saw him standing there. For it was her father who stood looking at her . . . her father as a young man. It was all those generations of Quade forebears, the family likeness passed from century to century and faithfully reproduced in the portraits that hung in the long gallery at Selbury.

'Nicholas,' she repeated, gazing at him with an intensity which clearly he found embarrassing. 'What I am about to say will cause you astonishment – perhaps shock. You may not believe it to begin with, but I shall convince you of the truth.' She paused and then her voice shook a little as she said, 'I am your sister. My name is Imogen Quade, and I have come from England especially to find you.'

Within an hour of the Suttons' arrival at Bealiba, Athol had proposed to Emily, who led him into the fern house for the event. The dark-green spears of fishbone ferns and graceful arcs of parlour palms provided an effective background to her white muslin dress as she accepted his proposal and allowed him to slip the diamond and sapphire ring upon her finger, then to embrace her. A short while later, champagne which had already been brought up from the cellar was poured into crystal flutes, and the young couple were toasted by the two families assembled in the drawing room. The fact that this engagement had been a foregone conclusion did not mean that the congratulations and good wishes were any less heartfelt.

Then suddenly – 'Oh, heavens above!' Amelia Sutton exclaimed. 'What with everything happening so quickly, we have clean forgotten Imogen . . . Mrs Quade. Where is she?'

'Perhaps she has dozed off in her room,' Athol Sutton suggested. 'I don't suppose she is used to rushing about the countryside the way we are.' He lounged easily on the sofa, one arm around Emily's slim waist.

Alice Robson rose from her chair. 'I shall go along to her room myself.' At the door she turned to smile at the assembled family. 'If she has been waiting all this time to be called, I dare say she will consider us real uncouth colonials!' She started along the corridor – then froze in astonishment as she saw that English gentlewoman, mistress of some splendid ancestral home in Somerset, as Amelia Sutton had informed her, walking towards her with her hand resting upon Nick Lockett's arm.

Years later, Emily Sutton was to tell her daughters, 'That wretched Mrs Quade almost spoiled the day your father and I became engaged. She quite stole our thunder.'

And indeed Emily and Athol found themselves relegated to the background of that day as Imogen calmly announced the astounding news that Nick Lockett, the orphan from Barnardo's Home for Destitute Boys, was in fact her own long-lost brother . . . Nicholas Quade, baronet, with an ancient house and estate in Somerset, and a family fortune to match. They all sat listening, silent save for the occasional exclamation of amazement as Mrs Quade related the strange history of her brother's abduction.

Finally she turned to Amelia Sutton and said quite charmingly, 'You must forgive me for not divulging my secret. When we met in Sydney, and you invited me to stay with you – and then, when I discovered you knew the Robsons so well . . . it seemed a sheer act of Providence.'

And Amelia Sutton smiled in a bemused fashion, quite forgetting that she had spoken of the Robsons the very first time she had met Imogen Quade.

Finally, Imogen announced that she and 'Nicky', as she called her brother, would travel back to England very soon, so that his claim and inheritance might be legally established without delay.

And all this time, Nicholas himself stood stiffly behind his sister, in a state of utter shock, trying to absorb everything she had told him during their hour-long talk together in her room, everything she was saying now . . . It was not only the sudden new identity she had bestowed upon him; it was all those other things he had learned about or realized as she spoke. He must ask her to relate everything again, slowly and carefully.

Everything . . . the story of the gypsy whose own son was caught in a mantrap . . . the tragedy of Marcus Newbold's death . . . It was far too much to take in at once. But it was all true, there could be no doubt of that. He really was Nicholas Quade, with a title to his name, and this self-assured English lady with her amazing flow of words was his sister. Imogen. Imogen . . . an echo floated down the years, became detached from oblivion and surfaced in his mind. *Midgin*. That was a name he used to know! Midgin . . . Imogen . . . it was the way a little child might try to say her name.

At dinner, Mrs Robson insisted he should take his place at the gleaming cedar table. He felt awkward and out of place, not knowing which fork, spoon and glass to use. They kept on calling him 'Nick', as they had always done, then correcting themselves and saying 'Nicholas' instead. It was quite funny, really. And there was Emily, who had always been so high and mighty where he was concerned, sitting opposite, fingering her sparkling new ring and actually smiling at him.

Then Mrs Robson said, 'How I wish Laura were here with us!' And that was the point at which Nicholas seemed to come to his senses, to revive from shock. Because – hadn't they sent Laura away on his account? He had not been good enough for her. Yet now – now that they knew who he really was, they wished that she was here. But he was just the same person, wasn't he? It was only his circumstances that had changed . . . those vital, important details: a big house in England, a fortune, a title to his name. Sir Nicholas Quade. (He could not resist a grin as he thought of the other jackeroos' astonishment when they heard about that.) Well, he did not care what Mrs Robson, or anyone at this table, thought of him. But Laura herself – that was a different matter altogether. What would she think of all this? Would it make a difference to her feelings for him? He had missed her very much during the past few months. There had been only those silly postcards. Yet that was what they had agreed. 'We can't write to each other, Nick,' she'd said. 'It would be too difficult – they'd find out for sure. It would only make things worse. Just remember that I shall be thinking of you all the time.'

And he had thought of her – not all the time, no one could do that – but every day, certainly. Now he looked across the table at Imogen . . . his sister. She had said they would go back to England very soon. He had to see Laura again before they left. He would insist on that.

'You must see Laura before you leave for England, Nicholas.' How extraordinary: Mrs Robson was echoing his own thought. Now she turned to Imogen. 'Perhaps when your ship puts into Melbourne, Mrs Quade, you would have time to visit my sister. My daughter Laura is staying with her, attending art classes in Melbourne. She and Nicholas are such good friends.'

Amelia Sutton exchanged a brief, somewhat incredulous glance with her husband. Imogen inclined her head. 'It may be possible,' she said coolly. And then she thought, why not? After all, Nicky would never return to Australia. Why should he not take a tender farewell of his little sweetheart before they sailed back to the place where he belonged?

They spent a few days at Bealiba, after which Imogen and Nicholas were to return with the Suttons, then travel on to Sydney. It was well understood there should be as little delay as possible in establishing Nicholas's claim.

During those few days, an incident occurred which Nicholas was to remember years later, when he received the news of Imogen's death. They went riding together, as far as the edge of some cleared land, where a group of eucalypts stood like survivors of a massacre. One had fallen; its trunk lay on the ground. Another, taller than the rest, was hollowed out. Imogen and Nicholas dismounted and sat down to rest upon the fallen log. Then Nicholas made a sudden grab into the air, and a second later opened his hand to show Imogen what lay inside it: a little native bee. To his amazement, she turned pale and her eyes grew fearful.

'It's only a bee,' he said. 'Quite harmless.'

'Only a bee!' she echoed, backing away. 'I have been stung twice by a bee, Nicky. Each time I nearly died.'

'But these are stingless bees,' he assured her. 'They couldn't hurt anyone. We call then "sugarbags" – they build their nests in hollow trees like that old fellow over there. The Aborigines will capture one and stick a tiny feather to it, then watch to see where it flies. That shows them where the nest is, and they climb up to take the honey.'

But Imogen was not reassured. 'Please kill it, Nicky.'

'I don't like killing things,' he told her; and opening his hand he watched it fly away.

The discovery of Nicholas Quade was a seven days' wonder, reported in every Australian newspaper, in England, even in America. To inherit a fortune, a great residence, a place in the hierarchy of the English class system . . . that was not only an archetypal colonial dream, it was a universal fantasy. To be transported from poverty to wealth, from obscurity to a position of respect and power, all in one delirious instant! Nicholas Quade had achieved all this.

While they waited to take ship in Sydney, Imogen and

Nicholas were besieged by invitations to parties and balls . . . and by begging letters from opportunists as well as unfortunates who had fallen on hard times. But they did not linger long enough to sample the social delights, nor to respond to those who hoped for handouts. Imogen secured early passages to England, then occupied her time outfitting her brother for the voyage home. Discreetly she refrained from comment on such details as his table manners . . . she was confident that, given time, he would naturally adjust to his new way of life.

She telegraphed Mr Pinchbeck: NICHOLAS FOUND STOP NO DOUBT WHATEVER OF IDENTITY STOP RETURNING ENGLAND IMMEDIATELY. As a consequence, it was not such a shock as it might have been when the solicitor opened *The Times* one morning to see a column headed DISCOVERY OF MISSING HEIR, and read that newspaper's sober account of the affair. But – no doubt whatever of identity? Cautiously Mr Pinchbeck reserved his judgment and awaited the return of Mrs Quade and her supposed brother with some trepidation.

Imogen telegraphed her agent at Selbury as well: SIR NICHOLAS QUADE DISCOVERED IN AUSTRALIA STOP RETURNING HOME IMMEDIATELY STOP INFORM STAFF. The receipt of this message sent the household at Selbury into a frenzy of anticipation. Sir Nicholas alive and returning to take up his inheritance! Mrs Quade was a dark horse and no mistake . . . going off to Australia to find him without dropping a single hint. A master instead of a mistress at Selbury once more. Mrs Arkney was glad now that she had stayed on, that she would witness this miraculous return. She recalled how Mrs Quade had said she wished Selbury to be looking its very best when she came back. Now they all knew the reason. Violet felt as though she were taking part in a real-life romance. 'I just can't wait till he gets here,' she declared. 'Oh lor', I just can't wait to see him!'

There was someone else who eagerly awaited Nicholas's reappearance, who had never ceased to mourn the little boy who had vanished from her life one day – Jessie, his former nursemaid. She read the newspaper report aloud to her husband and sons, marvelling at the details it contained. ' "Stolen by a gypsy" – poor little mite! "Worked as a climbing-boy" – well, I never. "Rescued by Dr Barnardo and sent to Australia as a farm labourer" – why, 'tes more than happens to most folk in a lifetime.' She felt that a secret part of her mind was unlocked at last, set free to revive memories she had suppressed all these years: a baby asleep in the high cot in the night nursery; a fair-haired infant taking his first tottering steps towards her; a sturdy little boy playing on the lawn. Then Jessie spared a thought for the governess, Miss Duval, who had left Selbury in such disgrace. She wondered again what had happened to her, and whether she would learn of Nicholas's return. 'I'd like to be able to tell her about it, that I would,' she told her husband. 'For I dare say she's fretted sorely on it all this time.'

Annette was visiting America, staying in a Philadelphia hotel, when she learned the news. The return of a lost heir to a British title and stately home was an item which could not fail to titillate the democratic readers of the Philadelphia *Courier*. The bold headline, MISSING ARISTOCRAT FOUND IN AUSTRA-LIA, caught her eye as the newspaper lay on her breakfast tray. She scanned it idly as she poured her coffee – then suddenly clutched the paper more closely as the name Nicholas Quade leaped out at her. Quickly she devoured the facts, then leaned back against her pillows. So Imogen had followed up her letter and succeeded in discovering his whereabouts. And now he would return to Selbury at last. So many years had gone by . . . She recalled all the sorrow, the trauma, the heartache of his disappearance, and was aware that a dark shadow had finally lifted from her mind. And it seemed to her that the part she had played in his discovery must expiate whatever guilt she carried for his disappearance. Quite suddenly, she began to cry. She was racked with sobs; joyful tears of inexpressible relief trickled down her face.

Later that day, before her appointment at Wanamaker's

store, where she was to complete details of their exclusive retailing of her range of products, she found time to send a postcard to England. It bore a photograph of the famous Liberty Bell, and on the back she wrote one sentence: 'Utterly delighted to learn news of Nicky – A.' It was addressed to Edwin Moulvey.

It occurred to Annette that this wonderful news was like a happy omen for her future. Tomorrow she was returning to New York, where a certain manufacturing pharmacist awaited her response to his offer to take over production of her cosmetics on a much larger scale. She found that offer tempting; she had reached a point where her business had to expand if she were to achieve greater success. And she wanted to go ahead with new ideas . . . including a long-cherished dream to create a perfume. She had just about decided to accept John Brownlee's offer, provided she herself would still be able to take a significant part in the business.

It would, of course, mean living in America. Well, she was quite prepared to settle in this exciting land, which seemed to offer unlimited opportunities. She would live in New York, which seemed to her the crucible of opportunity, excitement and new ideas. John Brownlee was a vigorous, successful, yet strangely idealistic man in his late forties. He maintained that real success might only be achieved by offering the public a first-rate product. In some respects he reminded Annette of John Barker. Like Mr Barker, he had recognized her products as first-rate, and was keen to make them available to a much larger market. Annette had met him several times in New York; she found herself looking forward to seeing him again with a feeling that went beyond the business in hand. He had made it clear he was unattached, a widower; she had an inkling his interest in her extended beyond taking over her business. How pleasant, she thought, to form a partnership based on mutual respect and endeavour. What romantic dreams she might have woven around that prospect in her youth! Now she was content to go to New York and await whatever Fate – or Providence – might hold for her.

There were flowers from the Robsons and the Suttons in Imogen Quade's cabin when the *Lisbon Castle* sailed out of Sydney harbour. Imogen herself decided to stay on board when the ship called at Melbourne, but Nicky, with unconcealed eagerness, took a cab to visit Laura at her aunt's Italianate mansion in East Melbourne, close by the Fitzroy Gardens.

Alice Robson's sister left the two young people to spend the day together; it was a joyful yet rather desperate reunion, overshadowed by Nicky's imminent departure. As for Laura, she could not help feeling a little awed by the events that had overtaken him.

'But, Laura, I'm just the same person I was before,' he told her as they sat in a little teashop towards the end of their day. 'Nothing has changed – I'm still *me*. Not Nick Lockett any longer, but what's in a name?' He reached across the chequered tablecloth for her hand and held it tightly. 'I feel just the same way about you as I did before. I love you, Laura.'

'Oh, Nick, I love you too. But what will happen to us? I'm so afraid that once you get to England, you will begin to forget me. It will be such a different sort of world. There will be so many new people in your life –'

'Then you can't have much faith in me, Laura,' he told her quietly. 'Look – I don't know what will happen once I reach England, whether I shall want to stay there or come back here –'

'Come back! To Australia? Surely you won't do that.'

'Who knows? At any rate, whatever happens, I shall never stop loving you, Laura. I shan't forget you, never fear!' He gazed at her solemnly. 'Would – would you come to England if I asked you?'

Suddenly the anxiety faded from her eyes and she gave a radiant smile. 'You know I would. As a matter of fact, Mother is already talking about the possibility of a trip Home. Oh, Nick, it's so – so shaming, the way she behaved towards you before, and how quick she has been to change her attitude

– towards both of us – once she learned who you really are.'

Nicholas gave a short laugh and shrugged philosophically. It was a gesture reminiscent of his father. 'I dare say your mother thought she was doing the right thing before – protecting you from an unsuitable alliance. And now – well, I suppose she considers she is doing the right thing again. Even if it does amount to a sort of contradiction.' He shook his head. 'I may be young, but I've met a lot of different people in my life, and I've been treated in all sorts of different ways. There are only three people I have really respected, I think . . . apart from you.' He paused. 'One was Dr Marcus Newbold, God rest his soul. Another was Thomas Barnardo. I owe him such a lot.'

'And the third?' Laura asked curiously.

'The third was my dear Polly. I've told you about her. It's really thanks to those three that I managed to survive at all.'

'And what about your sister – Imogen? She went to all that trouble to find you –'

'Yes, I know.' Nicholas hesitated. 'Somehow – I'm not at ease with Imogen. I daresay I shall get over that in time, but . . .' He frowned. 'I don't really understand the way she thinks. She was married, you know, for just a few years. But she doesn't talk about her husband, ever. I can't help wondering what happened. I know she went to great lengths to find me, and that she's giving away a great deal that for a long time she has thought of as hers. My inheritance, I mean. But somehow, I feel that she isn't doing it for me, but for some other reason. It may sound strange, but I don't know whether she even likes me. I have the feeling that she's – what can I say – making me dance to her wishes. As though I were a sort of puppet on a string. Everything that's happened in the last few weeks has been entirely arranged by Imogen . . . she even tells me what clothes to wear.'

Laura giggled. 'That's because she is determined to turn you into the image of an English gentleman, no doubt!' Then she went on more soberly: 'I haven't met your sister, Nicky, so I cannot express an opinion. But if you really feel you are a – a puppet, then you must snap the string and become your own person.'

'I will, don't worry!' he told her with a smile. 'I have managed to survive worse things than a domineering sister, don't forget.'

Their day ended all too soon; in a little while it was time for Nicholas to return to Port Melbourne and the *Lisbon Castle*. Imogen had expressed no wish to meet Laura, so he did not suggest that she come to see them off.

As Laura went back to her aunt's house she could not help wondering whether she would ever see him again, in spite of his reassuring words, their vow to write often to each other, and the farewell kisses they exchanged.

It was some time before Daniel MacMahon heard the news. When he came down on leave from the desolate ranges of the Hindu Kush, where he had been keeping watch over the enemies of the Queen Empress, a brother officer in the mess at Rawalpindi handed him a six-month-old newspaper cutting. He scanned it quickly, then crumpled the little piece of newsprint into a ball and tossed it into a spittoon without comment. But one sentence stayed in his mind as he ordered a bearer to bring him Irish whiskey. 'Sir Nicholas Quade's sister travelled halfway across the world to find him.' Did she, indeed? Daniel MacMahon's thoughts were unfathomable as he steadily began to empty the whiskey bottle. His brother officer was appalled by the expression on his face . . . it seemed clear MacMahon was about to embark on one of his notorious drinking bouts.

Chapter Twenty

'BUT NICKY, THIS is too exasperating. What do you mean, you won't be riding to hounds? I ordered your hunting pink especially – I know the Master expects you to turn out. Father always hunted, before he became too ill –'

Nicholas ignored the reference to a father he had scarcely known. 'I did not ask you to order any hunting gear, Imogen. I have no intention of chasing some wretched fox to a gory death. It's a cruel game, in my opinion. I enjoy a hard ride across country as much as anyone, but not to see some wild creature torn to pieces at the end of it.' He shook his head. 'Some idiot even imported foxes to Australia, just so that he and his friends could hound them to death. It wasn't long before they became another pest, like the rabbit.'

'So now they have to kill them.'

'We used to shoot them – a good clean death.'

Brother and sister were in the library at Selbury. It was the hour before dinner. Imogen carefully put down her sherry glass and acknowledged defeat with a petulant shrug. 'As you please, then. I shall explain to the Master.'

'Oh, I can explain for myself.' Nicholas frowned. These days, he and Imogen seemed to cross each other at every turn. But he had to make a stand, otherwise he really would do nothing but – what was it he had said to Laura – dance to her wishes. Something like that. And what had Laura said? 'You must snap the string.'

Imogen looked across at him and thought how right it seemed that he should be sitting there, in her father's wing chair. He wore the velvet smoking jacket which she had chosen for him at Gieves. She realized with satisfaction that he seemed to be rapidly absorbing the sort of manners that belonged to the people he mingled with these days. But she did not care for the rebellious attitude he was beginning to show towards a number of her plans for him.

In the beginning it had all seemed so perfect. Everything had happened just as she desired. Immediately after their arrival in England, they had stayed in London and kept several appointments with Mr Pinchbeck. That cautious man of law had pronounced himself entirely satisfied with their interviews. There could be no doubt that 'Nicholas Lockett' was indeed Imogen Quade's brother. Their last interview had coincided with one of the rare days when the venerable Mr Pinchbeck senior, who used to look after the affairs of Selbury in the old days, visited the chambers. As if to clinch the matter finally, he had shuffled into his son's office and, seeing Nicholas, hailed him as 'Oswald, my dear chap', prompted by a threadbare memory spanning almost seventy years.

Then, after a visit which Nicholas had insisted on making to Barnardo's home in Stepney, there had been the triumphant return to Selbury . . . and his gratifying gasp of admiration as the carriage rounded that bend in the long drive which revealed the house in its perfection of mellowed, honey-coloured stone, against green lawns and tall, ancient timber. The staff had assembled to greet them inside the great hall, the menservants bowing respectfully, the maids bobbing curtseys as the master of Selbury came home.

During the weeks that followed, Nicholas had thoroughly explored the house and estate and absorbed Imogen's educative accounts of family matters, beginning with the legend of Dame Margery, whose portrait greeted him each time he entered by the main door. He could scarcely avoid noticing the curious likeness between his sister and their ancestress. Every now and then, a vague, fleeting memory of time and place would come to his mind. The dusty, disused schoolroom, for example, seemed to conjure up early struggles to decipher letters and form rounded pothooks ... yet he could not tell whether this was something he truly recalled, or whether it was prompted by Imogen. 'This is where you did your first lessons, Nicky,' she told him.

In front of the house lay that green lawn he had seemed to recollect so often at Bealiba. Jessie, the buxom, kindly woman who had once been his nursemaid, it seemed, recalled the games of tag they used to play there, with two little dogs running around them.

Nicholas would venture only a few steps into Dame Margery's famous maze, recoiling from those narrow green passages which reminded him of his recurring nightmare. One afternoon he stood beside the lake, thinking, This is where the gypsy must have snatched me away. But he could not really remember what had happened. It was too long ago. He had been so little. And so much had happened to him since.

There were others who remembered him, strangers in his eyes: the old rector at St Michael's, who chuckled when they met and remarked it was just as well Sir Oswald had declined to install a memorial to his son; the Kittos, the old couple at the lodge, the first of the staff to greet him as the carriage rolled through the gates of Selbury on the day of his return; a retired head groom who talked about the Shetland pony he had ridden; and the comfortable cook, Mrs Robbins, who told him how he had come into her kitchen to stir the Christmas pudding and nibble at freshly baked jam tartlets.

Once, as he strolled on the lawn with Imogen, another recollection stirred dimly in his mind. 'Was there not a swing somewhere?' he asked. 'Hung from a great tree?'

Imogen's glance went involuntarily to the shrubbery at the

end of the lawn, but she said, 'There was no swing here, Nicky. Perhaps you recall one from somewhere else.'

He sat with Mrs Arkney in her sitting room one afternoon, rocking gently in a chair with a patchwork cushion as he told her about his life as a climbing-boy.

'Oh, Master Nicky – I mean, Sir Nicholas – if only we'd found you long ago!' she exclaimed.

Nicholas found it difficult to accept the business of being respectfully saluted by doffed cap and title wherever he went in the estate or village. 'I just can't get used to it,' he told Imogen.

She compressed her lips. 'It is the way things are done here – you will become accustomed to it.'

'It is not the way things are done in Australia.'

'England is not Australia.'

That was only too true. Nicholas had forgotten how the grey skies of England lay so leadenly and low over the landscape. Blue skies and fluffy white clouds seemed to last for so short a time. He had forgotten the depressing days of incessant rain that made the English grass so wonderfully green. And he felt restricted and hemmed in when he compared the little patchwork fields of Somerset, bordered by hedges and dry-stone walls, with the wide, unfettered acres that surrounded Bealiba.

Imogen arranged dinner parties, even a summer ball at Selbury that year to celebrate Nicholas's return. It was a chance for him to meet some of her aristocratic acquaintances and the county gentry. Quite soon, she thought, she would begin to look around for a girl of suitable family . . . Nicholas should marry before too long. She decided they should spend next season at the London house.

She invited their uncle, Edwin Moulvey, to Selbury for the ball. When he met his nephew again, she saw him wipe a tear from the corner of his eye. Uncle Edwin had always been a sentimental fellow . . . he was the first man she saw cry, she remembered. He brought his camera, and photographed Nicky on the terrace, the master of Selbury. Imogen put the print in a silver frame and placed it on a table in the drawing room, next to the miniature of Laetitia Quade, whose gentle spirit had once reached out to her, and been rejected.

There were long sessions with the Selbury agent, to acquaint Nicholas with the running of the estate. He did his best to demonstrate the interest so clearly expected of him. But in spite of his best efforts, in spite of all those painted ancestors in the long gallery whose names he now knew by heart, in spite of tenants and labourers and household servants who readily and warmly accepted him . . . in spite of everything, Nicholas Quade felt alien to his inheritance. It was not only his undeniable yearning for Australia . . . it was every experience of his hard youth that made it so difficult to accept this new way of life.

Gradually, inevitably it seemed, a new scheme for his future began to form in his mind. He said nothing of it to Imogen, knowing too well what her reaction would be. She had gone to such lengths to find him . . . she might well hurl accusations of ingratitude and irresponsibility at his head if she knew the tenor of his half-formulated plans.

In London, Augustus Pinchbeck had apprised him of the situation concerning Selbury and his cousin, Peter Wanslea. One day Nicholas decided to visit the Wansleas in Gloucester-shire. This created further difficulty with Imogen.

'Why should you want to see them?' she demanded in a hostile manner. 'They are nothing to us. It was bad enough when Daniel —' She bit her lip and left the sentence unfinished.

This was practically the only time Nicholas had heard her mention her husband's name. He would not be deflected from his intention to meet the Wansleas and spent a week with them, enjoying the relaxed atmosphere of their home and romping with their young son and daughter. Imogen did not enquire after their cousins when he returned. He found her attitude extraordinary. For his part, he did not tell her that Peter and Vera Wanslea had spoken of Daniel MacMahon in such friendly terms that he wondered anew about his sister's marriage.

It was the letters that brought things to a head between brother and sister. Nicholas had certainly kept his side of the loving vow made when he and Laura parted that day in Melbourne. He sent long and affectionate letters to Bealiba. And, after a suitable interval to allow for the long sea voyage, he began to look eagerly for letters with an Australian postmark, letters that would have crossed his own on the high seas. Gradually his eagerness declined into anxiety. No letters came from Laura. It was difficult to keep on writing when he received no response. Her silence puzzled and depressed him; he even went through a stage of feeling angry, resentful that she had not kept her vow.

One morning, he mentioned Laura's neglect to Imogen. They took breakfast together every day. Today, as usual, there was no missive from Australia among the letters brought to the table.

'I can't understand it,' he said moodily. 'She should have kept her promise.'

Imogen paused in the act of slitting an envelope with her paper knife. 'She is very young, Nicky. It is difficult for a young girl to realize what such a long separation really means. You are so far away . . . I daresay she has found a number of distractions at Bealiba. Her sister's marriage will be taking place quite soon, as I recollect. One marriage often gives rise to another . . . the happy excitement, all those preparations. A younger daughter often becomes engaged hard on the heels of her elder sister.'

'That is not very comforting, I must say,' Nicholas remarked bitterly.

'Nicky, dear, I only mention it for your own good. Surely your little romance with Laura Robson was just a charming flirtation? The sort of tender feeling many young people experience.' She looked with satisfaction at the embossed card she had drawn from its envelope. 'Ah, this is an invitation to a ball at Saltonbury – the Murrays' place. You remember the Murrays, I expect. They have a rather pretty daughter, Selina.'

'Oh yes,' Nicholas muttered uninterestedly. It was true, Selina Murray was pretty . . . but she was not Laura.

About this time, Nicholas began to take long tramps by himself. He would stride through Foxhollow wood, or perhaps take the field path to Selbury village, engrossed in his own thoughts. He was trying to reach a definite decision about his

293

future. He visited London again and paid another visit to Dr Barnardo. When he returned to Selbury, he felt happier in his mind than he had done for months. Soon afterwards he went to see Mr Pinchbeck, and then arranged to meet Peter Wanslea again. The lawyer furnished him with sound advice, and Peter Wanslea lent a sympathetic and understanding ear to what he had to say.

Imogen followed these comings and goings with a resigned air. Nicky was being rather mysterious, but she did not feel she could interfere. He seemed extraordinarily purposeful of late. Perhaps, she thought, he was making some arrangements to support Dr Barnardo's work. He had told her he would like to provide a cottage at the Village Home for Destitute Girls, in memory of some little waif or other he had once known. Well, he could easily afford to indulge such a whim.

Then, one morning, Imogen did not appear at breakfast. She had succumbed to a feverish cold and lay cocooned in bed, too miserable to care about anything for the moment. Nicholas breakfasted alone. As usual, there was no longed-for letter among the day's post. Afterwards, he went straight to the stables to saddle up for a ride. It was midday when he returned. He came into the library, went over to the massive desk to continue the lists he was busy compiling – and there, propped against the inkstand, was a pale-grey envelope, addressed to him in Laura's sloping hand. A letter from Australia at last! The footman must have overlooked it this morning, he supposed. He felt his heart beat faster as he reached out for it. So Laura had not forgotten him after all.

Eagerly he tore open the envelope and scanned the first sheet of paper . . . then paused in astonishment, frowning as he tried to understand:

'. . . at least six letters, and I have only received one short note from you,' he read.

Why have you not written, dearest? Are you ill? Have you perhaps [here her pen had wavered on its downward stroke] met someone else in England? I implore you to let me know the reason for your silence. I would rather know the worst, hear bad or disappointing news, than not hear from you at all. Please, please answer this. If you do not, then I shall never feel able to write to you again. I shall realize you did not care to let me know that your feelings towards me had changed, that circumstances unknown to me had altered them. I love you always –

Your Laura.'

This eloquent, despairing plea struck Nicholas with horror. She *had* written! Six letters – what had happened to them? Could they have miscarried? One, perhaps – but surely not all six. He went over to the fireplace and tugged the bell. After an interval one of the footmen appeared.

'Edward – this letter.' Nicholas held out the envelope. 'Do you know how it came to be here?'

'Why, I always put those Australian letters on your desk, Sir Nicholas, don't I. Mrs Quade's orders. She told me months ago to be sure to bring any letter with an Australian postmark straight here, so that you could read it in private. But you must know that, Sir Nicholas – Mrs Quade told me it was your wish –'

'I see.' Nicholas's voice was grim.

After the footman retired he sank into a chair, letting the full implication of Imogen's action sink into his mind. She knew he usually went straight out for a walk or ride after breakfast. So why ask for the letters to be placed here? The answer seemed only too plain. Imogen had used this device to withhold Laura's letters from him. She herself must come into the library each day to see if there was an envelope upon the desk. What had she done with those six letters? He had known she vaguely disapproved of his feelings for Laura – but it was appalling to realize she would really attempt to disrupt the relationship between them. And then he realized the corollary to this nasty business. His letters to Laura! She said she had received only one short note from him. That must have been the brief page he wrote as soon as he arrived in England. He recalled slipping it into a London pillar box. But none of his other letters had arrived, it seemed. Again, the reason seemed only too clear. At Selbury, letters for the post were left on a table in the great hall, to be collected each day by the postman when he made his delivery. It would have been very easy for Imogen to remove those letters addressed to Bealiba.

His instinct was to rush upstairs, confront Imogen immediately, demand the letters from her. But she was unwell; he would have to wait. In any case, she had probably destroyed them. Meanwhile, he could at least take action to repair the damage. He rang the bell again. 'The carriage, Edward. I shall be leaving for London. I believe there is an afternoon train from Yeovil.'

Three days later, Imogen felt sufficiently recovered to go downstairs after taking luncheon in her room. She met Violet coming along the bedroom corridor with a pile of clean linen.

'Do you know where Sir Nicholas is?' she asked her.

'Oh, he's just back from his trip to Lunnon, ma'am. He'll be that pleased to see you up and about, I expect.'

Nicholas stood at the bottom of the staircase, looking up at his sister as she came down to the hall. She looked pale; her pallor, he thought, emphasized her resemblance to the proud Elizabethan in the portrait behind her. It occurred to Nicholas then how truly alike these two women were: Dame Margery, their scheming ancestress – and Imogen, his scheming sister.

She put her hand on his sleeve as she reached the bottom stair. 'Nicky – you look rather done in. I hope you're not coming down with my wretched cold. Violet told me you had been to London again. Why did you go?'

'To telegraph Bealiba. To reassure my Laura. To let her know I love her.' He paused. 'I intend to marry Laura Robson, Imogen.'

Imogen raised a hand to her mouth as he took a letter from his pocket and held it out for her to see. 'This came from her the day you took ill – the only one of her letters that ever reached me. Where are the others, Imogen? And where are my letters to her?'

'Why, Nicky, you must try to understand.' Imogen spoke calmly, but suddenly she felt a little frightened of this tall young man, her brother, who stood before her like an accusing stranger.

'I understand more than you imagine. Where are the letters?'

'I – I destroyed them.' Imogen raised her head defiantly. 'It was for your own good. Laura Robson is simply not the right girl for you – to become mistress of Selbury. She comes from such a different background. You should marry an English girl, Nicky, someone used to the sort of life we know here –'

Nicholas clenched his hands, crumpling that one precious letter in his anger. 'I have had enough of your actions designed for my own good, Imogen. That is why I have been busy arranging my future for myself.' Containing his rage, he added more quietly, 'I think we had better continue our talk in the library.'

He stood aside to let her pass before him into the book-lined room. He felt no need, now, to break his news gently. 'I shall not be staying here,' he told her abruptly, standing beside the desk. He picked up a folder of papers. 'This contains the arrangements I have been making.'

Dismay and incredulity crossed Imogen's face. She sat down suddenly in a chair, as though her legs would no longer support her. 'What do you mean? Not stay at Selbury? But this is your place!' Her voice rose. 'Where else would you go?'

'I shall not be staying at Selbury, nor in England. I intend to return to New South Wales.'

'Go back to Australia? You cannot! If it is for Laura's sake –'

'Laura has a great deal to do with my decision, but that is far from being the whole reason for it. Oh, I can hardly expect you to understand. You, of all people. I – I feel imprisoned here. I was in Australia for just a few years, but I felt *that* was my place, where I belonged. I felt – free, released. I felt that my life was my own.'

Imogen's head was bent. When she raised it, Nicholas recoiled from her expression. Her eyes glittered, her mouth was drawn in a grim line. Perhaps, he thought, she was still feverish. 'This is a fine way to show your gratitude for everything I have done for you,' she told him vehemently.

He shook his head. His voice was harsh as he answered her.

'Not for me, Imogen. For yourself. And because of your – your peculiar attachment to Selbury. It is a lovely place, I grant you, and you must believe me when I say that its history, the history of our family, is far from meaningless to me. But you have allowed yourself to become obsessed – yes, that is the word: obsessed – by a pile of stone, a row of portraits on a wall. You seem to have thrown away your real-life chances of contentment. I do not know much about your marriage to Daniel MacMahon, and I dare say it is none of my business. Peter Wanslea tells me he seemed a pleasant fellow, but he and Vera sensed you were not happy together. I suppose you wanted children, an heir for Selbury –'

Imogen sat very still. At last she said slowly, 'I could never bear a child.' The bleak statement fell between them, slicing into their argument.

There was a brief silence. To Nicholas, it was as though the missing piece of a puzzle had been handed to him. 'I see,' he said quietly. 'That explains everything, I think. That was the reason you began to search for me. The true reason. Not for my sake, but as a substitute for the child you could not have. Because there must be an heir in the direct line for your beloved Selbury. Otherwise, of course, it would revert to Peter Wanslea –'

Imogen closed her eyes for a moment.

'– and you could not bear to think of that. And your first inkling that I might still be alive – so you say – came when Miss Duval sent you those Barnardo photographs.'

Imogen frowned. 'Do you doubt that? How could –'

He interrupted her. 'Listen, Imogen. I will tell you about an experience I had in London, yesterday. I decided to spend the night at the town house –'

'But it is all shut up!'

Nicholas smiled wryly. 'I have slept in worse conditions, I assure you. I obtained the key when I went to see Mr Pinchbeck.'

'You went to see him again?'

Nicholas nodded. 'Since I was in London, it seemed a good

opportunity to call in to sign some final documents.' He tapped the folder he held.

Imogen looked away, avoiding his gaze, then rose and walked over to a window. Then she turned towards him; he could not see her face clearly because her back was to the light.

He went on, 'I entered the house and went into the morning room. The furniture was covered in dustsheets, and there was a little fall of soot in the hearth. I daresay the chimney needs cleaning. I am sure that Manny Oliphant would be pleased to oblige.'

Imogen started at the mention of that name.

'Then, as I stood there,' Nicholas continued, 'a sudden flash of memory came back to me. I knew that I had been in that room before – as a little climbing-boy who had just come down the chimney. It was quite vivid – I almost heard voices in the hall outside . . . a little dog barking . . . and the dog's warm tongue rasping my sooty face. And then I seemed to hear someone telling me to leave go of the dog, scolding me because I had covered it in soot . . . I recalled quite clearly how I dared not look up – I saw only the hem of a lady's skirts.' Nicholas passed one hand across his forehead. 'I am sure it was *your* voice I heard, Imogen. Sam Oliphant must have been called to the house to sweep the chimneys that day . . .'

A little silence fell. Then Imogen said in an odd, almost mocking voice, 'And you think it likely I recognized that sooty little boy as my brother?'

'I cannot say. I think it very likely, however, that the little dog recognized me and came running. Jessie has told me how the dogs spent all their time with me. Angus . . . and Flora.'

'You are suspicious of me, Nicky.'

'There is something else. Something which puzzles Mr Pinchbeck as well as myself. Apparently, when his clerk went to check the records at Stepney, he got into conversation with Dr Barnardo. The doctor has an exceptional memory; he recalled that Marcus Newbold had mentioned the name of the master sweep who released me to him. Samuel Oliphant. The clerk managed to trace Oliphant's address and paid a visit to the house. Sam Oliphant is dead, it seems, and Manny runs his business now, but he spoke to his widow. She told him a lady had been to see her several weeks beforehand, and had asked the same questions about a certain climbing-boy.' He paused. 'That lady was you, Imogen, was it not? But you did not tell Mr Pinchbeck of that visit. And what neither he nor I can understand is why you should have gone there, how you would have known . . . Seemingly you only learned about Sam Oliphant from me, after I was found. Yet your visit to Mrs Oliphant was made weeks before you received the letter from Miss Duval.'

Imogen said tonelessly, 'And if all this is true – if your suspicions are correct – what then?'

'Why then – I cannot tell quite what to think. Except that if you did recognize me that day at Leighton Square and said nothing, keeping your knowledge to yourself, it must have been because you wanted so very much to keep Selbury and all that goes with it.' He added, 'I realize how hard it must have been for you to relinquish your inheritance to a younger brother.'

'Do you?' Imogen asked bitterly. 'Well, you are really very clever, little brother, to have worked out this puzzle. And what do you expect to gain from me now?'

'I expect nothing. I only know that I could never trust you again. Nor live beside you.'

'Well, you need have no worry on that score. After all, you are going to Australia.' Her voice was harsh. 'What else do you propose to tell me about your plans? That you have given Selbury away to that evangelical do-gooder, Dr Barnardo? So that he can turn the place into a home for little guttersnipes?'

Her rank words shocked him. 'Of course not. Selbury is your home, Imogen. It is all you have. I realize that very clearly. I have no intention of asking you to leave it. You must remain here for the rest of your life. That is what you want, I think. What you have always wanted.'

'And . . . when I die. What will happen to Selbury then?'

Nicholas shrugged. 'Who can tell? If my plans turn out as I

hope, I shall be well and truly established in New South Wales. Assuming I outlive you, I should not want a place like this in England as well as a property in Australia. I could not possibly look after both. I suppose I might approach the Wansleas to see if they . . .' Suddenly his voice took on a lighter tone. 'But I positively refuse to think about that now. Years and years lie ahead. You never know – I might have a son who will decide to return to England and live here when he inherits.'

When Imogen next spoke her voice sounded almost normal. 'I am more disappointed than I can say about your decision to go to Australia. I had so hoped that you would stay here – that I should see your children at Selbury –'

'– and know the previous Quade inheritance was secure.' He could not resist completing the sentence for her. 'Well, you did your best – or worst – to ensure they would not be Laura's children.' He shook his head. 'I have made my decision. The whole business is in Mr Pinchbeck's hands. I have arranged for funds to be transferred. As soon as I return to New South Wales I intend to look for land. I doubt if I will ever come here again.'

'If that is what you want I can do nothing to prevent you. I shall look after Selbury well, you may rely on that. Even if in the end . . .' Her voice died away. It was the end of their communication with one another.

During the few weeks that Nicholas remained in England, somehow they managed to maintain the semblance of a sibling relationship. In reality there was an unbridgeable gap between them.

Sir Nicholas Quade's departure for Australia was in marked contrast to his much heralded homecoming. There were no newspaper reports with dramatic headlines; an anti-climax is never newsworthy. Nicholas had arranged with Dr Barnardo that once he had found his land, four boys should travel out to work on his property. And the day before he left England, an anonymous cheque was received at Stepney, to provide a new cottage for the Village Home.

Pale narcissi, yellow jonquil, heliotrope and hyacinth, violets and orange blossom . . . mimosa, fragile tuberoses. It was a scented paradise, with the blue sky of southern France above and the little rocky bays of the Mediterranean coastline below the grey-green olive groves that clothed the gentle slopes. The Brownlees, designated by so many of their friends in New York City as 'the ideal couple', were visiting Grasse, that village of precious essences in the Alpes Maritimes. Ever since their marriage eight years ago, they had promised each other they would come here. It was part idyllic holiday, part business quest. Annette still dreamed of adding a perfume to their range of beauty products, a unique fragrance that would win for itself a special place in the world. Now she hoped that dream was about to become reality.

They had spent a few days in Paris, where they felt impelled to ascend the famous Eiffel Tower, newly completed.

'A thousand feet into the sky!' Annette had exclaimed as they viewed the city from that dizzy height. 'It's much prettier than the Tacoma Building, don't you think?' She clutched her husband's arm as she peered downwards. 'What was that word some journalist coined to describe the Chicago building – "skyscraper"!'

They took photographs with one of the new Kodak cameras you could hold in your hand. The days of the tripod were over at last. All you had to do was to insert rolls of film and send them away to be developed. Annette recalled how Edwin had once yearned to take pictures on the spur of the moment. Well, now there was a new word for that, too: 'snapshots'.

After Paris the Brownlees had come south to stay with the Morrissiers at their villa near Cannes. It was from the Villa Mimosa they made their pilgrimage to Grasse, to discover the processes that produced those precious flower essences, and discuss which blend of scents their own perfume should contain.

'Nothing too sweet or heavy,' Annette decreed. 'Simply a heavenly fragrance that every woman would love to wear.'

Each evening they dined on the terrace of the villa,

overlooking a moonlit sea. Annette and Lilian revived memories and gossiped about their neighbours, while Jean-Paul and John Brownlee speculated about the state of the modern world.

'I caught a glimpse of Prince Edouard yesterday, when I went down to Cannes,' Lilian remarked on one such evening. 'He had a new lady upon his arm and was smoking his eternal cheroot.'

'May *le bon Dieu* take pity on the Prince of Wales,' Jean-Paul responded. 'Why does his august mama not abdicate and allow him to gain the throne of England?'

'Surely you realize that Queen Victoria is immortal,' Annette teased him. She smiled across the table at her husband. It was good to see him relaxing here, away from the bustle of New York. Perhaps, she thought, it would be a good idea to look for a villa of their own in this idyllic spot.

'And how did you progress today with your search for the perfect *parfum*?' Jean-Paul asked.

'Oh, we've been shown the whole process now, from A to Z,' John Brownlee told him. 'From *enfleurage* and *maceration* to blending the *absolutes* and fixation of the final product. We know it all. And today we chose the chief tones for our scent –'

'Attar of roses with a touch of jasmine and clove, blended with musk and a hint of myrrh,' Annette went on. 'And the suggestion of one or two other ingredients,' she added mysteriously. 'We have to keep our formula a secret, you know.'

'Quite right,' Jean-Paul remarked approvingly. 'The formula for my *apéritif* is locked in here.' He struck his chest with such force that he emitted a doglike bark.

Llilian turned to Annette. 'It all sounds marvellous, *superbe*.'

Annette laughed. 'That is exactly what you said when I first told you about my complexion cream, all those years ago at Deauville, while the rain poured down outside. By the way, I never told you this. Do you recall that it was Marie Danton, the actress, who gave me the recipe for my cream?'

'I believe I do.' Lilian nodded. 'And both Jean-Paul and I advised you to forget how you had come by it.'

'I did not exactly follow your advice,' Annette confessed. 'When the product first proved its success, I felt I simply had to contact her. I sent a note and asked her to meet me. She couldn't have been nicer about it. When I told her that I felt I owed my success to her, she said she realized that was so, and proposed that I pay her a just reward.'

Lilian shook her head, while Jean-Paul waited apprehensively for Annette to continue. How like a woman to make such a mistake in her business affairs! But John Brownlee smiled quietly; he knew the story by heart.

'She asked me to arrange a permanent supply for her own use. That was all! And I have, ever since – she has received jars and jars of Duval's Nurturing Complexion Cream.'

Lilian looked relieved. 'I thought we were to hear some frightful tale of extortion. Well, I shall expect only one bottle of *parfum* from you, darling. Quite a large one, however.'

John Brownlee reached for his wine glass. 'I am intrigued, I must confess,' he said, 'to discover that besides the essences of exquisite flowers, the extracts used to fix these delightful fragrances derive from animal parts I dare not mention. Except, that is, for ambergris. And that, they tell me, is the waste product of a sperm whale suffering indigestion as a result of swallowing too many cuttlefish!'

Amid the laughter that followed, Lilian sniffed unappreciatively. 'I don't really care to hear such things. I prefer to imagine those beautiful scents are composed of nothing but flower petals.'

'We have to think of a name for our creation,' Annette said.

'Why do you not call it' – Lilian paused dramatically – 'Roses of the South, after that divine waltz we used to dance to when we were young?'

Annette shook her head. 'Much too long, Lilian. It has to fit on a tiny label.'

'Your *parfum* will give every woman a sense of beauty, of confidence,' Jean-Paul declared with Gallic fervour. 'Such a woman may achieve anything she may desire. Why do you not call it – *Femme Fatale*?'

'That strikes me as rather good,' John Brownlees commented.

'We have a great many customers of very conservative views, my dear,' Annette reminded him, smiling. 'Don't you think the middle-aged matrons who shop at Wanamaker's or Marshall Field's or Macy's might consider it a little – *risqué* to have that label on their dressing tables?'

'Their husbands might appreciate it,' John Brownlees responded. 'But I guess you have a point. Let's go for something simple. How about –' he glanced along the moonlit terrace, permeated with the heady scent of jasmine – 'Enchantment?'

'And in French – the same word – *Enchantement*,' Lilian exclaimed delightedly. 'It is good, just right.' She raised her glass. 'To *Enchantement*!'

A bumblebee flew in zigzag path across the law at Selbury. It was early summer, with blossoms in abundance for that diligent gatherer of nectar. It hovered above a flowering cherry tree, then set a course towards the lilacs below the terrace. Presently it took off again, heavy with plunder, and by mischance entered through the open door that led into the great hall. Bewildered, perhaps, by the sudden lack of sunshine, it flew above the staircase, and for a moment alighted on Dame Margery's portrait, crawling over the ivory-coloured fingers, narrow as fan sticks, that touched a painted parchment. Then it flew away once more, to come to rest at last among the carved oak leaves of a newel post.

For seven years, Imogen Quade had lived alone in that great house, served by a staff of obedient servants. She was over forty now. Gradually she had grown reclusive. She still saw a few people from the neighbourhood and kept up her church attendance as a matter of form, but she was beginning to be considered slightly eccentric. She had never been easy in her relationships, people reminded one another. A beauty in her day, but spoiled and wayward since girlhood.

The house was kept in perfect order, and Imogen saw that the Selbury agent sent regular reports of the estate to New South Wales. The property Nicholas had built up there had prospered, it seemed. He had named it Selbury Park. Imogen knew that he and Laura had four children, two sons and two daughters. At Christmas they exchanged formal greetings; apart from that, brother and sister remained out of touch.

It seemed to Imogen, brooding in her loneliness, that fate had played with her cruelly. All her brave designs had come to nothing. And she herself had been left with less than nothing. Though she still lived at Selbury, where she belonged, Selbury did not belong to her. And when she died . . . what might happen to this beloved place did not bear thinking of.

She walked slowly towards the house, carrying a few roses for the vase in her small writing room. These days, she hardly ever used the library and the desk where her father had so often sat at his papers. Lacking an everyday companion, she had taken to talking to herself. It had become her custom to greet Dame Margery's portrait each time she entered the house, almost as though she spoke to a woman of flesh and blood. Now she entered by the open door, crossed the great hall and paused at the foot of the staircase. She looked up at that arrogant painted face with its compelling gaze.

'The damask roses are in full bloom,' she said aloud. 'And the turf has grown over the bare patch of ground beside the elm tree . . .'

She rested the dark red roses upon one of the newel posts for a moment. She did not notice the insect that crawled out from among the carved oak leaves. Attracted by the scent of roses, the bee crawled onto a leafy stem. A moment later, her hand closed over the stems; the bee was trapped beneath her fingers. The painted face above her, with its unalterable expression, looked out unseeingly as Imogen Quade collapsed on the first wide stair, the poison from the sting spreading rapidly along her arm. The roses she had gathered lay scattered on the floor like a pool of blood.

Envoy

THE SIGHTSEEING COACH, filled with assorted tourists, was about to set off from Yeovil high street. Around the corner raced a young woman clutching a travel bag in either hand. She wore faded jeans and a cotton T-shirt decorated with a zany impression of the Sydney Harbour Bridge. Skidding to a stop beside the door of the coach, she climbed on board.

'You are going to Selbury Quade, aren't you?' she asked the driver breathlessly.

'That's right, miss. Half-day trip to one of Somerset's historic homes. Two pounds includes bus fare, entrance fee and guided tour.'

The girl rummaged in a wallet and drew out a few notes, peering at them dubiously. She selected two and held them out. 'There you go – I think that's right.'

'Right as rain. Just arrived in the old country, have you?' He glanced at her T-shirt. 'Not hard to tell where you come from.'

'I got in this morning.'

'Strewth, y'ain't wasting any time with the sightseeing, that's for sure.'

The other passengers watched as Midge Quade made her way to a spare seat. A middle-aged woman wearing an incongruous lolly-pink tracksuit nudged her husband. 'She's Australian.'

'How d'you know?'

'Call it woman's instinct,' she replied with heavy humour.

Her husband, a mild-looking man, craned his neck to look up the aisle. 'Why's she bringing luggage? You don't need luggage for a half-day trip.'

'Search me.'

Midge collapsed thankfully into her seat. She seemed to have been racing against time ever since the Qantas jet touched down early that morning. It was imperative she should reach Selbury by two o'clock; she'd promised faithfully she would be watching Emma play her semi-final at Wimbledon. No hope of getting a ticket actually to be there – and you had to line up all night for the unreserved seats, they said. Emma had found a place for Peter in the competitors' stand. But not for Midge. 'Sorry, just not possible,' she'd said on the phone. It was only what Midge had expected. Peter was even mentioned in the newspaper reports:

> Emma Sutton's boyfriend, Peter Quade, will be at Wimbledon tomorrow to give support to this rising young Australian tennis star as she faces the number one seed, last year's women's singles champion . . .

Midge's own romantic interlude with Peter Quade, their English cousin, had ended abruptly once he met Emma, who had asked if she might 'borrow' him to escort her to a woolshed dance. That was two years ago, during Peter's visit to New South Wales. 'You don't mind?' Emma had asked. And Midge had answered in her straightforward way, 'Of course not. He's not my property.' Well, Peter well and truly belonged to Emma now.

At the airport Midge had raced to the Underground and found her way to Paddington, where she caught the train for

Yeovil. She reached Yeovil only to find that she had missed the local bus she was supposed to catch. Infuriating to have come so far only to lose out on the last lap. She had promised her family she wouldn't hitch-hike – and there was no way she could afford a taxi. This visit to England was a break between the end of her course at agricultural college and joining her father on the property. She had saved up for it for ages out of the money she earned organizing the Selbury Park riding holidays for kids. She couldn't expect her parents to pay for the trip; she was only too well aware how difficult it was to keep up the property these days. And she knew the family at Selbury Quade were far too busy to come and collect her. 'It's opening week for the tourist season and we shall all be flat-out,' Cousin Letty had written. It was Letty who had provided the careful instructions for the journey from Heathrow, ending with the local bus that passed by Selbury.

Seeing Midge's downcast look, the woman at the information counter at the bus depot had said, 'There's a tour that goes to Selbury Quade – you might catch that if you hurry.'

And she had. It was lucky she had only the minimum of luggage with her, she thought. Now she looked out of the coach window eagerly as it moved off. She was here at last! In England – in Somerset – and soon she would see Selbury Quade.

Once clear of the town and its outskirts they travelled along a six-lane freeway, and eventually branched off at a point where Midge saw a sign that read, SELBURY 8 MILES.

And here they were. The coach slowed down to enter a pair of wrought-iron gates beside an old-world lodge overgrown with virginia creeper. A young man was working in the garden; he gave a friendly wave as they passed by. Midge recalled Letty telling her the lodge was rented by a young potter. Down a long winding drive they went, with tall English trees in full summer foliage on either side. Then suddenly . . . Midge gasped aloud as the next bend revealed the house itself, lovelier and more picturesque than she had ever imagined it. She had seen photos, of course – Letty had brought a whole swag of them when she came to Australia last year. But this was the real thing.

The coach drew up with a swirl of gravel before the main entrance, which faced a beautifully kept lawn. No problems with watering here, Midge thought. She followed everyone else off the coach. A young Japanese couple were already focusing their cameras on the house, and the pink-suited woman was wondering where the toilets were.

The driver recited a well-worn litany: 'Proceed through the main door, ladies and gents, where you will receive your entrance tickets. The toilets are situated in the stable block, madam, beside the gift shop and snack bar.'

Hefting her two bags, Midge went into the great hall. She had the strangest sensation that she was coming *home*. She looked to see if it was Aunt Grace handing out tickets beside the door, but saw instead a tweedy-looking woman who suggested she leave her bags beside the oak table where a row of leaflets, 'The History of Selbury Quade', neatly overlapped each other.

'Your ticket, dear.'

Midge accepted the slip of paper and glanced at her watch. Just midday. She had plenty of time to take this tour if she wanted to – and suddenly she decided that she did. It was really rather a joke, she thought, to arrive at Selbury with a bunch of tourists. So, like the others, she tagged after the guide, another tweedy lady with a plummy English voice.

'. . . fine example of an Elizabethan staircase. Note the garlands of oak leaves carved on the newel posts. The portrait above the stairs, by an unknown sixteenth-century artist, is of Dame Margery Quade, who built the house. The Quade family has lived here for almost four hundred years, and is still in residence.'

But that, thought Midge, was not quite correct. There had been that break of thirty years or so, when the Wansleas lived here. A Peter Wanslea had rented the house from her great-grandfather, who had come to Australia from England and founded Selbury Park. Then, during World War I, his eldest

310

son, another Nicholas, had come to England with the AIF and fallen in love, not only with Selbury Quade, but with an English girl. After the war he had settled here. Which was how Selbury Park in New South Wales had passed to Midge's father, the younger son.

Midge glanced up at Dame Margery's portrait and suddenly felt – what was that saying – as though a shadow had passed over her. Those painted eyes seemed to follow her as she walked up the stairs to join the others in the long gallery. And suddenly Midge had the most extraordinary thought. There was something about those eyes, that face, that reminded her of Emma! Surely she had glimpsed a similar expression, a certain ruthlessness, on Emma's face when she was determined to achieve something. Wasn't it known as 'the killer instinct' in the world of sport?

The long gallery was hung with more family portraits. 'Sir Nicholas Quade, Dame Margery's son ... Sir Carew Quade ...' the guide intoned. And, towards the end of the gallery, 'Sir Oswald Quade and Lady Louisa Quade, with their daughter Imogen.'

Imogen ... why, that was her great-grandfather's sister, for whom Midge herself was named. She did not know much about her, only that she had been unhappily married, and had died as the result of a bee sting ... the same way that the composers Mahler and Berg had both died. Midge was fond of music; they said she took after another forebear, the wife of that Robson who founded Bealiba Station. Her piano, which she had brought as a bride from England, still stood in the drawing room at Bealiba.

Midge looked at the little girl in the painting, her brown velvet dress tied with a big sash, standing beside her parents. She must have been about eight years old. Midge peered more closely. Why, there it was again, that look of the Elizabethan lady in the portrait – Dame Margery. Surely Dame Margery must have looked just like that when she was a little girl.

'Are they all sirs ... no dukes or duchesses?' a plaintive American voice enquired from among the group of sightseers.

'The Quade baronetcy was granted by Queen Elizabeth I,' the tweedy guide responded with a note of reproof in her voice.

The tour progressed into a bedroom corridor. One or two doors stood open, ropes looped across to discourage people from entering. From the doorways they gazed at old-fashioned furnishings: four-poster beds, washstands with elaborate fittings, huge clothes-presses, carved chests. There were artistic arrangements of fresh flowers in each of these show-rooms – Aunt Grace's touch, Midge guessed. Then they descended by the steep back stairs. The woman in pink clung nervously to the banister rail. 'Just fancy bringing coals and cans of hot water up these!' she gasped. 'Like they did in the old days. Slave labour, that's what it was.' Perhaps the ghost of a little tweeny would have agreed with her.

They were shown the library, where a great carved desk stood flanked by two huge globes on mahogany stands with clawed brass feet. Marble busts stood in shallow niches between the bookshelves, and recessed windows overlooked that pleasant lawn. Next the drawing room . . . then the music room – 'The spinet is a fine example of Charles Haward's craftsmanship; the Selbury account books show that Sir Nicholas Quade, Dame Margery's son, purchased it for the sum of five pounds.' And so they came to the huge kitchen with its scrubbed pine table and daunting array of pots and pans. The group's collective gaze swivelled to the big glass-fronted box high on one wall. Its indicators, marked with the names or numbers of different rooms, had stayed still and silent for years now.

Finally they were released through the morning room onto the terrace, where fuchsias spilled from stone urns and a freshly painted sign pointed the way to SHOP, SNACK BAR and TOILETS. Another sign pointed in a different direction: TO THE MAZE.

Midge stepped outside into the warm summer day. It was kind of England to greet her with blue skies and sun, she thought. Being here was like stepping into the history of her family . . . except, of course, for the electric lights, telephones and fire spinklers that had been installed in the house. How strange to think that she herself might have lived here, instead of half a world away, if Great-grandfather Nicholas Quade had not gone back to live in Australia. Midge knew by heart his romantic story – how he had been abducted by a gypsy, then bought by a chimney sweep, and finally restored to his title and fortune. There wasn't much of that fortune left now. Droughts and floods and agricultural depressions and taxes had seen to that. She thought of the little girl in the portrait, his sister Imogen. It was a pity no one knew much about her. But apparently Great-grandfather Nicholas had never spoken of her. They seemed to have been estranged for some reason.

It was intriguing to speculate that if he had not been abducted and had not come to Australia to work at Bealiba, he would not have met her great-grandmother, Laura Robson. Theirs had been a long and loving marriage. She herself would not have been the person she was now . . . She heaved a sigh as she followed the path to the stable block. It was all too complicated to contemplate, especially with jet lag setting in.

The stables had been skilfully converted. Tubs of pink and scarlet geraniums stood in the cobbled yard, with litter bins placed at discreet intervals. Midge stepped through the doorway that led into the shop. There, presiding over a display of home-made jams, lavender bags, recipe books – Aunt Grace had compiled *Dame Margery's Elizabethan Dishes* – pottery ashtrays, decorative tea towels and crested spoons, Midge caught sight of Letty – her cousin, Letitia Quade, who stood smiling patiently as the visitors hesitated over their purchases, proffered ten-pound notes for fancy bookmarks that cost fifty pence, shook out the neatly folded tea towels and sniffed at the lavender bags.

Midge went up to the counter. 'I'm here, Letty. It's really me!'

'*Midge!*'

Heads turned curiously as the tall, dark-haired girl behind the counter squealed in delight. 'You've made it in time! We were afraid you might miss the morning bus –'

'I did. I came on the sightseeing coach instead. I've just had a conducted tour.'

'That was clever. I'll have to take you round again, though, and tell you the real stories about Selbury. – I say, you must be exhausted. I can't leave here – but Mother's getting lunch ready in our flat at the top of the house. She was going to set up the video in case you missed Emma's match – we shall all watch it later, of course. It won't be quite the same though – we shall already know whether she's won or lost. Anyway, if you go back to the house you'll see a notice that says PRIVATE on the top floor.'

Midge went back, collected her bags, and duly arrived at the top floor, where the old attics and servants' rooms had been converted into a comfortable apartment.

'Midge, dear – welcome.' Aunt Grace, dark-haired and tall like her daughter, greeted her affectionately. They were courtesy aunt and niece, of course. Cousinly relationships were really too complicated for anything else.

Midge was set down in front of the television set with a plate of chicken salad and a mug of coffee. 'It's just about to start,' Aunt Grace said. 'I wish I could stay to watch with you, but I'm on duty at the ticket table now. Another coach will be arriving soon. – I just hope Emma pulls it off.'

'She probably will. She usually succeeds in whatever she really wants to do.'

Midge exchanged a rueful half-smile with her aunt. Both Grace Quade and her daughter Letty had been quite sorry when Peter had transferred his affections from Midge to Emma Sutton. Not that it could be considered a full-scale tragedy. Midge was so attractive, with such a sweet nature, she'd soon find someone else.

Aunt Grace went downstairs and Midge wriggled out of her chair to sit comfortably on the floor, munching her chicken and gazing at the screen.

'. . . here come the semi-finalists of the women's singles tournament walking onto Court Number One,' the commentator announced. 'Miss Deborah Layton of the USA, seeded number one, and Miss Emma Sutton of Australia, the young unseeded player who has taken Wimbledon this year by storm.'

Midge watched intently as her cousin appeared on the screen side by side with her opponent. Both stopped to turn and curtsy to the royal box before divesting themselves of extra racquets, towels and sweaters at the umpire's chair. Emma won the toss. After the knock-up – 'Miss Sutton to serve first. *Play.*'

Midge followed every stroke intently as Emma's crisp, brief-skirted figure darted about the court, serving faultlessly, slamming home passing shots along the sidelines, delivering that wicked backhand with the top spin. She was in her best form: that killer instinct was there all right today. Once she disputed a point – a linesman called 'Out!' to one of her returns towards the end of the first set. Emma lost the protest and did not look very pleased about it. The Wimbledon crowd gave an extra round of applause to the American, and Midge groaned inwardly. Emma could be quite unsporting at times. But the crowd's real sympathy lay with the Australian, you could sense that . . . and after the dispute Emma went on to win the next point, her confidence undiminished.

To her dismay, Midge found she had actually dozed off for a few points during the second set . . . but she was certainly awake at the end of the match, when Emma shook hands with Deborah Layton, smiling widely now, the winner in two straight sets. For an instant during the last game, just before the second match-point, the camera had swivelled towards the competitor's stand to rest briefly on 'Peter Quade, the young Australian's boyfriend, watching anxiously'. Midge's heart gave an unavoidable little jump when she saw Peter sitting there, leaning forward in concentration.

And while the crowd at Wimbledon applauded an Australian victory, the first tourist coach departed again for Yeovil.

'Funny,' the pink lady remarked to her husband, 'that Australian girl – she's not on the bus.'

'Perhaps she got lost in the maze,' her husband suggested.

The coach went back along the winding drive, through the avenue of tall trees, until the house was lost to sight. Then out of the gates onto the old highway, such a narrow, quiet road compared to that wide freeway with its ceaseless flow of traffic. They passed a crossroads where one way branched off to Selbury village. Beneath the smooth macadam surface was the place where a witch had once been buried with a stake driven through her heart . . . Agnes Selbury's bones had long since crumbled to dust, and the curse she uttered as she writhed in the cruel flames had passed beyond living memory.